# THE CREW *of the* Black Rose

Book Two
The Chronicles of the Deception

K.G. Ryder

Published by Spellwings Press

British Columbia, Canada

SpellwingsPress.com

ISBN: 978-1-0674771-3-4  Electronic book

ISBN: 978-1-0674771-2-7  Paperback

# Contents

"If you follow your star, you cannot fail to reach a glorious port." —Dante Alighieri, Inferno

For anyone who has landed in a situation that wasn't what they expected.

Who made the best of it...

...or didn't...

But still ended up with a hell of a story to tell.

Per aspera ad astra

...And for those who heard 'sexy pirates doing spicy things' and said: "Yes, please!"

This book is also for you.

# Prologue

## Pleading Progeny

Benjamina Johnson de la Rosa eagerly set about sorting the folios she had found in the sea chest beneath the floor of the Rose Academy's Archive Room. The books were all old, some dating back to the 1700s, their soft leather covers hiding a treasure trove of information. Mina began keeping notes of her own about the crew in a document on her tablet. Before long, that turned into a series of linked documents as the material quickly became unwieldy. She tracked the changes as she went, following the evolution of Ben/Roberto's relationships with his crewmates aboard the *Deception*.

After a few weeks of overwhelming, obsessive solo work, along with several stress-induced breakdowns and multiple low blood glucose alarms, Mina's parents and her abuela Beatriz, the current headmistress of the Rose Academy, called a family meeting in one of the school's conference rooms to decide what to do. The smell of fresh coffee reminded Mina to check her blood sugar. It was trending low, so she pulled an applesauce pouch from her bag. The moment she ate it, she wished she had not. Her stomach roiled, rejecting the cinnamon sweetness as the older adults began to speak.

"This is an important discovery," Tía Julieta said. Tía Julieta was Mina's great-aunt, Abuela Beatriz's youngest sister. As Mina's academic advisor in the history department, she knew better than anyone how the research was affecting her. Mina had broken down crying in her office three times and counting, and her blood sugar had repeatedly plummeted in the middle of lectures, a clear sign she was forgetting to eat. "Not just for us at the Academy, but for historians. We need to share this discovery and get Mina some help. A girl her age should be out having fun, not drowning in three-hundred-year-old papers."

"Who cares about some dumb pirate journals?" snarked Tío Flaco, Mina's uncle by marriage, who taught chemistry. "The only people who would want to read them are degenerates who like looking at dirty pictures."

Mina's face flushed, and her stomach turned, even as Tío Bernardo, professor of Latin American literature, chided his husband for the reductive comment. Mina liked the dirty pictures and the descriptions of how Ben experimented with his lover, the Black Rose. Not only was it incredibly sexy, it was romantic. The man had been so interested in his lover that he took a methodical, almost scientific approach to studying her body and learning how to please her. Mina would kill for a man like that.

Her thoughts snapped back to the room in a cacophony as her family squabbled around her. She tugged at a streak of teal in her chestnut-brown curls, then pulled it into her mouth and chewed on it for a moment. It calmed her a little. She spat it out and looked over at her mother, Isabel. Isa rubbed her temples, a low growl in her throat. Their eyes met, and Isa stuck two fingers in her mouth and let out a sharp, piercing whistle. Everyone froze.

"I think Mina should be allowed to speak, since she is the one doing all of the work right now."

A hush fell over the room, and fifteen pairs of eyes turned toward the young woman. Mina took a deep breath, her heart hammering in her chest. Beads of sweat gathered at her hairline, and she wiped them away with the back of her wrist.

"I think this is important, and I'll tell you why. Tío Flaco, name a famous pirate."

"Blackbeard," the scientist said with a scoff. "So what?" Tío Bernardo shot his husband a warning look before nodding at Mina to continue. Mina clenched her fist, her nails biting into her palm.

"Name any other member of Blackbeard's crew." She paused and waited, the way she did when leading a lecture. "Who was his quartermaster?" The next questions came rapidly, like rounds from a tommy gun in a gangster movie. "His cook? His boatswain? Who did their laundry? Who worked in the bilge? Did they have any animals aboard? What about the cabin boys? Cabin girls?"

Tío Flaco's mouth fell open as he thought, then snapped shut. Mina stood and strode to the portrait of the founders of the Rose Academy. While it was smaller than the large, grand one in the hallway, it was still more than big enough to prove her point.

Her voice rang out, loud and steady, as she listed not only the people in the portrait, her ancestors watching her with unblinking eyes, but also all the people who had helped build the very school they sat in. People whose portraits they recognized, whose names some of them knew, whose ghosts watched over their students and faculty every day. Mina needed her family to know these people, to love them, as she was learning to love them.

"And all because Roberto... Benjamin... saw these people as interesting, saw their stories as important and worth sharing. He saw fit to write them down. He drew color portraits of them! This isn't just about a man making sexy drawings of his lover. This is about a man who loved the family he found so much that he wanted them preserved. He wanted their memories to survive and live on. Years and years of work, all to make sure somebody would know these people existed."

She paused, panting, then lowered her voice.

"And if you don't think that is incredibly special, then get the hell out of here, because that is what this Academy was founded on, literally." She brushed curls from her eyes and pushed her glasses back up her nose. "The idea that everyone deserves an education, because everyone's knowledge and stories are important."

A smattering of light applause followed as she stopped to catch her breath.

"But," she continued, her stomach lurching again, "this is too much for just me. I love it, but I'm drowning. I think this is a golden opportunity, not just for my thesis, but for the Academy. This could bring us researchers, really put us on the map. The Rose Academy at the forefront of research on the Golden Age of Piracy in the Caribbean." She pointed at Tío Flaco.

"You're the one always saying we need new blood. This could bring in experts from all over. We could hire people who aren't family members. Or married into the family. People who haven't lived in Puerto Rico all their lives."

A ripple of laughter passed around the room, and even Tío Flaco's hard countenance finally softened. Mina turned to her grandmother.

"Abuela Beatriz, I want to share our findings and open the Academy to visiting researchers. There's so much here, and I love it so much, but I can't do it all alone. There are probably things I don't even know to look for, things I'm doing wrong. Please."

Abuela Beatriz studied her eldest granddaughter for a long moment, the soft wrinkles in her face making her expression hard to read. The only sound in the room was the air conditioner blowing with a faint, sharp scent of ozone. The silence and the chill raised the hair on Mina's arms as she waited for her grandmother's judgment. The fate of her thesis rested with the headmistress.

"Isa," Abuela Beatriz said at last, turning to her own eldest daughter, the mass of necklaces at her throat tinkling softly as she moved. "Do you and Mike still talk to that reporter in Florida?"

"Becks? Of course. He was Mikey's college roommate. Of course they still talk. They do that fantasy football league too."

Abuela Beatriz nodded.

"Ask him if he wants to come down for a long weekend and write a piece about our girl and her findings. Get her name and face in front of some nerds who might be interested in helping with the research."

Mina could hardly believe it. "Really?!?" she squeaked. "Thank you, Abuela Beatriz!"

She rushed forward and nearly bowled her grandmother over. The older woman let herself be swept into a hug before cupping a callused hand against her granddaughter's cheek.

"Of course, cariño!"

She winked at her own daughter, who smiled back. They shared a look, both thinking the same thing:

Maybe Mina will find someone worthwhile so she can finally settle down.

# Supplemental

## The Articles of the Deception

*R*esearcher's Note: *These were the rules that the crew members of the Deception agreed to and signed when they officially joined the crew.*

1. All aboard the ship shall obey civil Command.

2. The Captain, Quartermaster, Boatswain, Gun Master, and Sailing Master shall all have one share and one half. The Doctor and Cook shall have one share and one quarter.

3. All women and children are granted good quarter. Any man that offers to meddle with them, without their consent, shall suffer present death.

4. If any person should steal from the Company, to the value of a piece-of-eight, shall suffer what Punishment the Captain and the Majority of the Company shall think fit.

5. If any person should find valuables on a Prize, to the value of a piece-of-eight, and the finder does not deliver it to the Quartermaster in the span of twenty-four hours, he shall suffer what Punishment the Captain and the Majority of the Company shall think fit.

6. No striking one another on board, but all quarrels be ended on the shore with pistol and sword.

7. Any person that shall snap his arms, smoke tobacco, or carry a candle lighted without a lantern in the hold, shall suffer what Punishment the Captain and the Majority of the Company shall think fit.

8. Any person that does not keep his arms clean and fit for an engagement, or neglects his business, shall suffer what Punishment the Captain and the Majority of the Company shall think fit.

9. Any person found guilty of cowardice or drunkenness in times of engagement shall suffer what Punishment the Captain and the Majority of the Company shall think fit.

10. Any person that shall have the misfortune to lose a limb in time of engagement, shall have the sum of six hundred pieces of eight, and remain aboard as long as he shall think fit. Lesser hurts shall be paid proportionally.

11. No person is to game at cards, dominoes, or dice for money onboard.

12. Every person has a vote in affairs of moment; has equal title to the fresh provisions, or strong liquors, at any time seized, and may use them at pleasure, unless a scarcity makes it necessary, for the good of all, to vote a retrenchment.

# Chapter 1

## Pirates and Preparations

The Black Rose of Cartagena and her helmsman, Benjamin Harrington, walked along the path back to the three beached ships: the Black Rose's own *Deception*; the recently captured British weapons transport, the *Angelina Marie*; and the former slave ship *María del Mar*. Ben's shirt was full of bellfruit, and the Pirate Queen carried the stick with the flower crowns they had made together after making spectacular love beneath a waterfall, fulfilling one of the Captain's most cherished fantasies. The scent of the flowers was overwhelmingly sweet, almost cloying. Ben was trying to act nonchalant, to seem normal, though his world had been turned upside down by the realization that had struck him like a brick to his admittedly large nose.

He could not actually be in love with her. Right?

Not with his commanding officer.

What on earth was he going to do?

His brain was screaming a thousand incoherent things. It was so bad he could not even focus on his five senses, which usually calmed him when he was on the verge of a fit of nerves. He wanted to look at the Pirate Queen, to feast his eyes on the object of his affection. He wanted to take in the sun blazing off her bare bronze shoulders, her springy curls wreathed with plumeria, her deep mahogany eyes that always seemed to sparkle like stars. But he worried that if he let himself do so, he would make her uncomfortable, because he did not know how to gaze romantically upon his beloved without, to quote his wife Anne, "staring like a lunatic intent on murder."

His stomach turned at the thought of Anne. She had hated her husband and never wanted him to acknowledge her existence, let alone share her marital bed. Very, very different from the Pirate Queen, who could not seem to keep Ben from between her legs.

In the present, Ben's chest was tight, his palms damp against the fabric of his shirt, and the pungent flowers made his stomach churn. He settled for quick sideways glances as the Captain waxed poetic about her favorite fruits. Ben did manage to register that she was particularly fond of things called guayaba, maracuyá, and pitaya. He had no idea what any of them were, and did not want to interrupt her to ask. She stepped in front of him, walking backward, and looked at him expectantly.

"I'm sorry, what?"

"I asked what you like."

"I like fruit. Very much."

Genius. That was certainly going to secure her affections. Good work, Baffling Benjamin, he chided himself, using the derisive nickname once given to him by his Royal Navy cohorts.

To his relief, the Captain laughed heartily.

"So you don't have a preference?"

"Uhhh..." Ben instantly forgot every fruit he had ever heard of, read about, or tasted. At last, he remembered one in the context of eating pieces of it from her beautiful naked body two nights earlier. "Mango's good." Yes, good, that was a fruit, and he did like it fairly well. What else? "And bananas. And I like Xiang's tiny oranges."

"I don't care for oranges. I like the juice, but the flesh. ¡Qué asco!" She gagged theatrically. "And the white stuff under the peel is the worst."

She shuddered dramatically just as the trees opened before them onto the beach, where the three ships stood amid a bustle of activity.

Boatswain Talia and Doctora Julieta were leading a team building makeshift tables. Gunner Felipe, gun crew member Zsófia, and her wife Anya were setting small bonfires in metal braziers, adding herbs to keep the insects at bay, perfumed smoke curling on the breeze. Quartermaster Tobin moved through it all with a checklist tacked to a piece of wood. A kitchen team made up of Xiang, Natsuki, Frank, Li Mei, a woman Ben guessed was Samira, the cook from the *María del Mar*, and several others tended a large fire pit. Samira and Natsuki grilled flatbreads on a grate over the fire while the others prepared fish wrapped in banana leaves. Two enormous cooking pots bubbled nearby, filled with something orange Ben suspected was Samira's paneer curry. Beside them stood a massive, though somehow still tidy, stack of bowls and two large tubs of spoons.

Tobin, Felipe, and Xiang all stopped what they were doing to greet the Captain.

"Look. We found *pomme d'amour*!" she said excitedly, showing the men the fruit.

Felipe snorted. "Madame, this is not pomme d'amour any more than it is *pomme de terre*. But these are good, oui."

"Wait, what's pomme d'amour then?" Ben asked.

The Frenchman laughed. "That is a fancy way to say tomato, which these certainly are not."

Xiang took the fruit, chattering happily in Chinese and bowing to Ben, who bowed back.

Tobin thrust his list at the Captain, who handed the stick of flower crowns to Felipe.

"Put these in my quarters, in the shade, so they don't wilt."

She removed her own crown and rose onto her toes to drop it onto the older man's head. He delicately adjusted it so it did not fall into his eyes.

"Merci, Madame. You make me feel like a princess." He winked at her before loping away.

"That's a good look for him. We should have made him one too," Ben commented.

The Black Rose chuckled, then coughed and straightened. Tobin rolled his eyes, snarling almost imperceptibly at how well the Englishman's remark had been received. The Pirate Queen turned her attention to the checklist, her brows furrowing as she read.

"So what still needs to be done?" she asked, all business.

Tobin drew himself up to his full height, his dark umber skin glinting in the sunlight. His deep voice rumbled with authority as he pointed to the list with one large finger.

"We need to lay some planks down for the stage area, and if you'd like that decorated, we could get some palm fronds and flowers..."

The Black Rose looked up, scanning the beach. "Where is Alizée?" she asked. A freed slave like Tobin, Alizée was the Captain of the *María del Mar*, as well as Felipe's protégée and adopted daughter. She was nowhere in sight. The quartermaster sighed.

"She's keeping James out of everyone's hair," Tobin said. "He started on Andrew again, saying he has no drive or aspirations. James called Andrew 'Prince of the Pump,' so you know he's been thinking on that one for a while. Brazenly ungrateful, considering Andrew is the brains behind this little fiesta. And of course Eliza wasn't having any of it, so she pulled a knife on James. It took both Anya and Zsófia to hold her back. And the only reason that old bastard"—he indicated Felipe, who was climbing the gangplank to their ship—"didn't get involved is because he was taking a piss. James got very, very lucky."

The Black Rose gave a soft snort.

"So Eliza's having a cooldown in the brig of her own volition, Andrew is keeping her company, and if I know him, probably thanking her enthusiastically for her pains."

The Black Rose snorted again.

"And Alizée took James back to *María del Mar*. She said something about giving him a 'Captaining for Idiots' course. You know how good she is at improvising."

The Black Rose chuckled. Alizée was promoting James to captain of his own ship to get him off the *María del Mar* and out of her hair. While nobody thought it was an especially good idea, everyone agreed it was far less dangerous than allowing him to remain under Alizée's command.

"Probably just as well. Remind me to thank her for her trouble. And to offer my undying support to Eliza and Andrew. I'd hate for them to miss supper and the music."

Ben had not spent much time with Andrew, though he knew the man worked in the bilge. He had, however, spent quite a lot of time with Eliza, the *Deception*'s laundress, and thought very highly of her. She was an Irishwoman with a deep sense of justice and fair play. She had once threatened to blackmail Felipe on Ben's behalf, so he knew she was not above taking matters into her own hands to defend one of her crewmates, especially from an arsehole like James, who seemed to think everyone would do as he pleased simply because he was beautiful, with his golden-blond hair and sapphire eyes.

"¡Ay, Juanito! ¡Joder!"

Doctora's voice carried across the beach, and the Captain, Tobin, and Ben all slapped their foreheads.

"That boy," Tobin grumbled. Juanito, one of the cabin children, was exceptionally accident-prone. The sheer force of the physician's exclamation told them this was worse than usual.

The Black Rose sighed. "Benny, please go assist with the tables so Doctora can deal with whatever the hell Juanito has done this time."

Ben nodded, kissed her hand, gave her a wink he hoped looked suave, and headed toward Talia. Doctora approached from the other direction, carrying Juanito piggyback, drops of blood trailing in their wake.

"He dropped some nails in the sand and found one with his foot. Be careful," she grumbled, looking frazzled.

"Jules. Let me take this weight from you."

Felipe appeared out of nowhere, his sleeves rolled up, lifting the boy from Doctora's back. Though her name was Julieta, pronounced the Spanish way, the Frenchman called her Jewels, like the precious stones, a way of confessing his love without actually confessing it. She straightened slowly, her hands pressing into her lower back. Her eyes widened at once, drawn to the gunner's rippling tattooed biceps as he adjusted his grip. Ever since Ben had pointed out that the widowed Doctora always stared at his arms, Felipe had gone out of his way to show them off to her. She gave herself a small shake.

"Gracias, Felipe. He is a growing boy, and I am not."

They smiled at each other for a long moment before Juanito squirmed in Felipe's arms.

"You're squeezing me," the boy grunted.

"Maybe I squeeze some sense into you, eh? After you, Jules."

Doctora risked resting a hand on the Frenchman's flexed muscle under the pretense of steadying herself in the sand before they headed back toward the ship. Ben smiled and shook his head as he made his way to Talia.

"Och, Benny. Good. Watch yer feet, the wee bugger dropped some nails in the sand!" the Scot shouted as he neared.

"So I heard."

Ben helped Talia, Joaquín, the boatswain from the *María del Mar*, and several others build and set up the low tables. Once they were finished, all the benches from the galleys of the three ships were arranged around them, leaving plenty of seating. Tobin meticulously counted and annotated everything that came from each vessel, ensuring it would all be returned to its proper place. His organizational skills were truly spectacular, though, Ben reasoned, that was exactly why he was second in command.

No more nails found their way into anyone's feet, and the group amused themselves by inventing increasingly outlandish things to do with a drunken sailor early in the morning after they exhausted all the verses they knew. Some of the better new punishments included tying him up and making him listen to James, or putting him in charge of Juanito, early in the morning. At some point, Felipe returned with a small magnetic rock tied to a piece of twine and used it to pull the rest of Juanito's nails from the sand. The gunner took over for Talia to give her time to get ready, and large planks were placed atop an elevated dune to form a stage. A small table was added and covered with a cloth. Tobin came over with his list and smiled broadly as he checked off the final item with a flourish.

"We are ready. Everyone, freshen up, and officers, don't forget your pins!"

# CHAPTER 2

## PROMOTION FOR A PRICK

An hour later, everyone was on the beach making the final preparations. The Black Rose approached Ben carrying the stick of flower crowns. She had changed into her red blouse with the black cincher, and Ben was pleased to see she had covered her cleavage more than usual. While he believed the Captain could dress however she liked, James's obsession with her made everyone uncomfortable.

Ben did not want James getting an eyeful of her charms, and thankfully, she seemed to feel the same. The Pirate Queen also wore layered black and red petticoats beneath a ruffled black skirt, her bare feet peeking out from under the frills. Her ebony rose pin, signifying her rank as leader of the fleet, rested over her heart.

She offered Ben one of the flower crowns. His stomach had settled somewhat, so the strong scent of the plumeria was pleasant now rather than overpowering.

"Would you be so kind as to crown me again, Benny?"

"Yes, Mistress," he said, obliging her.

He bent to kiss her lips, but she turned her head. Damn it, he still was not allowed to kiss her in front of the crew. Recovering quickly, he kissed her cheek instead.

"You look lovely, Mistress," he murmured near her ear.

She smiled at him. She was pure starlight, and Ben could not fathom how deeply he adored her in that moment. James would never have her. Ben would do everything in his power to see to that.

They gazed at one another for a beat before the Captain shyly lowered her eyes and turned away.

"Felipe, would you please take Doctora her flowers?" she called.

The Frenchman looked as though he had been invited to glimpse heaven itself, nodding enthusiastically. He gingerly accepted one of the wreaths and made his way to where the physician was straightening the cloth on the small table beneath the box of pins for the new officers of the *Angelina Marie*.

Ben and the Captain watched as the gunner approached haltingly. Though the older man was fully twice their age, he turned back to them, and they waved him onward like parents encouraging a child on his first day of school. Ben and the Black Rose let their hands fall to their sides as Doctora looked up, and Ben instinctively reached for the Pirate Queen's hand.

She entwined her fingers with his, and Ben felt as though his heart might burst from his chest. He kept his face as neutral as he could while the Frenchman approached the Boricua, a word Ben had only learned earlier that week, meaning a native of Puerto Rico, though Doctora had explained that much of her ancestry was Spanish. Felipe's ordinarily pink skin had gone almost sunburnt, the back of his neck and the tips of his ears flushed bright red.

Doctora saw the flowers and tilted her head. Felipe said something Ben could not hear, and the physician smiled. She let the gunner place the flower crown on her head, and he brushed away a stray leaf with the back of his hand. They looked at one another for another long moment, his large hand cupping her cheek, and the Black Rose's grip tightened around Ben's.

"They're going to," she whispered, lightly knocking their joined hands against Ben's leg.

"Shush," Ben admonished, even as he too was certain this would be the moment the older couple finally admitted their feelings and kissed.

Until it was not.

Doctora's face went red, and she stepped back, nodding as Felipe stiffly turned and walked back toward Ben and the Captain.

"Joder," the Pirate Queen muttered. "So close."

"Shall I crown Alizée too?" the gunner asked when he returned, his face as red as his headscarf, his voice strained to a whisper.

"Yes, I think she would like that," the Captain said kindly, offering him another circlet.

He nodded and hurried away.

"These are lovely, Benny, thank you." Doctora had come up beside them, watching the gunner's retreating back.

"I'm glad you like them. My little sisters always loved flower crowns, and I couldn't resist the lovely plumeria."

"They smell divine. And so useful too," she sighed, watching Felipe bow theatrically to Alizée before crowning her, sweeping her into a great hug, and kissing both her cheeks. The faintest note of longing touched the older woman's voice. "Well, thank you for making them for all of us. It gives the female officers a sense of cohesion that will be very nice to see."

"How's Juanito's foot?" the Black Rose asked.

The physician sighed and rolled her eyes. "It was really in there. I was worried we might have to amputate, but Felipe managed to get it out. Juanito will need to stay off it for a few days. I ended up dosing him with the sleepy tea, so he'll be out for the rest of the night. He's asleep in the sick room. But I locked him in with a lamp, a book, some apples, and water just in case."

"Sick room?" Ben asked. He did not remember such a place, and he had thought he was getting to know every inch of the *Deception*.

"That door around the corner from ours, in the galley? It doesn't lead into our room. We have a small quarantine room just big enough for a bed. If someone is very ill and we worry they are contagious, we dose them with the sleepy tea and have them sleep it off in there, away from everyone else."

"Oh." Ben had never noticed the door, but it made sense.

"The sleepy tea is like the calming tea, floral, but much, much stronger. Xiang, Felipe, and I developed that blend together. But I am the only one who can authorize its use."

"Oh yes, I remember. You said Xiang could give Tobin half a dose after Los Roques."

She smiled sadly, adjusting her hinged spectacles. Ben, Tobin, and Felipe had endured quite a harrowing experience on Los Roques. The two men they had marooned fought back, trying to shoot Tobin and Felipe. The men of the *Deception* had come out of the ordeal alive, but not without a great deal of strain.

The Black Rose began waving hand signals across the beach. Ben turned and saw that she was communicating with Alizée. Felipe stood beside his Little Bird, making nonsense gestures with liberal use of middle fingers, which made Ben and Doctora laugh. The Pirate Queen responded seriously to the other captain while Ben pulled a silly face and flipped off the older man, whose booming laugh carried across the beach.

The Black Rose turned back to him, and he caught the scent of her flower crown once more. "Well, it looks like we should be starting soon. Benny, if you want to fetch your guitar, I think Talia is heading to the stage."

The ceremony went smoothly, just as the Captain had said it would. Ben and Talia played their grand, sweeping version of "Bully in the Alley," a joke at James's expense about his unreturned desire for the Black Rose. She, Alizée, James, and those soon to be promoted walked to the makeshift stage before the assembled crew. The officers of the *Deception* and the *María del Mar* flanked them. All the female officers looked lovely in their flower crowns, which helped the whole occasion feel a bit more normal, like an odd spring festival.

The Pirate Queen stepped forward, and the beach fell quiet. She lifted a hand and began to speak, a false smile fixed on her face. Ben noticed at once that the smile did not reach her eyes. She looked tired. It had been a long day, but she seemed like a completely different woman from the lively creature who had played the lusty mermaid that morning, swimming beneath a waterfall and making exquisite love to him in the pool below. Being so near James seemed to drain all her verve.

"Good evening, everyone. Tonight, we celebrate one of our own as he is promoted to Captain of his own ship."

There was light applause. James was beaming, oblivious to the fact that no one else truly wanted to be here watching him receive accolades.

The Black Rose continued, her voice carrying easily over the sound of more than a hundred people gathered on an open beach.

"I have known James since he was fourteen. He was a midshipman on the first Royal Navy vessel we ever captured. He was hiding in the galley, and Felipe, who was new to my crew at the time, quite literally scared the piss out of him."

Laughter rippled through the crowd, and James's smile faltered for a moment. Doctora lightly punched Felipe's thigh as the Frenchman looked ready to burst from the effort of holding in his laughter.

"I remember that," the gunner stage-whispered. "I grabbed him by the ankle and hoisted him upside down, and he made it rain on himself!"

That drew much louder laughter from the crew. The Black Rose herself snorted, then cleared her throat before continuing.

"As far as I know, he has grown up... at least a little... since then."

More laughter.

"Yes, hilarious," James said, rolling his sapphire eyes. "Never mind everything I have accomplished since then."

Now Alizée and the rest of the officers of the *María del Mar* started snorting and biting their lips to contain their amusement, while the new officers of the *Angelina Marie* exchanged increasingly uneasy looks.

"Anyway," the Pirate Queen said, her face once more composed, "James, we look forward to you adding to the strength of our fleet and our trading partners' enterprises. And now we will commence with the pinning. Talia, Benny, if you would."

Talia and Ben resumed their music softly as James removed his pin and held it in his hand. Alizée opened a small box for the Black Rose, who withdrew the captain's pin. James puffed out his chest as she fastened it to his jacket.

"How about a congratulatory kiss, Captain to Captain?" he asked quietly, his very words seeming coated in slime.

To Ben's left, Felipe reached for his belt, but Doctora grabbed the Frenchman's hand and shook her head.

"¡Ni en tus sueños!" the Black Rose replied, her tone poison-sweet through clenched teeth.

Ben had recently learned that *dulces sueños* meant sweet dreams, so he gathered she had said something close to *not even in your dreams*.

Then, more loudly, she addressed the crowd. "Congratulations, James. May the winds and waves carry you very, very far on new adventures."

There was applause again, this time a little more enthusiastic. The Captain's backhanded blessing had not gone unnoticed.

"And now, in his first act as Captain, James will pin his successor. Alizée, James, do you have any words for Fatima?"

"No, I'm good, thank you," James said, absorbed once more in examining his new pin: a coin-sized disc with a rose carved in relief and painted red, with a black ribbon cut into a swallowtail attached to the back. The officers beneath him would receive nearly identical pins of unpainted blond ceiba wood.

Alizée rolled her eyes and stepped forward. Fatima straightened her dark green headscarf and stood tall as Alizée took her hand. Ben could not quite tell from this distance, but it looked as though Fatima had burn scars on one side of her face.

"Fatima, over the past few years, it has been an honor to watch you grow. You came to us small, scared, scarred, and broken, but just as your flower garden requires care and the proper conditions to thrive, so too have you bloomed before us. We are all so very proud of you, my dear. May Allah keep your eyes sharp, your hand steady, and may He keep you safe as you keep us safe."

The two women embraced.

"James, please pin Fatima," the Black Rose said with a wide smile.

James finally tore his eyes from his own pin and sauntered over to Fatima. She stiffened slightly as he crookedly placed the pin at the bottom of her headscarf. He gave her an awkward nod, then stepped away.

Alizée turned to the gathered crowd. "The new gunner of the *María del Mar*!"

This time the applause was hearty, with a whistle from Felipe and a whoop from Doctora. Fatima wiped at her eyes and waved at the older pair with a broad smile.

"And now James will pin the new officers of the *Angelina Marie*."

Tobin handed the Black Rose a list while Alizée held open the box of officers' pins for James. The Pirate Queen read each name aloud and paused while James attached the men's pins to their shirts.

"Congratulations to the new officers."

There was another smattering of applause. The new gunner, Seth, looked visibly annoyed by the muted response compared to Fatima's pinning.

"Yes, that is certainly the man I would want in control of my weaponry," Felipe muttered, as though reading Ben's mind. "He's as bad as Frank. Good riddance to the lot of them."

"You are now representatives of the Black Rose and everything this fleet stands for. Your first mission is to head to Campeche and speak to Mama Tati. James, you remember Mama Tati, yes?"

James was once again absorbed in examining his captain's pin, but he nodded.

"Of course, M'lady. She's a jewel!"

A collective snort passed through the crowd, and Ben could immediately pick out every person present who had ever enjoyed the unique experience of meeting the tiny Mexican pawnshop owner. The Black Rose blinked and tilted her head, clearly not having expected that response.

"Uh... huh. Anyway, Mama Tati has a few leads on new routes. You will be able to choose from a few assignments, so you can all vote on what you'd like to pursue."

James stepped forward and took the Pirate Queen's hand. Doctora and Tobin both shot out their arms to stop Felipe from doing the same. The Frenchman's feet froze, but his hand still slipped into his belt, and Ben caught the gleam of one of his small, sharp throwing stars. James pressed an overenthusiastic kiss to the back of the Black Rose's hand. When he released her and swept into a low bow, she wiped her hand on her skirt with a grimace while he was still looking down.

"Of course, M'lady. We shall serve you bravely and with aplomb. You will be so proud of us come July."

"Of course, James, I'm sure."

She spoke as an adult might reassure an overexcited child who had no idea what he was doing, unwilling to crush his spirit despite seeing every flaw in his plan.

"And with that, three cheers for our new Captain and our new officers. Hip hip!"

"Huzzah!"

"Hip hip!"

"Huzzah!"

"Hip hip!"

"Huzzah!"

The final "Huzzah" was followed by several people, including a certain Frenchman standing immediately to Ben's left, chanting, "Fa-TEE-ma. Fa-TEE-ma," while the *María del Mar*'s new gunner smiled shyly. Alizée gave Fatima another squeeze before stepping forward and raising her voice.

"And now it's time to eat. Please form an orderly stampede so everyone can get a bowl."

As the crowd turned and the supper line began to form, James loudly shoving his way toward the front, the Black Rose slumped a little now that everyone's attention had shifted elsewhere. Ben leaned his guitar against the small table and went to her side. She smiled at him and pulled him into a one-armed hug, resting her head lightly against his shoulder for a brief instant.

"That wasn't terrible," she muttered.

Ben shook his head. "No, it was quite nice, all things considered."

"Yes, that went about as well as we could have hoped," Tobin agreed, appearing on the Captain's other side. Felipe, Doctora, and Talia came up beside Ben.

"Felipe only tried to get his throwing stars out twice," Talia said with a laugh. "That's probably the best we could hope for."

A faint chuckle passed through the group before they joined the supper line as well.

# Chapter 3

## Dinner and Discretion

Supper went off with only a few minor hitches. Thaddeus, the newly appointed cook of the *Angelina Marie*, did not care for curry or Asian-style cooking and loudly complained about it, telling anyone who would listen that he intended to run his new galley like a proper English kitchen. Ben thought of the traditional British food his wife and father-in-law preferred, compared with what his own family and neighbors tended to make.

Jamaican food was such an intense, vibrant kaleidoscope of flavors, shaped by Spain, Africa, Asia, and the indigenous people who had been there long before the British ever made landfall. Ben felt sorry for the crew who would have to subsist on the bland, greasy English fare the Baxters preferred when there were far more interesting options to be had. It hardly seemed better than hardtack and gruel, and Ben doubted he could ever return to a ship that fed its sailors that way.

Speaking of traditional foods, Ben tried some of Samira's paneer curry and immediately understood what Felipe and Doctora had been raving about. Especially with the wood-grilled flatbread, called naan, it was exquisite. Jamaican curry was nothing like this. The sauce was creamy and full of warming spices, and the cheese was firm while still absorbing the flavor beautifully.

"This is amazing," Ben said to Doctora, who kept stealing pieces of paneer from Felipe's bowl while he gamely pretended not to notice.

"I love Xiang's cooking, but Samira's paneer curry is quite a treat," she agreed, attempting to swipe another cube of cheese from Felipe with a piece of naan.

The gunner caught her hand.

"Jules. That is not very nice. You take all my paneer."

Doctora offered him the bit she had stolen, and the Frenchman let her feed it to him. His lips brushed her fingertips, and for a moment they looked happier than Ben had ever seen them. Then reality seemed to crash back in. Both flushed bright red and shifted a more respectable distance apart, staring down into their bowls while Talia groaned softly. Ben nearly did the same. Two near-misses in under four hours felt like a new record. He sighed and glanced toward the next table.

The Black Rose and Alizée sat with James and his new officers. A Colombian mestiza and a freed Black woman sitting as equals at a table full of Englishmen was remarkable enough on its own. The two women held themselves with grace and dignity, and the Black Rose in particular looked formidable, sitting tall and straight. Ben could not help staring at her. She was so regal, so composed, and he wanted nothing more than for her to tie him to her bed and make him beg for release. He wanted this fearsome Pirate Queen to dominate him so badly.

She noticed his gaze, and their eyes met. The Captain tilted her head ever so slightly toward the ship, her brows raised, a question in her eyes. Ben tried to answer in kind with a slow, subtle nod. She rose and excused herself, passing behind him. Fortunately, Doctora chose that exact moment to attempt to steal more paneer, this time from Talia, prompting shrieks of protest from the boatswain, hysterical laughter from Felipe, and annoyed grumbling from Tobin.

"Wait five minutes," the Black Rose hissed as she passed.

Ben nodded, laughing at the scene before him even as warmth spread over his skin.

After five minutes had passed, Ben excused himself, claiming he needed a few minutes of quiet before he and Talia performed. No one seemed to find it odd, or if they did, they said nothing.

He knocked softly on the door to the Captain's quarters, apprehensive and immensely excited. He was in love, and he was about to fuck that powerful woman again. What an glorious day.

The door opened, and the Black Rose pulled him inside. He barely had time to register the golden light of the setting sun and the lingering scent of plumeria before she shut the door, latched it, and pinned him against it with a kiss.

"We must be quick, Benny, but I cannot go without you a minute longer. Those men are so frustrating." She threw back her head, and Ben seized the opportunity to kiss her neck. She gasped happily. "No bruises this time, Benny. And I think you'll find a surprise under my skirts."

His hands could not get beneath the fabric fast enough as the Pirate Queen yanked his trousers down to his knees. She wore nothing beneath the petticoats.

"Yes, Mistress. Thank you, Mistress," he rasped as she stroked him roughly.

He slipped a finger between her folds before kissing her again. He wanted to bury his face between her legs. He wanted to lay her down and make love to her slowly, like a gentleman. He wanted her to tie him up again. He wanted to touch everything. He wanted too many things at once, but he kept his focus on what this needed to be: fast, mostly clothed, rough enough to relieve her frustration, yet gentle enough not to muss her hair or ruin her outfit. She had removed the flower crown, but everything else remained in place.

"Desk or wall?" Ben asked as his finger dipped deeper into her.

"Wall, please. Please, Benny."

Ben kissed her deeply.

"Your wish is my command, Mistress," he whispered, then spun the Black Rose around and pressed her to the door.

He leaned in, one hand feeling her breasts flattened against the wood, the other pushing aside her curls so he could kiss her neck. She shuddered as Ben gathered up her skirts and petticoats, exposing her backside. He growled as he crowded against her hips and drove into her hard, one fist bunching her skirts, the other seeking her pleasure through the forest of petticoats. He found it and set a hard rhythm, his hand working deftly as he thrust. It did not take long before the Pirate Queen cried out and struck the door, her inner muscles fluttering around him. He loved that feeling, loved knowing he had pleased her. He pressed into her, wanting badly to finish, but she swatted behind her.

"No. Don't. Back up."

Ben obeyed with a whine, though he could not complain for long, because his reward was her sweet mouth on his cock. Heat rushed through him, and he was already close.

Except she did not stop.

Oh, hell. He was going to come in her mouth unless she pulled away.

"Mistress, I'm... I'm about to..."

She looked up at him, lips tight around his length, eyes sparkling. Her mouth could not quite smile, but her eyes certainly did, and she nodded permission. Ben's head fell back with a groan as climax overtook him. The Black Rose licked him clean before pulling his trousers back up. Then she stood and kissed him, long and lingering.

"I can't believe you just did that," Ben gasped when they parted, still breathless.

"Anything else would have been too messy," she said lightly, kissing his cheek as though it were the most obvious thing in the world.

"Oh."

Ben wanted to tell her he loved her, to give voice to the realization that had struck him that morning, but she pulled away and stooped to retrieve a pair of short trousers from the floor, sliding them on beneath her skirts.

"Thank you, Benny. I really needed that." She took up a cloth and dabbed the sweat from her flushed skin with a smirk.

"Yes, Mistress. Thank you."

She rose onto her toes and kissed him again, quick as a heartbeat.

"Wait a few minutes, then come out. Are you ready for your performance?"

Ben nodded, picked up the flower crown, and gently settled it back onto her head.

"Thank you."

Ben cupped her cheek, memorizing the way she looked in that moment, then kissed her softly. They rubbed noses, and then she was gone, adjusting her skirts as she left. What an extraordinary woman.

The rest of the evening passed in a blur. Ben and Talia performed for the assembled crews, though they likely would have sounded even better with Tobin and Felipe joining them on drum and fiddle. The other men were too busy running interference to keep James from dancing with the Black Rose. The Captain's dance card was full as it was. Alizée and at least ten others stepped in at various moments to ensure that James never once got his hands on her.

Ben was pleased to see Felipe twirling Doctora through "Star of the County Down" while singing along in his deep French accent. He also spotted Eliza and Andrew off to one side, well away from James. Freed from her self-imposed exile, Eliza was laughing so hard she had tears in her eyes as tall, lanky Andrew performed a fantastically ridiculous dance, his shaggy blond hair flopping in the breeze. Tobin and Xiang managed to steal a quiet moment together at the back of the crowd during "Leave Her, Johnny," the African man resting his chin atop the smaller Asian man's head. Xiang looked almost peaceful with the quartermaster's large arms around his shoulders, while Tobin smiled broadly.

The evening ended with a rousing sing-along of "The Wild Rover," and Ben and Talia bowed to their audience. A surging mass of humanity immediately descended upon them, and Ben clutched his guitar for dear life, searching for an escape before he froze. A fist caught the back of his shirt and hauled him neatly out of the crush, leaving Talia to absorb the energy and accolades.

"Benny, come. We walk."

Felipe guided Ben toward the tree line, the younger man's knuckles still white where they gripped the neck of his guitar. Ben felt the rapidly cooling sand beneath his feet. He smelled and tasted the smoke from the gunner's pipe. He saw the last light fading over the jungle and heard frogs beginning to call nearby. Felipe took his guitar, and Ben sank down into the sand.

"You did very well today. Did you have a nice time with Madame this evening?"

"How did you—"

"Benny, why do you insist I am stupid? You know better. Unless you would like me to believe taking a piss made her that happy?"

Ben laughed, letting his head fall back.

"I'm in love with her, Felipe."

There. He had said it aloud. Perhaps now it would stop rattling around inside his head, drowning everything else out. The gunner tilted his head, incredulous.

"I ask again: why do you insist I am stupid?"

Ben shot him a look.

"Oh, *you* are stupid. You only just realized it. I thought since you wanted to sword fight romantically with her—" He broke off into hysterical laughter. "You mean to say that if she had not called those fruits pommes d'amour, you would not have figured it out? Oh no, Benny Boy."

Ben felt briefly insulted, then realized the Frenchman was entirely right. He started laughing too.

"I suppose so."

The older man laid a gentle hand on his shoulder.

"If I had to guess, it is because you thought you loved your wife, but this feels so different that you did not realize perhaps this is how it should feel."

Ben considered that.

"That... that makes perfect sense. You're very wise, Felipe."

The gunner waved a dismissive hand. "Non. Just old. And I have made a great many mistakes in my life."

He dropped down beside Ben, laying the guitar across his lap.

"The first woman I remember after Letty, after I came out of my grief..." Ben remembered Felipe's story of falling in love with an enslaved woman and trying to buy her freedom, only for her to be stabbed in the back by the overseer and die in his arms. So far, Felipe's and Talia's stories were the only ones Ben had collected for his project chronicling the lives of all the pirates aboard the *Deception*. "She was the reason I became entranced by opium. We were in China, and she invited me into her place of work for a smoke. She made me feel special. Her name was Hinata, and she is how I learned Japanese, since they will not allow anyone but the Dutch ashore on their islands. Apparently I was a fast learner on opium, because I learned Chinese that way too. We ended up staying for a few months while the ship was repaired, and then it was the rainy season. I thought she loved me. When we were finally ready to sail, I asked her to come with me. She said no. She felt nothing for me that she was not paid to feel, and she left me with a terrible habit. Well, you read my story."

Ben nodded.

"So," Felipe went on, "I became convinced people only cared about me if I paid them to, or because I could be useful to them. I thought I had missed my one chance at a happy story." He sighed.

"The thing about tragedy, Benny Boy, is that the stories do not show what comes next. We do not see whether Fortinbras executes Horatio, imprisons him, or lets him tell Hamlet's story. We never see who must clean up the blood. Sad stories do not tell us how to gather up the pieces afterward and try again. They just end. So you fumble around, trying to pull together the shards, and sometimes trying to hold everything together cuts you even worse.

"And then one day you find yourself in a situation where you realize everything is not what you thought. The shards are not as sharp. They do not cut as deeply. Not only that, the people around you are genuine. They care for you even when you do nothing for them. And then you meet someone kind and clever, and you do not have to pay her to spend time with you. She likes you as you are. She thinks you are funny and useful, and then…"

"Your heart gets stolen like a purse behind a whorehouse," Ben finished.

Felipe chuckled as Ben repeated the exact words he himself had once used to describe realizing he was in love with Doctora.

"You do pay attention. I suppose I see myself in you. You and Madame are not weighed down by tragedy as Jules and I are, and you may not yet know what love feels like. Especially because your wife, from what you have said, sounds like a salope vicieuse. So you do not know what it is to have a good woman like Madame, oui?"

Ben nodded.

"Then you are not stupid, only inexperienced. You have had misfortune, yes, but not tragedy. That is better than it is for many people you will meet. But come. The night grows cold, and there are insects and other nasties about."

The gunner helped Ben to his feet and handed him back his guitar. They had barely gone five meters when a voice came out of the darkness.

"What's this? Were Benjamin and the World's Oldest Prick having a tug in the jungle?"

James stepped into their path, his lips curled in a cruel smile.

"See, Benny? I told you there were nasties about," Felipe muttered. He cracked his neck. "James, I think you should reconsider whatever you are about to do, because Jules, Madame, Alizée, and Xiang are not here to keep me from killing you if you start shit."

"What are you two doing skulking around in the dark?"

"We could ask you the same question," Ben said.

"I was..." James began, then shook his head with a snarl. "You know what? I now outrank both of you, and I owe you no explanation if I choose not to."

"Ah yes, barely pinned and already making stellar leadership choices," Felipe groused.

"I should throw you in the brig and call for the cat-o'-nine-tails for grabbing my throat yesterday, you old fuck. And don't think I did not notice you doing everything you could to keep her from dancing with me. You're scared. Scared that if she experiences what I have to offer, she'll want me on her ship instead of you. I could replace both of you."

Ben scoffed. "You're in for an uphill battle, James."

James stepped uncomfortably close.

"Captain James to you, Benjamin. Fine. I will bide my time. She'll grow tired of you soon enough. Come July, she'll be bored and want something new. Then I shall step in and sweep her off her feet. I'll show her the most magnificent time, and you'll be left standing there with your cock in your hand while I become her new favorite."

Before Ben could answer, Felipe stepped between them, his hand on the hilt of one of the swords at his belt.

"I will duel you myself before I see you lay a hand on her again."

James clicked his tongue. "My, my, Benjamin. Having this senile old arsehole fight your battles for you?"

"No. I think I could beat you on my own."

James reached into his coat, removed a glove, stepped forward, and threw it at Ben's feet.

"Then I challenge you to a duel."

"In the middle of the night? Really? That's rather ungentlemanly, don't you think? Almost as tasteless and uncouth as threatening to steal a man's lover. Don't you think so, Felipe?"

Felipe nodded emphatically. "Mais oui. Very much against the rules of etiquette."

"You two are simpletons. Obviously not right at this moment."

"Oh, well, then I suppose we'll have to wait until July," Felipe said before Ben could answer.

The younger man bent, picked up the glove, and flung it back into James's face. It must have had sand on it, because James sputtered and shrieked, his hands flying up.

"My eyes! I'll have you flogged!"

"Come, Benny. Let's leave the new Captain to his business. James, we shall see you in July, and I do hope you'll be ready to have your arse handed to you."

Felipe grabbed Ben by the shoulders and steered him back toward the *Deception*.

"Now we truly have to work on your hand-to-hand combat," the Frenchman hissed.

Later that night, there came a knock at the door of the Black Rose's quarters. She rolled her eyes as she rose from bed. If Benny was there to beg for another audience in her bed, she would slam the door in his face. Was he not tired after today? Surely he must have sunburn on that very attractive backside of his. And after a quick, stolen fuck, he had still gone on to give such a splendid musical performance. He had to be exhausted.

She pulled open the door and was stunned to find Tariq, one of Talia's boatswain's mates, on the other side.

"Good evening, Captain," the Egyptian man said. He never smiled, but his eyes were large and expressive. Tonight they held a mixture of sadness and resolve. "May we speak?"

"Of course, Tariq. I would invite you in, but I know you cannot be alone in a room with a woman."

Tariq was Mohammedan and very strict with himself. He also refused to touch any of the women aboard for fear of compromising himself for his future wife.

He gave a mirthless laugh. "Captain always remembers. That is what makes this next part so difficult."

The Black Rose blinked. "What next part, Tariq?"

He drew a breath. "Captain, I wish to transfer to another ship."

"You want to go to the *Angelina Marie* with James? You cannot stand James."

He scoffed. "Anyone in the fleet with half a brain cannot stand James. No, I wish to transfer to *María del Mar* with Alizée."

"What? Why?"

The Egyptian shifted uncomfortably. "I know your... reputation, Captain, but it is one thing for me to know it and ignore it, and another for the... object of your lust... to speak so blatantly and brazenly about it. I would like to think you would have better taste in your paramours than to continue bedding a man who cannot keep his mouth shut about your... activities."

The Black Rose felt as though she had been slapped. Benny had been speaking about their lessons to other crew members? Tariq's eyes softened, concern showing in them as he saw how deeply the words had landed.

"So you did not know?"

She shook her head.

"If you are going to keep him, you may want to tell him that you do not appreciate it. I would say it is men being men, but he said it in front of Anya as well, so he did not even take mixed company into account."

The Black Rose let out a long breath and massaged her temples.

"Well, I thank you for your service, and I am very sorry to see you go. Especially since you did so well leading the second team in our last raid."

The man bowed.

"It has been an honor serving you, Captain, truly. Perhaps someday I will return to you, but you really must muzzle your lapdog before he ruins you."

"Thank you for telling me. I will certainly speak to him. Have you informed Tobin and Felipe?"

"No, Captain. And if you would prefer my discretion, I can tell them without revealing the exact reason."

She nodded.

"I would appreciate that. If you tell them you would like to see how you fare working under Alizée, I know Felipe will not fault you for it in the least."

She bowed back to him.

"Thank you again, and we will inform Alizée in the morning. She will be fortunate to have you."

"Goodnight, Captain."

"Goodnight, Tariq."

# SUPPLEMENTAL

## FROM THE PRIVATE JOURNALS OF BENJAMIN R. HARRINGTON - BLACK ROSE FOLIO

**A Running List of Xiang's Tea Blends:**

- <u>Amorous Blend</u>: spicy green tea. Makes me feel like I could either fight God himself or make love to the Captain for a week straight. I love this blend.

- <u>Calming Blend:</u> Floral tea made with jasmine.

- <u>Pep-Up Blend:</u> Citrus tea.

- <u>Stomach-Soother Blend:</u> Peppermint tea. Fresh mint added when available.

- <u>Cold Cure Tea:</u> Ginger tea. Served with honey.

The previous blends are brewed freely and can be requested at any time for any reason.

The following blends are closely guarded and only used in specific contexts:

- <u>Sleepy Blend</u>: Sweet flowery herbal tea with jasmine base. Given only on Doctora's orders, this tea is given when someone needs to be quarantined to keep them from infecting the rest of the crew, or they need to otherwise sleep for a long time.

- <u>'No Preg-a-nent' Tea</u>: Bitter herbal tea. Prevents pregnancy. Any woman who is not the Captain must ask her for permission before being allowed to use it.

- <u>Energy Blend</u>: Spicy citrus tea. Xiang keeps this blend closely guarded and only gives it if someone absolutely needs to stay awake. Makes me feel like every cell in my body is on fire and appears to cause me mild hallucinations. When it wears off, I drop into a dead sleep. *Note: I have been banned from this blend by order of the Captain.*

# CHAPTER 4

## PERTURBANCE, PONCES, AND POETRY

"A duel? Really, Felipe?" Doctora's voice was quiet, but a fiery anger burned in every syllable as she glared at the gunner over her bowl of porridge with chunks of bellfruit.

"Jules," the Frenchman said soothingly, patting her hand, "I am not going to duel him. Benny is."

"That is not better!" she hissed.

"First of all, James started it by threatening Madame again. Second, he made the challenge, not I, and not Benny. Third, we have until July. We are far too busy to do anything about it today."

Doctora's lips tightened into a disappointed line.

"Jules, if you had heard what he was saying, he was—"

Their argument was cut short by a whistle. The Black Rose stood on a bench in the middle of the galley, and Ben was once again entranced by her commanding presence. What a woman. Worth fighting a thousand duels for.

"Buenos días, my friends. I have a few announcements before we bid Alizée, James, and their crews farewell until July.

"First, we are suffering a loss. Dear Tariq wishes to sail on the *María del Mar* for a while."

There were sounds of disappointment mixed with light applause.

"What? No!" Talia's protest carried across the galley, and Tariq raised a hand. He was too far away for Ben to read his expression.

"I would like to try a more peaceful route for a while. I have always admired Alizée greatly, so I will try this new adventure until the Council convenes in July, and then decide where I belong. Thank you all for your friendship."

He turned to the Black Rose and bowed deeply.

"And thank you for your leadership."

She bowed back, smiling even though her voice sounded as though an ocean of unwept tears moved beneath it.

"Thank you for your hard work and your honesty, Tariq. Know that you are always welcome aboard the *Deception* if you choose to return."

She took a shuddering breath and continued with a smaller smile.

"But even as we lose one sailor, we gain another. While most of the crew of the *Angelina Marie* will return to their ship under James's command..."

There came a quiet "Boo" from a certain nearby Frenchman. The Captain rolled her eyes and continued.

"One of their number has requested to stay here with us. Everyone, please join me in welcoming Frank to the crew."

A smattering of skeptical applause followed as the man nodded, a blush creeping into his pale cheeks. He looked toward Li Mei and Xiang, who smiled at him.

"Merde, why him? Why does he want to stay?" Felipe muttered.

Tobin appeared behind them and flicked the older man's ear.

"Ow!"

"He asked to stay," Tobin murmured. "If I had to guess, he is interested in Li Mei and wants an excuse to get to know her better."

"Frank will be helping Xiang and Natsuki in the galley from now on, so we can expect the meal lines to move even faster."

"Now I definitely have to examine him," Doctora groaned.

Felipe took her hand again across the table.

"Jules, I will destroy him for you. Just say the word."

She laughed, adjusting her spectacles and smiling at the gunner.

"I don't need all that, cariño. I just need him to agree to let me examine him."

"He will agree, Jules. We will see to that."

"And finally, we will be making port next in Barranquilla. If you are feeling the Call of the Land and wish to stay ashore, please let us know as soon as possible. So finish your breakfast, we'll say goodbye to Alizée, Tariq, James, and everyone else, and we sail with the high tide this afternoon. Officers, a quick meeting in my quarters when you finish breakfast."

Some fifteen minutes later, the officers and Ben had gathered in the Captain's quarters. A map lay spread across her desk. Ben was itching to get in front of it, but he waited for permission from Tobin or the Captain. When the Black Rose entered, Felipe was on her immediately.

"Why Frank, Madame? What the hell? Have I done something to upset you?"

"Actually, yes, Felipe, you have, but that is not why I granted Frank's request to stay with us. I did so because, unlike the other crew members of the *Angelina Marie*, I think there is potential there. He seems to want to..." She waved a hand, searching for the right words. "He wants to experience life a little differently."

"I am sure you, of all people, can appreciate that. At the moment it may mostly be because he has taken a fancy to Li Mei, but we can use that to our advantage. So I need you to give him the benefit of the doubt and leave him be."

"He needs to let Jules—"

"He has already agreed to let Doctora examine him, and he will be signing our Articles this evening. Trust me, Felipe, this is something he wants. Do you believe me?"

Her large brown eyes searched his hazel ones, and he sighed.

"Oui, Madame. I trust your judgment. But you know you need only say the word, and I will take care of him for you."

"Which brings me to why I am upset with you. What is this I hear about Benny throwing sand into James's eyes? And a duel in July?"

The gunner let his head fall back with a groan.

"Jules. Why do you betray me like this?"

Doctora held up her hands and shook her head.

"I didn't. I promise."

Talia also raised her hands, lest the gunner turn his accusing eye on her next.

"No, it wasn't either of them. Captain James"—the Pirate Queen all but spat the name as she crossed her arms—"sent a representative this morning asking for Benny and his second to meet them on the beach at noon to discuss the terms."

She turned to Ben.

"What the hell is this all about?"

Ben and Felipe looked at each other for one beat before both started talking at once.

"He was saying some truly awful things, Mistress—"

"He is a *connard*, and he started all of it. Benny was—"

"You know we only want to keep everyone safe—"

"*Es un cabrón comemierda—*"

"Stop. Both of you, stop it."

She pinched the bridge of her nose.

"Benny, what happened?"

Ben swallowed.

"He was skulking around the ships in the dark. Then he started making threatening statements toward you, Mistress, and toward me. He challenged me to a duel. He threw a glove at me and everything. I did not even know people actually did that. I thought it only happened in books. This is... this is Knights of the Round Table nonsense."

The Black Rose blinked, confusion overtaking her anger. She turned to Felipe.

"El Rey Arturo, Ginebra y Lanzarote," the older man supplied.

Ben was once again in awe of the man's command of language.

"Oh."

"And clearly you were not raised with much money and an obsession with honor, were you?" the Frenchman asked, turning to Ben.

The younger man shook his head.

"My father discouraged dueling because he said it only separates the stupid from the lucky."

Felipe paused, his eyebrows climbing toward his headscarf.

"That… is not a bad way of looking at it, really. But it is a continental tradition. Trust me on this. I have had many gauntlets thrown at me."

"How many duels have you fought?"

The gunner paused to think, apparently counting on his fingers. Ben could not be entirely certain, but it looked as though the older man counted to around twenty-six before he stopped.

"Too many. And this is the only time I will admit to having been both stupid and lucky."

The Black Rose rolled her eyes and flicked a hand, swatting the conversation back toward relevance.

"But throwing sand at him, Benny? Playing dirty is so unlike you."

"That was an accident." Panic crept into Ben's voice. "I picked up the glove and threw it back at him. It must have gotten sand in it, but I promise you it was not on purpose."

She looked suspiciously from the younger man to the older. Felipe raised his hands in surrender, his voice softening as though she were a toddler on the verge of a tantrum and he an exhausted father.

"Madame, please. Do you trust that Benny and I want nothing more than to keep you, the crew, and this ship safe?"

The Captain made a strained sound in the back of her throat.

"I suppose I do," she conceded.

The gunner laid his large hands on her shoulders and leaned his forehead against hers.

"Then please, *s'il te plaît, por favor*, trust that we are doing what needs to be done to protect you, our crew, and this ship."

He kissed her forehead, ruffled her curls in a thoroughly paternal way, and straightened again. She stuck out her tongue at him, and he laughed.

"You are incredibly lucky that Alizée and I cannot stay angry with you for long. And Eliza too, though you certainly provoke her often enough. If anyone is going to snap and end you, my money is on her."

She chuckled, and the Frenchman laughed again.

"She has come very close. But I treasure all the darling daughters I have collected. I only wish to see them happy, safe, and well cared for."

"And my happiness at this juncture requires you making absolutely certain that Benny wins whatever nonsense comes of this."

"Oh, but of course, Madame. We shall preserve all the honor."

He thumped a fist over his heart and turned to Ben.

"It is fair to assume I will be your second?"

Ben nodded.

"I cannot think of a better person for this situation."

The gunner clapped his hands together, the crack loud in the small room.

"Very good. So we find out what our contest is, and then we prepare for that. In the meantime, Tobin and I get his hand-to-hand skills up to snuff, so if nothing else he can punch James very hard in his stupid, pretty face."

The Black Rose snorted with laughter even as Doctora gently slapped a hand to her own face. Tobin cracked his giant knuckles with a nod, and Ben suddenly felt uneasy at the thought of the quartermaster's fists rearranging his face. Or worse, winding up in a headlock in Felipe's massive arms.

Shit.

"Please do not cause any more trouble between now and noon."

The Frenchman bowed deeply.

"I shall do my best, but no promises."

The Captain gave him a look.

"Okay. Oui. Yes, promises. I promise there will be no trouble between now and noon. I will be in the armory at my workbench. I will even promise no explosions this time."

"Good. Thank you. Now I need to speak to Benny privately. The rest of you are dismissed."

Felipe moved toward the door, with Doctora and Talia behind him, but turned back.

"You will have him on the beach before noon, yes? It will not help our cause if we are late."

The Black Rose smiled.

"Of course, Felipe."

The gunner winked and held the door for Doctora and Talia to pass.

Tobin remained where he was, arms crossed, one eyebrow raised, as Ben giddily rubbed his hands together and approached the map.

*I'm going to talk to him. Stop worrying,* the Pirate Queen mouthed to her quartermaster.

He pursed his lips as though he did not entirely believe her, but nodded and walked out all the same.

Once the door clicked shut, the Black Rose tipped her head back with a sigh. She turned to find Ben already studying the map, disappointment shadowing his features.

"You already charted the course?"

"We did. That is not what I wanted you here for... unless you would like to make any changes?"

Now she was stalling. Fortunately, Ben did not notice. He was absorbed in the chart, muttering to himself. At length, he looked up.

"No, this course is quite good. We should be in Barranquilla in about five days. Well done."

"You can help us next time."

Ben straightened, smiling as he pulled her toward him, his head tipped like a puppy eager to play.

"So if I am not here to help with the map, what am I here—"

The Captain panicked.

She grabbed his chin and pulled him down into a kiss, cutting off the question. They parted breathing hard.

"I—"

Before the Pirate Queen could say anything else, Ben's fingers were tangled in her hair and his lips were on hers again. She melted into him. It was almost impossible to think about boundaries when Benny kissed her as though his mouth could melt clothes away. She did not want boundaries. She wanted his hands and his mouth and his cock. A small moan slipped out of her as she clutched his shoulders as if she might otherwise float away.

But she had to say something. This was why Tariq was leaving. Well, not this specifically, but Benny talking to other people about this.

But he certainly was not talking now. His tongue was in her mouth, challenging hers to a wrestling match she feverishly accepted. His hands slid from her hair to the back of her shirt, and his cock pressed against her stomach through two layers of fabric that needed to become zero layers as soon as humanly possible. He broke the kiss and pulled her tighter against him.

"Please tie me up and have your way with me, Mistress," he sighed against her cheek.

"Benny, it is a bit early for that, don't you think?" she said, trying to sound composed.

Ben did not answer. He had begun nibbling at her neck as though determined to leave another bruise.

"And don't bite me. At least not where everyone can see."

She gently pushed his face away. He made a low sound in his chest, took one of her hands, and kissed it. His long, slender fingers threaded with hers, and she could feel her resolve slipping further.

She had to say something before he—

"Last night you looked so strong and powerful sitting among those men. It was absolutely enrapturing. I wanted you to tie me up then and show me who was in charge. You wear authority so well. It is incredibly stimulating."

Well, shit. How was she supposed to tell him to stop talking when he spoke about her like that?

"Maybe tonight, once we're underway."

Her hand slid down his trousers and between his legs. Ben's eyes rolled back as she wrapped her fingers around something long, hard, and thick. She stroked him gently, feeling the silky skin move under her hand.

"Naughty boy likes being ordered around, does he?"

Ben drew a shaking breath.

"Yes, Mistress. I do. Very much so. I cannot really explain it, but it is incredibly attractive. You do not have to tie me up, but please, please at least favor me before I have to go down and talk to James."

"Very well."

Wait, no. She was supposed to be telling him how disappointed she was that he had been talking to other people about fucking her. She was supposed to be angry with him.

But desire took the helm.

Her blouse was over her head, her trousers on the floor, and Ben, now somehow also naked, was sitting on the edge of the bed, gesturing for her to join him. She moved to climb into his lap, but he turned her around and pulled her down onto his cock as though he were a chair, her personal throne of pleasure, drawing a gasp from her.

He planted his feet and lay back, guiding her up and down his length. She braced one hand on his thigh for balance while the other slipped between her legs to work at her pleasure. This was what she needed.

"Oh yes, Mistress," Ben groaned as the Captain swiveled her hips, chasing sensation. One of his large hands slid up her side to cup her breast, and the Black Rose let her head fall back. Her climax took her in a rush, her thighs shuddering as she nearly collapsed forward out of his lap. She knelt between his legs, trying to catch her breath.

"Finish yourself while I watch, you naughty boy."

Ben sat up, his hands going at once to his cock. He wanted to put on a show for her, but he was already so close. Her gaze heated, fixed on his hands as he stroked himself, baring the sensitive head and covering it again.

"Mistress, I would fight a hundred duels for you. I would die for you." He panted, flushed across face and chest. "Please touch me. Please, Mistress, I need—"

The Pirate Queen took over, stroking him with one hand while placing a soft kiss on the tip of his cock. That alone undid him. She squealed as he spasmed in her hand and spilled across her breasts. Ben fell back, breathing hard and wiping his face with his hand.

"Thank you, Mistress," he sighed as she handed him a cleaning rag and pulled him upright again.

"I do not want you to die for me, Benny," the Black Rose purred while he gently wiped her skin clean, kissing her as he went. She grabbed his curls, now growing long and unruly, and tipped his head back until they were nose to nose. "If you die, you will not be nearly as useful. Or as much fun. I like you useful and fun."

He shuddered, looking for a moment as though he wanted to tackle her back onto the bed for a second round.

"I shall do my best, Mistress," he whispered.

"Good. You are lucky that of all the people in this fleet, you chose to get on the bad side of the only one I truly do not like." She sighed as Ben buried his face between her breasts. "I am still very worried about all the crew from the *Angelina Marie* staying on their own ship with him, since he is former Royal Navy too."

"Well, you do not have to worry about me, Mistress," the man in her bosom said between kisses along her sternum, collarbone, and neck. "I certainly shan't leave you to go with them. And if we find he is a turncoat, we let Felipe have him. I am sure nothing would make the old goat happier."

"You don't miss being on a ship of all men?"

"Oh, heavens, no. I rather like the female company. Some more than others, of course."

He kissed her slowly. The Black Rose ran her fingers through his beard, and one caught on a tangle, making Ben pull away with a small "Ow."

"Benny, either before we leave or once we reach Barranquilla, you need a haircut. Maeve is excellent at cutting hair."

"Oh, I thought you might rather enjoy having something to grab and pull. I quite enjoyed it when you did it just now. And I know you like it when I pull yours."

He winked, wearing a wicked little smile, and it took every bit of the Captain's self-control not to pin him to the bed and begin experimenting at once.

"How about we wait until we make port? If we do not like it, I will speak to Maeve."

He nibbled at her ear, making her squirm.

"Your beard could certainly use a trim, though. I like it shorter, the way it was when you first came aboard. It is more sanitary, especially if your face is going to be between my legs."

He chuckled.

"Yes, Mistress. I was thinking the same thing."

"But please do not shave entirely."

"Of course not. I look like a child when I shave. I look like Juanito, only taller and ganglier."

She laughed, and he kissed her cheek.

"I'll trim my nails too. Can't have them scratching up this exquisite work of art."

She giggled, her cheeks warming.

"Very good. Clean yourself up and get down to the beach with Felipe. If you are a good boy, once we're underway, I can tie you up, and we can see whether we like your hair longer. If you want to do something about your beard and nails now, Tobin has all manner of razors, scissors, and tweezers. I am sure you have noticed how well maintained he keeps himself."

Ben had noticed that the quartermaster kept his head shaved, but it had not occurred to him until that moment that the only visible hair Tobin seemed to possess was his eyebrows, and even those were little more than thin lines.

"Why—?"

She held up her hands as she slipped out of his grasp to find her clothes.

"I do not ask, and he does not say. Far be it from me to tell him how to keep himself. I would be no better than that horrible man..."

She shuddered as she pulled her shirt over her head. Ben made a small, mournful "aww" as her breasts disappeared beneath the fabric.

"Don't worry. They will still be here tonight."

She handed him his clothes, and he stepped back into his trousers.

"Would you like me to..." He indicated his own chest hair.

"No. Not unless you intend to get tattoos there."

She ran her nails through it across his pectorals, which were growing more defined and beautifully tanned the longer he lived as a pirate.

"I like this just fine," she sighed dreamily. How was he this attractive? "You're beautiful, Benny."

He smiled broadly and pulled on his shirt.

"You're beautiful too, Mistress."

He drew her into his arms. The Black Rose noticed something different in his gaze, though she could not quite name it.

"You are so wonderful, and powerful, and—"

"Are you stalling with compliments again?"

He laughed and nuzzled her forehead.

"I do not want to leave without telling you I... I adore you. Like Felipe and Doctora, their little ritual. Felipe told me always to say goodbye."

She scoffed.

"Benny, it is not that serious. At least not at this moment. You are attending a conference, not a joust." She kissed his cheek. "But all the same, buena suerte."

They kissed once more before Ben headed off to find Tobin and borrow a grooming kit.

After the door clicked shut and she was sure he was out of earshot, Rosa struck the door with her fist.

She had not told him about Tariq. She had let herself be swept away again, let him make her feel as though they did not need boundaries. He said he adored her. What the hell did he mean by that? There had been something different in his eyes, hadn't there? Was Tobin right? Was she already too late? Was he already in love? Or was she imagining things that were not there?

This was all so confusing.

And now he was fighting a duel for her. What chivalrous nonsense.

She leaned her head against the rough wood and hit the door again.

Fuck.

At five minutes before noon, Ben, now with neatly trimmed nails and facial hair, and Felipe headed down the gangplank to the beach. Alizée met them on the sand.

"Pappy. Benny. What did you do now? James has been squawking all morning about how you tried to blind him."

Felipe sighed and swept his Little Bird into a large hug.

"I will say it until I turn blue. He started it. Does that ponce carry gloves solely to challenge people to duels?"

She shrugged.

"I do not think he has ever actually managed to fight one. He usually finds a way to get the other party in trouble before it can happen."

Ben and Felipe exchanged a look, brows raised.

"Well, that explains why he sent someone to tattle to the Captain on us," Ben said with a sigh.

"It got so bad that we had to change our Articles to ban duels outright. Before that, we had a rule that if you backed out of one, you automatically lost, but that was not fair to people who do not like to fight."

Felipe scoffed.

"He probably has no intention of actually coming, because..."

The gunner cupped his hands around his mouth, and his booming voice carried across the beach toward the *Angelina Marie*.

"James is a *connard*, a coward, and the dishonorable son of a flea-bitten whore!"

A commotion followed, and a figure in a tricorn festooned with enough feathers for several birds appeared at the rail.

"Fuck you, Felipe!" James shouted back.

"How about you come down here and do it for me? Maybe if you are a good boy, I will let you suck on my giant testicles!"

He lowered his voice and turned back to the others.

"That is not the word I wanted to use."

"I'm not sure what you intended to say, but I think it is effective regardless," Ben said with a laugh, and Alizée snorted.

There were more shouts and frustrated noises as James stumbled down the gangplank with someone following behind. Ben recognized not only the new gunner, Seth, but the same man who had made a snide racial comment about Felipe and Alizée when they first came ashore.

Fantastic.

"Well, well," James sneered. "Benjamin is looking rather different today. Trying to disguise yourself as someone worth a damn?"

Gods, Ben hated this arsehole.

"No, on the contrary. I simply wish to look my best, and you know it is bad luck to cut your hair and nails on the water."

"And you need all the luck you can get?" James asked dryly.

"No, actually. The Captain asked me to freshen up. Expressly for her pleasure, mind you."

Ben smirked as James's face twisted with confusion, as though he could not for the life of him imagine why the Black Rose might want Ben's nails and beard trimmed. Felipe was trying very hard not to laugh, and Alizée was shaking her head. Seth looked embarrassed to be part of any of it.

"Why does she—?" James began.

"Good God, man," Seth muttered. "He is making innuendo."

"I know that!" James snapped.

"Indeed. We squeezed in another quick tumble in the sheets, and she asked me to take care of that while we are still ashore," Ben said sweetly. "And then she gave me her blessing to utterly destroy you in July."

Now it was James's turn to plaster on a smile and speak through clenched teeth.

"And what does Benjamin want our contest to be, then? What has you so confident and cocky that you think you can even come close to destroying me?"

"I know it is not the traditional way to arrange a duel, but I will let you choose. Because I believe I can best you regardless of weapon. Swords, guns, or fists, I will put you in your place once and for all."

Ben could feel his confidence slipping. He had been hoping James would not call the bluff and choose—

"Fists, then."

Shit.

But Ben still smiled and held out his hand.

"Fists, after the Council convenes in July."

"And we will have the Black Rose choose the time and place," Felipe said quickly as James reached for Ben's hand.

James faltered and looked at Felipe in disgust.

"You are not worried about the two of you embarrassing yourselves in front of her?"

"On the contrary," Ben rumbled, dropping his voice as low as he could and channeling Tobin as best he was able, "I cannot wait to defeat you soundly and then make you watch me give her a big, sloppy victory kiss. Oh yes, it will be very sweet. Almost as sweet as the taste of her—"

"Very good," Alizée cut in. "We have our terms. Now shake on it, please."

James finally deigned to take Ben's hand, and they shook, each trying to make the other flinch by gripping too hard. Ben was pleased to discover they seemed fairly evenly matched. This might not be so bad after all. And he had two excellent men lined up to train him.

"Until July, then, Benjamin."

"Until July."

James looked toward Felipe and Alizée and snarled rather than speaking to them. Then he turned on his heel and marched back up to his ship, Seth hurrying after him. Felipe and Alizée both raised middle-finger salutes toward the new Captain's retreating back.

"Good riddance," Alizée spat.

Felipe put an arm around her shoulders.

"If nothing else good comes of this, I have one less worry tonight now that *cabrón* is off your ship."

She rested her head against the older man's shoulder, and he kissed her forehead the same way he had kissed the Captain's a few hours earlier.

"You and I both, Pappy."

Ben left Felipe and Alizée to their goodbye and climbed back up to his hammock to try for a quick nap before the tide came in and they could sail away. But since he would be at the helm when they departed, he felt as though his blood were crawling like ants through his veins. Not quite a fit of nerves, but close.

He pulled the key from his pocket and unlocked his lockbox, intending to make some drawings of that morning's lesson in his black rose-stamped journal. But the book of bilingual poetry caught his eye. He had been neglecting to ask the Captain for help learning Spanish, especially if they were going to Colombia next. If she really was from Cartagena, that would be close to her native turf. Barranquilla was only about a day's sail northeast.

Ben pulled out the volume and began leafing through it. He was not entirely sure what he was searching for, but so far the universe had been kind to him where falling in love with the Pirate Queen was concerned. Something that might tell her how he felt in a roundabout way, in case she reacted poorly to the prospect of a man she had only known for a month already being in love with her.

Glancing over the English versions of the poems, he found that Tobin had been right: some of them were filthy in the best possible way. He dog-eared a page containing a poem about the speaker licking every part of their lover and describing what each tasted like.

It was deeply stimulating, and Ben's mouth watered at the thought of licking the Captain's body... until the lover's slit was compared to an apple. That was so strange it looped back around into amusing. Ben decided to return to it later, if only to learn some of the innuendo and have a good laugh. He had only ever tasted one woman that way, but apples? How peculiar.

Then he turned the page and found the perfect sentence.

*I see all the stars in the sky in your eyes.*

Perfect.

Better still, because it was the first line, he did not have to go hunting for the translation in a sea of unfamiliar words.

*Veo todas las estrellas del cielo en tu mirada.*

And better still, it reminded him of stealing away to fuck her beneath the stars and watching one of his wildest fantasies come true. Which reminded him that he really ought to think up a few more wild fantasies in case they needed ideas. Ben copied the sentence into the back of his pocket notebook and went up to the armory to see if Felipe was there.

He was not.

Ben decided Felipe was probably spending every possible second with Alizée, so he went instead to see if Doctora might be free.

"¡Ay, joder, Juanito! You have to stay off your feet. Get back in bed, or I will make you drink more tea!"

"¡Pero Doctora...!"

"The only reason I didn't have to cut your toe off was because Felipe managed to yank that nail out. If you do not stay off your feet and get better, I definitely *will* have to cut it off!"

Juanito yelped.

"That's it. You're getting more tea!"

Doctora bustled out of the sick room looking harried. When she spotted Ben, she waved him over. Her spectacles were sliding dangerously low on her nose, and flyaway hairs stuck straight out from her bun. She looked as though she badly needed a break.

"Can you sit with him and make sure he doesn't get out of bed until I come back? Please?"

Ben nodded and slipped past her into the sick room. An astringent herbal scent met him at once. Behind him, Doctora made a noise of frustration as she headed for the stove.

She had not exaggerated about the size of the room. Juanito sat there looking sullen and defiant, arms crossed. A massive bandage wrapped his foot, and the bottom of it was already stained through with fresh, bright blood. He looked up at Ben, who waved awkwardly.

"Uh... hello."

The cabin boy sighed.

"I don't want to be in here. I have things to do."

"I understand that feeling entirely, but you are a bit young for a peg leg, don't you think?"

Then Ben was struck by inspiration. Felipe had threatened to make the children write lines, so they must know how to read.

"Can you read Spanish?"

Juanito nodded.

"We're all taught to read and write English, Spanish, and French. French is really hard, but Felipe said if I master French, he'll teach me Xiang's language so I can sail to China."

"Oh. Very good. What else do you learn here?"

"We learn about plants and herbs from Doctora. Felipe teaches us how to read maps and use and care for weapons. Tobin teaches us maths and how to work with money. Eliza helps us learn how to watch people and get information without asking directly, and she helps us mend and make clothes. That reminds me, I need her to show me how to let the hem out of my trousers because they're too short again.

Talia shows us how to fix things that aren't clothes. Maeve teaches us history and how to write stories and poetry in English and French. The Captain tells us about animals, and she makes us write daily journals for her in Spanish. Other people teach us things too, if they have time. Xiang taught us all how to make different knife cuts for different kinds of food. If you cut everything properly, it cooks evenly, so nothing burns."

Ben was astonished by how well rounded the children's education was aboard the *Deception*.

"And what do you like best?"

"I like learning from Xiang, and I like it when Felipe shows us maps of the world and tells us where he's been. He's been everywhere. I also like working with Talia. I want to be one of her mates when I get a little older. I love being up aloft. You can see the whole world from the nest, and I want to see the whole world."

Ben chuckled.

"Lofty aspirations for a lofty perch. But I agree, it's magical up there, isn't it?"

Juanito nodded.

"Can you do me a favor? Can you help me read a sentence? I want to learn to say it."

He pulled out the little notebook and showed it to the boy.

Juanito studied the sentence, then looked up at Ben. In a tone uncannily like Felipe's, French accent and all, he asked, "Well, how do you think it is said?"

Ben laughed and cleared his throat. His first attempt was dreadful. Juanito patiently explained the vowel sounds and helped him sound it out.

"Veo todas las estrellas del cielo en tu mirada," Ben repeated.

Juanito nodded.

"Felipe says that in Spanish you should build the words around the vowels. If you remember that each vowel only makes one sound, you can build the words from there."

"Huh. Thank you, Juanito. That was quite helpful."

"There are other things to remember too. Umm... two Ls make a y, like in *estrellas*. H is silent, and J makes an H sound, so when Doctora says *joder*, it's spelled with a J."

"Oh. All right, then."

Ben still did not quite know what *joder* meant, only that Doctora seemed to use it as a general expletive. He looked back down at his notebook.

"Veo todas las estrellas del cielo en tu mirada."

"I hope you aren't going to say that to Doctora. Felipe will kill you. He loves her whole lots, but we aren't allowed to say so because he gets embarrassed. And Doctora loves him whole lots too, but she gets sad about it because she's worried he'll die like her husband."

He sighed and scratched the back of his neck.

"Grown-ups are so weird. They tell us lying is bad, and then they turn around and do it. They'd both be happier if they just said they loved each other."

Ben could not help laughing at how perceptive the boy was.

"Right? I hate it when people don't say what they mean. All these stupid, unspoken rules everyone expects you to follow for no reason. Being an adult is terrible. But it is certainly better here than it was where I came from."

"Even though you had dragons?"

Ben smiled. He had meant the rigid social circles in Jamaica, but there was something sweet in Juanito remembering the story Ben had told him while treating his snakebite.

"Even though there were dragons."

"So who are you going to say that to? That is not something you should say to just anyone."

Ben was not sure he ought to tell him, since Juanito was only twelve after all, but the lad had been so helpful.

"Can you keep a secret?"

Juanito leaned in and nodded conspiratorially.

"I was going to say it to the Captain."

The boy gasped softly.

"Do you think she'll like that?"

Juanito nodded, then lay back and stared at the ceiling.

"You're so lucky you're old enough to be in love. I can't wait to fall in love. I hope she's smart, strong, and brave."

"All excellent qualities. And I am sure she will be worth the wait."

At that moment, Doctora returned carrying a large cup of floral tea.

"Here you go, Juanito. Drink up."

"But I don't want to go to sleep!"

Ben reached over and ruffled his hair.

"Maybe if you sleep for a bit, she'll visit you in your dreams."

The boy blinked, grabbed the teacup from Doctora, and chugged it in three large gulps. Then he lay back, folded his hands, and fell asleep within minutes. Doctora adjusted her spectacles, picked up the cup, and sighed, the wrinkles at the corners of her eyes deepening as she exhaled.

"I do not know what that was all about, but thank you."

Ben nodded.

"I have to put on a fresh bandage, and you will probably need to be on deck soon, but I appreciate whatever you said to him immensely."

Ben pulled the older woman into a hug, and she leaned into his shoulder.

"And thank you for the drawing. I love it."

Ben chuckled. He had left a drawing of Felipe conducting an experiment on her door the previous evening.

"I can assure you I have no idea what you're talking about, Doctora."

She lightly punched his shoulder.

"Get out of my sick room. But..." She looked up at him, eyes twinkling. "If you could perhaps suggest to a certain someone that I need a hug, I would be even more grateful."

"I'll see what I can do."

# Chapter 5

## Lore and Leaving

Ben made his way out onto the deck, pleased to see the tide coming in nicely. The *Deception* should be underway within an hour or two if the winds held. He looked down at the beach and saw Felipe, his normally pink face even more flushed than usual, enveloping Alizée in a huge bear hug. The Frenchman kissed both her cheeks, then her forehead, before making his way up the gangplank, wiping at his eyes.

"See you in July, Pappy!" she called after him.

"Not if I see you first, Little Bird! Fair winds to lead you forward!"

She blew him a kiss, which he pretended to catch in his fist before thumping it over his heart in salute. Then he turned and nodded at Ben. As the older man passed, the younger caught him by the elbow.

"I do not know if it will improve your emotional state, but Juanito was giving Doctora hell earlier, and she may have requested that you go down and give her a hug."

Ben was not sure how the gunner would take that, but he was startled when Felipe seized him by the shoulders, pulled him close, and whispered, "You are serious? You do not fuck with me?"

Ben nodded.

Felipe gave an excited little chortle. "¡Qué bueno! I shall give her *un abrazo muy fuerte*. Very strong."

They started toward the stairs together.

"Juanito is an interesting lad, isn't he?" Ben said.

"Oh, oui, he is a good boy, but maladroit... ah... *torpe*... no... merde... in-elegant? Clumsy? Clumsy. Yes, clumsy." Ben nodded to show he understood. "That is such a strange word, non?"

"Let me guess, he gave Jules a hard time because he wanted to fulfill his duties?"

Ben nodded again. Felipe sighed.

"He is very enthusiastic. That is why he hurts himself so often. He gets too excited to pay attention to his body, like... like a very large puppy with feet too big and a tail too long. But he is good with numbers, and he writes well in English and Spanish, and he will succeed at whatever he sets his mind to... if he can keep himself alive."

"I know he wishes to become a boatswain, but he will need to improve a great deal with ropes and tools. I think he would make a good quartermaster, so I am going to suggest that Maeve have him start assisting Tobin. Now, Gerda, on the other hand? She is boatswain material down to her bones."

He continued, "Where did Juanito come from? I know Gerda is here with Anya and Zsófia, Giselle is with Jean-Luc and Maeve, and Toñiete is with Arturo, but I do not think I know who Juanito belongs with."

"He is what you English call a... uh... guttersnipe. No family. He was begging in the street in Campeche, outside Mama Tati's. She and I had, eh, one of our little disagreements over price, and she threw me out."

Ben snorted. Felipe loved haggling in Mama Tati's pawnshop to the point of annoyance.

"I bought an *elote* to soothe my sorrow, and he kept staring at me while I tried to eat it, so I bought him one too. He was maybe eight or nine? About four years ago? He decided to follow me back to the ship and tried to stow away. I let him have his game, but the moment came when I had to ask him—or rather, the pile of canvas he was hiding under—whether he was completely certain this was what he wanted, because we were not likely to return to Campeche for quite some time."

"He begged, said he would do anything so long as I did not turn him back out into the streets. I made him promise to work hard, to study, and to learn, and he has kept every promise. He is an honorable one, and he holds himself to a high ideal. So yes, he may be awkward and clumsy, but he is a good boy. Being able to see so many places and work with so many different people at a young age is good for him."

He sighed, and Ben knew the Frenchman was no longer standing on the deck beside him.

"I think Jules gets frustrated with him because she substitutes him for her son. They would have been about the same age had Octavio survived the birth, so she is extra protective of Juanito. To her, he seems reckless, even though he is not, not really. He is a normal boy of that age. She has an idea of what a boy that age should be, but she has not experienced the reality..." He clicked his tongue. "So you and she have that in common, eh?"

Ben felt his cheeks warm. Doctora had not mentioned her son, but it explained the shift in her manner during his interview on his first day aboard, when he had explained that he married at seventeen to give proper parentage to a child who was ultimately stillborn.

"She told you about my daughter?"

Felipe raised both hands. "She said you understand her in the worst possible way. I inferred the rest, especially after the way you reacted when I told you about Jackie, Alicia, and Abbie back in Campeche. Really, Benny, you must stop thinking I am stupid."

He thumped Ben on the back.

Ben remembered how he had felt when Felipe told him about one of his former mates, Jackie, who had felt the Call of the Land. She and Felipe had walked up to her love's house only to find his massively pregnant wife, Alicia, at the door. Alicia had become so distressed that she went into labor on the spot, and Doctora had delivered her of a little girl, Abbie. The husband had reacted badly to the birth of a daughter instead of a son.

He had accused Doctora of witchcraft and tried to lay hands on her, which resulted in him being beaten soundly by the gunner. Later, the man drank himself to the wrong end of a knife in a tavern brawl, and Jackie and Alicia were now raising Abbie together in Kingston. That awful man had been handed a healthy, beautiful, living daughter, the thing Ben had wanted most in the world, and had answered it with anger and abuse. Ben still believed with all his heart that the man had deserved what he got.

"But you still have time, *mon frère*. Even if you do not succeed the way you intend, you are made to be a good husband and a good pappy. If you feel the Call of the Land, we would understand."

Ben shook his head firmly, and Felipe laughed.

"I know, you have set your heart on taming the wildest Rose on the seven seas."

He winked.

"Speaking of taming hearts, if you will excuse me, I have a *beauté ravissante* in need of an embrace. But I will be back before we set off."

He clapped Ben on the back once more and started away.

"Give her a kiss while you're at it!" the younger man called after him.

Felipe turned and threw up another middle-finger salute as he walked backward.

"I take it back. You are terrible, and I should cut out your tongue and let Mar have it for a chew toy!"

Even so, the Frenchman laughed and disappeared down the steps. Ben chuckled too, though he was fairly certain the ship's dog, a medium-sized shaggy brindled mutt, preferred living prey like rats and insects.

Roughly an hour later, everyone was on deck preparing to weigh anchor and get underway. Ben was pleased to feel the wind freshen considerably, somewhere around five knots. That would make things easy.

The *María del Mar* caught the breeze first, being the easternmost ship. Ben could see Alizée perched on her quarterdeck, waving. Everyone aboard the *Deception* waved back, and in his heart Ben wished her and her crew, Tariq especially, fair winds and following seas. Though he had only known her for a few days, he could already see why Felipe adored her, and he found he rather liked her too. And if she reminded Felipe of Letty, then Letty must also have been a truly exceptional woman.

Speaking of exceptional women, the Black Rose stood at his elbow, waving toward the *María del Mar*, grinning from ear to ear as she gleefully shouted orders. Ben had noticed it in Campeche too: she was often dour while coming into port, yet intensely excited to leave for some new adventure. Her excitement was contagious. He could not help smiling too.

The *Angelina Marie* pulled away next, and out of the corner of his eye Ben saw a certain Frenchman throwing two middle-finger salutes with such vigor that his massive arms were quivering.

Once the *María del Mar* and *Angelina Marie* were safely away, Ben threw back his head and shouted up to Talia.

"Hey, Tals!"

"What, Benny?"

"Come all ye young sailor-men, listen to me!"

"I'll sing you a song of the fish in the sea!"

Talia joined in, and a fair number of the crew followed, including the Captain. It was one of the boatswain's favorite songs, and she leaned forward through the ropes looking like a figurehead.

"Then blow, ye winds, westerly, westerly blow,
We're bound to the south'ard, so steady she goes!"

Ben drew in a deep breath of the salty wind, with the faintest perfume of tropical foliage bidding him farewell. Their next port awaited.

# Chapter 6

## The Recently Recruited

Soon they were underway, and most of the crew returned to their usual duties. The Pirate Queen still stood beside Ben, scanning the horizon, her curls whipping wildly despite the scarf's attempt to tame them, her eyes sparkling with reflected sunlight from the waves.

*Veo todas las estrellas del cielo en tu mirada,* Ben thought.

She was exquisite. A faint floral scent still drifted from her, delicious and sweet. She caught him staring and smiled.

"So how did you like my island?" she asked.

"It was fantastic. I already have some thoughts about the next time we go back."

She laughed.

"I'm sure you do."

She leaned in close and whispered in his ear, one finger trailing lightly along his arm.

"After we swear Frank in this evening, we'll do that thing you asked me about earlier."

She drew back and winked, and Ben's skin went hot.

"Trust me, I didn't forget," she said with a sly smile.

Then she was gone, and Ben set their heading for Barranquilla.

As expected, supper moved much faster now that there were three people working the line. Unfortunately, Frank's temper flared, and he got into a shouting match with boatswain's mate Arturo over cabin boy Toñiete's supper. Felipe sighed heavily, seized Doctora by the wrist, and dragged her with him to the front of the line.

The Frenchman walked around the serving station, lifted the English sailor a good fifteen centimeters off the deck by the back of his collar, and turned him toward Doctora as though he were presenting a misbehaving puppy.

Doctora's face flushed, though Ben could not tell whether from surprise, embarrassment, or lust. Perhaps all three. She gathered herself and calmly explained that Toñiete was going through a growth spurt and therefore needed a larger ration.

She assured Frank there would be more than enough food to go around and that Toñiete would certainly eat every bite of it. Frank, pale as death, nodded. Felipe set him back on his feet and glared until the smaller man added another ladleful of stew to Toñiete's bowl. The boy bowed politely, and his older brother gave a clipped thank-you before they left the line.

"All the children may eat as much as they like. I promise, nothing will go to waste," Doctora said with a kind smile before taking Felipe by the wrist and leading him back to the end of the line.

Frank kept his head down through the rest of supper service, and there were no more arguments.

After supper, Felipe escorted Frank to Doctora's quarters. He insisted on being present for the examination in case the man gave the physician any more trouble. Doctora asked Ben to stand guard at the door and turn away any non-emergency visitors.

As he waited with his arms crossed over his chest, Ben's thoughts drifted to the evening ahead. The thought of the Black Rose tying him up and pulling his hair was thrilling. But now that he was in love with her, ought he not to try making love to her like a gentleman? That might prove difficult if she would not allow him on top of her. That was her only real rule. He would have to think on it more. He wanted to experience the full spectrum of pleasure with her and hoped she wanted the same.

He did not dwell on the things he wanted to do with, and to, the Black Rose for long, because raised male voices sounded behind him. Then came the crack of a slap, followed by a second, quieter one.

"Stop it. Both of you, out. Now!"

Doctora pounded on the door, and Ben scrambled aside as she yanked it open, the smell of herbs flooding the hall. Frank and Felipe each had a hand pressed to one cheek. Frank's did a poor job of concealing the massive red handprint the gunner had left behind.

Felipe was pouting, but even so there was a spark of desire in his eyes. The physician's tawny cheeks were flushed, her jaw clenched, and her dark eyes blazed with barely contained fury. Felipe, meanwhile, looked at her as though she were the most beautiful thing he had ever seen.

"Even I must leave, Jules?" His voice was quiet, reverent, with the faintest hint of pleading.

"Obviamente. Who else do you think counts as 'both of you'?"

"Benny?"

She rolled her eyes.

"As far as I am aware, Benny is not trying to start any fights right now. Are you, Benny?"

"No, ma'am. One is enough for today, and certainly not with you."

"Benny, please inform the Captain that Frank is physically fit to remain aboard. You"—she pointed at Frank—"go gather anyone you wish to witness you swear in. And you"—now pointing at Felipe—"wait upstairs and keep your hands to yourself. I need a few minutes."

Felipe opened his mouth to argue, but she slammed the door in his face. He turned toward Frank, and the smaller man yelped and scrambled away. Ben stepped into the gunner's path before he could follow.

"What on earth was that about?" Ben asked, grabbing Felipe by the shoulders and physically turning him toward the stairs.

"That *connard* would not stop telling her how to do her job. Then he said he would not trust her to patch a leaky bucket. I informed him that Jules is as fine a carpenter as she is a doctor, and he rolled his eyes and said I only say that because I wish to..." He dropped his voice to a mutter. "...fuck her."

They reached the top of the stairs and the door to the Captain's quarters. Ben raised his hand to knock, then stopped and turned to him.

"He said that? In front of her? Oh dear. That's terrible."

"Do you see why I slapped him? He was disrespecting her. I should have knocked his teeth out."

At that moment the door to the Black Rose's quarters opened, and she peered out at them.

"Is everything alright?"

Ben lowered his hand.

"Uhhh, Doctora is done examining Frank. He is physically fit to remain aboard. However..."

"However I may have violated Article Six... again," Felipe muttered. "But Jules then slapped me, and I feel that is punishment enough."

"Even though you liked it," Ben fake-coughed.

The gunner whirled on him, pointing with a hard finger and a slight snarl.

"Benny. Now is not the time, and I already—"

The Captain stepped out and placed herself between them, keeping Ben behind her much the way he had separated Felipe from Frank moments before.

"Why does Frank upset you this much?" she asked, her voice calm. "Help me understand."

"He..." The Frenchman fumbled for words. "He disrespects Jules. He insulted her abilities, and then, when I defended her, he said I only did so because I wished to..." He dropped to a mumble. "...fuck her."

"But... you... do?" the Captain asked, plainly confused.

"That is not the point!" Felipe screeched, his face flushing with anger and embarrassment. "And he has a terrible temper, and he treats the women on this ship poorly. It is only a matter of time before he disrespects you too."

The Pirate Queen looked a little startled by her gunner raising his voice at her, but she straightened and poked him in the chest with one finger.

"Have you considered what he is doing to *your* temper? You have been so much angrier since he came aboard. Do you need to start meditating with Xiang and Tobin?"

Felipe stretched his fingers, then clenched them again, drawing deep breaths. The Black Rose gently touched his cheek.

"I appreciate that you're protective of us. I really do. And I understand that it pains you to see someone disrespect Doctora. But you cannot let it anger you like this. What would we do if you had an ah-nay-ooh-ree-sum?"

She opened her arms, and he accepted the hug, resting his chin atop her head.

"It is *an-yer-ism* in English," Felipe grumbled, though some of the fight had gone out of him.

"Aneurysm," she repeated.

"I do not like these Royal Navy types... present company excluded," he added, glancing at Ben and winking. His tone shifted then, and Ben recognized it as the same one Felipe used during their fencing demonstrations, when he wanted to showcase Ben's virtues to the Captain. "Benny is a very good man. We were very lucky to find him. And Andrew is excellent as well. But almost every other Royal Navy man we have encountered has been terrible."

"I know," she said, rubbing the older man's back. "But I believe Frank can become a better person. Perhaps not quite as good as Benny and Andrew, but they are rare bugs indeed."

Both of them looked at Ben, who shrugged.

"Most of the men I knew in the Royal Navy thought I was a poor example of an officer, so I much prefer being your... rare bug?"

"That is not exactly what she means. She is translating *bicho raro*, which means..." Felipe paused, waving a hand in a circle as he silently tested words. "Something like eccentric."

Ben lifted his brows.

"Ah, yes, like an odd duck. Doctora has called me *bicho raro* before. Eccentric is one of the nicer things I have been called, so I'll take it."

"It is a good thing to be. It means you are interesting. We like interesting people, Madame, oui?"

Felipe slipped free of the Black Rose's embrace, turned her gently toward Ben, and nudged the two of them together, wagging his eyebrows over the top of her head.

"I will wait for everyone on deck. I have two pistols on my belt that we can use."

Then he turned and walked away, humming something that sounded suspiciously like "Red Is the Rose."

The Black Rose's hand rose to Ben's cheek, and she ran her fingers through his freshly trimmed beard.

"I like this so much better," she murmured.

After making sure no one was coming, she kissed him on the lips. The kiss was brief, and Ben wanted more. Could they not just swear Frank in and be done with it so he and the Captain could have their fun? She lightly scratched his jaw, then caught his ear and pulled him down so she could whisper into it, her warm breath making both his hair and his cock stand at attention.

"I can't wait to get you into my bed tonight."

"Yes, Mistress," he sighed, nuzzling her cheek with his nose. "I have been very naughty, and I require punishment."

He straightened as they heard movement on the stairs behind them. Doctora, Frank, Li Mei, Xiang, and Tobin appeared just as the Black Rose stepped away and assumed an authoritative posture, which did nothing whatsoever to help Ben's arousal. Fortunately, no one seemed to be paying him any attention.

"Are you ready, Frank?" the Pirate Queen asked.

The smaller man nodded. The red handprint still blazed on his cheek.

The Captain turned and led him onto the deck.

Felipe stood beside the Articles with his arms crossed, a pistol in each hand, his expression sour but somewhat softened from before. Talia stood beside him, harness still strapped around her waist. Doctora crossed to Felipe's side and rubbed his back. He smiled down at her, and she gently bumped his hip with hers. Plainly, no real affection had been lost between them. If anything, Felipe was probably even more enamored of her for having slapped him.

The Black Rose indicated the papers tacked to the wall behind her.

"Frank, please take a moment to read over our Articles. We can answer any questions you might have."

Frank scanned the Articles, then turned and pointed at Felipe.

"He hit me. That—"

The Captain raised a hand calmly.

"I am aware. However, please read the rest of the sentence."

Frank huffed, but turned back to the paper. He mouthed the words as he read, then went pale.

**VI. No striking one another on board, but all quarrels be ended on shore with pistol and sword.**

"Oh," he said quietly. "No, thank you."

The Captain nodded.

"Exactly. So I suggest you both learn to get along. The best way for you to do that is to stop insulting my officers, Frank. Especially our good Doctora."

Frank glanced toward the physician. Felipe wrapped an arm protectively around her waist, subtly angling the pistol in his other hand toward the new recruit from the level of her hip. The Frenchman narrowed his eyes. Ben made a point of fixing the image in his mind to draw later.

Felipe looked very *dur à cuire*, and though Ben still was not entirely sure of the precise translation, he had gathered it meant something close to *tough*. This certainly qualified. Frank seemed to think so too, because he gulped.

"Yes, ma'am," he choked out.

He finished reading the Articles, then looked to Li Mei and Xiang, who both nodded encouragement. Frank drew a breath and let it out slowly.

"I am ready to swear, sign, and join your crew."

Then he turned to Doctora. Felipe instinctively pulled her closer.

"I am very sorry for how I acted earlier. I should not have insulted you. This is all very... different... for me."

"Different is not always so bad, is it?" the physician asked with sympathy.

Frank shook his head.

"No, Doctor Pérez, it's not."

Doctora nodded, and Felipe let his hand fall, stepping forward. He held the pistols crossed and level, though the threat in his eyes remained unmistakable. Ben was not always the best at reading people, but he knew exactly what Felipe was trying to convey without words:

If you wish to survive aboard this ship, do **not** insult my Jewels again.

The rest of the ceremony passed without incident. After the Black Rose dismissed everyone, she and Ben wandered to the rail to watch the sunset. Ben desperately wanted to put an arm around her, draw her close like he had on the beach, and kiss her as the pinks and oranges deepened into purples, blues, and finally black, but he restrained himself.

Her floral lotion mingled with the salt air, casting a tantalizing spell over him. Ben rested a hand on the rail, and she placed hers beside it. Not over his, but still touching. He turned slightly to look at her and found her doing the same. They laughed, and she lightly rested her pinky on top of his.

"Shall we?" she purred, glancing around.

"Yes, please, Mistress," he whispered.

"Wait five minutes, then come."

He nodded, and she walked away, her curls whipping behind her like a hurricane.

# Chapter 7

## Submission and Stories

Ben knocked tentatively on the door five minutes later and felt a rush as the Captain yanked him into her quarters by his shirt. He had been waiting for this.

His eyes adjusted to the low light as she latched the door. The Black Rose had spent the intervening minutes lighting lanterns and incense, so her room glowed as if he had stepped into heaven itself. The scent of spices and flowers only heightened the ethereal effect. Ben reached to take her into his arms, and she slapped his hands away.

"No," she growled sharply. "Clothes off and on your knees."

"Yes, please, Mistress."

Ben dropped his trousers and dragged his shirt over his head. Naked as ordered, he knelt on the floor with his hands in his lap, looking up at his Captain. His cock strained toward her, every nerve in his body aching for contact. She wore her delicate, sheer white gown, and her beautiful lips curled in a snarl as she bared her teeth at him. She ran a single fingernail up his arm and across his back as she circled him. Then she grabbed his hair and pulled gently.

Even expecting to like it, he had not anticipated the delicious ribbon of pleasure-pain that ran down his body. He moaned softly as she tipped his head back and made him look up at her.

"Is this what you want, Benny, you naughty boy?" she growled.

"Yes," he said quietly.

"Yes, what?"

"Yes, Captain. Please, Captain."

She bent just out of reach of a kiss, her fingers still tangled in his hair.

"Do you want to be allowed to fuck me?"

Ben nodded desperately, and the Black Rose tightened her grip.

"Use your words, Benny."

"Please let me fuck you, Mistress."

She turned and walked to the bed.

"Come, Benny. I would like to see how well you trimmed your beard before I tie you up."

"Yes, Captain."

Ben began to rise, then was struck by an idea. Instead, he crawled toward her on his hands and knees. His little display of submission earned him a slight moan as she spread her legs and licked her lips. She wanted him badly. The feeling was entirely mutual.

When he reached her feet, Ben lifted one and pressed a light kiss to the top of it, once again noticing the tiny glyph of a rooster. She had a small pig on the top of her other foot. He really ought to ask about that, but not now. He kissed up her ankle, her calf, her knee, and her thigh, feeling her body warm with every brush of his mouth and mustache against her skin.

By the time he reached the apex of her thighs, the Black Rose was nearly vibrating with lust. She traced her nails over his ear the way he liked, then tangled both hands in his hair and drew him closer.

"Lick me. That's an order."

"Yes, Mistress," he murmured before obeying.

The Black Rose placed one knee on his shoulder, opening herself to his worshipping mouth. He was her servant, devoted to her body. His tongue and fingers, now practiced, made an offering of love and lust that she accepted greedily, gently tugging his hair to guide him where she wanted him.

She came with a cry, falling back onto the altar of her bed and panting. Ben remained kneeling on the floor, his fingers lightly stroking her thigh while she composed herself.

"Very good, Benny," she said when she found her voice again.

She stood and helped him to his feet. Then she put an arm around his waist, twirled them both gracefully, and pushed him onto the bed.

"The naughty boy wants to be tied up, does he?"

Ben nodded fervently.

"Yes, Captain. Please, Captain."

"Sit with your back against the headboard."

Ben scrambled across the broad expanse of the bed and did as he was told. He sat upright and let her tie his arms outstretched to either side with ropes threaded through the headboard. From there the ropes ran up the wall and across the ceiling in a Y shape.

The Pirate Queen returned to the middle of the bed and pulled the trailing end taut, ensuring he would not be able to move his arms. Ben very much did not want to. Despite the ache in his cock, this was wildly stimulating. She was beautiful, and soon enough she would be on top of him.

Once the Captain was satisfied, she looked him over. He stared up at her, eyes bright with excitement, cock rigid, a hungry smile curving his lips. He really was the strangest man she had ever met. She grabbed another handful of his hair.

"Beg me to suck your cock," she whispered against his mouth.

"Please, Captain. Please suck my cock. Please." His voice had dropped deeper, roughened by need.

She slid down over him until she reached her destination.

"Are you sure you don't want me to play with it first?" she asked, tapping him lightly with one finger so he bobbed downward and sprang back into place.

Ben winced, his voice strained. "Whatever you would like, Captain. Please."

The Black Rose wrapped a hand around him and gently scraped her nails down the length. Ben shifted his hips, desperate for more.

"Yes, Captain. Please, Captain."

She kissed the tip lightly and flashed him a dazzling smile before taking him into her mouth again. Ben tipped his head back, closing his eyes and sinking into the sensation. The warmth of her mouth on his skin was as addictive as her kisses. She reached up and dragged her nails down his pectoral muscle, drawing a soft sound from her captive. He was enjoying this very much. Nothing else existed except the Pirate Queen's touch.

Then suddenly her mouth was gone. Her hands were gone. Ben's eyes flew open.

She was removing her gown.

Oh. Now it was getting serious.

The Black Rose smiled at him as she climbed over his body and sank down onto him, taking him into her willing heat. Perhaps it was the position, but he felt even larger than usual. She rolled her hips to accommodate his length and girth, her breasts brushing his chest as she settled into his lap. Ben gave a low moan and licked his lips as though hoping for a kiss. It was much more fun to deny him. She leaned in close but kept her lips just out of reach as she began to move. Twining a lock of his hair around one finger, she tugged lightly. Ben groaned, his eyes rolling back.

"You feel so good," he rasped as she rode him steadily, her hands gliding over his neck, shoulders, and chest. He was surrounded by her warmth.

She tugged his hair again, tipping his head back, then held her nose close to his, her lips still withheld. Unlike some of the times they had fucked, he was entirely present, looking at her with an intensity that made her shiver as though he had traced a finger across one of the most sensitive parts of her body.

"Should we play our game where you aren't allowed to come until I kiss you?" she whispered.

"I am at your mercy, Captain. I will do whatever you want, but please don't stop touching me."

She pushed his face down between her breasts, took another small section of his hair at the back of his head, and pulled. He exhaled in a soft moan, his breath hot against her skin.

"Exquisite. Fantastic. Marvelous," he muttered, his freshly trimmed beard grazing her sensitive flesh.

The Pirate Queen felt her release approaching and guided his face to her neck. He took the hint at once, kissing and licking just below her ear where he knew she loved it most. She felt the edge of his teeth and pinched his nipple.

"No biting. No bruises, naughty boy."

"Yes, Captain," he murmured.

She began to rock harder, grinding herself against him as if nothing in the world mattered except her own release. And she found it, moaning and trembling in his lap. Then she rose onto her knees, letting his cock slip from her body, and dragged his face up into a fierce, hungry kiss. Turning away, she gave him several hard strokes, and he came as well. Ben closed his eyes with a sigh as his body shivered under the flood of sensation.

The Captain leaned over for a rag and cleaned him up. Once she was done, the Black Rose settled back into his lap. Ben savored the warmth of her skin against his and felt her shifting slightly as she tilted her head first one way, then the other. Her rough but gentle hands moved over his chest and neck before coming to rest on his cheeks.

"Are you alright?" she asked softly.

"I am," he murmured. "That was excellent, as always. I enjoyed it very much."

The Captain tugged his hair again, and he opened his eyes. She gave a girlish giggle, kissed him on the lips, and untied him. She kissed his wrists as the ropes fell slack, then scrambled out of his lap. Ben stretched out on the bed, rubbing his arms.

The Black Rose flopped down beside him and snuggled into his chest. Ben pulled her closer and rubbed her back, savoring the feel of her skin under his hands after being denied the chance to touch her for so long. She looked up at him, candlelight reflected in her deep brown eyes.

"Veo todas las estrellas del cielo en tu mirada," Ben breathed as the Black Rose brushed her lips against his.

She paused and looked at him oddly.

"What? Where did you learn to say that?"

"Uh, Mama Tati sold me a bilingual poetry book. I told you, I want to learn Spanish so I can talk to you."

She studied him for a moment.

"Hmm. Bring it with you sometime. I'd be interested to see what sorts of poems are in this book."

"Did I say it right?"

"That you see all the stars in the sky in my eyes?"

"That was what I was aiming for, yes."

"Then I suppose you did."

They kissed again. Ben instinctively made this one sweeter, more tender, which made the Pirate Queen draw back slightly, disguising it as a stretch of her leg. With those words, all her unease came rushing back. While she still was not entirely certain, it truly did feel as though there was something in the bed with them now that had not been there before. He usually fucked her like a starving wild creature, all growls and claws and violence. Now there was softness in his gaze, gentleness in his touch, a purring note in his voice she was not sure she had noticed before. Had he always been like this, and she had simply been too ravenous to notice?

The obvious solution was to bury her face in his chest so she did not have to look him in the eye.

Obviously.

The sound of his heartbeat soothed her, and she relaxed against him. Ben stroked her hair, unaware that anything was amiss with his lover. He was never quite sure what prompted it, but the next question out of his mouth would become something of a ritual for them whenever they left land.

"What was your favorite thing that happened while we were ashore?"

The Black Rose blinked, then pursed her lips and thought, drumming her nails on his bicep.

"I want to say what happened under the waterfall, since that is something I have always wanted to do, but I think it was when we were on the beach and you tilted my chin up to watch the stars while you were fucking me. That was quite magical." She absently traced swirls through his chest hair with one finger. "What about you?"

"That was spectacular. It may also be my favorite. But I rather liked watching you swim. You are so beautiful I could have watched you for hours. Oh, and sneaking away to fuck right under James's nose during supper, knowing how badly he wants you? That was delicious. We should have taken Talia's suggestion and fucked in his bed."

She snickered. "Maybe in July, when I inspect the ships."

Then her smile faded.

"I wish he would turn his attention elsewhere. I'm sorry you got tangled up in all his nonsense. I still can't believe you're fighting a duel for me."

Ben waved a hand. "I will do everything I can to put him in his place. But Alizée did warn us he is a coward who likes getting his opponents into trouble, so we may have to worry about him trying to go to the authorities in Santo Domingo."

She scoffed.

"All these years in my fleet and he never learned a word of Spanish. You have learned more in a month than he has since he was fourteen. None of the rest of his crew speak it either. So unless they lied to us, I would love to see him try to get you in trouble."

The Black Rose stretched, and Ben caught her hand and kissed it.

"You're exquisite," he murmured as he kissed each finger in turn, then reached over and squeezed her breasts, drawing another lovely laugh from her. "But I suppose I'm dismissed again?"

She sighed.

"Indeed, helmsman... though what is this I hear about you collecting stories?"

The question was not accusatory, but Ben flushed anyway and began to stammer.

"I... uh... think these people are very interesting and I... uh... don't want them lost to history. So Felipe and I are collecting everyone's stories... for posterity. And I'm drawing portraits."

"I know. I saw the one of Felipe in Doctora's quarters. She likes it very much. She did tattle on you and Felipe today, just not in the way Felipe thought." She laughed. "You know I like my books, and I think a book about our crew would be very special. As you said, I do tend to collect interesting people."

"And you are, again, the most interesting of all." He kissed her forehead. "So we have your blessing to continue?"

She nodded.

"Doctora is mostly worried about it being used as evidence against us. If anything happens, if we are captured, I want you to bring it in here and hide it among my books. Any pirate trial would move too quickly for them to inspect every single volume for evidence, so that should keep it safe. And since many of these books are quite valuable, it also means someone important may one day read our stories."

"Very good, Mistress."

"And in the meantime, let us make sure our stories are worth hearing."

Ben chuckled, pressed another kiss to her cheek, and nuzzled her with his nose.

"Of course, Mistress."

"I know it will be difficult, but please let Tobin and Felipe train you so you can beat James so thoroughly that even he cannot twist the truth."

Ben nodded solemnly. "Tengo muy grandes cojones."

She shoved him away playfully.

"Sí, cojones muy grandes," she corrected with a titter. "Very big testicles."

That night, Ben brought the little pocket notebook to the armory. He found Felipe throwing a metal star into the wall beside his workbench. A small patch of wood, roughly the size of Ben's palm, was scarred from repeated assault, but the gunner's aim was excellent, his movements controlled and graceful.

Flick, thunk, pull, repeat.

Flick, thunk, pull, repeat.

"I wish that prick Frank had stayed with his own crew," the Frenchman muttered, continuing to throw the star.

"You thought I was a prat, a prick, and a ponce," Ben reminded him with a chuckle.

Felipe shrugged, though he did not laugh.

"I did not know what to make of you, surrendering to us when you could have gone merrily on your way with a hell of a story to tell back home. You could have been a legend in the Royal Navy, you know. The man who fucked a Pirate Queen and lived to tell the tale. I could not understand why you would want to stay. And now that I know you, I understand perfectly. I am surprised you rose as far as you did in the Royal Navy..." He held up both hands as Ben stared at him incredulously. "Not because I do not see your talent, because I certainly do. But the world is not built for men such as you and I, and many people would prefer that we not succeed."

Ben inhaled deeply. He had known this would have to come out eventually. At least Felipe would likely understand.

"Captain Reynolds, my commanding officer on the *Starling*... he sabotaged my navigation exam. He liked Thomas a great deal more than he liked me. He thought me argumentative and standoffish. I'm sure you've noticed that I don't tend to soften my opinions..."

The Frenchman clutched his chest theatrically as though seized by apoplexy.

"Non. Benny, please tell me more."

Ben chuckled.

"But how did he sabotage you?"

"Thomas and I were both ready to sit the exam. Normally in the Royal Navy, the first person to pass would have been promoted to navigator of their ship, and the second reassigned after the next tour. Unbeknownst to me, the Academy was planning to have us sit the exam at the same time and promote whoever earned the higher score. On a mock exam, I missed only one question, and that worried Reynolds enough that he gave me the wrong date and time. I had to call in a massive favor to be allowed to make it up, and I ended up with a perfect score."

"Of course you did." The Frenchman clapped him on the back like a proud father. "You are a very clever one. Far too clever for the Royal Navy. You are better off here with us. This is a far more fitting story for a man such as yourself."

Ben smiled at the compliment, but then remembered something.

"Oh, before I forget, we have the Captain's blessing to continue our project."

Felipe looked at him oddly, as though trying to solve a difficult sum. Ben wanted very badly to make sure he did not arrive at the correct answer, namely that Doctora had tattled on them to the Captain. So he blurted out the first believable thing he could think of.

"I told her about it. Sorry. It just slipped out."

Now it was the gunner's turn to snort dismissively.

"I miss being fucked so well I tell all my secrets."

"You may yet see those days again. Jules—"

Felipe sat up straighter and pointed the sharp little star at Ben. For a moment, the younger man genuinely worried he might throw it and flinched away from the tip.

"Benny, I promise, you do not want me thinking about how Jules fucks, especially not after that display today. She is astoundingly beautiful when she is impassioned, and that slap..." He smiled and sighed, his eyes bright as his hand drifted to his cheek. "I will make you very uncomfortable very quickly if I indulge this thought for any longer than the span of this sentence."

Ben theatrically snapped his jaw shut, pantomimed locking it, and tossed away the imaginary key.

The Frenchman chuckled.

"So, we have Madame's approval, and it no longer has to be secret. That is nice. Though nothing remains secret for long with Talia."

Ben laughed. "That is certainly true. And the Captain said that if anything happens, she wants me to hide it among her books in her quarters."

Felipe lifted his brows.

"That is a very smart plan. It means our work will not be wasted. I focus on Alizée so much that sometimes I forget Madame has very good ideas as well. Whom shall we interview next?"

"Still not ready for Jules?"

The older man shook his head.

"Then I think Xiang."

"Very good. You will like his story very much. Very adventurous. Tobin is *très dur à cuire*. Tobin does not become upset about many things, but he is very protective of Xiang and of Madame."

"I've noticed."

Felipe laughed again.

"He likes you well enough. He would not keep insisting you were useful if he did not. But you are, for all practical purposes, fucking his little sister, and he wants to be certain you are good enough for her, oui? You have a younger sister..."

"Five."

Felipe's eyes widened.

"Five! Mon Dieu. Then you certainly understand."

Ben nodded, though in truth he had never been especially involved in the romantic lives of his sisters. That had been more Nathaniel's domain, the second-eldest Harrington, who got into endless fights and duels with boys who ventured too close to the Harrington girls. Ben much preferred to leave his sisters to their own choices in matters of courtship. But now that Felipe had pointed it out, the parallel between Nathaniel and Tobin was uncanny, and Tobin's behavior made far more sense.

Felipe threw the star into the wall again before taking Ben's hand and squeezing it. Unlike James's handshake, this actually hurt, and Ben fought back a grimace even as he wondered whether the gunner might break his fingers. Felipe noticed and eased his grip.

"I think I would be much more hostile if I did not see so much of myself in you. I want so very badly for the two of you to be happy while you are still young, because I missed that chance."

Ben squeezed back before taking a deep breath.

"Felipe, I swear I will do my best to protect her and keep her safe."

Felipe patted his cheek and ruffled his hair.

"I know you will, *mon frère*. Now get some sleep. Tomorrow we begin training, and you will need all the help you can get."

As Ben headed for the stairs, he stopped and turned back to find Felipe wiping at his eyes again.

"Jules is right about you."

The gunner perked up instantly at the mention of his own lady love.

"Hmm? What did she say?"

"She said you would have made a wonderful father."

# SUPPLEMENTAL

## FROM THE PRIVATE JOURNALS OF BENJAMIN R. HARRINGTON - BLACK ROSE FOLIO

*Researcher's note: Written in the margins on the page describing his experiences on Isla Rosa. It appears as if fantasies were added over the course of Roberto keeping his journals; there are shorthand symbols next to most of them that the research team believes indicate he saw most of them become reality. Good for him! – Mina, 2023*

### New Fantasies

- Make love in a bed on shore (inn/tavern)

- Stay the entire night in her bed

- Time trials to see how quickly I can bring her to release using various methods of stimulation – record ≈ 6 minutes

- Make love in the grass in the rain

- Make love under a weeping willow tree in broad daylight

- Make love to her in every colony

- Tie her up and have my way with her - would she let me?

- Make love on the glowing beach in Puerto Rico Andrew told me about

- Rosa falls in love with me, agrees to marry me, and she bears my child(ren)

- Please her in front of someone who did her wrong, like James or Antonio

- Make Anne watch Rosa please me

- Anything that involves her touching me with her beautiful feet

- Master every position in that amazing book

# CHAPTER 8

## PULLING PUNCHES

The next morning, Tobin shook Ben awake. No one else was stirring yet, so it had to be early.

"Come on," he rumbled quietly. "The old prick is waiting."

Ben followed the quartermaster onto the deck. Felipe stood at the rail with a cup of citrus tea, watching the sunrise. He turned to the other men and smiled widely.

"Bonjour, mes frères. It looks to be a beautiful day."

He finished his tea and delicately set the cup on a barrel.

"We will start simple." He slapped his thighs and planted his feet. "Benny. Hit me as hard as you can."

"What? No, I—"

The Frenchman held up his hands.

"Fine. Then hit Tobin."

Ben looked from one man to the other, eyes wide. It was far too early for this.

"We need to know where we are starting, Benny. I promise, we can take it. Look."

He turned to Tobin.

"Hit me."

Tobin drew back and let loose with a hard right to the older man's cheek. Felipe laughed, then answered with a quick one-two to Tobin's stomach. Ben stood dumbfounded as the two men began trading blows while carrying on an almost normal conversation.

"You are going soft. You have not even drawn blood yet."

"Xiang told me to be gentle with you both."

"Jules slaps harder than you are punching right now."

"I know you like it rough. Maybe if Doctora hits you hard enough, she'll break the lock on your chastity belt. Your hosepipe is probably dusty from disuse. Maybe if you got some of that pent-up lust out, you would actually be useful when she's around," Tobin grunted, hauling the older man into a headlock.

"That is a low blow indeed. But I! Am! A chivalrous! Gentleman! And once a lady! Owns my heart! She is the only one I want!"

Felipe twisted out of the other man's grip and flipped Tobin over his shoulder like a particularly troublesome sack of flour. Tobin landed hard on his back, and Felipe planted a bare foot on his chest to claim victory.

"Also, I have noticed you are not as, shall we say, free with your body since you and Xiang reached your... understanding." He offered the younger man a hand. "So once again, we have much more in common than you would like to admit."

Once they were both standing, Felipe bowed theatrically to Ben, who started to applaud out of habit.

"Don't clap, you idiot," Tobin groused, rubbing the back of his head. "What did you learn?"

Ben froze. What had he learned? He was fairly certain the quartermaster did not mean anything about their bedroom habits. Felipe snorted, as though reading his mind.

"You were paying too much attention to the conversation and not enough to what we were doing, oui?"

Ben's cheeks burned as he nodded. Tobin slapped a hand to his forehead while Felipe clapped him on the shoulder.

"Very well. Tobin, we do it again, no talking this time. Benny, would you like it at speed or slow?"

"At speed is fine. I promise I can keep up."

The men returned to where they had started, and Ben shifted his mind toward angles and calculations. He saw the fine curves of Felipe's stance and the sharp, straight lines of Tobin's. Though the Frenchman was older, he was very agile. Tobin relied more on his bulk and youth.

The two men began to fight again, and with the conversation replaced by snarls and grunts, Ben saw just how ferocious they really were. The punches landed hard enough to bruise, and soon Tobin had Felipe in a headlock once more. The Frenchman lifted a hand and stopped struggling.

"Now pause, Tobin. He needs to really see this. We do this part slowly."

Tobin nodded. The Frenchman explained the process as Ben followed along, his mind diagramming the movement and filing it away.

"Bring your chin in close to your neck. That will buy you a few breaths you may need. You want to step back on the side where he has you."

He slapped Tobin's flexed arm.

"Tobin is right-handed, so it is his right. I step back so my right leg is outside and behind his. Do not lean back. Lean forward... then turn..."

He swung his left leg around and elegantly twisted out of Tobin's grip.

"I do not think I will throw you again, since you seem to be getting tired."

"I'm not getting tired, you old prick!" Tobin roared, grabbing Felipe around the waist.

The gunner twirled out of his grasp, slipped under Tobin's arm, followed through, and pinned it behind his back.

"Ow. Fuck. Mercy."

The moment Tobin said *mercy*, the Frenchman put up his hands and stepped back.

"Now you try, Benny. Tobin, stand up straight and attack him."

The quartermaster nodded, stepped behind Ben, and locked a huge arm around his throat. The gunner crossed his own arms and watched his experiment with pursed lips. Tobin began to squeeze. Ben felt panic bubbling up as his air dwindled. He slapped at Tobin's arm.

"Calm down and think, Benny. What did I tell you about your chin?" Felipe asked, his face marked with disappointment.

Ben paused, then tucked his chin tightly to his neck. At once it became easier to breathe.

"Très bien. Now what?"

Tobin was right-handed, and his right elbow was around Ben's neck. Ben stepped back with his right leg, moving it outside and behind Tobin's. His body wanted to lean backward, but a voice rumbled against him.

"Don't give in to the temptation. If you do, you have no leverage, and I strangle you."

Ben leaned slightly forward and planted his right foot. With all the elegance of a drunken, one-eyed crane, he swung his left leg around and broke free of the quartermaster's grip. His hands flew immediately to his throat, rubbing the skin. The gunner nodded.

"Again."

Tobin grabbed him once more, and this time Ben protected his throat at once with his chin. His movements were still awkward and uncertain, but he escaped more quickly.

"Good. Again."

Ben practiced escaping Tobin's headlock at least a dozen times before Felipe had him try a left-handed version. Ben fumbled as his muscles wanted to go right, but he still broke free of the gunner's grip. The skin of his throat was red from pressure and friction, yet Felipe made him do it once more.

Ben let Tobin put him into another headlock, but this time the quartermaster spun him around, and suddenly Ben found himself face to face with the Black Rose.

"Good morning, Benny."

She smiled brightly, and Ben felt his cheeks heat.

"Oh. Um, hello."

He waggled his fingers in a ridiculous little wave, and she chuckled, planting her hands on her hips.

The arm around his throat tightened slightly, and Ben remembered what he was supposed to be doing. He tucked in his chin, slipped free of Tobin's hold, and somehow, more gracefully than he would have thought possible, ended on one knee at the Captain's feet.

"Captain."

He took her hand, kissed it, and winked up at her. He was delighted to hear her sharp intake of breath and feel the warmth rush into her skin. If nothing else good came of this morning, the radiant smile on her face made it worthwhile.

*Vale la pena.* It is worth the pain.

And her eyes were sparkling, reflecting the light off the waves.

*Veo todas las estrellas del cielo en tu mirada.*

A large hand shoved his shoulder and knocked him off balance. Ben sprawled inelegantly across the deck, making the Black Rose snort with laughter.

"Tobin. That wasn't very nice."

"Pay attention to your surroundings, Benny boy," Felipe said, hauling him back to his feet. "Do not let your guard down around a known enemy, even if the distraction is as lovely as Madame."

He ruffled her curls as she swatted at his hand playfully, like a kitten batting at a feather.

"You have earned your breakfast. Tomorrow we review, and then you will punch at least one of us, oui?"

"I suppose..."

"Maybe you should punch Tobin, since I'm sure it will not hurt him very much."

"All the more reason he should punch you, you old sack of shyte."

The Black Rose laughed again as she led them down to the galley.

Once inside, with the air thick from the heavy, warm scent of the morning porridge, Xiang scurried over carrying the fruit bowl on his shoulder. It looked freshly stocked. He presented it to them with a bow and spoke rapidly. Ben thought he caught the word *shuǐguǒ*, which he had lately determined must mean fruit.

"Yes, yes, we went easy on him this morning. We taught him how to escape a headlock," Tobin said with a slight smile.

"Ah."

Xiang looked expectant. Before Ben's brain could interpret that expression, Felipe had him in another headlock, this one from the right. Ben had begun to suspect the gunner was ambidextrous, favoring his right for fighting and his left for writing. He slipped out of the older man's hold, and Xiang clapped his hands.

"Zuò dé tài hǎole!"

"He says very well done," Felipe translated. "Xiang may help us with more defensive tactics if we need them. He was the one who suggested teaching you how to escape grapples. Defensive maneuvers are his specialty."

"Oh. Xièxiè. That will be very helpful, I'm sure."

Xiang held the bowl out to Ben, who chose a bellfruit, as did the Captain. Felipe took an orange, and Tobin selected an apple.

"Xièxiè. And let us know how Frank does today, oui?"

When Xiang answered, his voice sharpened, and the smaller man reached up to poke the gunner in the chest. Felipe looked indignant.

"I am not being unreasonable."

He switched to Chinese, and the two of them bickered for a moment. Ben thought he heard Felipe say *Jules*. Then Xiang confiscated Felipe's orange the way a mother might take away a sweet from a misbehaving child. The Frenchman's jaw dropped, and his cheeks flushed at being chastised like that in front of everyone.

He lowered his eyes and mumbled something that sounded apologetic. Xiang handed the orange back while speaking with the grand authority of a man preaching gospel, so Ben assumed he was delivering wisdom or perhaps some proverb from his deity. Felipe nodded.

Xiang returned to his station.

Tobin was nearly vibrating from the effort of holding in his laughter. Felipe looked ready to sharpen his tongue and tell the quartermaster off, but then Doctora appeared at his side. At once, every bit of fight went out of the older man as she greeted him with a one-armed hug.

"You need to listen to him. You are too angry right now. We are very worried about you, cariño."

The gunner wrapped an arm around the physician and leaned his cheek against her forehead.

"You will not be rid of me so easily, Jules. I still have much left to do."

# Chapter 9

## Breaking Beautifully

The next day, Tobin woke Ben at around the same time and brought him up to the deck. They reviewed the previous day's lesson, with Ben escaping a left-handed grapple from Felipe and a right-handed one from Tobin. Then Felipe and Tobin stood shoulder to shoulder.

"Now you punch us. Left, right, oui? Two punches each."

Ben froze, feeling very much like a rabbit flanked by a pair of hunting dogs. Though the three of them were roughly the same height, the experienced pirates suddenly seemed much larger.

"Why... why do you make yourself small?" Felipe seemed to be struggling to reconcile his concern with his annoyance. "You will not get in trouble. The Articles do not apply right now! This is training! Madame wants you to fight us. Stand up straight and punch us!"

"Fine then," Tobin growled, stepping forward and taking a swing at Ben.

"No!" Ben squeaked, throwing his crossed arms in front of his face to block a blow that never landed. He peeked through his wrists and saw the two men staring at him with concern. He had to explain himself.

"I like my teeth where they are, in my mouth, thank you. And I don't want to break my nose again."

The Frenchman's concern gave way to confusion. "But we could just as easily break your nose or knock out a tooth with a bō staff or with a sword. How is this different?"

"Because..." How was it different? It certainly was. "There are only so many things you can do with a bō staff or a sword. But people and their bodies can do so many strange and terrible things, it's hard to predict and counter and... there's just too many variables! And if we assume James will fight dirty, then the numbers just go entirely out the window!"

Ben was breathing harder than he would have liked, and he felt an attack of nerves coming on. His throat tightened as though Tobin had put him in a headlock, and he dropped his gaze to the deck, choking out,

"I don't want to embarrass her. Or lose her. Especially not to James! And what if I do win and she ends up hating me anyway? I'll have gone through all this and inconvenienced you both for nothing! And what if...?"

Felipe put his hands on the younger man's shoulders and gave him a small shake.

"Easy, Benny. Cálmate, pues. That is...you have very much happening in your head. Es como una jaula de grillos...uh...like...a cage full of crickets. Crazy, many thoughts, and very noisy, yes?"

Ben nodded. The gunner poked the helmsman in the chest to emphasize his pep talk.

"Fear is a reflex. Courage is a choice. Why do I see Jules before I do something dangerous? Because I fear leaving her alone. Then I decide to do whatever I must to see her again. Every choice I make is what will get me back to her. So, too, must you decide that you will do whatever you must to get back to Madame. You chose to be here, to stay with us. You chose to go along with my gauntlet. You have made so many good choices. Choose again. And again. Choose to do what you must to win!"

Tobin put a hand on Ben's shoulder and spun him to face him. "Do you know what hoisam is, Benny?"

"Umm...no. If I didn't know what a moonfish was when we caught it, why would I know what... whatever you said...is?"

"Sunfish in English," Felipe corrected gently.

Ben paused and turned to the older man. "That's ridiculous! It's a big, round, silver thing. Moonfish is a much better name!" He exhaled in frustration. "Fine, sunfish. Is it an animal?"

"Yes. Imagine, if you will, an animal that looks like a long, thin, straight squash, about..." He approximated fifteen centimeters.

Ben stared at him.

"Oui, it is exactly like you think, it does look exactly like a *bite*," Felipe deadpanned, using the French word for male anatomy.

"If you cut one open, do you know what you find?"

Ben shook his head, uncertain.

"It doesn't have a brain, it doesn't have a heart, and it doesn't have a spine."

Tobin stepped right into Ben's face. "So, are you a hoisam, Benny? All cock, no brain, no heart, and no spine?"

Ben gritted his teeth and narrowed his eyes.

Felipe appeared at his side, whispering like the Devil himself as he pulled the younger man's shoulders up and back so he stood straighter.

"Oh, Benny, are you going to let him talk to you like that? Are you going to stand for him calling you stupid and worthless? He thinks Madame only likes you for your cock. He thinks you don't deserve her. He says you are a coward. What will Benny do about it?"

Ben was caught somewhere between anger, embarrassment, and panic. What was he going to do? He didn't want to fight the mountain in front of him, but he also didn't want Tobin and Felipe to think he was a pushover, or that he agreed with them that he didn't deserve a place on the Black Rose's ship, in her bed, or in her heart.

An answer came from the strangest place: a memory of Jacob from the *Angelina Marie*. The young man had once passionately defended his decision to be marooned with his uncle, the ship's captain, and had pulled back and headbutted one of the men, Thaddeus, now the cook aboard the *Angelina Marie* under James. While that decision had ultimately led to Jacob and his uncle's demise after Jacob tried to shoot Tobin, the headbutt itself had not been a terrible idea.

Ben pulled back and tried to smash his forehead into Tobin's. Unfortunately, Tobin flinched, turning his upper body just enough that Ben's ample nose smashed into his very well-developed deltoid.

"'Uck!" Ben shouted as pain shot through his skull. His eyes watered, and he could feel liquid pouring from his nose. Oh, shit, had he broken it again?

Fortunately, Tobin and Felipe were both calm in the face of this new development, even as the Frenchman let out a heavy sigh of annoyance. Years of dealing with Juanito had accustomed both men to sudden, violent, inconvenient injuries.

"Merde," he grumbled. "Jules is not going to be pleased with us."

The gunner pulled out a handkerchief, tipped Ben's head slightly forward, and pinched his nostrils shut. "You hold this, I am not your Pappy."

Ben took over, pressing the cloth to his bleeding nose. Tobin surveyed his shoulder and then looked at him.

"Eliza is going to be pissed. Look at us."

"Looks like most of my pay is going toward buying her supplies. Again. Merde. I had much different plans for that money..."

Ben's eyes finally focused, and he saw that Tobin's vest was slick and dark with blood, as was his own shirt. The handkerchief he was bleeding all over was pale blue and embroidered with initials in the corner: JPdC.

"Whose handkerchief is this?" Ben asked, his voice thick.

Felipe's face went white. "Merde!"

He looked as though he might try to snatch it back, but thought better of it, his fingers grabbing helplessly at the air. Tobin started laughing.

"She's been missing that handkerchief. You know it's her favorite color. My, my, how are you going to talk your way out of this? Did you bribe Eliza to let you have it?"

"Non."

Tobin raised his eyebrows.

"Possibly...but...well, what is done is done, and it's all bloody now, so we may as well take him down to her. Maybe she will be so angry about Ben she will not notice the cloth."

Tobin and Felipe each took an arm and steered Ben toward the stairs. Finally, logic cut through the fog of pain.

"Julieta Pérez...?"

"De Colón," Felipe supplied curtly.

Tobin rolled his eyes. "Hispanic women don't normally take their husband's last name, but Doctora took Gustavo's name, and for some reason that makes this old prick angry."

"It does not bother me that she took his name. That is tradition in many countries. I am bothered by why she was compelled to take it."

"Love?" Ben asked, now sounding like the honk of a goose.

"If it were something as normal as love, it would not bother me in the slightest. I wanted Letty to wear my name very badly as well. Non, it is because many people have...unfortunate opinions...about intelligent, talented women who become healers. Satan does not go about giving women brains. He did not teach her how to make salves or tinctures. She learned that from other intelligent, talented women, and it is not sorcery in the slightest. It is science! She is a scientist, not a fucking witch!"

"Gustavo was a childhood friend, and his family was very important in San Juan," Tobin explained. "He married her to protect her with his name so she could continue to study and practice medicine."

The three men arrived at the physician's door. Tobin looked over at Ben.

"I really hope you didn't break your nose, but it looks like you gave yourself a black eye."

"Yes, easiest fight you ever won, right, Tobin?" Felipe said with a sigh, steeling himself before tentatively knocking on the door.

The door opened, and Doctora stood there in a nightgown the same pale blue as the handkerchief Ben was currently soaking with blood. Her hair was down, she was not wearing her spectacles, and Ben heard the Frenchman's breath hitch. She was quite beautiful, even with the sparkling silver streaks beginning to spread through her hair. She squinted.

"¡Ay, joder, Felipe! What did you two do to him?"

She pulled the door open farther and drew Ben inside to sit on her bed. Once he was settled, she retrieved her spectacles and set them on her nose. Then she looked at the gunner expectantly, arms crossed, head pulled back like a coiled snake.

"What did you do?"

"I did nothing! And Tobin did nothing! Benny tried to give Tobin a headbutt and missed terribly."

Doctora brought a hand to her forehead.

"No, it's true," Ben honked. "I have a large nose, and Tobin has a large shoulder, and I suppose in the moment I wanted them to be friends."

Ben's silly comment was enough to crack her, and she started laughing. Ben joined in while Tobin and Felipe exchanged a silent conversation of shifting pupils, nods, and waggled eyebrows.

Doctora pulled the handkerchief away from Ben's face.

"Oh, no! My handkerchief! Where did you get this?"

She looked from Ben to Felipe to Tobin. The tips of the gunner's ears had gone pink, and Tobin raised his eyebrows, lips tightening into a thin line.

"I found it," Ben volunteered. "I didn't know who JPdC was. I suppose I should have figured it out, but you told me to call you Doctora, and I sometimes forget you have a given name."

"Hmm."

She did not seem to believe that entirely, but she began to poke and prod at Ben's nose. He winced.

"The good news is, I don't think it is broken. However, you will have a black eye for a few days." She stuffed gauze into his nostrils. "Keep these in your nose and come see me in a few hours."

She picked up her handkerchief and sighed. "I hope Eliza will be able to wash this properly. I embroidered this for my trousseau before I got married."

"It's a lovely color. It looks very nice on you."

She smiled at Ben. "Thank you. It's my favorite."

Then she turned to Tobin and Felipe. "I will let you know when I check it later if you can continue or if he needs to rest for a few days. But please be careful. You know the Captain will be upset if you hurt him too badly."

"She will be even more upset if James brings a knife to a fistfight and he gets gutted like a fish!" Felipe countered, frustration simmering in his words. "He needs to be able to defend himself, adapt, and overcome!"

Doctora shot him a look, and he deflated a little.

"But we have time. And this is good, makes him tough!"

"Kintsugi," Tobin muttered.

Felipe began to laugh uproariously. "Yes! We will get some gold to fix his nose. That would be a sight; Madame would like that."

Doctora started laughing too, her eyes sparkling as she looked at the gunner.

"What is that?" Ben asked, thoroughly lost.

"The Japanese have a method of mending broken things with gold or silver," Doctora explained, showing Ben a tiny ceramic bowl from her dresser. A delicate vein of gold ran through the dark blue like a lightning bolt. "The object was broken, so it has history, and its repair should be highlighted and showcased instead of hidden. It is still whole, it is still useful, and it is even more beautiful."

She looked up at Ben and smiled kindly. "People are like that, too. The things that break us make us stronger, more interesting, and more beautiful."

The physician was far too busy talking to Ben to notice that behind her the Frenchman had melted into a puddle of pure adoration, one hand clasped over his heart. Tobin rolled his eyes and cleared his throat.

"Doctora, is there anyone in the sick room? We need to use it for a few minutes."

"No, Juanito vacated last night." She lifted a hand and made a face. "For how long? Who can say? But it is empty for now."

Tobin nodded and indicated that the other men should follow him. "Thank you, Doctora. Benny will come back in a few hours."

# Chapter 10

## A Shocking Secret

The three men left Doctora's quarters and went around the corner to the small room. With his nose stuffed full of gauze, Ben couldn't smell anything, but he was sure it still reeked of sharp, bitter herbs. Tobin pointed to the bed, and Ben sat.

"It's not that bad, I don't need a lie down," he protested.

"No," Tobin snarled, frustration evident in every syllable. "I don't want you to have a nap..." He turned to Felipe, resigned. "We have to tell him."

The gunner nodded and sighed deeply. "Now we must tell you about James. You promise you will not tell Madame?"

"I promise."

"And it stays out of the books?"

"I promise."

The older man nodded and sat beside Ben on the bed with a small groan, suddenly looking every one of his fifty-some-odd years. Tobin closed the door and leaned against it, indicating that Felipe should tell the story.

"We got James on a Royal Navy ship, the *Cunning Nymph*, eight years ago. He was a freshly made midshipman, so fourteen or so? The Captain, she was..." He looked at Tobin and waved a hand. "Seventeen or eighteen? I know you are the birthday police, Benny, but I do not know when hers is. But that was the first raid I took part in with the Black Rose, and right away, he had eyes for Madame.

This was before she started her challenge of bringing the highest-ranked prisoner to her quarters."

Ben winced at the thought of other men in her bed.

"He came aboard the *Wolfhound*, and he was... distressingly interested in getting the Captain alone. Fortunately, she is a decent judge of character..."

"Usually," Tobin interjected.

Felipe waved a dismissive hand at the quartermaster's slight against Ben.

"In this case, she was correct. She would never allow him to corner her. She asked me to put a latch on her door for him, a habit that carried over to the *María del Mar* and the *Deception*.

"We freed *María del Mar* some months later, taking on Alizée, Jean-Luc, and the others. James is very jealous of them, especially my Alizée. I suppose he thought that I wasted my time and energy on her, given that she is a Negro woman. He was always quite disrespectful to her.

"Then why—?"

Felipe held up a hand.

"I will explain in a moment. But this part is going to be upsetting. Know that it all turns out fine in the end, but..."

The gunner clenched and unclenched his fist. Tobin growled quietly, shifting his weight. Ben braced himself, fearing he knew exactly what the older man was about to say.

"On his eighteenth birthday, he decided that he had done enough and that Madame owed him something. At his celebration, he kept refilling her cup when she wasn't looking, and she got quite drunk. He..." The normally pink skin of the Frenchman's hands had gone white, and he pounded them against his thighs.

"She didn't latch her door, and he got into her quarters. I happened to be passing by, carrying Andrew...very drunk...down to Jules. I noticed her door was not all the way closed. I caught him, quite literally, with his pants down, trying to climb into bed with her while she was asleep."

Ben's heart lodged in his throat. Now he understood why Felipe had not told him this on Isla Rosa. He was quite sure he would have marched off at once and challenged James to defend her honor. Now he had even more reason to beat the living shit out of him come July. He would have to be as good a student for Felipe and Tobin as he was in the Black Rose's bed, if not better.

Felipe reached over and squeezed Ben's hand again, shaking with rage even as his voice wobbled with regret.

"Yes, I know. I dragged him down to the galley, screaming the whole way. Tobin and I, we beat the absolute hell out of him. Xiang intervened, so we did not kill him, but it was very close. I had a knife to his throat. That is why James does not like us."

"The old bastard and I do not agree on many things, but we agreed we needed to get James off that fucking ship," Tobin continued. "The two of us, Xiang, Doctora, and Alizée, made sure she was never alone with him after that. The ladies don't know the full extent of the situation, and we never told the Captain. She's a heavy sleeper. Never even turned over. Andrew likewise slept through the whole thing, curled up in the hallway outside her quarters."

"Honestly, so much could have been avoided if I had been allowed to castrate James as soon as he came aboard the *Wolfhound*, but I digress," Felipe muttered. He continued:

"Then the Captain won the *Deception* and decided this should be the flagship of the fleet. She asked if we had anyone we thought was ready for command. I spoke to Alizée, and we had a long talk about whether we thought she was ready. In the end, we were both confident in her abilities, and she said she would take James off our hands.

"James was never interested in Alizée for a few reasons. One, he likes his women older. While we do not know for certain how old Alizée is, it is certainly not old enough.

"Two, as I mentioned, he has...unfortunately, common attitudes towards Africans. While he views the Captain as exotic," Tobin gagged slightly, "he sees Alizée as beneath him because of the accident of her birth in that body."

Felipe pointed at the quartermaster.

"He also doesn't respect Tobin nearly as much as he should, but look at Tobin. James may be incredibly stupid, but not stupid enough to directly challenge a man built like an ox."

"Remember how I told you when you first came aboard that most white boys have to be taught how to address me properly?" Tobin asked, and Ben nodded. "I was thinking of James specifically."

"But Alizée has on many occasions put James in his place." Felipe proudly puffed out his chest and smiled. "It is a privilege to watch her hand him his pride in shreds, as it will be watching you do so in July."

"And three, since Alizée does not feel the sexual attraction to men or women, she is not blinded by his bullshit like many others are."

"The greatest sin is that man is as beautiful as he is," Tobin agreed. "How terrible to have such a beautiful face and body, and such a rancid personality and a maggot-ridden soul."

"So how did he fare under her command?" Ben asked. "It seems like he would have made her miserable?"

Felipe laughed derisively, and Tobin snorted.

"Oh, he tried very hard to make her miserable. Fortunately, she is much calmer and slower to anger than I. I...well, I already told you, I wanted to kill him, castrate him, any number of things to rid us all of him. He is a menace. For four or five years, she has tolerated him. Each passing year, he grew more resentful, harder to work with, less willing to compromise. That is why she finally decided it was time to set him to his own devices."

"The Captain thinks the crew of the *Angelina Marie* will convince him to go back to the Royal Navy."

The gunner laughed coldly. "Would that not be nice, if he were their problem instead of ours? But he is just competent enough to be worth worrying about, even if he is selfish and cannot see beyond his own nose most of the time. In that case, we will have to hope his lust for Madame keeps him on the stupid side."

Ben and Tobin both groaned quietly.

"I hate feeling like I have to compete with someone so terrible," Ben muttered.

Felipe waved a dismissive hand. "It is not much of a competition. It is a competition the same way Mar fighting a rat is a competition. In this metaphor, you are Mar."

"Oh, well, thank you," Ben said dryly.

"And I realize it may seem strange to you that we are keeping this from her," Tobin said, "but we do not think she needs to know how close she came to having her honor forcibly taken. She only allows herself to get drunk when she feels safe, and she obviously would not have allowed herself to get like that with James around. It was luck that saved her that night, pure and simple. We think that knowledge could be catastrophic for her mental state... especially if she knew it was at James's hand."

Felipe let out a long breath. When he spoke again, his voice was much quieter.

"I also personally hate being reminded of how little control I really have to keep my poulets safe. I still do my best. Otherwise, despair would swallow me whole if I let myself think too long. If there were going to be ladies aboard the *Angelina Marie,* I would have been compelled to say something, but non, he will be surrounded by sausage on all sides, as he deserves."

Ben and Tobin both nodded. Felipe started poking Ben in the chest again.

"And we tell you all of this, so you have an incentive to obliterate that connard. We need you angry, but we need you smart angry." His long finger poked into Ben's forehead. "What you did today? You panicked. Panic makes you stupid. I know it is a lot, there are many variables, but if you learn some techniques that can apply to multiple situations, then you can improvise. We believe in you! Right, Tobin?"

The quartermaster stared hard at Ben, his mouth a thin line. "You are...better than the alternative."

With that, the other man turned, opened the door, and left, closing it behind him. Felipe clapped a hand to Ben's shoulder.

"He blames himself for not watching her more closely. It does not matter what I say, he holds the shadow of what could have happened that night even more closely than I do."

He turned Ben to face him.

"But you have your affections for her to guide you. I know I would burn entire continents to the ground to ensure Jules was safe and cared for. You would do the same for Madame, oui?"

Ben nodded.

"Good. It is frightening, but you have the choice: Show her you are brave, and that you are strong even though you are broken; or you can drop yourself overboard right now and save me the trouble."

The gunner's hazel eyes met Ben's grey-blue. Ben clasped the older man's hand.

"I choose to fight for love."

Felipe smiled widely.

"Good man! Now, if you excuse me, I must go throw myself at Eliza's feet and beg for mercy. She hates washing blood out of clothing."

# CHAPTER 11

## PAST DAMAGES AND PLAYING DOCTOR

Ben avoided the Captain for as long as he could. Not only did he not want her to see him with a black eye and his nose stuffed with gauze, he was also worried he would take her into his arms and never let her go. Then she would probably want to know why, and with Tobin and Felipe's tale still so raw in his mind, he was not sure he would be able to keep the secret contained.

But alas, he still had a job to do.

He made his way onto the deck and approached the helm. Felipe was talking animatedly to the Captain as she kept a light hand on the ship's wheel. When the gunner saw Ben approaching, his face shifted to panic. The Frenchman took the Black Rose's face into his giant hands, squishing her cheeks in a decidedly insubordinate manner and holding her so she was looking him in the eye and nowhere else.

"You know we are trying to train Benny to fight James, oui?"

"Obviously," she grunted, trying to wiggle out of his grasp.

"You also know accidents happen, oui?"

She stopped struggling, and though Ben could not see her face, he recognized her tone. He could all but picture her narrowed eyes.

"What did you do?"

"We did nothing, Princesa, but..."

In a move Ben knew in his heart the Captain had learned from Felipe himself, the Black Rose dug her thumbs into his wrists. The Frenchman bit his lip even as his face turned red. He cracked, making a strained noise and dropping his hands from her face. Now that the tables had turned, she kept a firm grip on the gunner as he tried to escape her grasp.

"Ow! Mercy, Madame!"

Just as the gunner had immediately backed off from Tobin when the quartermaster cried for mercy, so too did the Captain release him the moment he beseeched her. She wheeled around, saw Ben, and jumped back, startled.

"¡Ay! ¡Joder, Felipe! No wonder you didn't want me to see him."

She came closer and brushed a gentle thumb beneath Ben's eye. It was feather-light, but he still winced.

"What did mean old Felipe do to you," she purred, as if comforting a child.

Felipe scoffed, incredulous, rubbing his wrists. Ben smiled at her and took her hand.

"He didn't do anything, Mistress. I smashed my face into Tobin's shoulder. I may as well have tried to headbutt a rock."

She clicked her tongue sympathetically. "Yes, I imagine that did not feel very good. Oh, Benny..."

"Jules does not think it is broken, but she will look at it again after his duty," Felipe said.

Ben nodded. "It probably looks worse than it is."

The Pirate Queen turned back to her gunner.

"Do I need to start attending these sessions? I will wake up early if I must."

Ben and Felipe both threw up their hands.

"No! That's not necessary, Captain!"

Ben tried very hard to keep the panic out of his voice and was not entirely certain he succeeded. It would be impossible to concentrate with her watching. Felipe was much calmer, his tone even, once again sounding as though he thought he was her father.

"Non, Madame, you need your sleep. We need you on deck with a ready mind and clear eyes. It will not do us any good to get you dependent on the energy blend when we can take perfectly good care of Benny. If Juanito has not yet managed to get himself killed on our watch, I think we can manage a clumsy library rat."

"I'm not that clumsy," Ben protested. "Also, what is a library rat?"

The Frenchman paused, blinking uncomprehendingly for a moment as he cycled through all the languages floating around in his brain.

"Oh...in Spanish and French, you are a library rat. In English... uh..."

"Bookworm!" the Captain supplied enthusiastically.

Felipe smiled. "That is exactly correct! Bien hecho, Madame."

The Black Rose beamed, sparkling in the sunlight.

"And not only that," the Frenchman continued, "I believe we had a breakthrough this morning that will make Benny more...shall we say, cooperative."

The Black Rose pursed her lips. "Very well. But if anything worse happens, we may have to switch tactics."

Felipe nodded. "I am sure it will be better. Now that one of the worst things Benny was expecting has come to pass, he can concentrate on what is happening and not what he fears will happen."

"Excellent! Benny, I would like you to deliver Doctora's recommendation to Felipe when you receive it."

The bell sounded, signifying the end of the shift.

"Now I shall hand this over to you."

She stepped away from the wheel, allowing Ben to take her place.

"Felipe, about your business."

The gunner bowed deeply. "Of course, Madame."

After he loped away, the Black Rose pulled her lover down to whisper in his ear.

"I think I should like to give you an examination of my own in my quarters this evening. Would you like to be my patient?"

Ben's breath caught in his throat. Her hand had slipped beneath his shirt and was resting on his bottom, so there was no mistaking what she meant.

"Absolutely nothing would please me more, Mistress."

She gave his backside the slightest squeeze before disappearing as well.

The prospect of another sexual adventure with the Black Rose only hardened Ben's resolve. Tomorrow, if Doctora approved, he would imagine Felipe was James and punch him in his beautiful, stupid face. He would make whatever choices were necessary to maintain his place by the Captain's side and in her bed.

"The fook happened to you, Benny?"

Ben turned to find Talia hanging upside down from the rigging beside him like a buxom spider. He gently pushed her away, and she laughed as she flipped upright and landed gracefully on the deck beside him.

"I tried to headbutt Tobin."

The boatswain chuckled. "On purpose, ya daftie?"

"He and Felipe are training me for my duel with James."

Talia snorted and patted Ben's shoulder. "Och, dinnae fash yerself. James looks all big and bad, but he's a wee pansy. I dinnae ken if he's ever taken a proper punch. Scaredy cat."

She clapped him on the back.

"I have every confidence in ye, Benny."

After his shift at the helm was over, Ben went down to Doctora's quarters. He found the physician examining Juanito's foot, which she said was healing nicely. Once Juanito left, she invited Ben in to sit. She carefully removed the gauze from his nose and asked him to try blowing gently into another handkerchief. Ben did so, and while a few blood clots dislodged themselves, there was no fresh bleeding.

"Very good! Yes, it's not broken. It may be a little sore for a few days... and your eye..."

She lightly brushed her fingers over the bruise.

"I do tend to bruise quite easily, especially around my eyes. Honestly, part of the reason I decided to grow my beard was to hide bruises."

Doctora cocked her head. "You don't strike me as the type to get into fights with other men, Benny. That's why this whole thing seems so strange to me."

"I never said it was to hide bruises from other men, Doctora."

Ben's voice came out small and wispy.

"At least people would accept that as a good reason to have bruises."

She looked a little confused.

Ben sighed. He may as well tell her.

"My wife... Anne... she gave me a black eye on our wedding night when I tried to...fulfill my husbandly duties. She was very adamant that I not touch her. Ever. Very adamant."

The Boricua's face shifted into a look of pity. "Oh, Benny! You're such a sweetheart, why would..."

Whatever question she had intended to ask seemed to answer itself. They looked at one another for a long moment before Doctora pulled Ben into a crushing hug. He did not realize he was crying until she gently wiped his eyes, ghosting the pads of her thumbs along the bruised skin.

"Would you like to tell me more about her? Get it off your heart?"

"May I? I don't want to impose if you have something else to do."

She smiled, handed him her giant mortar and pestle, and added some herbs to the bowl.

"Talk to me while you grind these herbs."

Over the next half hour, Doctora listened as Ben poured his heart out while mashing massive roots and delicate leaves. He told her about his infatuation with Anne, his elation when she agreed to make love to him, the immediate disappointment and regret, and how she slapped him when they were done.

He told her how he had been forced to marry her to protect her reputation, and of the threats against his family from her father, the Magistrate. He had heard scuttlebutt that she had been forced to marry him as punishment.

He told her about her violent reaction when he tried to consummate their marriage, and the honeymoon she spent locked away. Her throwing things, breaking things, screaming at him, insulting him. Ben was fully sobbing by the time he told her about the stillbirth of his daughter and the possibility of divorce, even after he had tried so hard to be a good husband.

Doctora took the pestle from his hands, set it down on the small table, and wrapped an arm around him. She snuggled into his shoulder, took his hand, and let him cry. When his sobs had settled into sniffles, she stood and crossed to her dresser. She returned with a locket and handed it to Ben. He popped it open, and inside was a small painting of a handsome man with a mustache.

"Gustavo...my husband's name was Gustavo. He never desired me, either. He loved me, but he was not...in love with me. We were best friends from the time we were children. When I began to study and practice medicine, people in San Juan did not like that. Said medicine is man's work. I wanted to be a surgeon. But even when I changed to midwifery, and women's and children's health..."

She closed her eyes.

"I was put on trial because I never lost a mother and only lost one baby. That's unheard of."

They called it heresy, witchcraft, brujería. Said I made deals with the devil to keep everyone alive. Gustavo...bless his heart...Gustavo surprised me. He made a big, public show of proposing to me at my sentencing, saying he couldn't live in a world without me in it. He was very quiet and reserved, so it was a lot for him to do that in front of so many people. And since the Colón family is so important in San Juan, it was a very big deal. They couldn't very well put me to death after something like *that*. I had to say yes. Without exaggeration, he saved my life."

She sighed, gazing at the portrait.

"We had a huge public spectacle of a wedding. Obnoxious, really. While we were happy to be the very best of friends and share a home and a bed, I think he may have been more like Tobin and Xiang, or perhaps Alizée.

"He would give me hugs and kisses as you might give a very dear friend, but he had to get incredibly drunk to be intimate with me. People began to talk, and it became clear that if anything happened to Gustavo, they would pick up right where they left off, and I would be up on the scaffold again before Gustavo was cold in the ground.

"I became convinced that if I gave the Colón family an heir, I could protect myself. It took a few tries, and Gustavo was always hungover and resentful in the morning, but I fell pregnant. While Gustavo understood why I wanted to give him a child so badly, he never spoke of it as anything but an inconvenience."

"That's terrible," Ben said quietly, giving her a squeeze.

"Don't speak ill of the dead, Benny. We can call your wife a harpy because she is still alive, but I will not have you slighting my Gustavo. He was my very best friend, and I owe him my life. Besides, not every man is as eager for fatherhood as you are."

Ben nodded. "Touché."

She took a deep breath, her grip on his hand tightening.

"I asked my best apprentice to deliver my baby. But something went wrong, and she didn't check his neck. My beautiful, perfect boy, my Octavio..."

She sniffled. Ben leaned his cheek against her forehead. There was a long beat of silence.

"I don't even know what happened to my daughter. The only information I got from bribing the midwife's apprentice was that it was a girl. We never even gave her a name. I wanted to name her Abigail, but Anne never spoke of her. After a month or so, it was like it never even happened."

Doctora sniffled. "Gustavo was like that, too. I wanted to try again, but Gustavo was vehemently opposed to it, so I figured it would be wise to let the matter drop. I was ready to broach the subject once more when Gustavo was taken from me. He passed in his sleep, and I never figured out what happened, or whether there was something I could have done..."

She laughed without humor. "Life can be quite cruel, no?"

"Indeed," Ben agreed, giving her another squeeze.

He paused as a memory of something she had said drifted to the front of his mind.

"How come you didn't reinvent yourself when you joined the crew?"

"Hmm? Oh, the thing I said when I told you about Felipe helping Alizée choose her name?"

Ben nodded.

"Well, many pirates want to appear tougher and scarier than they really are. But if you say the name Doctora Julieta Pérez de Colón in certain areas of San Juan, that is enough to drive fear into the hearts of many. I suppose I thought I'm already terrifying enough as it is."

She shrugged and wiggled her fingers in a sarcastically mystical way.

"Boooo!"

Ben chuckled, and she laughed too.

"Well then, why didn't you?"

Now it was Ben's turn to shrug.

"I didn't know I was supposed to. It never occurred to me that all these famous pirates are not actually using their Christian names. I should have realized it, because who names a baby Blackbeard? I mean, honestly!"

Doctora dissolved into giggles, and Ben started laughing too.

Once they had both recovered, Ben cleared his throat and continued.

"Although I suppose I did become Benny. Nobody ever called me Benny, not even as a child. My family all called me Ben, and everyone else called me Benjamin if they didn't call me Harrington or Lieutenant. I guess I carry myself like a Benjamin."

"I think Benny suits you. It's sweet. And you're sweet, like a friendly, curious dog. I know that is strange to say..."

"Not all that strange. I think it's quite a compliment, thank you."

"Tobin and Felipe want you to be tough, but please promise me you will not become cruel. Especially because R-...uh, the Captain...the Captain has also had a difficult life and has experienced immense cruelty from people who claimed to love her and were supposed to protect her. She deserves someone sweet and gentle, just as you deserve someone enthusiastically giving of herself."

She patted Ben's cheek.

"I think you will both find what you seek in each other, if you both open your hearts."

"I promise, I will do my best."

"I know you will, Benny. But it's almost suppertime. You are cleared to continue training tomorrow morning. Be careful of your nose for a few more days. Just because it's not broken now doesn't mean that a hit at the correct angle won't finish the job."

"Yes, Ma'am."

Ben paused. He badly wanted to suggest that Felipe might be the man she needed, that he would love her passionately and deeply as she should be loved, but he decided against it. Doctora had laid a good portion of her past bare to him, and if he tried to put in a good word for the gunner, she might not take it as intended.

"Thank you for listening, Doctora. It felt good to tell someone."

She smiled and patted his cheek again.

"I know you carry Anne's voice in your head, and I know she's heavy on your heart, but she can't hurt you anymore, Benny. Don't let her ghost keep you from the good things you have in front of you."

He nodded, gave her another hug, and then left to share the physician's recommendation with Felipe.

As expected, Felipe was thrilled to hear that Ben could train again in the morning so long as they were careful of his nose.

"I realize it is quite a large target," Ben joked self-deprecatingly, "but you'll have to prove how good your aim is."

"Très bien, Benny. And tomorrow you will punch me good, oui?"

"Indeed, so I hope you're prepared!"

"I anxiously await my beating," the Frenchman said with a laugh. "Go tell Madame, too."

The Black Rose was nowhere to be found, but Giselle handed Ben a note tied with a thin black ribbon before skipping away.

> *Benny, you have an appointment in*
> *my quarters this evening after supper.*
> *-Doctor R.*

After supper, Ben snuck up to the Captain's quarters and knocked on the door. It swung open, and the Black Rose pulled him inside. To his immense delight, she was wearing her sheer white dressing gown that left nothing to the imagination.

"The Doctor will see you now," she purred, holding him at arm's length. "Please take your clothes off and have a seat."

"Yes, Doctor," he whispered.

Ben could not get his clothes off fast enough.

"Have a seat," she said, indicating her desk.

Ben obeyed, and she leaned in close to inspect his bruised nose and eye.

"Are you feeling alright? You don't think I'll hurt you?"

"Mistress, I know you won't. At least, not on purpose."

"Does it hurt if I do this?"

She asked it before gently kissing the tip of his nose.

"It doesn't hurt at all. In fact, I think you may have made it at least a little better."

The Captain chuckled. "Then let's examine the rest of you. Do you have any concerns besides your nose and your eye?"

Her hand was gentle on his cheek.

"My lips, to start," Ben whispered, hoping she found it as seductive as intended. "They are incredibly dry right now."

"I can certainly see what you mean. Let me try something."

Exactly as he hoped she would, the Black Rose leaned in to kiss him, careful not to put too much pressure on his nose. Ben pulled her close, licking at her lips. She opened her mouth, allowing their kiss to deepen. After a few moments, they parted, faces red, breathing hard.

"Is that better?" the Black Rose asked.

"Yes, very much so. Now, I also seem to have something questionable happening to my cock, if you would be so kind as to take a look at that."

The Black Rose gave him a wicked little smile before pushing him to stretch out on her desk. His legs hung off the edge, so she put a chair beneath his feet for support. She ran a finger along the length of his manhood, and Ben sighed, closing his eyes.

"Oh, goodness! Look at this! Can you tell me a little bit about how it ended up like this?"

"Well…there's this woman…she's spectacular! Every time I see her, it gets like this."

The Pirate Queen smiled radiantly, her fingers stroking along his thigh.

"I see. And how does she react when it does this?"

She was enjoying their little game as much as he was.

"She seems to rather like it. I would like to think it excites her, too. She is quite enthusiastic, which I appreciate immensely."

"And what does she do with it?"

"Whatever she wants," Ben rasped.

The Black Rose purred low in her throat.

"No, I want you to tell me," she stage-whispered. "Tell me about the naughty things we do. Spare me no details."

"Oh, of course, Mistress…Doctor! Uh…sometimes, she takes my cock into her mouth and licks it like it's a sweet. It is divine…"

"Like this?"

The Captain licked a long stroke up the shaft before gently pulling the foreskin back and licking around the head of his cock. Ben's head fell back as he entwined his fingers in her curls.

"Yes, Doctor. Very much like that."

She stroked him, littering his skin with kisses as she did.

"Yes, she has magical hands. She can always bring me to release."

"Is that what you desire right now?" she asked. "Or would you like to tell me more?"

"I don't think Doctora would approve because I need to be careful of my nose, but I rather enjoy exploring between her legs with my mouth and tongue. She seems to like it as well."

The Black Rose broke character with a laugh.

"I do very much enjoy when you taste my wares, but you are correct, we need to be reasonably gentle. Maybe once you've healed, I will put you through your paces."

Ben smiled up at her and gave her a wink. "I look forward to it! We have been experimenting with many different ways to make love, but I must say my favorite is when she is on top of me. I have never been so happy to be someone's prize pony."

The Captain climbed onto the desk with him, and Ben was thankful for its sturdy construction. As she balanced herself over him, she took his hands and entwined their fingers. She leaned forward and ghosted a kiss over the tip of his nose, and Ben stretched his neck to meet her lips.

"Now, Benny, I would like you to demonstrate for me, if you would please."

Ben gently tugged the sleeve of her dressing gown.

"Are you going to take this off first? It's quite lovely, and I would hate to ruin it."

"I can always have another one made," she purred.

"Yes, but what will you wear from now until then?"

She pursed her lips and narrowed her eyes slightly before delicately slipping out of the fine mesh and tossing it onto her bed. Then she leaned down until they were once more nose to nose.

"Now your challenge is to make good on that threat. Show me how you would have ruined my lovely robe."

"Is that an order Cap-...Doctor?"

"Very much so. Now is the true physical examination. Do your worst!"

The Black Rose slid herself down onto his cock, and Ben immediately grabbed her waist. His rough hands gripped tightly, holding her hips still as he thrust up into her. The Captain's head fell back, and she moaned, flattening her palms against Ben's chest.

"Ohhh, so good, Benny!"

Ben hauled her harder against him, dragging her forward and pushing her back to grind her pleasure nub against him. She took over from there, moving her hips while Ben reached up to pinch her nipples the way she liked. She gasped as the pleasurable pain radiated through her. Ben shifted his grip, holding her breasts in a tight, claw-like grasp. The Captain answered by raking her nails over his pectoral muscles. Now it was Ben's turn to groan.

"Yes, please, Mistress!"

The Pirate Queen leaned down once more, lightly brushing her lips against his.

"Is this really your worst, Benny?" she asked, a little smile on her lips.

Ben growled playfully and pulled her down until her breasts pressed against his chest. He wrapped one arm around her back and once again pinned her hips in place so he could drive into her harder, this time with even more fury.

Here he was, having what James wanted most, because he, Ben, was not an immense arsehole. He had earned the right to be in her bed, and he would be damned if he let just anyone take it away. The friction of his cock inside her was making her quite noisy.

"Yes, Benny! Like that! Please!"

After a few more minutes, Ben was struck by inspiration. He held her still, and she cocked her head, panting. Her honey skin was flushed a warm reddish pink, and she was glistening with sweat. Gods, she was stunning. He was a lucky man indeed.

"Mistress, I am sorry to interrupt our game, but I have an idea."

"Oh, do tell, Benny."

"I need you to get down, please."

The Black Rose lifted herself off him and rolled gracefully to a standing position on the floor beside the desk. Ben sat up, a giddy grin on his face. He took the chair from beneath his feet and moved it in front of her large mirror. Then he sat in it like a naked king on a throne, slapping his thighs.

"Mistress, please watch me fuck you."

The Pirate Queen smirked. Why had she not thought of that? She turned to face the mirror and eased herself back down onto his cock. She spread her legs wide for balance and watched with fascination as Ben's manhood moved inside her. He pulled almost all the way out before thrusting hard back in.

The Black Rose stretched her arms behind her on either side of Ben's head, gripping the back of the chair and holding on for dear life. Ben reached around, his wonderful fingers rubbing circles over the sensitive bud. Watching herself ride him was so stimulating, and when he once more held her hips still so he could pound into her again, it proved too much.

Her skin grew hot as the head of his cock rubbed exactly what it needed to inside her channel, and release hit her like a hurricane. She let out a yowl, spasming as her internal muscles clenched tight. Ben desperately wanted to follow, still wanting to claim her entirely.

He cursed under his breath when she pulled off him again, then dropped to her knees on the floor to take as much of him into her mouth as she could, working him furiously with her hands and tongue.

She looked up at him with her big brown eyes full of… well, Ben was not entirely sure what emotion it was, only that it was a good one. Love, lust, desire, joy. The specifics did not matter right now. What mattered was knowing she enjoyed fucking him. That alone shoved him right to the edge.

"Mistress," he croaked.

She nodded, watching intently as the muscles in his cock rippled, pushing his seed out of his body and onto her breasts. Ben's eyes rolled back and closed as his body twitched, pleasure coursing through him. He slumped in the chair for a long moment. Then he felt the rough cloth of a rag against his skin as she cleaned him up, followed by a feather-light kiss on his forehead.

"Come cuddle."

The Black Rose led Ben to her bed, and he flopped onto it, careful to avoid her discarded robe. Once he was settled, he took her into his arms and kissed whatever he could reach. He began muttering to himself, and she felt the vibrations more than she heard the words. She focused her ears.

"Fucking ponce bastard! He will never have my place between your legs! He can challenge me to all the duels he wants, but I belong here!"

Ben pulled the Captain on top of him and buried his face in her curls. He could not see the look on her face, because if he had, he might have known to shut his mouth.

"So, what you're saying is that this duel isn't about protecting me from James in a general sense, but this is very specifically him challenging your place in my bed?"

"Mmmhmmm."

Ben was rubbing his mustache over the sensitive skin of her neck and taking small nips. He was clearly still love-drunk from his climax, reveling in her warmth and weight on top of him.

"And how did he know you were in my bed? I didn't tell him..."

"I may have mentioned it..."

Ben answered with careless ease, picking a spot on her shoulder to nibble.

"I admit, I was antagonizing him a bit. James did start it, though. He was calling us names and being quite awful. It felt nice to knock him down a few pegs, letting him know I'm getting something he wants. Felipe and Alizée thought it was hilarious."

The Pirate Queen felt as though she had been kicked in the stomach. She knew Tariq was not a liar, but hearing Ben admit that he had talked about what the two of them did in private? That he did not seem to care whether he was in mixed company? And to fucking detestable James of all people?

Ben needed to get out of her room before she screamed at him.

She needed to think.

He needed to leave.

Right the hell now.

"I'm sorry, I have to take a piss. Goodnight, Benny," she said, wriggling out of his grasp.

He pouted, but quickly retrieved his clothes, dressed, and left. He was in such a hurry to give her privacy that he did not kiss her goodnight, much to the Captain's relief.

She had to think. She needed a plan for how to talk to Ben about setting ground rules.

She did not want to lose his company in bed entirely. He was spectacular in bed, and on her desk, and on her island, and everywhere else. If she was being honest, he should brag about his prowess.

Especially to James.

Especially if it made James angry or made him feel bad about himself.

Prick.

She sighed. This was all incredibly confusing. She would sleep on it, and perhaps things would look clearer in the morning. She would write out a list. That would likely help.

Ben liked lists.

Tobin did too, and he would probably be smug about the whole thing. He would probably want to tell her, "I told you so," but would refrain because she was the Captain.

Fuck.

The next morning, Ben jumped out of his hammock as soon as Tobin shook him awake. Today was the day. He was going to punch James today, and hopefully not break his hands in the process. How thrilling.

But when he and Tobin got up on deck, Felipe was nowhere to be found. Then, from above, in the crow's nest, came a whistle, followed by the gunner's voice.

"Tobin! Wake Madame."

"What do you see? Do you really think it's worth waking her?"

"French colors on the horizon, mes amis."

The Frenchman threw back his head and cackled with excitement.

"Today looks to be a beautiful day!"

# Chapter 12

## Raining Blood on the Bouclier Rouge

Ben followed Tobin to the Captain's quarters. The quartermaster pounded on the door. They stood side by side, the same height, though Tobin was twice as wide as Ben.

"Captain! Sails on the horizon," Tobin called, knocking again.

A groan sounded from within, and after a few moments the Black Rose opened the door, wearing an incredibly fetching red nightgown, rubbing her eyes and yawning massively.

"¿De dónde, Tobes?" she asked mid-yawn.

"French," Tobin replied, unfazed.

Once the Captain finished yawning, she shook herself slightly and seemed to finally register Ben's presence beside her second-in-command. Her hands flew to her hair, her face flushing before she slammed the door in the men's faces. Tobin rolled his eyes.

"What do you think?" she called through the door.

"You know how Felipe is. He wants to take it."

"Of course he does. He's the gunner, that is his job! What kind of French ship?"

"Not sure, Captain."

"I'm not entirely certain," Ben interjected, "but it looked like a cargo ship. It's probably headed toward the French Antilles from Haiti. It didn't look like a slaver. Best case scenario would be sugar, indigo, and cotton; worst case scenario, cows."

"Cows?"

The door opened again, and the Pirate Queen now stood dressed in her raid outfit, the very same one she had been wearing the day she and Ben first met: a soft red blouse, a black cincher at her waist, black trousers, and high black boots.

She tied a crimson headscarf around her forehead and began braiding her curls. Ben knew that once they left, she would tuck pins, nails, broken glass, and other sharp things into it to deter enemies from pulling her hair. A clever lesson hard-won, as evidenced by the large crescent-moon burn scar around one shoulder blade.

"Yes," Ben confirmed. He willed himself to stop talking, but the torrent of information came pouring out before he could stop it. "I've heard they have an ungodly number of wild cows on Hispaniola, and they tend to favor the western side of the island, which is Haiti."

*Please stop, you absolute twat*, he thought to himself. But Baffling Benjamin, the anxious know-it-all who lived in Ben's mind, still had more to say.

"And from personal experience, cattle are an absolute nightmare on a ship. Getting them on, getting them off, keeping after them... rather disgusting and quite dangerous in small spaces. And that's not even counting how much they eat! You would think they would be docile, but crowd them and they just get so damn nasty."

Why couldn't he shut the hell up and be normal for one godforsaken moment?

Ben was not sure what the Black Rose would do with all that information from Baffling Benjamin, but he certainly had not expected her to chuckle, her deep brown eyes sparkling.

"I can imagine, Benny. Cows can be bastards. Are you saying it looks worth our while to try to take it?" she asked.

Tobin nodded. "Even if it is cattle, we can sell them to a butcher in Barranquilla," he rumbled thoughtfully. "Might be able to get more for it as exotic French beef. If there's cotton and indigo, we can make a tidy profit. And if there's sugar, Xiang will be quite pleased indeed. He wants to try making small sweets in addition to the fruit bowl. That way, his experimentation will not come at a detriment to our own coffers."

The Black Rose squealed happily and clapped her hands. Ben made a mental note that she liked sweets.

"Very well. Tobin, tell Talia to wake the crew. Benny, please calculate how long we have before they're upon us, and then help Felipe in the armory."

Ben and Tobin nodded before turning away. Tobin went down the stairs, and Ben turned right to go back onto the deck.

Ben climbed up the rigging and joined the gunner in the crow's nest. Felipe handed the younger man a sextant, and Ben began calculating, talking through his process out loud. The numbers wrote themselves in the air in the corner of his vision. Finally, he arrived at an answer.

"I'd say about two and a half hours before they're upon us."

"Très bien. I shall not be making bets against you again. Do you wish to be a feather this time?"

Ben nodded excitedly. The older man pulled out a scrap of paper and pencil and began scribbling notes.

"I would very much like that. I've been itching to get back up there again."

"Very good. We will need to get a volunteer to give up their spot to you. You will likely owe them a favor for borrowing their strap. Most members of the Air Team develop special relationships, so if you mix up the straps and feathers, they do not tend to work as well together..."

He paused to think.

"Or Talia may agree to strap for you again. We shall have to ask."

He fell silent for a long moment, and Ben could practically see the wheels turning in the gunner's mind. The *Deception* had an air team during raids, where feathers, smaller or thinner crew members, swung from ropes, throwing smoke bombs, shooting targets, or otherwise deploying Felipe's experiments. Their partners, the straps, controlled the ropes from the crossbeam, which allowed the feathers to swing much longer than they would have managed on their own.

Talia, short, plump, and buxom, was a feather because of her extensive acrobatic and tumbling experience. Her strap, Arturo, had massive arms, much like Felipe. Speaking of the old goat, he snapped his fingers, signalling an idea.

"I have been working on something. Remember when I mentioned making it rain blood during a past raid?"

Ben nodded.

"I still have not let go of that idea. Come! To the armory!"

Once in the armory, Ben pressed himself against the wall to stay out of the Frenchman's way while the man buzzed around his workbench. He produced a series of bags that looked like waterskins with pipes sticking out of them. They looked rather like bagpipes. One of them certainly did not look like the others, covered in strips of plaid fabric.

"Is that Talia's missing bagpipe that nobody wants her to have?" Ben asked with a laugh.

Felipe's face went blank for a moment, though the tips of his ears turned pink, a sure sign of guilt.

"Possibly...but you must understand, Benny, she is not as good with them as she says she is. I do not hate cornemuse, but she is... non, she is not good. This serves better. Come, help me fill them up."

Felipe showed Ben where a large barrel of blood was hidden in a false wall in the kitchen, carefully stowed where it would not get too warm. It was half empty and did not smell nearly as terrible as Ben would have expected, given how old he guessed it to be. Ben held the bags while the Frenchman filled them with a large serving ladle and a funnel.

"Talia suspects you took it, at the behest of Tobin and Doctora," Ben said with a snicker, still finding the situation highly amusing.

Felipe nodded. "Tobin gets headaches very easily, and they are much worse when she tries to play. So yes, I took it as a favor to Tobin. But he does not need to know that. All he needs to know is that the noise miraculously stopped. I am working on something for him that I think might help the headaches, though. I was thinking to give them to him for his birthday, but he might need them sooner. Maybe I will give them to him for Xiang's birthday."

"When—?"

Felipe chuckled. "Of course, birthday police. Tobin's birthday is in September, but early. Mine, if you remember, is the last day of September. Xiang's birthday is when it is almost summer, sometime in early May. I do not know the exact dates, but I know the order of birthdays on this ship, and when they should be coming around. Next will be Juanito. We do not know his birthday, so we celebrate the day he joined our crew. Beginning of April sometime. Jules and Andrew know for certain."

Once the six bags were filled with blood, Felipe and Ben took them back to the armory and gingerly laid them on the workbench so they would not spill. Talia, Arturo, and Doctora came around the corner. Talia's emerald eyes flashed when she saw the workbench.

"It was you, ye auld bastard!"

The Scotswoman stood on her toes and smacked Felipe up the back of the head. The older man was not as tall as Ben and Tobin, but he was close, and it was still a reach for the boatswain.

"My poor wee Brunhilda Bagpipe!"

"Talia," Doctora admonished, even as she gave Felipe an exasperated look.

"She serves a greater purpose! For the science of warfare!" Felipe declared grandly, waving a finger in the air like a man delivering a political speech.

"What greater purpose, ya big wee nasty beastie?"

She picked it up, and her anger melted away, replaced by dawning understanding.

"We rainin' blood again?" she whispered, hopeful excitement in every syllable.

Felipe nodded, and the two of them started cackling while Doctora put her face in her hands. Arturo bit his lip, though he too was shaking with concealed laughter.

"Just make sure ye remember to warn Eliza this time," Talia said once their laughter had subsided.

"Oui, yes, of course, of course."

The gunner pulled out some paper and began hastily writing notes.

"Tals, Benny would like to try the air team for this experience. Would you strap for him?"

Talia considered for a moment, then nodded. "Ye ken I wanted to make it rain blood again, so ye now can owe me a favor."

Felipe held out his hand before thinking better of it and pulling it back.

"As long as it is not building you another perdu bagpipe..."

Talia pursed her lips, clearly annoyed that he had seen her request coming.

"Then I'll have to think on it," she said through a clenched-teeth smile, but they shook on it all the same.

The older man nodded, then turned to Arturo, Talia's strap.

"Arturo, I will give you the choice: Retreat Team or Second Team?"

"Second Team. It should be Tenoch and Aisha's turn for the Retreat Team."

Felipe nodded. "Oui, you are correct. I think I shall put our dear friend Frank on the retreat team as well... Hmmm... I think to let Anya try to lead the second team, oui? She did well last time..."

Felipe presented his list to Talia and Doctora, who both nodded. Talia walked to the stairs and blew an all-hands-on-deck whistle as she climbed up, with Arturo and Doctora following her. Felipe stared at the physician's retreating backside, shaking his head slightly.

"C'est une femme parfaitement merveilleuse!" he whispered breathlessly before clapping Ben on the back. "Come, Benny!"

Much like the *Angelina Marie* raid, the pirates gathered for their assignments and other announcements. Breakfast would be late, but Xiang's fruit bowl was stocked. Felipe would lead the first team. A cheer rose from the crowd when Anya was named leader of the second team, even as Zsófia and Gerda looked apprehensive.

Zsófia, Anya's wife, was a member of the gun crew and part of the retreat team. She would be below with the cannons and would have no way of knowing what was happening to her beloved. Their daughter Gerda, as one of the cabin children, would likewise be below deck, cared for during the raid by Doctora. This rotation, they would be joined by Aisha and Tenoch. Tobin would escort the Black Rose.

As everyone was dismissed, Ben saw Eliza and caught her arm as she passed, also heading down as part of the gun crew.

"Eliza?"

She grasped Ben's hand defensively and moved quickly, as though she meant to break his fingers. It startled him. He had no idea the laundress had reflexes like that. She checked herself and smiled at him, though the smile did not reach her eyes. The blue orbs flashed, sharp and observant.

"Yes, Benny?" she asked sweetly. Far too sweetly.

Ben cleared his throat, unsettled. "Uhh...Felipe is having us rain blood on them again. Thought you would like to know."

Eliza's head fell back, and she pinched the bridge of her nose.

"That auld nutter. That's going to be..."

She sighed in frustration. Then she straightened, shook her head, and inhaled deeply through her nose before letting out a long breath through her mouth, a trick clearly learned from Xiang.

"Thank ye fer warning me. Now I know to expect it."

She made her way down to the cannons, grumbling to herself. Ben went back to the armory to collect his kit.

Felipe had requested an audience with the feathers to explain their kit for this raid.

"First, you throw the smoke bombs as normal. Then you blow air into the smaller back pipe while you squeeze, which will send the blood shooting out the larger front pipe. I put a mesh in the front pipes, so hopefully it should..."

He stopped, clamping his mouth shut with a snap of his teeth.

"Sorry, it is very boring," he said quietly before the showman returned. "But hopefully it will look more like rain this time, so make sure you guide the big pipe side to side in big arcs for more coverage, oui?"

The feathers all nodded.

It suddenly struck Ben how much he and Felipe had in common. The older man must also have a voice in his head that told him to shut up, just as Ben was always trying to talk Baffling Benjamin down. Except the gunner did not appear to listen to himself most of the time. Perhaps that was the benefit of being older and caring less about what others thought.

But Ben really had found his people, hadn't he? Odd as they were, strange as it all seemed, in this unlikely place.

"Alright, air team! To the masts!"

Talia clapped a hand onto Ben's shoulder, steering him and the rest of the team toward the steps as Felipe headed for Doctora's quarters for their pre-doing-something-dangerous ritual.

Shit, he had not gotten a good-luck kiss from the Captain.

He tried to turn back, but Talia kept a firm hand on him.

"Nae, Benny, we all need to get aloft."

"But—"

"Nae buts! We need to get aloft before they see us! Ye need harnessed!"

In short order, they were fully harnessed and waiting with bated breath. From his position at the front of the ship, Ben could not even see the Black Rose. Terrible luck indeed.

The French ship put a gangplank between itself and the *Deception*, and once more Felipe limped across, pretending to be a doddering old man. He spoke in animated French to the two men who came to meet him. Then the gunner turned and motioned toward their colors, which Matilde unfurled. The crimson banner bled once again against the brilliant blue spring sky, revealing the Black Rose's symbols: a black skull and a lacy ceiba flower. Felipe pulled two pistols from his belt and shot both men flanking him as he shouted in a voice that carried on the wind:

"Allez!"

Ben ran along the mast, stepped off as he had been taught, and felt the rush as the wind caught him full in the face. He had missed this feeling. Ben threw his smoke bombs as hard as he could. His aim was true, and they exploded right in front of a group of rival crewmen advancing on Felipe.

Ben felt Talia tugging the rope above him, and he swung back like a pendulum. That gave him time to position his blood-bagpipe. He blew into the bag and gave it a squeeze as he flew over the deck of the rival ship. He made broad side-to-side sweeps, pleased to see that Felipe's mesh seemed to be working as intended, splitting the liquid into multiple streams. It really did look like rain as it fell into the smoke.

Then came a sound unlike anything Ben had ever heard before.

A chorus of terrified, discordant screams rose from below as Ben swung backward. More tugging on the rope above him sent him forward again for another pass. More screams, and through the smoke he saw the other crew slipping, sliding, and scrambling. Anya howled like a wild dog as she led her team across, her white-blonde hair flopping in the wind.

As the smoke cleared, Ben finally caught a glimpse of the Black Rose.

The Captain and Tobin advanced through the smoke toward the helm of the French ship. Tobin once again flitted around his charge with remarkable speed and grace for a man of his size and build, sunlight glinting off his bald head. The Black Rose reached the helm, raised a red scarf, and waved it triumphantly. Ben felt Talia release his rope for a moment so she could bring her boatswain's whistle to her lips. She blew a short tune, and everyone stopped to cheer.

Ben reveled in the happy energy he had been longing to feel again, the thrill of being thrown into a precarious, potentially deadly predicament and emerging unscathed. The excitement made him grin wildly as he let out a great whoop from his perch.

He sat in his little rope swing, admiring the beauty of the day, both ships, and his lover, tiny below on the deck.

Wait a tick.

She was coming back aboard.

All the adrenaline fled him at once as Ben watched the prisoners file onto the ship and line up.

No.

No, he had to get down there.

What if the highest-ranking officer fucked the Captain?

That was *his* place. His place was in the Black Rose's bed and between her legs, not dangling from the mast like a worm on a hook.

"Tals, get me down!" Ben shouted up to his strap.

She shook her head as she slowly, methodically wound up the rope.

"Sorry, Benny Boy, cannae do that. Air teams's responsible for a fair wee bit o' clean up after a raid. Ye need to give me a moment, and then ye need to get yer arse up here and help."

All the anxieties from the last raid came flooding back.

What if the other man couldn't satisfy her?

Or, even more distressingly, *what if he could?*

Why had Felipe not told him the air team had so much to do? How was Ben supposed to win the Black Rose from up here while another man was in her bed?

Ben followed Talia's directions to the letter, seething with resentment toward Felipe the entire time. The longer it dragged on, the harder he spiraled. He hated the old bastard with all his heart. How could he ever have thought the man was on his side, much less that they were two sides of the same coin? Maybe he really would make like Captain Kidd after all and spill the gunner's blood all over the deck.

The instant Talia dismissed him, Ben all but ran to the Captain's quarters, hoping against hope for a miracle. He found Felipe guarding the door. The Frenchman's face lit up, and he threw his arms wide over his head in welcome.

"Benny! How did you enjoy being a feather? Was it everything you hoped?"

Ben felt wild, his anger and frustration surging through him. He gritted his teeth, pulled back, and let his fist fly. It connected, striking the gunner squarely in the chin. Felipe shook himself a little and rubbed his jaw.

"Why didn't you tell me there was so much clean up as a feather?" Ben hissed, trying to keep his voice down so as not to attract the Captain's attention, though he could not remember ever being this angry. "What is happening? Is she... has he... is she?"

He pointed at the door.

"Oui, she just went in. However, I get the impression...he is more like Tobin and Xiang, if you understand my meaning. Another of his officers was quite upset when he was taken away, even after I reassured him that no harm would come to the prisoner."

He shrugged.

"I did tell you before, Benny boy, that you must come to terms with this. This will keep happening."

"You suggested sabotage. And I thought you *liked* us together as a couple."

Felipe's head fell back in exasperation. "I suggested sabotage to give you some feeling of control, oui, but obviously the circumstances are not always for you to control. You must learn to adapt. This is why you worry me."

The older man lit his pipe, and the sweet smell of burning leaves filled the hallway. The scent was oddly comforting, and Ben's body relaxed against its will. His mind, however, was still a spooked horse with no rider astride it.

Before Ben could say anything else, a frustrated noise came from inside the Black Rose's quarters. She yanked open the door, wearing her dressing gown, cheeks red, eyes flashing.

"Get him out of here," she growled. "Take him down with the rest of them."

"Mistress, would you like...?"

Ben reached for her, but she slapped his hand away.

"No! No, Benny. I...I just...ugh, no. Get him out!"

"Oui, Madame. Come, Benny."

Felipe and Ben untied the officer, who was hysterically sobbing in French. The gunner nodded as he listened, but did not translate. Once the man was dressed, they took him down to the brig. Anya was once again guarding it, her teeth still red from the fake blood capsules. She opened the cell door, and the prisoner flung himself into the arms of another man. The second man risked a kiss on the first's forehead, making soothing little sounds as they clung to each other.

Felipe spoke calmly and authoritatively, explaining the situation. The man who had been tied to the Black Rose's bed wiped his nose on his sleeve and stood a little straighter. He said something, his voice wobbling, barely holding back a sob. One by one, the other crewmen laid a hand on him, and even without understanding French, Ben knew the decision they were making: we stay together at all cost.

Felipe nodded and turned to Ben, who was still seething. The older man sighed, and then his eyes flicked toward the laundry area. He jumped slightly, a panicked whisper escaping him.

"Merde! I forgot to warn Eliza about…"

As though summoned by name, the laundress leaned backward into the doorway that separated the brig from the rest of the hold.

"Benny warned me, ye old goat."

She came into the room, and though otherwise unable to smell much of anything, Ben could still faintly pick up the lye clinging to her apron. She pointed a stern finger in Felipe's face with a snarl. The Frenchman cringed away from the Irishwoman.

"If ye cause any more messes to cross my basin before we make Barranquilla, I'll charge ye yer whole damn share! So much fookin' blood, ye thrice-curséd maniac!"

She grumbled darkly before moving back to her station. Hefting a large sack over her shoulder, she disappeared up the steps, leaving the two men alone.

"Thank you for warning her," the gunner said quietly. "I get too excited, and I forget sometimes…often…"

He turned to Ben, his eyes soft.

"As I forgot to tell you, the air team has a lot to do after raids are complete. I will not put you as a feather again unless you ask. You seemed so excited, and that made me excited, and now you are angry with me, and Eliza is angry with me, and I owe Talia a favor, and Lord knows what that woman will ask for."

The frustration in the older man's eyes deflated what remained of Ben's anger. Felipe really was a lot like him after all, wasn't he? Right down to the anxious spiraling. Ben would never have guessed the Frenchman thought so negatively, but it was oddly comforting to know someone else's mind worked much the same way.

Felipe tipped his head back, staring at the timbers overhead.

"Regardless of how I feel about you and Madame as a pair, she is the Captain. This is how she wishes to conduct her business. The day she requests my opinion, I will be certain to put in a good word for you. In the meantime, I can help you become more appealing to her, and I shall continue to make sure you are better than James, but Benny…"

He raised his hands, then let them fall again.

"I told you previously, and I shall tell you again: it is not personal. As I told you on the beach, it is about choice. You cannot be so insubordinate as to presume to choose for her, but you can choose your reaction. So, what will it be? Drop yourself overboard, or work to make yourself more appealing?"

Hazel eyes met grey-blue ones, and though the younger man wanted to argue, he knew the older man was right. Much as he hated it, he could not expect one of the Black Rose's officers to choose Ben's desires over the Captain's.

Besides, he could always take that frustration out on Felipe and Tobin during training.

"I'm sorry I struck you," Ben grumbled quietly. "Are you going to…?"

Felipe waved a giant hand. "Non. Tobin and I have been begging you for days to punch us. And now I know how you hit. You have good aim, but you will need much more power if we are going to obliterate James. I want you to break his stupid, beautiful jaw so he cannot speak ever again. So I will take my well-deserved punch in the face in the service of wrecking him entirely."

Ben nodded, and though he tried to feign indifference, the muscles in the Frenchman's shoulders relaxed.

"Come, we must return to Madame. I am interested to hear what this other ship hides beneath her stays."

# Supplemental

## From the private journals of Benjamin R. Harrington - Small Pocket Notebook

### Questions for Xiang

1. What are your favorite dishes to prepare?

2. What is one dish that you will never prepare again? Why?

3. What are ingredients that you will buy whenever you find them, no matter how much they cost?

4. What is the most creative meal you have ever put together with limited ingredients?

5. How do you reconcile your nonviolent belief system with the life of a pirate?

6. What is your favorite saying or teaching from your faith?

# CHAPTER 13

## BECALMED AND BEDEVILED

Ben and Felipe made their way to the Black Rose's quarters for the debrief. The Captain was sitting behind her desk, sulking, still wearing her green dressing gown. Ben wanted nothing more than to ask if she wanted him to stay after the meeting, but he also knew her well enough by now to realize that if he offered himself to her, she would likely reject him out of stubbornness.

She most enjoyed their 'lessons' when they were her idea...or, at least, when she *thought* they were her idea. And Ben had to admit, even to himself, that if he had his way, he would never leave her bed. Her deciding when and where they made love ensured they could both fulfill their duties.

But he certainly wished making love to her could be one of his assigned duties. He would certainly never neglect his business if she were his business!

Talia, Doctora, and Xiang filed in. Doctora and Felipe lit up to see each other while Talia rolled her eyes. Shortly thereafter, Tobin came in, looking bewildered.

"You are not going to believe this," he said as soon as the doors closed, "but we have encountered Benny's worst-case prediction."

"Cows?" Ben and the Black Rose asked at the same time. The quartermaster nodded.

"Cows. Forty-five head and five calves."

"Tell me you're joking," Ben said. Tobin shook his head. "What bad luck!"

"Not bad luck. An opportunity!" the Black Rose countered. Ben wondered if she actually felt that way or was just being contrarian. "As you said earlier, Tobin, we could sell them in Colombia."

"Yes, but we have to get them there!" Ben felt like he was losing his mind, his residual frustration tightening the muscles in his neck. Was he crazy?

"We'll worry about that in a moment," the Black Rose waved a hand before addressing Felipe. "What sayeth the prisoners?" The gunner had Doctora in a loose one-armed embrace, his arm draped over her shoulder with hers around his waist. When they realized the Captain was speaking to them, they both stiffened, and Felipe stood at attention, his arm dropping away from the pouting physician and snapping to his side.

"I have spoken to the captives. They wish to stay together. I say, next island we come across, we put them all in some lifeboats and set them off together."

"That's unusual," Tobin grumbled. "They usually sell each other out to save their own skins."

"Well, if you do not believe me, you can learn French and ask them yourself," Felipe responded, sarcasm dripping from each syllable.

Tobin scoffed. "I didn't say I don't believe you, you old prick, I just said it was unusual."

The Black Rose pulled out a map, unrolling it on the desk, and the officers all gathered around. Ben hung back a little, feeling a little presumptuous as he was still not yet a full officer.

"We should be passing by a small island later tonight or early tomorrow. I suggest we take their ship in tow to Barranquilla. If cattle on a ship are as difficult to deal with as Benny thinks, it may be easier than trying to estimate how many people would need to man a skeleton crew. How many prisoners from the captured ship?"

"Fourteen, Madame," Felipe supplied. "Many members of their crew fought bravely and died honorable warrior's deaths. Quite a waste, but if you can say nothing else of the French, they certainly have conviction! And this crew is very close. *Fraternité*, like brothers. Maybe that is why they do not sell each other out.

Maybe it is because our last few captures have been English, and the English are... well..." He waved his hand vaguely. "No offense, Benny." Ben shook his head. He would very much *like* to take offense, but not in front of the Captain. Not like this. Despite that, he tried to soothe the anger in his chest by making a self-deprecating comment. Maybe if the Black Rose laughed...

"None taken. If I hadn't surrendered, I know my crew on the *Starling* would have tied me to the anchor and dropped me overboard themselves if I had been left in charge." Nobody laughed. In fact, there was a flicker of something that looked like pity on the Black Rose's face. Ben's annoyance wavered toward hope; that could mean an invitation to make them both feel better later.

"So, we take the ship in tow to Barranquilla and try to sell it there. Time to put it to a vote. All in favor?" Everyone except Ben and Doctora slapped an open palm on the desk, signifying a yea vote. "Very good. Five in favor, two abstentions."

"I still cannot vote, Mistress," Ben corrected quietly. The Black Rose's head fell back.

"Still carries," she growled, frustrated. "You're dismissed. When we sight land, we can send our new friends off, and then it should be smooth sailing to Barranquilla. We should be there in two or three days. Easy!"

Except it was not that easy.

That evening, they passed a small island, and the fourteen members of the *Bouclier Rouge* were filed into their own lifeboats and set adrift. Felipe and Xiang saw to it that the crew had provisions, and distant fires on the beach told them the island was in fact occupied. They were pirates, and they could be ruthless when the circumstances called for it, but heartless they were not. Certainly not with a man like Xiang aboard. Their Buddhist cook made sure prisoners were treated fairly in addition to keeping everyone well-fed.

Ben hoped the Black Rose would summon him to her quarters, but no such invitation, written or otherwise, materialized. What a spot of bad luck! First, fucking cows, and now this.

And then, the next evening, even worse luck: the wind stopped entirely.

For almost two weeks, the *Deception* sat trapped, becalmed in a doldrums very unusual for that part of the Caribbean. The air was thick, hot, sticky, and still. The sun beat down. The sea was so calm that it barely splashed against the ship. It was like living in a cursed book, nothing to move the ink from the page.

The crew swabbed and cleaned everything they could think of. Especially with a whole second ship full of cows, there was plenty to clean, but soon the *Deception* was completely spotless.

A gangplank was put down between the *Deception* and the *Bouclier Rouge* for ease of movement between the two. Ben helped Tobin devise a duty rotation for taking care of the cows. Tobin exempted the officers and the kitchen staff. Ben suggested that Eliza also be exempted, and Tobin agreed. Ben's duty would be to coordinate the children in feeding the animals. The children liked Ben and were likely to follow his orders without arguments. Ben found that agreeable.

The cows also meant the crew did not have to worry about food, but soon almost everyone was missing fresh vegetables and fruit. Xiang, Natsuki, Frank, and Li Mei made every beef dish they could think of, to varying degrees of success.

The children tried to teach Mar so many new tricks that the poor mutt had taken to hiding under Xiang's bed, refusing to come out for anyone except Xiang and Ben.

Felipe was most well-adjusted for the long period of free time, where he could tinker and experiment, but after a few days of everyone else's complaints of boredom, he arranged some activities for the crew. First was target practice with their cannons to make sure they were still in top form, as they had not been used recently. The novelty wore off quickly when the rest of the crew realized how much work went into a single shot.

Ben was quite impressed by how well the gun crew worked together, and marveled at Maeve's spectacular aim. They managed to hit all of the empty barrels thrown overboard as targets. Ben knew from experience that aiming a cannon was quite difficult, and he wondered if the Haitian former slave woman could see diagrams in the air like he could; however, Maeve scared him a little, and he didn't want to ask.

The Frenchman then set up target practice on the rail, and invited everyone to try shooting from his impressive collection of guns: pistols, muskets, and a blunderbuss that was certainly older than Ben was. Gun shooting was much more popular, and everyone was stunned to find that Doctora and Gerda, neither of whom were involved in their normal raids, were both natural marksmen.

While musket shooting, Doctora was able to hit a tea saucer Felipe flung out to sea like a discus, and the gunner had been so impressed Ben was surprised the old goat hadn't proposed marriage to the woman on the spot. Gerda, Anya and Zsófia's daughter, and the youngest of the children aboard, was not only able to shoot a bottle on the rail from the opposite rail, but repeat the feat three more times. She was also able to load the pistol again herself after watching Anya do it once, which Ben thought was even more impressive.

The Frenchman and Ben gave some more fencing demonstrations, and Ben's hand-to-hand combat training attracted much more attention than the younger man would have liked. Learning to block punches in front of so many people was distracting, and Ben was covered in bruises the entire time. Fortunately, he was also starting to gain more power in his own punches, so Felipe and Tobin were likewise sporting discolored skin by the end.

Other people, inspired by Felipe, also pitched in to give lessons or provide distractions to the crew: Anya led a workshop on using grappling hooks, aiming for the rail of the *Bouclier Rouge*; Halima gave lectures on some of the plants she kept in her little garden below the bowsprit on the prow of the ship that Ben hadn't realized was there; Maeve hosted a poetry contest; and the cabin children were given 'secret missions' by Eliza to gather information about the adults without directly asking for it and without the adults realizing they were giving it.

Toñiete, the quiet lad he was, took exceptionally well to subterfuge. While Juanito and Giselle would interrogate Ben point-blank while they were feeding the cows, Toñiete first posed queries to Ben about maps and charts, and inquired how Ben had learned certain things.

By the end of their conversation, Ben had all but told Toñiete his life story, and the lad said, with a small smile, "Eliza will be most pleased that I got everything on her list, and so quickly! You are certainly very open with your life if asked the correct way!" Ben didn't know how to feel about that, but the boy was so pleased with himself that the helmsman couldn't bring himself to be cross with him, and he knew better than to get on the laundress's bad side.

Felipe also took the opportunity to interview Xiang for *The Chronicles of the Deception*. Ben tried to sit in, but when he kept interrupting with questions, asking for translation, and trying to read over the Frenchman's shoulder, Felipe lost his patience with the younger man. He threatened to drop both Ben *and* the folio overboard if Ben didn't get out of his hair, and Ben was fairly certain the gunner meant it this time. Ben retreated, leaving Felipe to weave Xiang's tale.

Almost all members of the crew were sporting new tattoos: Talia and Felipe got compass roses on their left wrists to match Ben's as a symbol of their brotherhood. Xiang and Tobin finally agreed on one of Ben's designs and got their matching key and cooking knife tattoos, with Xiang also getting a pair of chopsticks and a bowl of noodles.

Andrew requested a raven on his left front shoulder. The man from the bilge was gangly and almost as tall as Ben, with shaggy, sandy blond hair, a closely cropped goatee and small mustache, and clear brown eyes that sparkled with mischief and something Felipe called *joie de vivre*. Ben found him chatty (but agreeably so, not overwhelming like Talia could be), and as another former Royal Navy man, they had quite a bit in common.

He was also hysterically funny, to the point that Ben had to stop multiple times for a few minutes because they were both laughing too hard. After spending time with him, Ben was incredibly confused as to why such a vibrant, interesting man would want a raven etched on his skin, especially after Andrew mentioned the Morrígan.

Ben knew from his Irish grandmother's stories that the Morrígan was a Celtic goddess of war and fate, but he was concentrating very hard on getting the beak just right, so he didn't verbally question it. Despite all that, the smile Andrew gave him when he was finished made Ben feel like he had made a wonderful new friend.

The next day, Eliza asked Ben for a parrot on her right front shoulder after gushing about how much she loved Andrew's raven. Ben thought this was an even more outlandish request, pondering how much more sense it would have made if they had gotten opposite tattoos. If Andrew were to be represented by a bird, a parrot seemed much more fitting, colorful and talkative.

But alas, Andrew was already inked, and Ben wasn't about to argue with Eliza, especially not when she had reflexively attempted to break his fingers. She was much more like a raven: solidly built, not a stranger to tricks or blackmail if necessary, and very protective of the nest she had found on the *Deception*. How odd that they should etch incorrect representations onto their skin permanently.

But Ben kept his mouth shut and drew the laundress the most darling little parrot he could manage. She burst into tears when she saw the finished product, thanking Ben profusely. Confusing, but a job well done nevertheless.

Doctora spent the better part of an afternoon with Felipe punching drawings of different flowers and herbs into the skin of her upper left arm, including a tiny *fleur-de-lis* iris. A tiny fleur-de-lis design that Felipe had absolutely no idea how it got there.

*Just what exactly are you trying to imply, Talia?*

Seeing the physician's new garden on her arm, the Captain asked Ben to draw a blooming rose on her collarbone. He deeply regretted it almost immediately as they sat together on the deck in front of everyone. Being so close to her, drawing so delicately in such an intimate place when they both were still *so frustrated* from the last raid, got both rather flustered.

Ben needed to excuse himself and disappear below deck. He emerged sometime later to find Felipe had finished the Black Rose's tattoo, and she was wearing her shirt off the shoulder to show it off. It looked very sweet and dainty on her if he said so himself, and Ben swore that the moment he got the Pirate Queen to admit she loved him back, he would get a matching one over his heart.

The crew sang every song any of them knew, and even some they didn't, making up words to fill the rhythms and rhymes of half-remembered snatches of melodies. There had even been a full day where Ben and Talia taught each other their respective versions of "The Jolly Roving Tar," and then had debated until long into the night which version was superior, ending in a stalemate, as each was convinced they had won.

Tobin had taken inventory of every item on the *Bouclier Rouge* and then moved on to the *Deception*. He even took inventory of people's personal effects, which had caused more than a few arguments. The biggest and loudest of these was when the quartermaster deigned to start parsing Felipe's hammock and the armory.

Tobin threatened to scuttle all the junk the gunner had acquired, and Felipe insisted it was all useful; they just didn't *know* the use yet. Tobin threatened the Frenchman bodily before Doctora intervened, causing Felipe to immediately concede. That had kept the quartermaster busy for a solid day, and when it was done, he had a giant list and nothing else to do.

The entire crew was absolutely, completely, unequivocally bored.

The Black Rose herself was taking the boredom very poorly. Ben realized it likely had to do with the cycle of her monthly courses, and she was probably still agitated because of how 'negotiations' with the French captain had gone. Ben observed her, wishing she would invite him to her quarters for one of their 'lessons' to relieve them both.

He had hoped that since she had been just as hot and bothered by him drawing on her chest as he had been, he would have been invited to see, touch, and taste the finished product, but no such luck. Bunking with the rest of the crew, there was little privacy to take care of his desires, but he was used to having to sit with his lustful feelings. At least his loveless, frigid marriage to Anne had trained him well in that aspect.

Finally, after supper on the twelfth evening, Xiang handed Ben a note in the Captain's elegant script.

*Please come to my quarters for a lesson as soon as you are able.*
*– R*

Ben almost ran to her room. Finally. He knocked, probably a little too loudly and enthusiastically, and was roughly pulled inside before the door slammed behind him.

The Black Rose was naked, and she pointed to the bed with a feral growl.

"Get your cock hard and get it inside me this instant. That is a fucking order."

Ben opened his mouth to say something, and she clawed at his clothes, yanking off whatever fabric she could grab.

"No. Do not say a fucking word, just get on the bed before I have you thrown overboard. You don't need to speak, you don't need to 'Yes, Mistress,' you need to get your goddamn pants off!"

Ben put his hands up in a submissive gesture and stripped as quickly as physics would allow. Fortunately for both of them, her demands had turned him on far more than he would have expected, and she groaned when his trousers hit the floor and his large cock stood at attention.

Before he could even sit on the bed, she tackled him. He fell back, momentarily worried they might break the frame, and the Captain scrambled over him, desperate to align their bodies. Once she found the right angle, she impaled herself on him, throwing her head back in relief.

"Mistress—"

"No," she said through gritted teeth, slapping a hand over his mouth. "If you say a single word, I swear to God, Benny, I will have you flogged."

Ben bit his lip, and the Black Rose began riding him frantically, cursing up a storm as she did.

"Fucking son of a bitch, you bastard," she growled, before switching into Spanish.

Ben had not the slightest idea what she was saying, and figured it would be smarter not to ask. Her nails dug into the muscles of his shoulders. The sting of pain, their mutual desperation, the stream of poetic nonsense hissed over him, and the sheer novelty of having something, or someone, to do was intoxicating. He thrust into her as forcefully as she drove down onto him.

He felt her tightening, felt her begin to shake on top of him, her breathing turning ragged and her diatribe climbing in pitch. He caught a few snatches of something that sounded almost like a prayer. She leaned back just a little and unraveled on top of him, loudly calling out for Santa María. Two pumps later, Ben was seized by his own climax, spilling himself into her. He closed his eyes, exhaled, and muttered without thinking,

"I love you."

And in that moment, whatever post-release calm and delight the Black Rose had been feeling vanished completely.

First came the slap.

Ben's eyes flew open at not just the force of it, but the sound. It cracked so loudly his ears rang, as though he had been standing beside a cannon without covering them. The Captain loomed over him, face flushed red with fury, eyes wild. Ben was transported back to the day he lost his virginity, right down to the slap.

But while Anne had been silent, the Black Rose showed all the passion in the world. Ben realized the knee to the groin he had suffered when he dared kiss her in front of the whole crew during their fencing demonstration was nothing compared to the wrath about to be visited upon him.

"How dare you!" she screamed, drawing back to slap him again.

"What? What did I do?" Ben asked, voice wobbling as he threw up his hands to protect his face while blows rained down on him.

Somewhere deep in his mind, he was glad Felipe and Tobin had been spending so much time teaching him to block punches. It was coming in quite handy. Also, fortunately, the Captain did not hit nearly as hard as the gunner and quartermaster did.

But her nails were longer and sharper, and Ben still took several scratches, as though he had decided to wrestle a large jungle cat.

"You released inside me, pendejo cabrón! And then you said you love me? What the fuck?"

She slid off him and yanked him out of her bed, her nails biting into his arm.

"Get out of my quarters, you...you dumbass...you...fucking...walrus!"

Ben felt as though he had been slapped again, this time in the brain.

"What the hell is a walrus?" he asked, but got no answer as she shoved him out the door. He turned just in time for it to slam in his face, the latch dropping into place.

Ben's head tipped back toward the ceiling, then fell forward again. He noticed something rather important. Or rather, the lack of something important.

"Can I at least have my trousers back?" he called quietly, trying not to attract attention from the deck.

"No," she barked.

"What am I supposed to do now?"

"I care a fucking cucumber!"

Now what the hell did that mean? Was he having an apoplexy? Had she slapped him so hard he'd lost all grasp of English? Or was she translating a Spanish idiom that made no sense out of context? What on earth was happening?

"Go see Tobin," she continued, "and maybe go fuck yourself while you're at it!"

At least those were instructions he understood and could follow, so to speak. That slowed his mental spiral, even if it did not stop it.

Ben stood there for a moment, still staring at her door, his mind reeling, his chest tight. Maybe he had not meant to say he loved her, but had he really deserved that reaction?

He looked around for anything he might use to cover himself. Seeing nothing, he cupped his manhood in both hands and quickly, quietly made his way down to the kitchen, where he guessed Tobin and Xiang were probably indulging in their own pleasures in the little room beside the pantry.

Fortunately, nobody was about, not even to nick one of the last sad apples from the bowl. Most of the crew were either out on deck trying to stave off boredom as best they could, or already asleep below.

Ben reached the cook's door and knocked softly.

"What?" came Tobin's deep bass rumble, and Mar whined behind the door.

"Um...it's Ben. I...need a pair of pants. Please."

A small laugh sounded from within. Xiang.

Ben heard Tobin get up, and then the door opened. The quartermaster's eyebrows rose.

"Even though you said you needed pants, that's still not what I expected to see. What did you do to make her mad?"

"How can you tell?"

"Well, you're naked, you smell like a whorehouse, and you have a red hand-print on your face and scratches on your arms and chest. The only people aboard with hands that small are Xiang and the Captain, and Xiang has been in here with me the whole time, and his nails wouldn't do that sort of damage. Ergo, you fucked the Captain, made her mad, and she threw your ass out. So how did you piss her off?"

Ben's head fell back, and he tried pleading his case to the ceiling. Mar had a different idea, shoving her snout into his crotch and making him jump at the cold of her nose.

"Can I answer that after I have pants? Please?"

Tobin shook his head.

"No. I don't want to give you trousers if we're going to end up stringing you up or tossing you overboard, so I need to know what you did."

Ben sighed.

"Can I come in? Please?"

Tobin glanced at Xiang, who shrugged.

The quartermaster stepped aside to let Ben pass. Xiang said something in a jocular tone, and Tobin snorted.

"He said keep your raw buns off his bed."

Under normal circumstances, Ben would have found that funny, but he was drowning in embarrassment, rejection, confusion, and pain.

"I just cannot win today," he grumbled.

"Well, you got to fuck today, so you were winning, and then you ruined it. Out with it, man. Is she going to want to keelhaul you, or is this walk of shame all?"

"I...finished inside her."

Tobin and Xiang shared a grimace. Ben's voice climbed in pitch as panic rose.

"I didn't do it on purpose, we finished at almost the exact same time..."

Tobin held up a large hand.

"Is that the first time you've finished inside her?"

Ben nodded. While it was something he had wanted for weeks, he was not about to admit that to Tobin. And in the moment, it had been the furthest thing from his mind. It truly had been an accident.

"Okay. As much as you two little bunnies are going at it, I'm surprised it took you this long to slip up." He turned to his own petite lover. "Xiang, we're going to need to keep the Captain's special tea in stock. Actually, she will probably feel better if you brew her a cup now."

Xiang nodded and pulled a vial from the shelf. He held it up to Ben and spoke in halting English.

"No. Preg-a-nent. Tea."

He pushed past Ben and Tobin into the kitchen to set a kettle on. Ben's mouth dropped open in shock. Tobin shook his head.

"Are you a simpleton? Don't you know that if you get her pregnant, you'll ruin everything she's built? Not to mention she'll probably have to leave."

Ben shook his head.

"No, no, I understand that part. I just didn't know Xiang could speak English at all."

Tobin shrugged and went on.

"So that's it? She slapped you that hard for not pulling out?"

Ben ran a hand through his hair to the back of his neck. Realizing modesty no longer mattered, he dropped his other hand from his manhood. Tobin had seen him naked on his first day aboard; it was hardly new.

"I also, maybe, possibly might have said 'I love you' after I released."

Tobin looked as though he might smack Ben too, but settled for slapping his own face with his palm.

"That's what we've been worried about."

"You talk about me with her?"

Ben felt his face grow hot. What else did she tell Tobin about him? Tobin looked exasperated.

"Don't get insubordinate, Benny! I outrank you, and I am still having trouble deciding if you deserve pants. Yes, the Captain does confide in me, and yes, she does talk about you. And if you want to know any more, you will shut the hell up and listen."

Ben closed his mouth and bit his lip.

"She has been trying to avoid fucking you these past few weeks, especially right now, when everyone is bored and...desirous. You are the first person to please her in a very, very long time—if ever, honestly—and the only one who asked to stay. She's not used to having someone who satisfies her so well on board, just existing, since she makes it a point never to fuck her crew. She thinks it takes away her authority, like she slept her way up the chain of command instead of starting at the top.

"She has a reputation to uphold. And as such, you and she need to reach an...understanding...but she's been having trouble deciding her terms. I imagine this experience will make them much more concrete for her. This will likely result in a set of rules for your...relationship...so be prepared for that. And honestly, she should have laid down some rules the moment you asked to stay. I'm not going to tell her, 'I told you so,' because she is still the Captain, but..."

The quartermaster shook his head.

"Also, I think she's worried you're going to ruin her if she gets too dependent on what you offer."

Ben nodded. Much as he desired the Captain, it made all the sense in the world that she harbored complicated feelings about wanting him in return.

"She did seem quite angry at the start. She wouldn't let me say anything, and she was speaking Spanish the whole time."

Tobin nodded.

"Yes, she's been incredibly frustrated. Like a jaguar in heat. She has been grappling with that frustration ever since that man from the *Bouclier Rouge* couldn't get it up. She knew that if she came to you for relief, it would probably feed into whatever odd notions you have about being in love with her. And you are terrible at hiding it, by the way. You're worse than Felipe and Doctora."

"Is it so wrong to love her, though?" Ben asked, wounded.

Tobin sighed, pinching the bridge of his nose.

"Are you actually an idiot, Ben? Truly? You don't get the keys to the kingdom because you fuck her correctly. You are infatuated with her because she is something you want that was clearly missing in your life before. And it's not just you, Benny. Plenty of men get their cocks wet once and think they've found everything they're looking for and tie themselves down.

"And think like a logical adult human for a moment: if she is worried about being forced to give up her life for a baby, don't you think she's worried about how a husband would sideline her the same way? Demanding she stop 'negotiating' with other men, keep a house ashore, pop out an heir every year?"

"But..."

Ben started to protest, but Tobin raised a hand again.

"No buts. You clearly want to be a husband so badly, and you are trying to make her see you as such. She is not there yet, and she may never get there. And if you really think you love her—which you don't, by the way, at least not yet—you need to respect that she might never feel that way. You haven't even known her for two whole months, and this is not a romance story. This is real life."

Ben realized this was likely what Tobin had been holding against him since Campeche. Everything began falling into place. The quartermaster sighed, his face softening a little before he continued.

"So, you have a choice: either you hold onto her as gently as you would a butterfly, and please her when you can, while you can; or you find another crew next time we make port and you both put each other in the past. Her job is difficult enough without you trying to complicate it further. And if you keep trying to push your weird love agenda on her, I will throw you overboard myself."

Xiang appeared in the doorway with a large steaming cup of tea. His eyes flicked down to Ben's nakedness, and understanding washed over his face. He said something before handing the cup and saucer to Ben.

Ben cocked his head, and Xiang gently poked his arm with one finger.

"You. Apologies. Now."

"He thinks you should apologize by taking the Captain her tea," Tobin clarified.

Ben accepted the cup and looked down.

"So...can I have some trousers?"

Tobin and Xiang shook their heads in tandem.

"No."

Ben sighed, but nodded.

"Say you have her tea, and she will at least open the door," Tobin suggested. "Either she'll pity you and give you your pants back, or she'll be turned on and ask you to fuck her again. Do it correctly this time, and you may yet tame the beast. Good luck."

Ben stepped away, the bitter herbs of the tea wafting up to his nose. He quickly replayed the Black Rose's words in his mind, trying to gird his loins, so to speak. Xiang, Tobin, and Mar emerged from the room and headed toward the galley. Still, one thing the Captain had said continued to puzzle him.

"Oh, one more question..." he said, following them, trying not to spill his precious cargo.

Tobin looked up expectantly from the fruit bowl.

"What in God's name is a walrus?"

Tobin rolled his eyes.

"You really don't know shit about animals, do you?"

Ben shook his head.

"At some point, if she decides she's done being angry, you can ask her to show you her animal book. They're…interesting. Now, please take the Captain her tea before you ruin everything."

# CHAPTER 14

## DOLDRUMS AND DEMARCATION

Ben heaved another heavy sigh, shoulders slumping, before making his way back to the Captain's quarters. His hands were full now, trying to balance the cup so none of the precious liquid would spill, and he prayed nobody would come into the galley and see him.

As he crossed back toward the stairs, he thought about what Tobin had said. Tobin had known the Captain for a long time, perhaps even before she became the Black Rose. Of course she would trust him more than she trusted Ben. As Felipe had said, Ben was basically fucking Tobin's little sister. Of course he would want to protect her from ruining what she had worked so hard to build.

But something else Tobin had said stung with its truth: *You want to be a husband so badly, and you are trying to make her see you as such.* It bruised his pride, but it was not necessarily wrong.

He had tried to settle into the familiar routine of what he thought marriage ought to be, because she was his ideal of what a happy wife should be. He had felt that way from the first time she had ridden him, excited, beautiful, and enjoying herself fully.

But she did not want or need a husband. She wanted and needed a hard-working, trusted sailor and navigator whose company she also happened to enjoy in bed...and everywhere else they had experienced each other, and would no doubt continue to experience each other. He could do that, right?

And if she were ever ready to settle down, he would enthusiastically put a ring on her finger and buy her a gown.

"But for now, just try to have fun when you can," he muttered to himself as he arrived at her door, though he was not entirely certain he believed it.

He gingerly knelt in supplication, ready to beg forgiveness, took a deep breath in and out, and knocked.

"Captain," he said quietly, "I have your tea. And an apology."

To his surprise, the door opened.

The Captain stood on the other side of the threshold in her dressing gown, tied loosely enough to expose a deep V of honey skin down to her navel. She held a large fan, sweat glistening at her throat in the fading twilight as she snapped it shut.

She unconsciously licked her lips at the sight before her. Ben shifted his angle slightly to better admire the glimpses of her beautiful breasts, as though they were fighting to be liberated from the heat of their fabric prison.

But the Black Rose was still angry, her jaw set, a small snarl on her lips. She considered taking the tea and slamming the door in his face again, but she knew it would be unfair not to hear his apology. She took the cup from Ben and stepped aside to let him in while she swallowed a large gulp. The bitter herbs made her wince, but she relaxed a little as the heat slid down her throat into her chest. She hated this tea, but it worked.

"Sit," she said, indicating one of the chairs by her desk.

"You wouldn't rather I sit on the bed?"

She shook her head. The Captain swallowed more tea until the cup was empty. She felt much better now that she did not have to worry about that.

Then she produced a neatly folded pile of fabric and set it on her desk.

"Here is your shirt. And your trousers. But don't put them on yet. Depending on how this conversation goes, you may want to leave them off. Just in case."

"So you're not mad?"

"Oh no, I'm still mad. I'm absolutely furious. I thought what we did earlier was a hate-fuck. But I could still hate-fuck you again, even harder and with much more hate, and have Tobin and Felipe toss you overboard after I am satisfied. Leave your blue balls to buoy you up to the surface."

Ben winced. She did not like being this cruel to him, but in that moment it was cathartic.

"But you said you had tea and an apology, and I've only seen one of those things. So, make with saying you're sorry and we'll go from there,"

Ben nodded and knelt on the floor, taking the Pirate Queen's hand in his own.

"Captain, I am incredibly regretful that I accidentally finished inside you. In the heat of the moment, I didn't realize that finishing inside you could create a... predicament... that you are very responsibly attempting to avoid. I promise that in the future, I will be more cognizant of my body and warn you when I am getting close."

The Captain nodded serenely.

"Apology number one is accepted, Benny, thank you. I appreciate your understanding. Now for the second part?"

"I... uh... I'm sorry that I said what I said. It may not have been completely untrue or total nonsense, but I understand why it upset you."

The Black Rose tilted her head.

"This is the part where you promise not to say it again," she prompted in a stage whisper.

Ben shook his head. "I don't know if I can make that promise. Even though Tobin explained it to me quite plainly, I don't want to deny that we have something...special...between us. Maybe I could be more than some...elaborate fuck-toy...to you...someday...I don't know. But I do know that I don't want to force you into something you don't want. Trust me, I have plenty of experience with that. I just..."

Ben sighed deeply, clenching and unclenching his free hand into a fist. The Pirate Queen waited while he collected himself. When he finally spoke, it was so quiet she almost did not hear him.

"You are everything I ever dreamed of, Mistress. I have always, always wanted a woman such as yourself. If I cannot have you as entirely mine, then I want any crumb you deign to give me. A smile, a wink, a touch, a kiss, or the most mind-boggling perfect fuck I've ever had, it doesn't matter; I want up that ladder and back down it, repeatedly, until I am called back to the dust."

He drew in a deep breath, seemingly steadied by the admission.

"But you cannot prevent me from adoring you, and possibly even loving you. I don't want to have to leave you. And I think you'd also be most put out if I decided to leave you for another crew. Am I right?"

The Pirate Queen clicked her tongue, frustration clear on her face, but she knelt to his level, her deep brown eyes searching his grey-blue ones.

"I hate that you're being this difficult, but I appreciate that you know your worth, because you're right, I would be very upset if you left. And not just for the loss of this beautiful treasure..."

She ran a finger along his cock, and his manhood swelled eagerly under her touch. She wagged a finger at it, as though that would do anything to contain his lust for her.

"If we are going to keep studying together, we need to come to some agreements."

Just as Tobin had warned him.

"I am ready to listen, Mistress."

She stood and began to pace around him.

"First, you do not verbalize what we do to anyone, even if they ask. You are simply following your Captain's orders. Do not talk about the lessons, the demonstrations, or any other time I invite you to my quarters, my bed, or wherever else we decide to have a lesson. It can be an open secret, but you will not fan the flames of rumor. Especially not to that pendejo James."

"Yes, Mistress."

"Secondly, you absolutely do not finish inside me unless I expressly invite you to. I probably won't, but don't pull this nonsense again. And if you do, you will immediately get me a cup of my tea, or your place between my legs is forfeit."

"Yes, Mistress, and again, a thousand apologies. I will strive to be better in tune with my body."

"Thank you."

She paused, then continued.

"Next rule: When I ask you to leave, you do so immediately. No attempts to dally, no trying to get me back in bed, and certainly no attempts to spend the night with me unless I ask."

"Well then, I want quarters closer to here so my Walk of Shame isn't quite as embarrassing."

Ben was confounded by his own audacity, but it was something he had been wanting for a while. The lack of privacy had been a problem these past weeks, when he had no way to relieve his tension. The Captain blinked and raised her eyebrows, but did not argue.

"That is fine. I was thinking about that anyway, since we'll likely be promoting you at our next big holiday gathering. I like to do promotions during celebrations, as it makes them more fun. Passover, Easter, and Eid are coming up, so it will likely be then."

She gestured toward the door.

"The room at the bottom of the stairs currently belongs to Tobin and Felipe, but Tobin has all but moved into Xiang's room. So, you can take his spot."

"Wait, you're promoting me again? Already?"

She shrugged. "We have to vote to make it official, but I think you've earned it, Lieutenant. Why delay the obvious and inevitable? Talia, Felipe, and I are having a terrible time trying to do our own jobs and failing to be navigators. We are all suffering for it."

She threw a hand up to indicate their stalled ship.

"Obviously."

"Obviously," Ben agreed quietly. "May we seal that contract with a kiss?"

They leaned into each other and kissed deeply. The Black Rose made a small, strangled sound. Ben pulled back. Her cheeks were flushed.

"Mistress?"

"I think that was probably my biggest mistake, kissing you on the mouth and letting you do it to me. But you're just... intoxicating."

"You are, too," Ben mumbled as their lips met again.

This time they kissed slowly, eagerly, until Ben was sure he might never breathe again. When they finally parted, the Pirate Queen rubbed her nose against his.

"Next rule: At absolutely no point do you say you love me, expecting me to say it back. I'd rather you not say it at all, but if I must hear it, fine. But don't get all sad and strange when I don't reciprocate."

Ben gritted his teeth, but nodded. This would probably be the hardest rule of all.

"Yes, Mistress."

"I'm not saying I will never feel that way, but I don't feel that way right now. Does that make sense?"

Ben nodded.

"It does. And as I previously stated, I will content myself with whatever you give me."

She touched his cheek gently.

"Don't be sad, Benny. I do like you very much, though," she purred, running her nails along his shoulders. The sensation made him groan quietly. "Additionally, I am very sorry I struck you. And scratched you. And screamed at you."

She looked down at him.

"This is why I walk away when I'm angry, because if I don't, then things like that happen. Or worse."

"Apology accepted, Mistress."

He paused. He could not remember a superior officer ever apologizing to him before. As Felipe had said, that was leadership. That was why, while the old goat would burn the world to the ground, he would follow the Black Rose into the mouth of Hell itself. Ben decided he would, too.

The Captain cocked her head.

"Do you have anything you would like to add?" she asked.

Ben shook his head.

"No, no. Once again, I am truly, very sorry, Mistress. May I please try again to make it up to you?"

She smiled faintly, shaking her curls.

"And already breaking a rule by trying to get back in my bed."

Ben scoffed, indignant.

"We just had the most serious conversation with me sitting here completely naked because you told me not to get dressed. I hardly think that makes me the wrongdoer in this scenario."

The Black Rose laughed, a giggle that dropped back into a deeper growl as she untied the belt of her dressing gown and let it fall open. She advanced on Ben, running her fingers from his knee up his thigh. He shuddered.

"You're so fun to play with, Benny, you really are. But don't you think it's too hot to fuck?"

Ben shook his head fervently.

"No! Never. I..."

Then inspiration struck.

"I have an idea."

The Black Rose licked her lips again as Ben stroked himself to full hardness and settled on the bed.

"Now climb onto my lap, facing me."

The Pirate Queen gingerly climbed over him, the heat and sweat making their bodies slick and sticky.

Once she was settled, Ben eased her back against the sheets. Grasping her thighs, he guided his cock down into her womanhood, drawing her onto his length. The Black Rose moaned, using her fingers on her pleasure bud while Ben also lay back. She let him take control, pulling her down to meet him and then pushing her away. The only places their bodies touched were the tight slide of her channel on his cock and her thighs draped over his.

Yet despite the lack of full-body contact, the result was still deeply sensual.

"Benny?" the Captain whispered in the dark.

"Yes, my lo...Mistress?"

Ben groaned, eyes closed, as he eased her back until only the tip of his cock remained inside her, then pulled her forward again so their bodies bumped firmly.

"Ignoring that... I am very glad you are well-endowed. This feels so nice. If you could give me kisses, it would be perfect."

"How are you going to say you don't love me, then turn around and say you want me to kiss you?" Ben murmured. "Although I do wish I could bury my face in your bosoms. That's my absolute favorite place to be."

"Benny, for someone so intelligent, you're being a willfully ignorant walrus."

There was that word again. He really did need to know what the hell she meant by it. But that would have to wait. He had to please her. He had to show her how badly he wanted to be here with her.

"And I didn't say I don't...oh, yes! I care for you...greatly...especially...especially when you...when...you...do things...like this! Oh, gods! Benny! Benny!"

His concentration was rewarded within a few strokes by her thighs quaking against him as she reached release. Feeling her inner muscles clutch around him and shiver made him realize how close he was too.

Unwilling to test the waters any further than he already had, Ben sat up, pulled out, and stroked himself hard, spilling onto the Black Rose's stomach.

"I do appreciate that you learn from your mistakes."

Ben pulled her into an embrace, nibbling at her ear.

"Even though I'm sure you attempted to break..."

"You told me not to expect you to say it back, but you did not, in fact, ban me from using the L-word."

She sighed, her forehead dropping onto his shoulder.

"You're a pedantic arsehole."

"Indeed. Hence why I was so popular in the Royal Navy."

He had not meant to say that, but he was relieved when she chuckled, running her fingers through his beard and turning him to face her. She kissed him deeply, and he could feel the smile on her lips. When they parted, she rubbed the tip of his nose with hers.

"Are you still angry, Mistress?"

She shook her head, her nails still gently scratching his chin in a soothing rhythm.

"No, Benny, I think you fucked the frustration out of me. And I think our rules will help, should you actually follow them."

They kissed again.

"Excellent. Now, may I ask you a question before it drives me to madness?"

"Hmmm?"

"What the ever-loving fuck is a walrus?"

The Black Rose sat bolt upright, scrambled out of bed, and scampered over to her bookshelf. She pulled down a large, well-worn, obviously beloved volume: the same book she had used to look up the snake that bit Juanito during the gauntlet.

"You're going to love this!"

She brought it to the bed and flipped through the pages until she found it. Then she turned the book toward Ben and pointed.

"That is a walrus."

Ben stared at the drawing. It looked like a seal crossed with an elephant, with massive tusks hanging from its mouth.

"You're joking."

"No!"

"That's real?"

"Yes!"

"Have you ever seen one?"

"No. They're cold-climate animals. But I want to, someday. They're huge! How do you not know about walrus?"

Ben shrugged.

"I am not as interested in animals as I am in, say, geography. I like dogs and cats well enough, but I don't know different birds or fish like I probably should. Or snakes. I am rather good with plants, though!

"Actually, that reminds me, does Tobin and Felipe's quarters have a window? I should like to try my hand at a window box with some herbs. I'll obviously let Xiang have the harvest. I'm worried smaller herbs will get lost in Halima's garden."

The Pirate Queen bit her lip.

"I don't think so. But you're welcome to keep a box at one of my windows."

Ben leaned toward her, a smirk on his face.

"So, you're saying you want me to keep plants in your quarters."

She nodded.

"Plants that will need regular watering, trimming, and attention."

She laughed again as he moved closer.

"In your quarters. That you are trying very, very hard to keep me out of..."

He stopped nose to nose with her, lips almost touching.

"Am I understanding properly, Mistress?"

She shoved his face away, but he did not miss her smile.

"You are reading far too much into it, and you must stop thinking with your cock. Really, it's truly a character flaw. But your clothes are returned, I am no longer angry with you, I look forward to awarding you your promotion, and..."

Whatever she had been about to say was interrupted by a massive gust of wind, and the *Deception* began to move.

"Oh, thank the gods," the Black Rose shrieked. "Get dressed, we're finally moving!"

# SUPPLEMENTAL

## XIANG'S TALE

*(Excerpt from The Chronicles of the Deception)*

*Preface, on Japan: Japan is Sakoku, 'locked country'. If you are not Dutch, you are not welcome. The Dutch Catholics and their converts treat other religions the way countries like Spain treat Mohammedans and Jews: convert, leave, or die. While many other religions fight back, Buddhism is a religion of nonviolence. — Fd C*

Xiang was the second son of a family of tea merchants in China. When he was five, he was sent to a Buddhist monastery in Japan known for cultivating tea. Xiang believes his father hoped his second son would learn secrets that would allow the family to grow tea, while his elder brother would sell it. They never came back for him.

Xiang's sunny disposition made him a natural choice to work with children. The monastery kept a basket at the gate with a bell to ring whenever a baby was left there. He was allowed to name the first child he found. He called her Summer's Hope, Natsuki.

Not long after, a baby boy was left at the monastery and named Daichi, Great Wisdom. These are the very same Natsuki and Daichi who sail with us now. That is why they call him Older Brother, and why they have forged a bond deeper than blood.

Xiang lived happily for over twenty years, gardening and learning to cook. Then, seven years ago, that peace was shattered.

A contingent of Catholics arrived at the monastery. Because the monks would not lift a hand in violence, it was a slaughter. Xiang watched as they killed every child older than an infant but too young to be sold as a slave. Everyone else was herded onto a ship.

The prisoners endured the brutal journey around Cape Horn, losing many of their number to exposure and starvation. The ship, the *Gouden Zee*, finally made port, and the captives were stripped of what little they had left.

The *Gouden Zee* landed in Portobelo, Panamá. By strange fortune, they happened to dock beside a pirate ship called the *Wolfhound*—just before the pirates aboard her took the *María del Mar*. It is still unknown why a Dutch ship ended up in Panamá, but however strange, a gift from the universe is a gift nonetheless.

The *Wolfhound* was in port for extensive repairs after a disastrous raid. Her Captain—barely eighteen and desperate to prove herself—paced the deck skittishly, while her quartermaster, Tobin, and gunner, Felipe, treated the port as their own personal paradise, spending all their time in houses of ill repute and brawling in taverns. In nursing the wounds of a recent falling out, Felipe indulged Tobin's every reckless whim.

Tobin was curious about the Dutch ship, even more so when a small stand appeared in front of it selling trinkets: mostly jewelry, some combs, ribbons, and makeshift toys. It was such an odd assortment of items that the pirates had to take a closer look. Tobin showed Felipe a piece he was considering buying for the Captain, thinking it was the helm of a ship.

But having spent as much time in the Orient as Felipe has, he knew what it truly was: a Dharma Wheel, a symbol of the path to Enlightenment, with no business being sold as a trinket in a pirate port. The most damning object, a blood-spattered Ohm, confirmed by a surreptitious taste, told them these were not trade goods. They were trophies.

So Felipe did what any naturally curious person would do: he asked how the man had come by these items. He did his best to be nonchalant, all the casual wondering of an old man thinking of buying something nice for his daughter.

The man quietly but excitedly told the pirates that there was a cargo of slaves from the Orient on the ship behind him, skin as fair as sand, and that they would be put up for auction in three days' time. The *Wolfhound* was meant to leave in two.

He offered to take them on a tour of the ship to see the wares, adding that while Felipe's "manservant" looked very strong and capable, perhaps he might also be interested in something daintier. Tobin thankfully held his tongue, but the look in his eyes told Felipe he had reached the same conclusion.

They had to help these people.

Adopting the airs of wealthy buyers, Felipe and Tobin followed the man aboard. While the horrors and stench of a slave ship were familiar enough, the language was different. Felipe recognized the sharp cadence of Japanese from his previous relations with Hinata, but there was also something else: a mournful song in a slightly different tongue. They followed the singing to a group of terrified children huddled around Xiang.

Xiang looked up, and when his eyes met Tobin's, the air in the room changed with the strike of a lightning bolt.

The prisoner did not beg for his own life. Instead, in soft, urgent Mandarin Chinese, he begged the "buyers" to save the children. Tobin's entire demeanor changed. Where he had previously looked ill, there was now a spark of cold, violent resolve.

They had to break these people out and destroy that ship.

In the suffocating darkness, Xiang was stunned to hear his own language spoken to him for the first time in over thirty years. He was even more shocked to see an African man for the first time. But in the midst of all the terror and suffering, Xiang claims he could, for a moment, see the Hóng Xiàn, or Red String of Fate, connecting him to Tobin.

That put him at ease, knowing these men would be their salvation. Xiang claims to see silken threads connecting people in moments of stress, and says it reminds him that love is real. When Felipe pressed him about the connections between other crew members, Xiang smiled serenely and insisted the gunner already knew the answers he sought...which may be his gentle way of suggesting that Felipe is an idiot.

The pirates left the ship, and Felipe tossed the man a coin—a final, ironic payment before they ruined his entire life. The air between Tobin and Felipe was heavy with unspoken rage and heartache as they made their way back to their own vessel. Once out of earshot, they agreed: they would not leave Portobelo without freeing those souls.

Back aboard the *Wolfhound*, they cornered Madame. She met Tobin and Felipe's enthusiasm with pragmatism: attacking a Dutch ship in a Spanish port could start a war and land the whole crew on the end of a rope. A miscalculated explosion could further damage their own ship.

Not only that, but the *Wolfhound* was far too small to carry nearly a hundred refugees. But Tobin and Felipe painted a vivid picture of suffering children and peaceful monks, and it struck her tender heart. This, she decided, would be the way to reclaim the honor lost in the last raid.

Geraldo, the boatswain, was from a village outside Portobelo called Buenaventura, so they brought him in to help shape the plan. There was a natural harbor hidden from Spanish eyes by a peninsula thick with tall trees. It was a perfect place to vanish, provided they could get the prisoners off the *Gouden Zee* and across the water without being seen.

Madame was overwhelmed and stepped out onto the deck of the *Wolfhound* for air. She paced for the thousandth time and rubbed at her cheeks beneath her eyes. Then she turned to her officers, her eyes sparkling with an idea.

Madame could predict hurricanes with startling accuracy.

The plan relied entirely on the chaos of the coming storm. Geraldo was sent to Buenaventura with a purse of pooled coin to secure lodgings. As the sky darkened, Madame set about clearing the port, not with weapons, but with a warning. Playing the role of a distressed local girl concerned for the visitors, she went from ship to ship, urging the foreign crews to seek shelter before the storm swallowed the docks.

From the crow's nest of the *Wolfhound*, Felipe and Tobin watched Madame move from ship to ship, driving sailors inland. She met a barrier at the *Gouden Zee*, as the crew spoke neither Spanish nor English. Fortunately, one of the Dutch sailors made a comment in *rromani čhib*, which she also speaks.

Whatever omens of the coming terror she whispered worked; the Dutch captain ordered an evacuation without a backward glance for his "cargo." There were mutterings of a Hendrick being left behind, but they fled to a tavern on land all the same.

The first fat raindrops began to fall, and Madame sprinted back to her ship. The stage was set, the *Gouden Zee* was deserted, and the pirates' window of opportunity would not wait.

As the gale roared in, three pirates made their way to the *Gouden Zee*. While Geraldo kept watch, Felipe and Tobin ransacked the table of stolen treasures, the Dharma Wheel necklace heavy in Felipe's hand as they entered the hold. In the stinking, sweltering dark, Felipe spoke to the captives in Japanese, assuring them of their safety. Tobin set to work using a skeleton key to unlock their shackles, while Madame arrived to help shepherd them onto the deck and into the storm.

The commotion woke Hendrick, the large drunken enforcer, who came barreling into the hold with a cutlass drawn, swaying on his feet. He slashed at Tobin's shoulder, but the pirate stood bravely between Xiang and the drunkard. Steel met steel, and the rattle of chains was replaced by the clash of swords. The lightning bolt Tobin had felt earlier now manifested as desperate, protective fury.

Tobin disarmed the brute with ease, and the Dutchman sank to his knees on the floor. Yet he hesitated to put the man out of his misery, his eyes flicking to the beautiful stranger beside him. As Tobin grappled with what to do, young Daichi dealt the killing blow. When freed, he asked Felipe for a sword and used it to run Hendrick through from behind. It was a cold, necessary execution—a reclamation of Natsuki's honor. Daichi spat in the man's face as he died.

Hendrick convulsed and went still, and the spell upon Daichi broke. Eyes wide, he fell to his knees and turned the blade toward his own stomach, meaning to commit seppuku and reclaim his own honor after violating a sacred tenet of his faith.

"I have done something dishonorable, Big Brother!" he cried.

But Xiang was already at his side, his voice calm and soothing. He told the boy that protecting his community was the highest wisdom and no sin. With that affirmation, Xiang eased the sword from Daichi's grasp, and it clattered to the deck as they embraced. Tobin finally managed to unlock the shackles at Xiang's ankles.

As Tobin led the last of the captives to the *Wolfhound*, Felipe rigged a delayed explosive, lighting the fuse with a single, practiced shot of his pistol. He did not linger to watch. The smell of fire filled the hold as he ran up to the deck, where he found the Captain, Tobin, Xiang, and Daichi waiting in the torrents. The rain fell so hard it turned their skin red with the force.

Back aboard the *Wolfhound*, Natsuki waited like a figurehead on the bowsprit, wind whipping her long black hair behind her, refusing to go below. Daichi collapsed to his knees and confessed what he had done, his tears mingling with the rain.

Natsuki did not recoil in horror. Instead, she pulled him to his feet and into their first kiss, desperately grasping at a future she had not believed they would live to see. Xiang watched them proudly, whispering to Felipe that they had been in love since childhood, before Older Brother led his siblings down into the warmth and safety of the *Wolfhound*'s hold.

Madame, Tobin, and Felipe turned just in time to feel the vibration in the water—a muffled crack that shuddered through the planks of the *Wolfhound*.

As the rain continued to pound, the *Gouden Zee* split in half and was swallowed by the deep within minutes.

Everyone had been saved, but there was now a new problem: a hundred shivering, starving souls aboard a small pirate ship with nowhere to go and only one person able to understand them.

Madame asked Felipe to translate as she welcomed the prisoners aboard her ship. She offered them no easy lies about returning to Japan. Panama's west coast could be reached by an overland journey, difficult but free of Dutch shackles.

She spoke of the haven offered by Geraldo's countrymen in Buenaventura, and finally of a third option: a place on her crew for anyone willing to trade their chains for the dangerous life she and her tiny fleet led. She promised roles that required no bloodshed, as well as safety and protection for the village of Buenaventura, whatever choice they made.

A heavy silence followed, broken only by the drumming of the storm against the ship.

Then Daichi stepped forward.

He said that with the spilling of blood, he could no longer follow the old path, and so he would instead pledge himself to the woman who had freed them. He fell to the deck, prostrate, and Natsuki joined him, her hand finding his as they swore themselves to the crew of the *Wolfhound*.

Then the abbot monk, the *jūjishoku*, stepped forward and bowed to Madame. On behalf of their people, he offered their profound gratitude. All the rest bowed as well, foreheads pressed silently to the deck in thanks and respect.

That moment saw the birth of the Black Rose.

In that moment, a young pirate woman stopped chasing prizes and began chasing an ideal.

As the storm raged, the pirates fed their new friends and helped them dry off and get warm. Xiang, naturally shy, asked to be introduced to Tobin. He gave not his birth name, but the name he chose the moment he stepped aboard the pirate ship: Xiáng, for he felt lucky to have found them.

Xiang vowed that he would follow Tobin wherever he went.

Tobin replied that his own path was to remain always at Madame's side.

Xiang then introduced himself to Madame and offered his life—and his skills as a cook—to the Black Rose.

The pirates returned the jewelry and trinkets, and they discovered the bloody Ohm belonged to Natsuki. She refused it. Later, once the *Wolfhound* had cleared the harbor and those remaining had signed the Articles, Daichi took Natsuki to the rail, and she dropped the Ohm into the sea as an offering, a way of leaving their suffering behind.

By sunrise, the *Wolfhound* dropped anchor in the hidden harbor at Buenaventura, and a new era dawned there. The cultures of the Panamanians and the Japanese Buddhists blended beautifully, the tiny village growing into a much larger town. And in the year of our Lord 1716, one of the Panamanian men, Raúl, married a Japanese woman, Keiko, merging their cultures once and for all. We have that hurricane to thank for the vision the Black Rose now holds dear.

When asked how Xiang reconciled his beliefs with his life as a pirate, he said that he shared Madame's vision for communities like our allies in Panamá. Breaking the shackles of slaves, disrupting oppressive systems, bringing people together, and offering financial assistance are all ideals the Buddha would approve of, and the ends justify the means. He has seen the good we do, even for the smaller sufferings we cause along the way.

Additionally, he had a "See No Evil" mindset. He does not participate in raids, instead staying below deck with Jewels and the children, and he does not usually come back up until everything is well over. Then he and Jewels see to the well-being of any prisoners to the best of their ability.

Xiang also says he feels Jewels is another kindred soul aboard. He has always admired healers, and being able to work so closely with one so talented gives him great joy.

He is also happy to have continued cooking, and to experiment with ingredients in ways he never could back in Japan. He is most pleased to recreate dishes from China that he remembers from childhood, though it took practice to get them right. His favorite dishes to prepare are Chinese noodles in garlic pepper sauce, ropa vieja with rice (the Captain's favorite), and plantain mash (Tobin's favorite). He also appreciates any chance to build a grill pit ashore. He most likes to grill salted fish.

If he could make only one thing for the rest of his life, he would choose coconut sweets. They are simple—only sugar, water, and grated coconut—but taste very nice. He loves them dearly, and everyone else does too.

It has not all been pleasant cooking, however. One time, he agreed to make a haggis for Talia's birthday. He says it was disgusting, made worse by her watching over his shoulder the entire time. It also smelled terrible in the heat of summer. She enjoyed it. He says never again.

He also said Mitsu (currently on the *María del Mar* with Alizée) once tried to teach him how to make a traditional Japanese dish involving a live octopus. Xiang found it immensely upsetting and freed the creature instead. Mitsu took it in stride, but they have not exchanged recipes since.

There are a number of ingredients Xiang will buy whenever he finds them, no matter the cost. One is *jiàngyóu*, a fermented sauce made from soybeans. He can make his own, but if he finds it bottled, he will buy it, because if it has made its way to the Caribbean, it is probably aged to perfection. (Researcher Note: soy sauce.) He also says he goes through a ridiculous quantity of garlic. He will likewise spend a great deal on good-quality black pepper, vinegar, and a decent cooking wine.

Xiang does not care for hardtack, but we keep a supply just in case. One time, he soaked some in a little water to soften it and turned it into dough. He then used it to make dumplings filled with leftover scraps of meat and vegetables. After that, he made a broth from dried fish flakes, seaweed, and spices, turning it all into a soup. He feels this was the most creative meal he has ever made.

He has two sayings by which he lives.

The first is: "If you light a lamp for another, it also lights your own path."

He likes this one because it reminds him that when helping and teaching others, you are also helped, and you also learn. It reminds him of all the children he helped raise at the monastery, as well as the friendship and camaraderie he has found among our crew.

The second is that the same fire that scalds skin and scorches wood can cook nourishing food and brew comforting tea. We are each a fire, and we choose how we burn.

His greatest wish is that we always remember what we are fighting for: a better world for tomorrow.

# Chapter 15

## Schemes and Shanties

The *Deception* sighted Barranquilla the following evening. The Black Rose pulled Ben into her quarters to "help decide the next course." It had quickly devolved when she grabbed his chin and began kissing him fervently.

"I'm so sorry," she murmured into his mouth. "I missed you so much."

"I missed you, too," he agreed, wrapping her in a tight embrace.

They let themselves get lost in the passionate meeting of their lips, and Ben had just begun tugging at the hem of her blouse when pounding sounded at the door. An excited French voice accompanied the knocking.

"Land ho, Madame! We must decide how we bring our prize into port."

The Captain's head fell back with a sigh.

"Good thing we didn't go any further than kissing," she muttered.

"Mhmm," Ben agreed, a silly smile on his face, lips swollen, cheeks flushed, and a few hairs at the back of his head sticking straight up.

The Black Rose pulled him to his feet before opening the door.

Felipe entered first, holding paper and pencil, followed by Doctora, Talia, Xiang, and Tobin. No one batted an eye at the sight of Ben in the Captain's quarters looking slightly disheveled. At least he was fully clothed this time.

Felipe lightly clapped a hand to Ben's shoulder, the faint scent of burnt tobacco clinging to his sleeve, and stealthily passed him a small scrap of paper with a wink before spreading his larger pages across the desk. Ben unfolded the note and glanced at it.

*Agree to whatever I say. Trust me.*

Ben gulped, disguising it as a cough as he crumpled the paper in his fist and tucked it into his pocket. He stared hard at the gunner, who ignored him completely, choosing instead to gently sweep a loose tendril of Doctora's hair behind her ear. Fortunately, everyone else was also staring at the pair with varying degrees of annoyance. But Felipe and his Jewels had eyes only for one another.

The Pirate Queen cleared her throat loudly, and the spell broke. The gunner and physician both blushed profusely and turned away from each other. Felipe shook his head.

"Madame, I have surveyed the crew. None feel the Call of the Land at this time."

"Thank you, Felipe."

"We will not be able to make port before nightfall," Tobin said. "We'll have to drop anchor for the night and dock tomorrow. We'll need to divide the crew and cut the towline. Less suspicious that way."

Felipe pointed to his list.

"The *Bouclier Rouge* should be staffed with those we believe best suited to negotiate the sale of the cows and the ship itself. Better still if we can convince someone to buy the whole lot. Here are my recommendations."

"We should use this evening to settle the scores and pay everyone before we separate the ships."

The Black Rose took the list and looked it over. Her face fell.

"Why do you want to take Benny?" she asked, the barest edge of frustration in her voice.

Ben was heartened by her concern and equally annoyed by the suggestion. He had rather hoped he and the Captain would be able to continue where they had left off. Two weeks without her touch had been brutal, and Ben had no desire to go without her again so soon.

*Agree to whatever I say. Trust me.*

"It will be good practice for him. The art of negotiation, if you will. Besides, he is very good at the helm, and these docks are a tight squeeze."

The Black Rose growled, agitated, clearly thinking much the same as Ben.

"He doesn't speak Spanish. He won't understand."

The Frenchman's face was uncharacteristically stony. Ben could not tell whether the older man had forgotten that detail or whether it simply did not matter to whatever scheme he had concocted.

"It is not important what we say. It is important how we say it. Don't you agree, Benny?"

Felipe and the Captain turned to him.

Shit.

He had to pretend this was a marvelous idea, even though at that moment he badly wanted to punch the Frenchman in the face again.

"Of course! Perfectly reasonable," Ben said, with a smile he prayed did not look as fake as it felt.

"And I have a plan. You will see, everyone else I have chosen to come aboard with us is either *hispanohablante*, a freed slave, or both."

"What is your plan, then?"

Felipe once again placed his massive hands on the Captain's shoulders as though he were her father.

"Do you not trust me, Princesa?"

The Black Rose narrowed her eyes.

"Not when you ask like that. You only call me Princesa when you have an idea you aren't sure will work. And not telling me is quite out of character for you."

She pointed a sharp fingernail at the Frenchman's nose.

"If anything happens to Benny on your watch..."

Felipe's voice turned smooth and soothing, like a higher-class salesman in the shops Anne had frequented in Kingston.

"Nothing will happen, and it is an excellent plan. Benny will be safely out of the way where he may observe, and his language skills will not be questioned. I promise, it shall work out very well. Everyone simply needs to play along."

The Black Rose grimaced as though she wanted to argue. In truth, Ben rather hoped she would. At last, she sighed and decided to trust her gunner's tactical mind. She certainly let her disappointment show, pouting and grumbling.

"Well then, I suppose Tobin and I had better settle the scores and get everyone's pay ready. Talia, Doctora, Xiang, about your usual business. Felipe, Benny, inform the temporary crew of the *Bouclier Rouge* of their new assignment. And whatever ridiculous plan you've cooked up. *Chiflado*."

Ben nodded, and Felipe chuckled at whatever she had called him before bowing theatrically low, nearly folding himself in half. Ben wanted nothing more than to kick the Frenchman in the arse and knock him face-first onto the floor.

Talia, Xiang, and Doctora filed out of the room. Felipe offered the Captain and Tobin some paper and a few pencils before he and Ben followed.

The moment the door clicked shut behind them, Ben flicked the gunner's ear, like he had seen Tobin do on occasion. It seemed a better idea than a full punch to the face.

"Ow!" The older man swatted at him.

"What the hell, Felipe?" Ben hissed, keeping his voice low.

Fortunately, Felipe understood the need for discretion and lowered his own voice in turn.

"Come, and keep your mouth shut!"

The gunner grabbed Ben's arm and steered him down the stairs into the quarters they would soon share if the Captain got her way and Ben was promoted. Once they were safely secluded, Felipe turned to him and raised his hands.

"Benny, thank you for trusting me. Xiang told me what happened last night, and, since it looks like you and Madame made up, I am trying to help you."

Ben crossed his arms, but held his tongue.

"Every once in a while, you must give Madame the opportunity to miss you. I promise you, it will help."

"But—"

"No buts! It is only because of the darkness that we can appreciate the light."

Ben stared at him for a long moment.

"Talking to Xiang really got to you, didn't it?"

Felipe blinked, then threw back his head and cackled.

"I believe it did! I swear, I have been speaking in proverbs for days. But in seriousness, abstinence makes the heart grow fonder!"

"Absence," Ben corrected with a chuckle.

"Absence? What did I say?"

"Abstinence."

The two men stared at each other for a beat, then burst into laughter again.

"Abstinence makes other things grow, too!" Felipe said, wiping his eyes before continuing. "But I know Madame, and I truly believe this is a good strategy. It is not as though we are going off to start our own fleet. It will only be for a night or two. Give her time to marinate on how much she enjoys your company, oui?"

Ben sighed.

"I don't particularly like it, but I suppose I do trust you. And I did notice you left Jules on the *Deception* as well."

Felipe clicked his tongue with a frown.

"That is also purely strategic. As much as I would like her with me, Jules needs to be where Juanito is. And I do not want him anywhere near those beasts."

Felipe began rifling through his possessions and pulled out a faded, tattered Spanish flag. The *Deception* kept the flags of all the colonizing countries to ensure safe passage through various ports around the Caribbean. They were stored behind a false wall in Eliza's washing area. The ship had several such hiding places, courtesy of Felipe, Talia, and Doctora. But while those flags were well-kept and pristine, this one looked as though its last better day had been twenty years ago.

"So, are you going to tell me what we're doing?" Ben asked as Felipe handed him one end of the banner to help fold it.

"I will when everyone is aboard the *Bouclier Rouge*. I wish to explain it only once. And Madame will be playing a part in it. She simply does not know yet. She is a better actress when she does not know what it is. Much more natural."

Some time later, Talia's all-hands-on-deck tune rang through the ship. The Black Rose poked her head out of her quarters just as Ben came up the stairs and handed him his guitar as he passed. Ben took up a place between Talia and Felipe.

"Didja decide on a name for yer wee instrument yet?" Talia asked as Ben checked the tuning.

Unlike the guitar he had left behind—a second- or third-hand thing of questionable origin—this beautiful piece held its tuning remarkably well, though Ben made a mental note to acquire more strings at the first opportunity.

"I think I shall call her Euphonia. It's a songbird from Jamaica."

Talia chuckled.

"I thought ye didnae ken different birds."

"I saw it in the Captain's animal book, and I recognized it. They're everywhere in Jamaica. The males are little blue-grey puffballs with yellow bellies, and the females and juveniles have olive green wings. It also means 'good sound,' which she certainly provides."

Talia clapped her hands.

"Perfect! Johnny Jump-Up and his wee friend Euphonia! I love it!"

Johnny Jump-Up was the name of her own guitar, after the folk song about cider.

Once everyone had assembled on deck, the Black Rose addressed her crew.

"Amigos, we will be making port in Barranquilla in the morning. We will be splitting the crew for this venture. A number of you will be going over to the *Bouclier Rouge* with Felipe and Benny. They are in command in my stead, so follow their orders as if they were mine, Tobin's, or Talia's. Felipe, please name your team."

The Frenchman had retrieved his magnifying spectacles, which made him look as though he had mouse ears. He stepped forward with his list.

"The following crew are with myself and Benny. Bring what you will need overnight. If you are on rotation to care for our cow friends, you are still on rotation, so do not think you have avoided your fate."

A few groans rose from the crowd, and Felipe read through the names.

Natsuki for the kitchen. Daichi had cow duty, so he would also be coming.

Arturo and Toñiete. Jean-Luc and Giselle. Inés, Azucena, Mateo, Diego, David, Auguste, Jamaal, and Maeve.

With Felipe and Ben, there would be sixteen aboard. The crew would be a little small, but they could make it work.

Ben noticed the look of disappointment on Doctora's face when Felipe did not call her name.

Once Felipe had finished, the Black Rose spoke again.

"Now, since we are dividing the crew to make port, we are going to distribute your pay now. The profits from the sale of the other ship and the cows go toward our next score. *Bouclier Rouge* team, you will be paid first if you would be so kind as to line up. Benny, Talia, will you lead us in our anthem?"

Ben chuckled, turning toward the Captain and Tobin, who buried his face in his hands.

"Pay me, you owe me! Pay me my money down!

You've got to pay me or you'll go to jail! Pay me my money down!"

After a few raucous choruses, the quartermaster looked as though he was about to lose his mind.

"Why? What have I ever done to you people?" Tobin grumbled as Felipe clapped him on the back.

"If you had not told us how much you hate that song, we probably would not sing it nearly so often. If you had lied and said you hate 'Leave Her, Johnny' instead, we would sing that for you."

Upon hearing this, Ben immediately began strumming the other tune as well.

"I thought I heard our Captain say, 'Leave her, Johnny, leave her,

Tomorrow you will get your pay, and it's time for us to leave her!'"

Tobin's dark face broke into a wide grin as everyone joined in. Ben deduced this must be one of his favorites, remembering the quartermaster swaying with Xiang on Isla Rosa. When the song ended, Ben turned to the assembled crew and prayed he was not overstepping.

"Motion to make our new pay ritual both songs?"

"Seconded!" Talia, Doctora, and Tobin all raised open hands in support.

"Very well, I suppose we'll put it to a vote," the Captain said, her eyes sparkling with mirth. "All in favor will raise an open hand, all opposed will raise a closed fist, and no raised hand will count as an abstention. As this is not a serious vote, we may keep our eyes open. On the count of three... Uno... dos... tres!"

On *tres*, a flurry of open hands rose into the air. Ben didn't see any closed fists. Felipe abstained.

"Motion passes, and we now have a new pay ritual! Thank you, Benny!"

Ben nodded and smiled at the Captain, then looked at Tobin. The quartermaster clasped his hands together in front of his nose and bowed slightly, mouthing, *Thank you.*

Once everyone had been paid, they were dismissed. The *Bouclier Rouge* team would have until the next bell to gather what they needed and prepare to cross to the other ship. Xiang, Frank, and Li Mei hurried down to the kitchen to help Natsuki collect what she would need for breakfast. Felipe and Ben went down to the armory, where the gunner promptly found himself cornered by Doctora.

"Why don't you want me?" she asked, looking genuinely upset.

She seemed to realize how that sounded and quickly corrected herself, clearing her throat.

"Why don't you want me to come with you?"

"Jules," he murmured, taking her hand. "It is not that I do not want you. Far, far from it. *Non*, you know that you need to be where... certain other people are, in case they need you. If I did not have to worry about them, I would certainly have called for you."

She sighed and nodded.

The gunner pulled her into an embrace and nuzzled her forehead with his salt-and-pepper beard. The physician absently stroked his bicep.

"Besides, there is nothing dangerous this time. We are going to dock the ship and try to sell it. Simple."

"Given how you behave with Mama Tati, I doubt that."

All three pirates chuckled at the thought of the tiny pawnshop owner in Mexico, who regularly threw Felipe out of her establishment for haggling too much.

"*Non!* This will be the opposite. I will try to make the price *higher*."

He pulled her back just enough to look into her eyes and gave her a silly little smile, which made her laugh. She rose onto her toes, and Ben was convinced she was about to kiss him.

And she did.

On the forehead.

Ben swallowed his groan, but Felipe looked as though he had just won the greatest prize in the world. He kissed her hand, and she melted. Ben shook his head. What was he supposed to do with these two?

Felipe gave Doctora a wink before hefting a rucksack older than Ben over one shoulder and heading back out to the galley to help the kitchen crew. Ben returned to his hammock to fetch his satchel. Gathering some pencils, his personal journal—the black folio stamped with the rose—and his brown *Chronicles of the Deception* folio gave him time to think.

Felipe was taking him on this assignment to make him more appealing to the Captain. What, then, could Ben do to help the gunner win Doctora? What invisible walls needed tearing down before the two of them would allow themselves what they so clearly wanted?

Ben sighed. He was terrible at this sort of thing. He even found himself wondering whether it would be such a bad idea to steal their clothes and lock them in the sick room together until they finally sorted themselves out.

Once he had packed what he needed, Ben stopped by the Captain's quarters to return her guitar and, if possible, steal a good-luck kiss. The Black Rose gave him an unexpectedly passionate one, lamenting how that "mean old prick" was separating them when she had planned such a lovely lesson for the evening. Ben shrugged, pulling her body flush against his as she ran her fingers through his hair.

"I'm sure it will be worth it. I know I'm going to learn a great deal."

She pursed her lips.

"I don't like it when I don't know what's going on. I'm the Captain. I should know everything."

Ben gently touched her cheek, rubbing the tip of his nose against hers.

"He says you have a part to play, but it will be better if you don't know what it is. He hasn't even told us the plan yet, likely so we wouldn't tell you. But he seems to think it will work, and that is good enough for me. Against my better judgment, I trust him."

She rose onto her toes and pressed another kiss to his lips.

"You're going to be a wonderful officer for us. I hope you know that," she whispered, eyes sparkling, as she led him toward the door.

Before she could set her hand on the latch, Ben caught it. He did not know what possessed him, but he kissed the back of her hand and whispered against her skin,

"*Mi princesa de las estrellas.*"

My princess of stars, cobbled together from what Felipe and Juanito had taught him.

Then he winked at her.

The Black Rose pressed her free hand to her chest, her breath hitching. When she spoke, her voice came out as a growl dripping with desire, every syllable aching to tie him to her bed and demand satisfaction.

"How dare you say such beautiful things when we can't act upon them, you awful walrus!"

Ben laughed.

"Then I suppose we shall have to have a very special lesson when I get back. But now we truly must be going..."

He reached for the door.

"One more," the Captain muttered, tugging his face back to hers.

Ben poured everything into that kiss—his desire, his longing, his lust, and his love. It felt as though the Pirate Queen might have been trying to do the same, for she clung longer than she usually did. For someone who did not want to fall in love with him, she was certainly very affectionate. Ben now felt fully confident that Felipe knew exactly what he was doing.

A bell sounded, and Ben slung his satchel over his shoulder once more as they stepped out onto the deck.

# CHAPTER 16

## FRATERNITY AND FABLES

The Black Rose and Ben walked to the rail, where Anya, Zsófia, and Tobin were preparing to secure a gangplank to the French ship. Each held a grappling hook, which they cast with practiced ease, their aim true.

Once the hooks caught, the team and the Captain hauled together to draw the *Bouclier Rouge* closer to the *Deception*. The Black Rose ended up directly in front of Ben, who did his best to steady her whenever she looked in danger of falling on her backside.

Fascinating woman. She always wanted to be in the thick of things, always ready to help. He really ought to start taking notes on her leadership qualities so he could better emulate them.

*Don't be afraid to get your hands dirty.*

Once the gangplank was secured, Natsuki, Daichi, and the kitchen crew crossed first to set up the galley for breakfast. The Captain gave Ben's hand a squeeze before he crossed. He wished it could have been one more kiss, but there were far too many witnesses for that.

Once the *Bouclier Rouge* crew had crossed, Felipe unhooked the grapples and tossed them back to Anya, Zsófia, and Doctora. The Boricua's eyes were full of longing as the women wound the ropes back up to return them to the armory. Tobin removed the gangplank and cut the towline.

Ben hurried to the helm to steer the French ship away from the *Deception*. Once they were a safe distance off, they dropped anchor for the night, and

Daichi and Arturo rigged the old Spanish flag. The *Deception* did the same. Though the pirate ship still lay fairly close, it felt a world away.

The Black Rose felt a world away.

Xiang had prepared something Felipe called a *charcuterie* for supper. It was a spread of dried meats and fish, hard-boiled eggs, cheeses, pickled vegetables, dried fruits, and crackers. This must have been the last of their stores after two weeks of sitting still. Strange as it looked to Ben at first, it was lovely in execution, rather like the picnic the cook had packed for him and the Black Rose the night they had made love on the beach beneath the stars.

Once the humans and cows had all been fed and tended, the skeleton crew gathered on deck for Felipe's grand explanation of the plan. But before he could open his mouth, Maeve pounced, her tongue as sharp as one of the gunner's folding knives.

"So how are we going to sell everything, Mistah Big Smart Man? Most people won't buy from pirates, even in a friendly port, and a shipment like this likely had a buyer elsewhere. Nobody off the street is going to buy it."

"I am very glad you asked!"

It was obvious from his tone and tight smile that Felipe was not glad at all, and was rather annoyed that Maeve had stolen his thunder.

"I have a wonderful idea for how we came to be in possession of this ship and the cows, and I think it makes excellent sense."

He paused for effect.

"So what are we going to do?" Jean-Luc asked.

The younger Haitian was well used to the Frenchman's theatrics and knew the quickest route to the point was to play along. Felipe beamed, practically vibrating with excitement.

"We are going to stage... a mutiny!"

The gunner threw up a fist and punched the air. He had clearly expected a different reaction from the one he got: confused silence. His face fell, and he deflated a little. Maeve crossed her arms and cocked her head.

"Against who? You?"

"What? *Non*, I am leading the mutiny, of course."

Maeve only looked more confused.

"Then who are we...ohhhh."

Ben looked around in bewilderment before realizing Maeve was staring at him.

They all were.

His skin went hot and cold at once.

"But I have to berth the ship," Ben said weakly.

"Oui, I know. Barranquilla has no one observing who is steering the ship. And if you look around us, you will notice how closed off the helm is from onlookers on the docks."

Felipe was on a roll now, once again sounding like a salesman.

"So, you moor the ship, we tie you to the mast, put a gag in your mouth so you cannot speak, and we tell everyone we have bravely made a stand against an unjust Captain. Part of his punishment is seeing his ship and his cows sold right out from under his nose."

"But mutinies are normally frowned upon! Won't they...?"

Ben willed himself not to panic, but there was only so much he could do. A squeak escaped him anyway.

"Barranquilla is actually quite friendly to mutineers," Jamaal conceded. "You chose a good port for this particular scheme."

"But how do we prevent anyone from hurting Benny?" Arturo asked. "What if a mob decides to take care of him?"

That brought Ben right to the edge of the abyss, and he began to tremble. Felipe placed a hand on his shoulder to steady him. The effect was not as immediate as it was with the Black Rose, but the weight of the gunner's hand did help tug him back into reality. Ben drew a few deep breaths, thinking of Xiang.

"Do not worry. Nothing will happen to you. That is why I invited Giselle. Giselle is very fast. She will run to the *Deception* and tell Madame a man needs saving from a mutinous crew. You know she will rush over, thinking either you have all finally had enough of my nonsense and are letting me have it, or I have done something terrible to Benny."

He turned to Giselle.

"She will come even faster if you imply it is Benny."

Giselle nodded, clapping her hands excitedly. She loved feeling she had important jobs to do, so her inclusion was strategic indeed.

"When Madame arrives, if I know her, she will argue with me to release Benny to her so she can rehabilitate him into a better man. She is very popular in Barranquilla, so we use that to our advantage."

"What about you?" Ben asked. "Surely they will recognize you?"

Felipe grinned like a trickster god. When he spoke, his French accent vanished entirely, and Ben finally understood how the crew of the *Angelina Marie* had not attacked him the moment he opened his mouth. He sounded exactly like Ben, like James, like Andrew, like any other proper son of the British Empire. The man was a linguistic chameleon.

"Not without my pin. I speak Spanish well enough that I do not have a discernible accent. Nobody can quite place where I am from, but I am still understood. We are merely a random crew aboard a ship, nothing special about us. This is not like Campeche, where everyone knows us. In Barranquilla, without my pin, I am invisible—just another sailor in port, like a thousand others. And we will use that to our advantage. Any further questions, Lieutenant?"

Ben shook his head. Felipe's usual accent returned at once.

"I just know this will work, as long as everyone plays along, oui?"

A chorus of "Yes, sir" answered him in various languages.

"Très bien. Now get some rest. We make port at first light."

The night felt longer aboard the *Bouclier Rouge*, almost longer than nights had once felt aboard the *Starling*. Felipe's plan was meant to make the Captain miss Ben, but Ben could not help how much he missed her in return.

Felipe refused to take the Captain's cabin for the night, insisting instead that Maeve, Giselle, and Toñiete share it. The Frenchman sat on the rail staring across the water at the *Deception*, at the light shining from the Captain's quarters. Or perhaps the light below it. A light with a faint red glow that must have been coming from Doctora and Talia's room.

Ben was beginning to wonder whether the older man ever slept. He had only seen the gunner asleep once, in Doctora's quarters after Juanito's snakebite. Felipe had fallen asleep kneeling beside her bed, a lock of her hair wrapped around his fingers.

He certainly could not sleep in the hammock in his own quarters, filled as it was with assorted junk, but Ben rarely saw him enter that room unless he needed something from his magpie's nest. Stranger still, Felipe kept drinking from a flask. Alcohol ought to make him more tired, not less, shouldn't it? Ben's curiosity got the better of him.

"She kissed you," the helmsman said softly, approaching the older man.

"Oui, she did. I do enjoy it when she is affectionate with me. We have not had a cold season this winter, but my favorite thing is when she invites me to share a blanket and we read together. That is how I taught her English. That was a cold winter, and she had some very nice blankets."

He smiled to himself, and Ben caught the scent of what was in the flask: Xiang's citrus energy tea, but laced with something spicier, like the amorous blend. Ben guessed it was meant to keep Felipe awake. So many questions crowded his mind, but the way the gunner sat gazing at the distant ship made him look almost like a painting. That reminded him.

"Thank you for helping me with my project. I know I got on your nerves while you were interviewing Xiang, but I just find him so fascinating."

"I was going to let you stay until you made the joke about me licking wares for sale in the market," the Frenchman chuckled. "That was not funny at the time. It is quite funny now, but at the time that was the final drop, and the frustration overflowed my barrel of patience. Xiang did tell me off for threatening you, by the by. That was the other lecture I received from him that evening."

"No hard feelings, truly. That story was quite a read. Very exciting."

"And he would not let me embellish any of it, not even to make Tobin more *dur à cuire*. He says that, while Tobin was very brave that day, that is not what attracted him. Xiang said he saw a light in Tobin's darkness, and the light within Xiang called out to it. Like a *luciole*, a firefly."

He shrugged.

"He asked me not to write that down because he says it is not a good enough description to explain how beautiful the process was. I think he gave a lovely description, but I honored his wish. Because of this, Xiang calls Tobin *Dēngtǎ*, Lighthouse. It amuses me because...well, I suppose I have already shown you my hand, but if I win Jules for my own, I wish to call her *ma belle soleil*, my beautiful sun. I know many people think she is a little thundercloud, but when she smiles, it is like a ray of sunlight after a hurricane."

Ben looked up at the sky.

"And the Captain is like starlight. I have always loved the stars, obviously, but the astronomically small chance that we would ever have met makes me think our meeting was fate, or destiny. Written in the stars."

He sighed dreamily, thinking of those beautiful brown eyes always full of reflected light.

"Also, I love it when her eyes sparkle. *Veo todas las estrellas del cielo en tu mirada.*"

He nodded to himself.

"Yes. Starlight."

Felipe sighed, smiling.

"Amazing how many languages describe love as a light, *non*? And life without it as darkness."

The older man clapped the younger on the back.

"I am happy for both of us that we found a light. Tobin and Xiang, too. None of us should ever have met, but I am glad to have my string of fate entangled with people such as you."

"Even though you are leading a mutiny against me?"

Felipe threw back his head and laughed.

"It is an improvisational play in service of selling the ship and the cows. Non, if I did not feel kinship with you, we would not have matching tattoos. Never forget that. I…"

He paused.

"I will tell you a secret."

Ben leaned closer.

"I hate sitting for these. I know that seems odd to say, as I have so many, but I do not like being poked, and I do not like soot and piss rubbed into my skin. But each one of these means something. Some are badges of honor, like the shellback, my swallows, and the ship on my back. Others are things important to me, like our shared compass rose, or…"

Felipe tugged down his collar, exposing the small tattoo over his heart. Ben had seen it before: a sprig of pointed leaves and red berries. He had never been sure how the gunner got the red pigment, but did not wish to ask.

"This is *l'houx*… in English, holly. European holly, so it looks a little different from what you are probably used to."

Ben nodded. He knew holly as long smooth leaves and berries hanging on long stems. The gunner let his shirt fall back into place.

"In Europe, holly is the symbol of the month of December. Jules—her birthday is in December. I would have liked a *Flor de Maga*, but that felt too obvious, especially since she is not fully mine. If I fully win her, perhaps I will get one, but this is a symbol of my love for her. I am not sure she even knows what it is. But holly is an evergreen, and my feelings for her are likewise constant and unchanging. That is why it felt right."

Then he pulled up his sleeve to expose the compass rose on his wrist. Ben instinctively did the same.

"This is the same. I did not get it merely because I like the design. The design is very nice, oui, but I would not have done this if I did not care for you a great deal. This means I shall always have your back, as I hope you will always have mine. Even if I must lead a mutiny against you.

"And just as Madame is like my daughter, so you are becoming like my son. I want what is best for you both, truly…"

The Frenchman stopped and cocked his head.

"Why do you cry?"

Ben reached up and discovered his cheeks were indeed wet. He wiped them frantically and tried to speak; his voice came out quiet and halting.

"No one has ever done anything like that for me before. And I did not leave things on good terms with my father, and now it is too late, and..."

He sniffled.

"I'm sorry..."

Felipe pulled Ben into a tight embrace and kissed him on both cheeks. Then he set his giant hands on Ben's shoulders.

"It is nice finding where you belong, oui? And everything makes sense?"

Ben sniffled and nodded. Felipe patted his cheek.

"Good. If you are not stupid, and you work hard, you will continue to belong with us. So no matter what I say about you tomorrow, know that you and I are family now, oui?"

"Well, if you do it according to plan, I won't have the slightest idea what you're saying anyway."

Felipe began to laugh, and Ben joined him.

"Very fair, very fair! Now go get some sleep. Tomorrow will be a great performance!"

In the morning, the crew of the *Bouclier Rouge* had a quick breakfast before weighing anchor. They were to dock first, before the *Deception*. This would give Felipe time to stir up a scene. Ben was still a little nervous, but their conversation the night before had steadied him.

Felipe viewed him as family. It was possible Talia did as well, since she had the same tattoo. Ben had never felt this kind of kinship with anyone outside his blood relations, and even then his relationship with most of them had been strained, especially after their father passed. When their mother died, he had been estranged from all of them except Sarah.

He wondered briefly how they were all faring, and how they had taken the news of his presumed death at pirate hands. Did they even know? Did anyone besides Sarah care? Sarah sometimes picked up extra money running errands for Anne and her father, so perhaps his youngest sister had learned it from Anne—or, more likely, from the Baxters' servants.

Ben shook himself. Now was not the time to think about the other Harringtons. Now was the time to think about the family he was building with the crew of the *Deception*.

"Bonjour, Benny! Did you sleep well?" Felipe asked, taking another long swallow of the spicy citrus tea from his flask.

Ben nodded.

"Excellent. Now you will show us what you are really made of! It is one thing to beach us; it is another to navigate an unfamiliar port. But we will help you, if you trust us."

Ben smiled and clapped the older man on the shoulder.

"I trust you have my back, as I shall have yours."

Felipe grinned broadly and clapped his hands.

"Très bien! Weigh anchor and make ready!"

"Aye!" came the answering chorus.

Guided by the crew, who knew every sandbar and hidden reef, Ben brought the *Bouclier Rouge* into Barranquilla. Though her name was the Black Rose of Cartagena, she treated this port as one of her bases, and the ease with which they berthed an unfamiliar ship showed just how deeply this city was written into their souls. Ben successfully brought the ship to a central pier in the heart of the port.

Once the vessel was moored, lines tossed to the dockworkers and tied fast, Ben left the tiller and took his place by the mast for the next stage of the plan. Felipe soon joined him, whistling to gather everyone on deck.

"You did very well. You are quite talented," he said. "But you are also terrible, and now we must take over the ship, oui?"

Ben nodded.

Once everyone was assembled, Felipe gave last-minute instructions. Toñiete was to remain in the crow's nest, and the moment he spotted the *Deception*, he was to signal with a whistle. At that signal, they would all make a tremendous fuss and draw a crowd.

Mateo, who was from Barranquilla, would go to the butchers' guild to see whether they might be interested. David and Diego would try a few local taverns. Arturo and Azucena would make offers to anyone passing through the port who looked rich.

Once they had enough of a crowd, Giselle would run to fetch the Black Rose.

Daichi and Natsuki would stay hidden until the crowd grew large enough for them to slip away unnoticed, since two Japanese people aboard the ship would do nothing to lend credibility to the story.

Everyone understood their part.

Some time later, a whistle sounded from the nest.

The *Deception* was coming in.

Ben dutifully allowed Felipe and Jamaal to tie him to the mast. The Frenchman made the ropes appear tight, though Ben was quite comfortable. Then Felipe gave him a swallow of the flowery calming tea from a tiny corked vial. It tasted sweeter than Ben remembered. The Frenchman handed the empty glass to Maeve, who slipped it into a pocket with a tiny clink.

"Are you alright?" the gunner asked.

Ben nodded.

"Good. Just try to look pathetic, yes? Like a puppy who does not understand why his master has kicked him, oui?"

Ben nodded again and let the Frenchman tie a gag over his mouth.

"Also, Benny, I am very sorry, but I must give you some bruises."

Felipe drew back, and a vicious left hook landed against Ben's cheek.

"Uck!" Ben shouted against the gag.

"You may repay me later, but we must rough you up a little."

Ben's face throbbed, but he knew the gunner was right. Maeve also mussed his hair until it hung tangled over his eyes.

Either Felipe hit him harder than intended, or the tea was astonishingly strong for such a small dose, because the rest blurred together. Maeve's task was to make sure Ben had water regularly and that no one got too near him.

A steady stream of people came to gawk at the overthrown former Captain, and before long there was a respectable crowd. Fortunately, Maeve's normal expression was frightening enough that no one bothered him.

Soon Felipe and some of the others began working the crowd, raising their excitement as though the whole thing were a festival performance or public auction. The air crackled with energy, like the deck before a thunderstorm. The gunner launched into a long, dramatic story that seemed to hold the entire port enthralled. He had missed his calling by not becoming an actor. He would have made a magnificent Falstaff, or perhaps King Lear.

Ben lost all track of time in the haze of the tea. It might have been an hour. It might have been five. He had no idea. Then, suddenly, a great commotion broke out as someone climbed the gangplank to the *Bouclier Rouge*. There were gasps, cheers, and excited whispers. Ben craned his neck, shaking the hair from his eyes, and watched the crowd part.

A stunningly beautiful woman approached.

Honey-bronze skin. Deep brown eyes. Curls barely tamed beneath a crimson headscarf. A delicate blooming rose tattooed at her collarbone. She glowed like starlight.

The Black Rose, wearing her pin on her white blouse, black cincher tastefully amplifying her bosom.

She bit her lip to stifle a laugh at the sight of Ben tied to the mast, gagged. Then she turned to Felipe, fully understanding her part in the performance.

"¿Quién es él?" she demanded, pointing at Ben.

Even through the fog, Ben understood that.

The crew quailed melodramatically, but Felipe stood tall, his hazel eyes twinkling at the promise of a good improvisational performance. The gunner and the Captain went back and forth, voices rising, fingers stabbing toward Ben. The crowd gasped at various moments, and Felipe was unquestionably having the time of his life. Ben wished he could understand what was being said, but it was probably better that he could not.

At last, the Black Rose snarled something with finality, and Felipe clutched his chest as though wounded. He hung his head and sank to his knees. The Black Rose stood over him, chastising him. Then she hauled the gunner to his feet and led him to the mast. Felipe untied Ben to loud applause from the onlookers.

Once released, Ben let himself crumple to the deck like a man who had been bound for days. He hid his face and fake-sobbed to cover the fact that he could not speak Spanish. Pressing his forehead to the Captain's boot, he felt her bend close.

"I need you to say 'Le prometo' to whatever I'm about to say," she whispered, that familiar flower lotion filling his nostrils as she untied his gag and helped him into a kneeling position.

Then she stood and launched into some grand declaration. Felipe later told him that she had said his ship and cargo now belonged to the mutineers to do with as they pleased. In exchange for her mercy, Ben then promised to renounce his life of greed and cruelty, renounce his title as Captain, free his slaves, and serve her. He swore to all of it as desperately as he could.

Ben was so overwhelmed by the sheer number of people that he felt a freeze rising in him. He reached for the Black Rose's hand and pressed his forehead to the back of it. Her touch steadied him and kept the panic at bay. He could do this a little longer. She was right there.

She said something else, looking down at him, her eyes soft. Ben would never tire of looking at this woman.

Holding her hand, he drew a deep breath and, hoping against hope it made sense in context, shouted, "¡Sí! ¡Vale la pena!" before once again falling to her feet and pressing his forehead to her boot.

That was one of the phrases she had taught him—that something was worth the pain and effort.

He wanted her, and everyone watching, to know that he was worth the pain.

And, hopefully, that she would believe it.

Apparently it was good enough for the scene, because the crowd erupted in cheers. The Black Rose hauled him to his feet and guided him off the ship, leaving "Captain" Felipe to preside over a bidding war for the cattle and the vessel.

"He is ridiculous," she muttered once they were down the gangplank and onto the pier. "Did he hit you hard?"

"Not as hard as he could have," Ben conceded.

She took his hand and laced their fingers together.

"Let's get you back to the *Deception*. I believe we have some business left unattended."

# SUPPLEMENTAL

## FROM THE PRIVATE JOURNALS OF BENJAMIN R. HARRINGTON - BLACK ROSE FOLIO

*This list was written in the margin of the description of this trip to Isla Rosa.*

<u>Guitar Names:</u>

*Sweet William*

*Barbara Allen*

*Orpheus*

*Tam Lin*

*Rousing Rosie*

*Celestial Cadence*

*Banshee's Ballad*

*The Wild Rover*

*Randy Dandy-O*

*Sloop John B*

*Black-Eyed Susan*

*Cassiopeia*

**Euphonia**

# Chapter 17

## Pledges and Parcels

Once back aboard the *Deception*, the Black Rose pulled Ben into her quarters. Lingering incense left the air heavy with cinnamon and spice, and her hands went immediately to his backside, drawing him hard against her. As much as Ben wanted her, Felipe's suggestion to let her marinate in her desire rose to the forefront of his mind.

"We should wait," he mumbled into her mouth as she kissed him. "It would be terrible for Felipe to interrupt us by telling us how much he got for everything."

The Captain let out a frustrated noise, her head falling back. She sighed, though it sounded more like a growl.

"You're right, and I know you're right, but I want you so badly!"

She punctuated the sentiment by squeezing his bottom possessively.

"Later, you can show me how much you missed me," Ben suggested with a smirk.

She pinched his cheek.

"You awful walrus... kiss me again."

As Ben had predicted, it was not long before someone knocked on the Captain's door. Ben was seated in one of her desk chairs, the Black Rose straddling his lap and rolling her hips against him while he fervently kissed the rose tattoo at her collarbone, careful not to leave another bruise. They were both red-faced and breathing hard, though still fully clothed. The Captain swept her hair back from her face, slid off Ben, and helped him to his feet.

"Madame! Open the door! Look at this!" Felipe called.

She unlatched the door and pulled it open, and Felipe and Tobin came barreling in with a chest that, though small, looked quite heavy. They set it on the desk, and the Frenchman flung it open with a flourish.

Gold, silver, and two kinds of green stones glittered inside, and the Black Rose lit up.

"Gold, silver, jade, and emeralds, courtesy of the butchers' guild. They were quite taken with the quality of the cows, especially the calves, and they have lately been in talks to commission a ship. We got very lucky that they had this capital gathered! What do you think, Princesa?"

The Black Rose picked up one of the smaller emeralds and held it to a finger, as though imagining a ring. She smiled at the gunner.

"I'll likely be docking some of your share for roughing Benny up, but this is wonderful!"

"It all worked out beautifully!" Felipe said, puffing out his chest with pride as yet another plan proved the work of hidden genius. "A terrible, greedy man was overthrown and offered the chance to turn over a new page by the beautiful and benevolent local hero, the Black Rose. We helped a local guild, and we shall help the economy further when everyone goes on their sprees. Our legend grows! I would say that was worth a punch to the face, Benny, oui?"

"It was, yes. But I certainly need to learn more Spanish. And probably French."

"*Oh!* I almost forgot!" Felipe pulled his rucksack from his back and carefully removed two bottles, setting them on the Pirate Queen's desk. "Speaking of French! Maeve found these hidden in the Captain's cabin on the *Bouclier Rouge*. Tobin told me that you shortchanged yourself yet again so that everyone could have their fair share, so we would like you to have these. It is Sauternes, a sweet white wine from my home in France. I think you will like it."

The Captain smiled shyly, blushing at having her generous spirit praised so openly.

"Thank you, that's very kind of you both."

She looked up at Tobin.

"I suppose we should count this and get the gems appraised while we're here?"

The quartermaster nodded.

"That will probably add a day or two in port, but after being trapped at sea as long as we were, I hardly think anyone will complain."

Felipe clapped his hands.

"I am going to take Benny out shopping and stop for a pint. He deserves it after today!"

The Black Rose nodded, cupped Ben's cheek, and gave him a quick, gentle kiss on the lips. Tobin rolled his eyes while Felipe smiled giddily, clasping his hands under his chin like a tittering schoolgirl. The gunner looked as though he were having the best day of his life.

Once Ben and Felipe had left the Captain's quarters, Ben froze, his hands slapping at his hips.

"Where is my satchel? Did I leave it...?"

"*Non*, mon frère. Natsuki and Daichi took it off the ship when they left. I gave Natsuki a skeleton key to get into your lockbox. You can check whether everything is there."

The gunner's face turned deathly serious.

"However, Jules is right to be worried about our project. If you take those books off this ship again, you must be certain of where they will end up. I know they are incomplete, but both could be quite damning. The butchers' guild would likely have many opinions if they got hold of them. As popular as Madame is, I hardly think they would appreciate learning that their lovely new ship is technically the product of an act of war."

The older man caught Ben's face in his giant hands.

"We are trusting you with our stories, Benny. Please, handle them with care. This may be the only way any of us are remembered. Especially my Letty."

He gently squished Ben's cheeks as he spoke of his lost love. His and Letty's story was the first in *The Chronicles of the Deception*, and he was adamant that her memory live on. He had carried the weight of her death longer than Ben had even been alive, and his love, sorrow, and determination not to let her death be in vain had made him the pirate he was today. That alone made the project worth finishing.

"I shall endeavor to take better care of them," Ben said as clearly as he could with his face sandwiched between two massive ham hocks.

Felipe patted his cheek.

"I know you will. Come, we shall go shopping. Do you need anything?"

"I would like some extra guitar strings. Do you know where I can get some catgut?"

The gunner thought for a moment.

"I know someone here. I require some colophony and horsehair. I need to rehair the bow of my fiddle."

He chuckled to himself.

"That would have been a good use of our time while we waited for the wind to return. It is such a pain, but I need to keep everything in order. Anything else?"

"I don't think so."

The older man cocked his head and considered him for a moment.

"We should get you a new shirt or two. Madame hinted we would be voting on something soon. I presume it is about your promotion, since Easter, Passover, and Eid approach. I know how she likes you in blue, but it may serve to have another. Make a statement."

"What do you suggest?"

They arrived at Ben's hammock, and he found his books and pencils in his lockbox exactly as promised. His purse lay untouched at the bottom, and his satchel had been neatly folded in the hammock. Felipe pulled out Ben's crimson headscarf and held it to his chest, considering.

"I think red, certainly, and perhaps a green one as well. You know that dark green thing she wears? That is her favorite color. It suits her, and it might suit you..."

He clicked his tongue.

"Although it may be too dark for you. We shall look at green. But certainly red. Red will get her attention."

"And I suppose you have a blue shirt for Doctora?"

Felipe scrunched up his face.

"Unfortunately, that clear blue she likes best does not suit me. I look like a *porcelet* in that color. However, she has told me many times that I look pretty in black, so I have a nice black shirt for special occasions."

Ben looked again at the red headscarf.

"Do you think we care too much what they think about us?" he asked, feeling rather foolish. He had once cared deeply about what Anne thought of him, and had been rewarded with violence and scorn. He could not bear the thought of giving up everything he had known only to end up in the same place again.

But Felipe laughed.

"Care too much? *Non.* No such thing. We live in a world where they are told again and again that their thoughts and opinions do not matter because of the bodies they were born into. It does not hurt us to show them that we care what they think.

"And I do care what Jules thinks. I want her to be happy, like keeping a fire lit. If seeing me in black, or showing off my arms, or cuddling and reading beneath a blanket brings warmth and light into her life, why would I not do that? The moment I stop working toward her happiness, then one or both of us is likely dead, because I will never stop trying to make her smile."

Ben nodded. Reasonable enough.

"Very well. We'll see what they have at the shops."

The gunner clapped him on the back, nearly knocking him into his hammock.

"There is the spirit! Come! Barranquilla wishes to make your acquaintance!"

A few hours later, Felipe and Ben returned to the *Deception* with their purses noticeably lighter. Both had bought supplies to care for their instruments, and the Frenchman had talked Ben into two new shirts: one a crimson that matched his headscarf, the other a green that made Ben's grey-blue eyes flash bright peridot, a lighter version of Talia's deep emerald.

The young women at the shop had seemed quite taken with how well the green suited Ben, with his golden-tanned skin and black hair. Felipe whispered translations of what they were saying, and Ben was once again astonished to find himself the object of very lusty advances. The older man, thankfully noticing how uncomfortable it made him, kindly but firmly told the women that Ben did not understand them and that his heart was already claimed by another.

The two men bustled down to Felipe and Tobin's room with their parcels. Ben told Felipe what the Black Rose had said about him moving into that room, so the gunner offered to keep Ben's purchases there until it was official.

"And once you do move in, we can put some hooks on the wall to hang your guitar and keep it safe!"

As they came back out, they found Talia stepping from her and Doctora's quarters across the hall.

"Tals, is Jules in?"

"Nae, ye old goat. She went shopping with Juanito, Jean-Luc, Giselle, and Maeve. I dinnae ken how long they'll be out."

Felipe's face fell slightly.

"Why? Were ye finally going to confess yer love after a wee night away?"

The Frenchman scoffed.

"And what if I was? Then what?"

Talia rolled her eyes.

"Lying disnae become ye. If ye want, she has invited me and the Cap'n to play a wee game of cards later. But she heard ye were takin' Benny out for a spree, so she decided to go as well."

"Very good. And tonight is the night, Tals! You will see!"

# CHAPTER 18

## THE ALEHOUSE AVENGERS

As soon as Felipe and Ben were back on land, Ben caught the gunner's arm. The older man looked slightly ill, his pink skin faded to pastel, as though being removed from the ship sapped all his vigor and bravado.

"Are you serious about confessing your love tonight?"

"I panicked," Felipe squeaked, his voice much higher than usual. "I know that does not become the gunner of the fearsome Black Rose. I can stare down a room full of men with pistols drawn and believe I will get myself out alive, but the thought of Jules..."

He began to tremble, then took a few slow, deep breaths with his eyes closed.

"She won't reject you, I promise."

Felipe shook his head without opening his eyes.

"Do not make promises you have no control over. But I need something to loosen my tongue at any rate, so let us find a tavern and strategize. I cannot simply barge in and say, 'Good evening, Jules, I love you. Please kiss me now.' It needs to be as special as she is."

After a few minutes' walk, Felipe found a tavern with a pig roasting in a pit outside. The sound of fat sizzling as it dripped onto the coals, and the sweet smoky scent rising from it, hit Ben like a physical blow. It reminded him of the first time he had gone to Los Roques. He had been twelve, and the choice had come down to starvation or survival in the midst of a civil war between mutineers and those loyal to Captain Llewelyn. He had chosen the Captain, who had been the only other survivor, and—

"Benny."

Felipe snapped his fingers beside Ben's ear. Ben jumped as he came back to Barranquilla, feeling as though all the blood had drained from his body, leaving him cold, hollow, and sweating.

"I... I don't eat pork. Bad experience when I was younger."

Thankfully, the Frenchman did not argue or pry. His voice turned uncharacteristically gentle, as though he were speaking to one of the cabin children.

"Will it upset you if I get some? We have so many people aboard who will not eat pig, but it is a nice treat for me. If it will make you ill, I will get something else. Or we could go elsewhere."

Ben shook his head, but the wind shifted and blew the smoke directly into his face. He gagged, covering his nose and mouth.

"Of course not. Get what you would like. I'll be fine. But please, let's go inside."

He gagged again and yanked the door open.

They stepped into the bustling tavern, Ben's legs heavy and unsteady. In the cooler, darker room, he huffed the smoky scent of roasting pork from his nose, though it still clung stubbornly to his clothes. Felipe stopped a serving girl and asked her something.

She nodded and pointed to what looked like a menu board, with drawings of a fish, a chicken, a cow, a pig, and cheese. The two men quietly discussed their options, and Ben settled on a stew called *sancocho* made with chicken, though his stomach was still roiling. Felipe found the same serving girl and gave her a coin. She introduced herself as Frida and happily seated them.

She took their order and brought them both a small glass filled with something that smelled strongly of herbs, sharp enough to stab at the sinuses on either side of Ben's nose. The Frenchman tossed his back without flinching, but Ben tried a cautious sip first. It was somewhat sweet, with a biting anise flavor.

"Aguardiente," the gunner told him. "It is a specialty here in Colombia. It reminds me of a liqueur we have back in France, but this tastes much better than wormwood."

Ben considered the liquid for a moment, then threw back the rest of the shot as well, stacking his glass atop Felipe's. The older man laughed and clapped him on the shoulder. Oddly enough, it cleared away the memories of his past and settled his stomach.

Yes. He could eat.

They sat for a few minutes. Ben was not sure whether it was the alcohol already taking hold or whether the men behind them were simply very loud, but the table at their backs was suddenly all he could hear: a group of about seven men who appeared, judging by their absurd fashion choices and the fact that most were speaking English, to be pirates as well.

"I think I need to eat before I have any more to drink," Ben muttered, resisting the urge to clap his hands over his ears. He could not think through all the noise.

"Sancocho is good food for drinking. Very hearty. You will get some rice to dip into the soup, make it nice and filling…"

Felipe suddenly reached out and yanked Ben's head downward as though meaning to smash it into the table. But having trained with the man so much, Ben felt no malice in the movement. What he felt instead was gentleness and care.

He did not fight it, but turned his head and caught the glint of a dagger passing through the space where his eye had been moments before. The man behind him was telling a drunken, animated story and had lost all sense of spatial awareness. He did not even realize he had nearly stabbed the person sitting behind him.

"Sit over here," Felipe whispered, his eyes boring into the other man's head.

The pirate paid them no mind, nor did his companions. Ben shifted his chair closer to the Frenchman.

"Thank you," he muttered as he settled beside him.

"Cannot have a navigator missing an eye, now can we? But I do not like these ones. We must keep a weather eye on them. They look like trouble."

Their food arrived shortly afterward, along with some ale, and Ben tried to make conversation with Felipe even as the gunner watched the other pirates like a hawk. The plan to confess his love later that evening seemed to have been forgotten in the face of a more immediate threat. The other men still paid no attention to the people around them and were growing louder by the minute.

"I've been meaning to ask you," Ben said, dipping a spoonful of rice into the stew. As Felipe had promised, it was hearty and delicious, though Ben wished it were a little spicier. The scent of onion, garlic, and cilantro was comforting, but he thought a sharper heat on his tongue might help distract him from their noisy neighbors. "Why did you tear out the first page of the folio? Did you start off being a massive prick and then have a change of heart?"

Felipe sighed and shook his head, suddenly very interested in his beer.

"I cried too much and smeared the ink. It was completely illegible. I am sorry. Once I stopped crying, I decided to be a prick to try to get it on the paper again while less sad."

Ben had been about to comment on the older man's soft heart, but the group behind them interrupted again. Frida had come over with another round for their table, and the man who had nearly stabbed Ben earlier grabbed her, making her spill the beer all over herself.

"Thah's okay, luv," the man slurred, grabbing her braid and trying to drag her head down. "Ye can jus' lick it up."

Felipe kicked the man's chair hard, jolting it enough that he released her hair. He turned, bleary-eyed, toward the men behind him.

"Sorry. Convulsion," Felipe muttered, his French accent gone.

That apparently served as explanation enough for the drunken pirate, and it gave Frida time to escape. She returned a few moments later with more small glasses of aguardiente. Felipe motioned for her to lean down between him and Ben.

"Do you speak English?" he asked quietly. "¿Habla Usted inglés?"

She nodded.

"I understand more than I talk," she whispered. "Thank you for to help me. This is gratis."

"Do those men bother you?"

She nodded, biting her lip.

"Do you wish for us to do something about it?"

She nodded again, her eyes wide.

"Very well. My name is Felipe. The moment you wish us to take care of them, you say my name, and we will."

It did not take long.

The next time Frida had to approach their table, a different man grabbed at her chemise and yanked it downward, trying to expose her breasts. She did not even have to say Felipe's name. He was on his feet at once, though bent slightly to meet the other man's level.

"Let her go," he growled, taking the man's wrist.

Ben was once again impressed by the disappearing accent.

"Or what, old man? D'ya think you're me father?"

"No. Because if you were my son, I would have taught you better than that."

"Oh, like this little ponce?"

The man gestured toward Ben.

Ben took that as his cue to stand. At his full height, he towered over the other men. Felipe straightened as well, and the two of them looming above the pirate crew was enough to startle the man pawing at Frida into letting her go. She scurried away.

"We can do this the easy way," Felipe said quietly, "or we can do this the hard way."

Too quietly.

Terrifyingly quietly.

The other man was so emboldened by lust, drink, or stupidity that he failed to grasp just how precarious his situation had become. He spat in the gunner's face.

"I only take orders from me Captain, and you ain't him. Piss off, and let me get me jollies with that there lass."

Felipe wiped the spit from his face as though it were sea spray, his expression unreadable.

"This is most unfortunate," he murmured. "You just made a very bad decision, and we are doing this the hard way. Very well."

Then the Frenchman smashed his forehead into the other man's.

Chaos erupted.

The man with the knife lunged at Felipe, but Ben punched him in the back of the head, sending the blade flying into the wall where it stuck fast.

Even though it was seven against two, the fight felt more than evenly matched. Ben used every tactic Tobin and Felipe had taught him to avoid punches and managed a few solid jabs of his own.

It also became immediately clear that Felipe had, in fact, been going easy on him.

The famous European prizefighter was on full display, and he fought dirty. Kicks to groins. Knees to noses. At least one man got bitten. The gunner used none of that in training, honoring Ben's wish to beat James fairly. Ben began to suspect he might have to rethink that position, because fighting honorably was not proving very effective in practice.

Yet for all Felipe's viciousness, there was grace in it too, a kind of elegance, as though he were dancing steps his body had long since memorized while these other louts badly needed better instruction. Next to him, Ben felt like a drunken goat as he tried to kick the man who had nearly taken out his eye. He missed and lost his balance. In his scramble to get up again, Ben grabbed the first solid thing within reach.

Which happened to be the other man's crotch.

The man howled in pain, startling Ben, who had not even realized what he had grabbed. But once it dawned on him, he squeezed harder until the other pirate sank to the floor. When the man was level with him, Ben punched him as hard as he could, and the man toppled over.

"Very good, Benny boy," Felipe chortled, even as he deftly dodged attacks from two directions and sent the enemy combatants crashing into each other. Then he grabbed both men by the collars and bashed their heads together.

"You're just having the very best day today, aren't you?" Ben panted, sweeping a kick that knocked another rival pirate onto his backside.

"This is quite exhilarating, oui?"

"I fucking hate the French," one of the men shouted, swiping a knife at Felipe.

Felipe twisted the other man's arm behind his back and rested his chin on the man's shoulder. His disguise broken, his French accent returned in exaggerated force.

"Well zen, zat is convenient, because I fucking hate people who disrespect women. So zen I suppose zat we are even. Benny, please kick zis man where it will hurt ze most, *tout de suite*."

Ben obeyed, kicking the man in the groin as hard as he could. Felipe took the knife and threw it into the wall beside the first one so it could not be used again. His accuracy under pressure was almost absurd.

Within a few minutes, only one man remained standing from the English pirate crew. He raised his hands in surrender and fled.

Felipe and Ben looked around.

Six men lay on the floor, unconscious or too hurt to get up.

Frida was clutching the arm of a man who looked old enough to be her father, with a huge mustache. He held a pistol and wore an expression of amusement. Fortunately, none of the other patrons had seen fit to intervene. Felipe straightened and began speaking calm, apologetic Spanish to the man Ben later learned was Frida's father, the *dueño*, the owner of the tavern.

The *dueño* pointed at Felipe's pin and asked about *la Rosa Negra*. The gunner nodded, puffing out his chest with pride, displaying the disc of blond ceiba wood carved with the relief of a rose, a black ribbon cut in swallowtail fashion attached behind it. The other man then indicated Ben, and Felipe draped an arm around the younger man's shoulders.

Whatever Felipe told them must have been excellent, because the entire tavern cheered. Frida let go of her father's arm and gave both Ben and Felipe a hug and a kiss on the cheek before inviting them back to their table. Some burly men employed by the tavern dragged out the other pirate crew and dumped them onto the street, while Frida brought Ben and Felipe more aguardiente, lining up three shots apiece.

"Those men have been causing trouble for the past few nights," Felipe whispered to Ben. "Armando here was about to shoot the man who groped his daughter, and he thanked us for helping her. Since we are part of the Black Rose's crew, our drinks are free in gratitude. We are still paying for the food, though."

Ben nodded and tapped his glass to Felipe's before they both tossed back the shots. Ben exhaled and finally took stock of the aftermath. His knuckles were red, though they did not hurt as much as he would have expected. He would probably have bruises on his backside and knees. Then he looked up at Felipe and started.

One side of the gunner's face was slick with his own blood, and he seemed not to care in the slightest.

"Do you realize you're bleeding?" Ben asked. "You have a very large cut over your eye. Do you think—"

Felipe waved off the concern with a smile.

"Non, we can have some more drinks. Let Jules and the girls enjoy themselves. And if drinks are free, I can drink myself into a looser tongue. To our ladies, and to Cupid."

He threw back another shot of aguardiente, and Ben did the same.

# Chapter 19

## Covert Cuddles

Many hours later, Ben and Felipe sloppily carried each other back to the *Deception* while the older man tried to teach the younger a French shanty. Through the fog of drink, Ben decided he would like to learn it properly when the gunner was sober.

And when he was sober.

They stumbled up the gangplank to their ship, and Felipe looked around.

"I want to see Zzjjuuules," he mumbled.

Ben nodded. All the adrenaline from the fight, and from their drunken reward afterward, still coursed through him, and he felt strong and virile. He wanted to see the Captain and demand an audience in her bed while he still felt like this. Perhaps this was exactly what Felipe needed as well, enough courage to finally confess himself to Doctora.

Ben helped Felipe down the steps and knocked on the door of the physician's quarters. She answered and opened it wide, the scent of herbs rushing into the narrow hall. The Black Rose and Talia were also inside, playing cards over one of the bottles of wine from earlier. It still looked three-quarters full.

"Ay, joder, Felipe," the older woman sighed.

Ben realized the cut over the gunner's eye was still weeping blood.

"Benny, what the hell happened?"

"We went to a tavern and these men..."

Doctora's head fell back.

"Felipe, can you just once go to one *estupid taberna* and not get in a fight? One time."

"Zzjjuuules," Felipe intoned, drawing out the *u* with a tiny chuckle.

Doctora, entirely unamused, held up an accusatory finger in his face.

"One time. The next time you do this, I will never speak to you again."

Felipe pouted.

"Never? But that is so long. You do not mean that, Zzjjuuules."

She grabbed him by the collar and sat him on her bed. Then she angled the lantern for a better look and adjusted her spectacles, one balled fist still clenched at his throat. Felipe smiled at her through the haze, a single finger stroking over her hand.

"Zzjjuuules, these men would not leave the serving girl alone, and she asked us for help. How could we say no? We cannot simply sit by and not do the right thing."

His eyes widened, and he pushed his lower lip out further to make himself look pleading and pathetic. The physician exhaled with a shudder, momentarily softening before gathering herself back into icy annoyance.

"That may be so, but you are going to need stitches."

She turned to the Captain, Talia, and Ben.

"I don't think you want to be here for this. We will play cards again soon."

The Black Rose poured some wine into a cup and shoved it at Felipe, who drank it quickly, never taking his eyes off Doctora as she bustled about gathering what she needed. The physician handed the gunner a wooden dowel, which he dutifully put in his mouth as the Black Rose, Ben, and Talia filed out. Talia turned left toward the galley, and the Pirate Queen took Ben's hand and pulled him up the stairs to her quarters.

Once inside, with the door latched, the Black Rose set the bottle down and began lighting lanterns around the room. When her cabin glowed softly, she took Ben into her arms, her lips hungrily seeking his. Ben held her against him, still feeling manly and powerful even as he sobered quickly. She broke the kiss just enough to speak against his mouth.

"Benny, we are going to cuddle and drink this wine, and then you're going to fuck me while we are good and drunk. Yes?"

"Yes, Mistress."

In the back of his mind, he remembered what Tobin had said.

*She only lets herself get drunk when she feels safe.*

And she wanted to get drunk.

With him.

And she trusted him with her body while drunk. She might not love him yet, but surely that counted for something. He would have to make certain her trust was not misplaced.

They sat on the bed, and the Captain poured wine into a pair of glasses from her desk, handing him one before taking a gulp from her own. Ben swirled the liquid and sniffed it, just as he had often seen Anne and her father do. Yes, it definitely smelled like wine.

"What are you doing?" the Black Rose asked, curious.

Ben chuckled.

"No idea. I think you are meant to be able to tell things about the quality of wine by doing this, but I don't know what I'm supposed to look for. Or smell for. They never explained it to me."

"They? Your parents?"

"Oh, heavens, no. If my parents knew anything about wine, they certainly would have taught me properly. They knew how to explain things so I understood them. No, my...my wife, Anne, and her father. They were very particular about wine."

"You're going to have to tell me about her..."

Ben shook his head.

"At some point, I will, I promise, but please not right now. The last thing either of us needs is for me to become the sad, sobbing drunk."

"You're right. We need you to be an amorous Don Juan drunk."

"Who is Don Juan?"

She crossed to her bookshelf and pulled down two books. One, in Spanish, was called *El Burlador de Sevilla*; the other, in English, *The Libertine*.

"He is a *mujeriego*... I don't remember the English... he pursues many women."

"Womanizer? Rake? Cad?"

"Something like that," she muttered, pouring more wine into her glass.

Ben did not particularly care for wine, preferring a good Jamaican rum or Irish whiskey, but there was magic in this bottle. Perhaps it was the company, or perhaps the lingering influence of the aguardiente, but the sweet white wine left him warm and pleasantly blurred. The Captain and her cabin shimmered in the lamplight. She looked ethereal there, giggling softly, and Ben knew she must be feeling much the same.

"Benny," she purred, "touch me."

"Yes, Mistress."

They helped each other out of their clothes and collapsed in a tangle on the bed, hands sliding gently over skin.

"I missed you," the Black Rose whimpered, lightly scratching Ben's backside as she clumsily tried to climb over him.

"I was hardly gone two days, Mistress. Compared to the past two weeks..."

The Captain let her head fall onto his shoulder as she settled beside him, and he looped an arm around her back.

"No, it's different. I could have had you at any point those two weeks. If I wanted, you would have had your pants off before I finished asking. But I was being stubborn because I knew Tobin was right about needing rules, and I did not want him to be. Then he *was* right, and I took it out on you. It was my fault. And I smacked you. That was not nice."

Of course. The reason Tobin knew about the rules was because he had told the Captain she needed some. Count on the quartermaster to want a list.

Ben realized the Black Rose was no longer speaking.

Nor was she moving.

She had gone completely limp in his arms.

For one panicked instant, he thought he had somehow killed her. He felt for the pulse at her neck and was relieved by the steady throb beneath his fingertips. She gave a tiny snort and burrowed more comfortably into his embrace.

She had fallen asleep.

Ben sighed, kissed her forehead, and tried to decide what to do.

Did he carefully untangle himself and leave her to sleep off the wine?

Or did he accept this opportunity to let a beautiful naked woman sleep curled in his arms?

The hopeless romantic in him desperately wanted this to feel like being a proper husband, even if the logical side of him knew that was entirely absurd. Ben snorted softly to himself. Perhaps, in addition to Baffling Benjamin and Horsecock Harrington—the nickname he had earned for being well-endowed, with the joke that no woman would ever get far enough past his anxious over-thinking to find out—there was also Ridiculous Romantic Robert living in his head.

And in Ben's tipsy state, Robert was winning.

He looked around and saw that the books the Captain had pulled down were still within reach. He had not had much opportunity to read since joining the crew, so busy had he been with ship's business, his journals, illustrating *The Chronicles of the Deception*, and, of course, his lustful lessons. Ben reached over to grab the books, and the Pirate Queen clutched him tighter in her sleep.

He supposed that answered the question.

She was comfortable. He was comfortable. He had a book. Apart from the unfinished business of his own pleasure, it was very nearly ideal. And knowing she felt safe with him outweighed the disappointment.

Ben gently rearranged the pillows and blankets to make them both cozier, kissed her forehead, and settled down to read *The Libertine*.

It was a play, which initially threw him off. He was appalled to discover what a vile creature this Don Juan—Don John in English—truly was. A violent, remorseless womanizer who thought only of seduction and his own appetites. He reminded Ben of someone, though he was not sober enough at first to place him. Surely this could not be the kind of man the Black Rose actually wanted. Ben could not have been that man if he tried.

And he did not want to be.

The only woman he wanted was asleep against his chest.

She was more than enough.

As Ben finished the play, silently cheering as Don Juan and his wretched companions finally got what was coming to them, the Pirate Queen began to stir. She opened bleary eyes and seemed startled to find him still there.

"Hello, Starlight," he said quietly, trying not to spook her. "You fell asleep on me, and then you would not let me leave."

He indicated her arms, which were still wrapped around him rather tightly. She noticed the book in his hands.

"I was naked in bed with you, and you read a book?"

Ben shrugged.

"Well, I was not particularly tired, and I have not had much chance to read lately. I must say, this Don Juan character is quite terrible, by the way. He..."

Now that he had sobered, a series of connections clicked into place. Don Juan reminded him of James. James, who, when presented with the Captain passed out in her bed, had later tried to force himself on her. How many other men, when presented with a naked sleeping woman, would have simply sat there and read a book?

The thought made him feel faintly sick.

The Black Rose, however, seemed to take exactly the meaning he hoped she would, and she chuckled.

"As honorable as he is well-appointed, our Benny," she said, stretching and throwing a leg over him. "I take it we did not get very far in our mission?"

Ben clicked his tongue and nuzzled her cheek with his nose.

"No, Mistress, we did not."

"May I make it up to you now?"

She climbed over him until they were nose to nose.

"I would like that very much."

She took the book from his hands and tossed it over her shoulder. Then she stroked his ample manhood back to readiness.

"And Don Juan is not meant to be sympathetic. He is meant to be… lecherous and lustful. But that is ultimately his undoing."

"Just as you are mine," Ben breathed.

The Black Rose chuckled and lowered herself onto his cock. She moaned softly, her head falling back, and Ben's hands gripped her waist.

"You would not believe how much I missed this feeling," she sighed, going still for a moment. "You under me. Inside me."

She leaned forward and kissed him as she slowly rolled her hips. Ben's hands slid up her back, lightly tugging at her hair.

"Yes," she breathed. "Just like that."

Ben felt as though he had a fire burning in his groin, and found himself split in two. Part of him—Ridiculous Romantic Robert, perhaps—was enthralled by the slower, gentler pace, by the way they could savor every shift of her body, every touch, every kiss.

The other part of him was ravenous.

That part wanted the beautiful, brutal friction until she screamed. Then her hands and mouth would finish him off, and he would have the release he wanted.

"What do you desire, *mi princesa de las estrellas*?"

The Black Rose smiled and leaned forward until their noses touched.

"I'm due to start my monthly course soon, so we had better make this count."

"Yes, Mistress," Ben said quietly, and pulled her close enough to brush their lips together.

She moved faster, then slowed almost to stillness, then quickened again, as though she were playing with the very edge of his restraint. She brought him right up to the point where he nearly needed to pull out, then let him ease back again. She was having a marvelous time, squirming and moaning happily as she tormented him with exquisite care. Ben ran his hands over her skin, reveling in the warmth of her as she moved closer and closer to her own release.

At last she bent for another kiss, and her breath hitched.

"Benny," she cried, guiding his hands to her breasts.

He squeezed them exactly as he knew she liked while thrusting hard to meet her. Her head fell forward, her curls dropping around them like a curtain that shut out the world as they kissed deeply. Her body shook, and her inner muscles clenched around him, then loosened.

When it was over, she lifted herself off him and took his cock into her hands, stroking him with vigor. All the tension snapped. Ben spilled across his own stomach, panting, while the Captain made sure to work every last drop from him. She cleaned him up before drawing him into a sitting position.

"I do believe this is the latest you have ever been in my quarters," she murmured as she slid into his lap.

"You are probably right," he agreed, trailing kisses down her neck. "And you have not asked me to leave yet. I shan't complain. I think this has been rather lovely."

"You should not have stayed..."

Ben opened his mouth to protest.

"...but I'm glad you did. And I'm glad you got some reading done. I do like my officers improving themselves with intellectual pursuits."

"So when do you think the vote will be?"

The Pirate Queen stretched her arms around his shoulders. Ben let his face fall into the crook of her neck and rubbed his mustache against her skin, earning a snicker.

"Probably tomorrow night. Tobin and I will have to get the gemstones appraised. We likely will not sell them here, since they will fetch a better price outside Colombia, but it is good to have a baseline. We will probably get more for them in an English or French port, so we will also need to vote on where to go next."

"Very good, Mistress."

Ben yawned, and the Captain did too.

"Time for you to get dressed and go to bed. You have had a very long day."

"Yes, Mistress."

This time Ben did not argue as he wriggled back into his clothes. He cupped the Black Rose's cheeks, rubbed their noses together, and gave her a gentle kiss on the lips.

"I promise we will have a good drunk fuck at some point. We shall simply have to plan for it earlier in the evening."

"Of course, Mistress. Or else leave a stack of books where I can reach them."

She snorted and gently smacked his bottom as he passed through the door.

"Goodnight, Benny."

"Goodnight, Mistress. Sleep well. I know I shall."

He kissed the back of her hand with a wink and was gone.

Once Ben had left, Rosa grabbed her large fan, let it unfurl, and all but swooned back onto her bed.

He called her Starlight.

And his Princess of Stars.

How lovely.

*Stop that,* the voice of reason scolded. The voice in her head sounded like some dreadful mixture of Tobin and her father. *Do not let him ensnare you.*

She waved the fan at it.

*It is fine. Did you not see how easily he left? No argument. No sad puppy faces...*

*But look at you. You are the one swooning on the bed, thinking about how he gave you pet names like some spoiled little girl. Highly inappropriate. Insubordinate...*

"Oh, hush," she muttered aloud, snuggling back into the sheets and hoping Ben might visit her dreams again as a merman.

He did, though she remembered little of it by morning.

Ben also dreamed beautifully that night. He and the Captain became mer-people, and he took her hand and led her to a brilliant coral reef. The Black Rose swam ahead of him, giggling, and Ben chased after her while shining silver fish scattered in all directions. She slowed as they neared the shallows, letting him capture her in an embrace before pointing up above them.

It was sunset.

They broke the surface of the water beneath a blazing sky. A great outcropping of rock rose nearby, and the Captain pulled herself onto it, her crimson tail flicking seawater playfully at Ben while golden light played across her breasts. She beckoned him to join her, and he did, settling his blue-grey tail beside hers.

She leaned against him and rested her head on his shoulder as he put an arm around her waist. Together they watched the sun sink and the moon rise, trading kisses every time a star fell.

Right before Ben woke, the mer-Captain looked at him, her eyes full of starlight, and spoke the only words either of them said in the entire dream. Words Ben would carry in his heart for the rest of his life.

"El amor vale la pena. Le prometo."

Love is worth the pain. I promise.

# Supplemental

## From the Private Journals of Benjamin R. Harrington - Black Rose Folio

Leadership Qualities Aboard the *Deception*

- Generosity to your subordinates: the Captain shortchanges herself sometimes to ensure all other shares are equal. She often keeps it a secret between herself and Tobin.

- Trusting your fellow officers: even if we don't understand the plan, or even know the plan, trust that we are surrounded by capable people.

- Getting your hands dirty: the Captain never expects others to do things she wouldn't do herself. She has not let her hands lose their calluses, even as the other officers exempt her from duties unbefitting a Captain. She did eventually ask why she never had cow duty, but Tobin waved it off, saying she had other things to do, like run the damn ship. She didn't seem to like that answer, but Tobin's tone said it was not up for debate.

- Organization: A checklist can lower stress levels, especially if there are many moving parts. While Tobin's lists may be overly thorough, they are incredibly helpful when you have three ships and are trying to keep track of what goes back on which ship.

- Skill matching (need to find a better term for it): finding people whose skills complement each other and have them work together to fill in each other's gaps. Felipe and Doctora are a good example, as are myself and Talia. The Strap and Feather system seems to live and die by this concept as well.

- A clear, shared vision: while not apparent at first glance, there is an understanding of how the *Deception* operates. They mainly attack Guineamen, prison ships, and military ships. None of the officers are in this trade for wealth. They are more interested in...well, for lack of a better descriptor, being people who would make Xiang proud. Redistributing wealth, helping women and children, disrupting oppressive governments, freeing slaves and prisoners. It is codified in the Articles, and it seems that everyone aboard understands that to some extent.

- Apologies: admit when you are wrong and apologize. Put in the work to make it right. The Captain does not want to be feared (at least, not by her crew). She listens to their concerns and makes changes as needed.

- Know your team's strengths and limitations: Talia and Andrew would have been fantastic to try to sell the *Bouclier Rouge* and the cows, but their Spanish is almost as bad as mine. But this exercise gave Arturo the opportunity to flex some improvisation and acting muscles by allowing him to go toe-to-toe with a master like Felipe. Arturo only seems quiet because he's one of Talia's mates, and she overshadows him considerably. He is just as talented and charismatic, but defers to his superior. Of the two brothers, Toñiete is much quieter. He wants to train to be a navigator, so once I am promoted, I will see if he has a head for it, and then perhaps take him on as an apprentice when he's a little older. Maeve said he is the best student of the children, so my hopes are high.

- Be open-minded: as Felipe told me during the Gauntlet, with crew from all over, everyone aboard knows something or has experienced something I have not. While it is difficult to no longer be the smartest in the room, it is good to know that if there is a problem, we have a wide variety of ways to look at it and come up with ideas and solutions. And empathizing with these people helps to strengthen our shared vision. Every member of the crew feels seen, known, valued, and if not understood, they know we will do our best to try. I think this is a big reason why nobody has been able to usurp the Captain, despite her being fairly young. Felipe says a handful of people have tried, and they always lose the vote spectacularly. These people truly believe in the Black Rose. And so do I.

# Chapter 20

## Ink and Incredulity

The next morning, Ben found Felipe in the galley with a large bandage wrapped around his head, looking sullen over a cup of strong citrus tea and an orange.

"So did you confess to her?" the younger man asked quietly.

*Had Doctora rejected him after all?*

Felipe shook his head.

"Non. It did not seem a good idea to do that while she had a needle so close to my eye. Talia has already given me hell about it."

Ben sighed. "Just as well. You wanted to make a grand declaration, and we didn't really get to plan one, with the fight and everything."

The Frenchman waved a hand. "That is also part of it. I could not bring myself to tell her I love her when she was angry with me. That makes it seem as though I only say it to soothe her anger. Non, I must tell her when we are both in good spirits, and I do not have to worry about her stabbing me."

"Fair enough," Ben conceded with a snort as he started to peel his own orange. "Oh, I would like to go back out and purchase some more quills and inks today, if we can. I saw a shop last night when we were coming back to the ship. They had inks in a little wooden case in the window. It isn't too far."

Felipe nodded and leaned forward, lowering his voice. "We could not let them do that to Frida, oui? We had to help...yes?"

Ben nodded. "We did. I'm sure Doctora was just frustrated because you got hurt. How many stitches?"

"Ten. But Jules makes very small stitches. Doc Finnegan, he would probably have done it in five or six, but Jules does hers small so the scar is less obvious."

Ben remembered how fine the embroidery on Doctora's handkerchief had been. That seemed like an excellent quality for a midwife to possess.

"Got in another fight, you old prick?"

Tobin sat down next to Felipe. The quartermaster peeled a banana and started cutting chunks into his porridge.

"Oui, we did. But it was for a good cause! And Benny did quite well! He even fought unjustly!"

Tobin raised his eyebrows, eyes wide with surprise.

Ben blushed a little. Was that supposed to be a compliment? His throat tightened as he tried to keep his voice low, hoping Felipe would take the hint and lower his as well. "I think I need to learn to fight dirtier. James certainly can't be trusted to fight with honor."

The quartermaster nodded, his deep obsidian eyes glinting. "Very well. We can add some of that to your training."

Felipe pointed a stern finger. "I know that look. Do not do any damage that will make her hate you! His nose is one thing…"

Tobin scoffed. "Please. You know R–… the Captain would never hate me, no matter what I did."

"She might if you do what you are thinking."

Ben felt like he should know what they were talking about, but whatever they were implying was just out of reach of his mind this morning. "What on earth do you mean?"

Tobin snorted, and Felipe sighed, squeezing the bridge of his nose. "Do you remember what you did last night? To the man who tried to put out your eye? When you fell?"

Ben nodded, and then the coin dropped, and he understood, his hands instinctively covering the area in question.

"Tobin likes to go for that area."

The quartermaster sneered, incredulous. "So do you!"

"Yes, but it is stronger to use your legs and feet! Using your hands leaves you too close and too vulnerable. It is an unwise tactical decision!"

Tobin waved a hand dismissively. "It's better to have a proper grasp of the situation, and you can adjust as necessary. In more ways than one."

"And if you are wrong, you are in very much trouble. In more ways than one."

Felipe dropped his voice to mimic Tobin's deep, rumbling growl, but could not get the sound far enough down into his chest.

"And if he is no longer just her playthi—"

Tobin slapped a massive hand over the gunner's mouth. There were muffled, angry French noises as the older man tried to bite the quartermaster. Tobin paid it no mind and stared hard at Ben.

"Don't get any strange ideas about what you mean to her. We've already had this conversation, and I do not wish to have it again."

Ben held up his hands in submission, holding his tongue lest Tobin decide to take it out on him during their next training session. Tobin released the Frenchman, who rubbed his jaw.

"And yet you say it is I who is the prick! Mon dieu, quel connard tu es!"

The quartermaster ignored him.

"Also, the Captain said we are having an officers' meeting at two bells after supper. She and I must go get the gems appraised, but we should be back before supper."

That news seemed to placate the gunner. Ben was sure Felipe was imagining the younger man wearing one of his new shirts and sweeping the Black Rose off her feet.

"Très bien! I am most excited for Benny to become a full officer!"

"Are you excited on Ben's behalf, or are you excited because next time we get caught in the doldrums, nobody's going to blame you?"

The gunner looked indignant. "Just because I am good at many things does not mean I must be good at everything! It was just as much Talia's fault as my own!"

Then, a little quieter, the Frenchman said, "It is about seventy percent proud of Benny and thirty percent happy not to have another fucking thing to do when I could be experimenting."

Ben snorted, and Felipe clapped him on the back.

"And I know you will be happy to finally have the title you have worked, studied, and trained for!"

"Indeed," Ben agreed.

"We haven't voted yet," Tobin grumbled, and the older man rolled his eyes, then said something to Tobin in Spanish. Ben caught the word amor and something about Xiang, but could not make head or tail of anything else. Tobin cracked his neck, patience wearing thin.

"Would you like to lose your other eye, you old prick?"

"Non, which is why I must be going now. Come, Benny! We go back shopping!"

After their chores were tended to, Ben and Felipe went back down into the town. Despite having been drunk when he passed it, Ben was easily able to find the shop he had seen the night before. He pointed at the case through the window, rising onto the balls of his feet like a child pointing out a toy to his father.

"Hmm..." Felipe pursed his lips, looking quite paternal in his own right. "I do not think I know this shop. Let us see how much they want for it. It seems a place that may not take kindly to us."

He adjusted his rose pin to be a little more noticeable on his chest.

Ben followed the older man into the shop and immediately understood what Felipe meant. Back in Campeche, Ben had been worried about being too low-class for the soap shop that Tobin and Xiang took him to. Xiang had reassured Ben then that if he could afford their wares, he definitely belonged. Here, he felt even more out of place.

While Eliza took excellent care of his clothes, Ben still seemed shabby compared to the elegant outfits worn by the salespeople. Felipe looked no better, and his clothes, although well-maintained, were at least a decade out of fashion. And unlike Campeche, Ben didn't know if he could afford anything in this shop after buying catgut, two shirts, and supper the night before. He still had some money, but there was no indication of how much anything in here cost.

The room smelled of old metal mixed with leather, parchment, and ink. There was a heavy, stale stillness, though, like nothing ever came in and nothing ever left.

A man built like a rectangle standing on its short edge came around the counter, regarding them with a sneer. While Ben couldn't understand the words he spoke, he understood the patronizing tone of someone who definitely didn't think they belonged there.

Ben looked at the gunner, eyes wide with low-level panic, but Felipe's gaze was fixed unflinchingly on the other man. He stood up straighter, pasted a fake smile on his face, and mimicked the elegance of the other man's tone. Ben heard the phrase cuánto cuesta, which he remembered meant how much? from Campeche.

"How much do you have?" Felipe whispered out of the side of his mouth while still in his staring contest with the salesman. As polite as he was acting, Ben could feel the contempt radiating off the Frenchman. Ben told him, matching his volume.

"Un momento, Señor." Felipe steered the younger man back toward the window.

"He is asking for twice what you have," the gunner whispered as they pretended to look over the box and the inks. The lid of the case had an intricately carved map of the world on top. It was beautiful, and Ben ran a finger along the smooth relief of the Spanish Main. "I do not think he will let me argue like Mama Tati."

Ben's face fell. "That's a shame. It's so lovely. Maybe we shouldn't have…"

"Oh no, we are buying this," Felipe growled, baring his teeth. "I cannot stand men like that. I will give you the rest of the money."

"You don't have..."

"Yes, I do. Look."

The Frenchman pointed into the corner of the box. All the inks had little tags with a small blob to indicate the color, and Ben understood immediately. One was a lovely dark green that was very close to the color of the Captain's dressing gown. The second was a clear, bright blue that matched Doctora's favorite shade.

"We must buy this, and not only to spite him."

"What do you want in return? Do you want me to pay you back? Or would you like a favor?"

"One portrait of Jules in this color," he said, indicating the blue ink. "As beautiful as she is."

"Wearing that color or the whole drawing in that color?"

"I allow you to make that creative decision when the time comes. Give me your purse. We are going to give this connard what he asks for, and next time we come to Barranquilla, he will not speak to us like this. Pick out some quills, quickly."

Ben nodded. He found a table covered in writing implements, picking a couple that looked like they would be cheap without completely sacrificing quality. He also saw something that made him stop, his skin growing hot.

There was a large, fluffy white feather that would likely make a terrible pen, but it looked soft. He gently stroked it, and his suspicion was confirmed. He immediately imagined tickling the Captain with it, running it over her breasts and down her sides. He grabbed it.

Felipe cocked his head, confused. "That will be a very bad pen."

"I know."

"You will put it in a hat?"

Ben shook his head. "No, I intend to use it..."

He stopped. The Black Rose had made him promise to stop talking about what they did behind closed doors. But he and Felipe had an understanding...did that count? He cleared his throat.

"She's...uh...quite ticklish. I think this might be quite effective for making a...romantic evening."

Felipe chuckled. "Very good! Yes, plan special things for her! She will like that indeed!"

They made their way back to the salesman, who looked perturbed to see them carrying so many things.

"What did you say to Tobin this morning? When you spoke to him in Spanish?" Ben asked as the vendor tallied up their purchases.

"Benny, if I had wanted you to understand, I would have said it in English," he responded flatly. He sighed, and his tone softened. "But Tobin needed to be reminded not to overstep. He is not her father, and she is not a child."

The salesman said something, and Felipe made a big show of pouring out the purse of coins onto the counter.

"Gracias, señor," the Frenchman said with a contemptuous smile as he efficiently stacked the money, pushing a few piles of it to the man before putting the rest back into his little black coin purse.

"Thank you for helping me buy these. I will be sure to save them for something special."

Felipe shook his head. "Non, you will pay me back by using them as intended. I did not help you buy them for you to only use as much as it will take to draw Jules, and then to never use them again because nothing is special enough. If *The Chronicles of the Deception* is not special enough for colored illustrations, then I do not know what will be. There will always be more ink."

He lowered his voice conspiratorially and winked.

"And I hope you get very good use of that feather!"

# Chapter 21

## Ballots and Blackbeard

Later that evening, after supper, the officers and Ben gathered in the Captain's quarters. Since they would be voting on his promotion, Ben expected to be asked to leave the room again. However, the Captain seemed confident it would be a quick vote and asked Ben whether he wanted to turn around or see it. Even though his logical mind was sure the outcome would be in his favor, Ben was suddenly overcome by a wave of nerves.

What if he had not convinced these people of his usefulness?

What if they all secretly couldn't stand him and were just humoring their Captain? His logical mind knew this was complete bullshit, as long as Felipe was in the room.

What was the majority needed to carry a vote? Simple? Two-thirds? Three-quarters?

What if he were accepted as their navigator and then suddenly forgot all his training? He had never actually done any work with the title of navigator. What if he couldn't do it after all? What if someone on the crew was better suited, and better trained, and better...

There were multiple hands on his person to bring him back to the moment: Felipe and Xiang each had a hand on one of his shoulders, Doctora and Talia each held one of his hands, and the Pirate Queen had a gentle hand on his cheek. Ben let out the breath he hadn't realized he had been holding.

"Sorry," he muttered.

"We really must work on that," Felipe groused. "Freezing from stress is no good. It is dangerous."

"He's been getting better," Tobin countered, surprising Ben. "He doesn't tend to do it while fighting. It's when he is thinking too much, or there is too much happening at once, that he does it."

"Still," the Frenchman grumbled, even as he squeezed Ben's shoulder.

"So, Benny, would you like to watch the vote?"

Ben shook himself. "You know what? I would. Face my nerves head on."

The Black Rose smiled. "Very well. In the matter of Benny's promotion to navigator and sailing master of our ship, we vote on the count of three. Uno... dos... tres."

Six open hands rose into the air, five of them attached to smiling officers. Tobin looked stern, but the quartermaster's eyes were a little softer. Perhaps the Captain and Ben, now having rules and boundaries, with Ben fully understanding what was at stake, placated him. The Black Rose clapped her hands excitedly.

"Excellent! Motion passes! Congratulations, helmsman Harrington, you are now the navigator of the good ship *Deception*. You will continue to serve as helmsman until your ceremony, but you are now able to vote with the officers."

She gave Ben a hug and a quick peck on the cheek as the other officers applauded with various degrees of enthusiasm. Xiang and Felipe were the most excited, while Tobin was the least, rolling his eyes.

"And speaking of voting, that brings us to the second matter at hand: where we want to go next. Tobin and I counted the gold and silver from the butcher's guild. That will likely be the next pay everyone receives, unless we encounter a prize along the way to our next destination. However, we will not be distributing the jewels. I'm sure I don't need to remind everyone what happened last time."

"Non!"

"Certainly not!"

"Oh, goodness, no!"

"Bù!"

Felipe, Tobin, Doctora, and Xiang looked pained. Ben blinked, looking around the room, hoping someone would favor him with an explanation. He expected it from Felipe, but it was Tobin who provided it.

"Maybe six or so years back, we took a prize and distributed some gems as pay without getting them appraised. None of us is trained in that way, so we did it by size without even considering quality. That was the most massively unbalanced distribution of shares we have ever made."

"We lost a sizable number of the crew over it. Many retired from the sea, fortunes now secured, and some quit and left for other crews because of how severely we underpaid them. We had to take on almost an entirely new crew. Ever since then, we have gotten professional appraisal and distributed the shares as coin, so everything is as equal as possible."

Ben cringed. "That sounds awful!"

"It was awful," the Black Rose growled, "an awful way to learn an important lesson."

She exhaled and allowed a serene smile to come to her lips. "Do we have any suggestions for our next destination?"

To Ben's surprise, Xiang raised his hand.

"Yes, Xiang?" the Black Rose said, nodding.

Xiang said something, but Ben caught Panamá and Yuánliào, which Ben was now pretty sure meant ingredients.

"Okay, so we need to go to Buenaventura within the next month or so. But if we want to offload the jade and emeralds, we will likely want to go to a non-Spanish-speaking port to do that."

"Maybe it's finally time to visit our friends at the Repub-..." Felipe began.

Doctora whirled on him, evidently still upset with him over last night's fight.

"NO!" she shrieked, an accusatory finger pointed at him again. "It is too soon! The last time we went to the Republic of Pirates, you almost ended up in a gibbet!"

Felipe raised his hands, attempting to placate the angry Boricua. "I ask again, how was I supposed to know who he was? There are hundreds, thousands of men named Ed with long black beards running around the Caribbean! How was I to know that this specific one was Ed Teach?"

"Ed Teach? The Edward Teach? As in Blackbeard?" Ben asked, agog. "You met him?"

Talia laughed, but it was uncharacteristically mirthless for the boatswain, who never took anything seriously. "And pissed him off somethin' awful."

Felipe lifted his hands slightly in an exasperated shrug, then let them fall back to his thighs with a small slap.

"I told him his ribbons and bows made him look very pretty! I still do not understand why he was so angry! I like being told I am pretty!"

"Because 'pretty' is feminine in English, you dolt!" Tobin said, each syllable dripping with frustration. "And I've told you at least a hundred times, you cannot tell Englishmen they are pretty!"

"And I maintain that is ridiculous! Beauty is not male or female!"

"How did you survive?" Ben asked in complete awe. This was as if his grandmother were telling him that the fae are real and she had won a drinking contest against them in a pub back in Ireland.

As soon as he asked, the Black Rose's honey-bronze skin flushed red, and she looked intently at the floor.

"Madame went to Hornigold and played him in a hand of cards," Felipe explained, clapping the woman on the back. "Madame is quite a talented card player. That is how she came into possession of the *Deception* as well."

Suddenly, the way everyone spoke of the Captain and her flagship made sense. They always spoke of how she won the ship, not that she had taken, conquered, or captured her. The *Deception* had literally been a prize for besting someone at cards. Ben had to laugh at the absurdity.

"You...challenged Captain Hornigold...to a card game...to spare Felipe...from being hanged...by Blackbeard?"

"That's a good summary, yes," the Black Rose said quietly, her cheeks still matching her crimson headscarf.

"What did you offer...?"

"No, we aren't going to the Republic of Pirates," the Pirate Queen interrupted. "How about Tortuga? Or Saint Thomas? Saint Lucia?"

Each suggestion went up slightly in pitch, and her eyes darted nervously from one officer to the next.

"Surely everyone is getting tired of Spanish ports?"

There were some shrugs and waving hands among the officers.

"Spanish ports have the best food," Felipe said with a grin.

"And most of me best tickle partners," Talia said by way of agreement.

"How about Saint Lucia? Check in on Doc Finney and see how retirement suits him," Tobin suggested, his voice steady and soothing. "We should be able to get what we need for Easter, Passover, and Eid there."

The Black Rose nodded, taking a few breaths before continuing, standing up ramrod straight. "Very good. Benny, while you will not receive your pin until our celebration, you are now able to vote. Remember: an open hand is a yea, a closed fist is a nay, and not raising your hand is an abstention. We require a simple majority, so if it is four to three, the four win."

Ben nodded. Perfectly sensible.

"In the matter of our next port of call being Saint Lucia, we vote on the count of three. Uno... dos... tres."

Ben raised an open hand, as did Tobin, Felipe, and Talia. Doctora and the Captain did not raise their hands, and Ben was surprised to see Xiang pouting and raising a fist. He obviously still wanted to visit Panamá. The Pirate Queen clicked her tongue.

"Four in favor, two abstentions, one against. The yeas have it. And we will visit Buenaventura soon, Xiang, but it's only a three-day sail from here. You know how everyone gets when we don't spread out our visits to ports."

The cook sighed and nodded.

"Is there any other business we need to discuss?"

Six heads shook no.

"Very good. Everyone..." she hesitated. "Everyone but Benny is dismissed. I... I wish to discuss your ceremony. The rest of you, to your business or to your pleasure."

# Chapter 22

## Phantoms of the Past

When the Black Rose dismissed everyone, they nodded and filed out. Felipe clapped Ben on the back with a wink. Ben was pleased to see that Tobin did not try to argue with the Captain about Ben staying behind. She must have told him about the rules, which placated him. Maybe she even told him about how chivalrous Ben had been the night before.

But Ben also noticed Doctora looked a little confused, which seemed unusual. Of all the people on this ship, Doctora was the one who *definitely* must know how often Ben and the Captain were making love. Trying to lie to the physician would certainly invite an accident that could ruin everything, so Doctora was probably intimately involved in keeping the Black Rose child-free.

Once everyone was gone, Ben stood, waiting for the Captain to make the first move.

"Congratulations, Benny," she said quietly, opening her arms. Ben took her into an embrace, kissing her on the cheek.

"Thank you. I look forward to serving you. But do we have to plan it all out now if it's almost two weeks away? Wouldn't you rather...?" She shook her head.

"Remember last night I told you we needed to make that count because my monthly course was starting soon?"

"Yes... ohhh." Ben frowned slightly, which made the Captain chuckle.

"Exactly. It's a good thing we didn't try to put it off any longer."

"That also explains why Doctora looked confused." She nodded.

"Indeed. I was in her quarters earlier asking for some supplies, so she probably thinks we're about to make a mess." A look of horror washed over Ben's face.

"Oh no! Eliza will be so upset! She hates cleaning up blood!"

The Captain snorted quietly. "We aren't going to be doing any of *that*. We don't have to talk about your ceremony. It won't be nearly as complicated as the one we had on Isla Rosa.

"But I would like to have some private company, so you don't feel forsaken." She laughed again. "Do you remember saying that to me last month?" Ben did remember, but it felt like he had lived two lifetimes since then. It felt like so much more happened on a pirate ship than a regimented Royal Navy vessel, where most of his days had been planned down to the minute.

"I remember. And you didn't think I would still be here in a month."

"You certainly showed me," she said, rubbing the tip of her nose to his, but not allowing their lips to touch. Not quite yet.

"And I am still having a *fantastic* time on my little adventure." The pair kissed, deep and slow, Ben entwining his fingers in her curls. "Promise you won't fall asleep again?" She smiled, pressing her forehead to his.

"I promise. But remember how far you can go right now, and don't push that boundary."

"Uh-huh," Ben mumbled, trailing a line of kisses along the Pirate Queen's neck. He wasn't sure how good he could make her feel in her current state, but he was still going to try. And she really liked it when he kissed and licked her neck. He kept his hand on her knee. If she wanted him to touch her breasts, she would certainly let him know. After a few minutes of this, she sighed deeply, tapping his hand on her knee.

"Ben?" Ben stopped nipping her delicious skin and sat up straight. The entire time he had been aboard, she had never once called him Ben. It was always Benny, Lieutenant, or helmsman. And lately, of course, whenever he was particularly sappy, lustful, or overly romantic, she called him *walrus*. Even though it had been born of upsetting circumstances, Ben found it funny now. He had never had any private in-jokes with Anne, so it was unexpectedly heartening to find their relationship becoming more intimate in non-sexual ways.

But there was also a slight sense of panic. Was he in trouble? Was something wrong?

"Umm, yes, ma'am?"

"Ben, what sort of life did you leave behind when you joined me?"

"Umm, well, I left the Royal Navy and my rank as Lieutenant... I was likely about to be promoted to navigator and assigned to a new ship..." The Black Rose waved a dismissive hand.

"Yes, I already know that. But where did you live? Where was your home?"

"Jamaica. Kingston, specifically."

"How long has your family been in Jamaica?"

"My grandfather, my father's father, was a soldier from England sent to fight the Spaniards in Jamaica. My grandmother was an indenture, and, as far as I can tell, came from Ireland to escape...something. I'm not entirely sure what; nobody ever spoke of it. He took her on to keep his home, they fell in love, and he forgave her remaining debt so they could be married.

"My mother was the product of a priest and a nun who fell in love, left their respective orders, and married. I'm not sure how long they were in Jamaica, or where they came from. My mother had bronze skin, almost like yours, with black, black hair," Ben indicated his own mop of black curls, "which I inherited. So, I'm probably some sort of *mestizo*, or octoroon, or something. But I have my father's English and Irish complexion, and this *very* European nose, and light eyes, so nobody ever asked questions."

"Most of my siblings are fair, but my littlest sister, Sarah, whom I've mentioned before, is all but our mother's twin. In addition to being a sickly child, she also had a difficult time growing up because people treated her like she was illegitimate. Even though my parents loved each other dearly, and my mother would *never*..." He stopped and cleared his throat.

"Would you please tell me about the lady in Kingston that I stole you away from? Anne?"

Ben laughed coldly. "Mistress, please remember, you didn't steal me so much as I flung myself at you and begged you to take me away."

The Black Rose took his hand, entwining her fingers in his. "But can you tell me about her? I know it's upsetting, but I...I want to know. Please?"

Ben sighed. He knew he could no longer weasel his way out of it.

"She lived up the hill from me. Our home was just on the edge that separated the rich people and their big, fine houses on the hill from the poorer community. We were city people, not plantation people. I haven't the slightest idea what to do with most farm animals. Hence why I was not thrilled about finding the cows on the *Bouclier Rouge*."

"What about horses?"

Ben chuckled. "Can I tell you a secret?" The Captain nodded and leaned in. "I'm *terrified* of horses. I don't like the front end, I don't like the back end, I don't like being on them, nothing. They're pretty to look at, but I don't want to be near them if I don't have to be."

"Oh, I agree completely! Horses are lovely, but I don't want to own one. They're a lot of work, and I don't want to have to care for one ever again."

Ben paused, still trying to avoid the inevitable. "Before I continue, I think it's only fair for you to tell me something you're afraid of. Admitting I'm afraid of horses is information you could use against me." The Pirate Queen thought for a moment, and Ben thought she would dismiss it. But her eyes were kind, and she humored him.

"I'm afraid of lampreys." Ben's face went blank, and she chuckled. "You really don't know anything about animals, do you?" Ben shook his head. The Captain stood and retrieved her animal book once more.

"I'm going to make you read this. It's very informative. I know exactly where it is because I always avoid it. The drawings are disgusting." Without looking at the page she opened to, she turned the book to Ben with a full-body shudder.

Ben took the book and was treated to pictures of an eel-like fish with a circular jaw full of sharp teeth that apparently attached to prey via suction, bored a hole in it, and sucked its innards out. He closed the book and handed it back to her.

"That is absolutely revolting!" he said calmly, even as he wished he could scrub the image from his mind. "No wonder you're scared of them. I think I am now, too."

"Sorry to give you something else to fear in life," she said with a laugh, "but at least it's something tangible and real that other people can understand." Ben raised his eyebrows at this, but she continued, steering back to the conversation at hand. "So, there was a lovely little rich girl up the hill, and you have questionable family history."

Ben exhaled. No turning back now. "Yes. I adored her for many a year, since I was about seven or so. She had these light green eyes that looked like peridot, long fiery red hair down to her waist, and she was thin and elegant as a swan.

"She's the reason I learned to play guitar, because I read in a book about how in Spain men play music for their sweetheart under their window. My mother thought it was sweet. She encouraged me to learn, even she didn't care for Anne or her family one bit. But she would pick up extra money doing errands for them sometimes, which is how Anne and I met.

"For years, I tried to build a friendship with the Magistrate's daughter, but she was standoffish and always treated me like I was beneath her. As we got older, I went calling. I begged her to go courting. She would never agree."

"You can certainly be infuriatingly persistent, Benny."

Ben shrugged. "Persistence taught me guitar, and taught me astronomy, and how to make and read charts and maps." Ben turned so he was nose to nose with the Pirate Queen, dropping his voice to barely above a whisper. "It is also helping me as a student of the bed, so you are *directly* benefiting from my infuriating persistence in *multiple* ways." She let out a shuddering breath as her skin flushed slightly.

"Touché, Benny. Carry on."

"Then one day, after ten years of trying to get her attention, she suddenly agreed to see me. She wanted to steal away with me that very moment. I think she'd argued with her father, for she was quite angry. I took her up to my room, to my bed, and things...passed the point of no return. But it was not how it should have been. She was quite...dispassionate? Bored, even? She wouldn't kiss me; she just stared at the ceiling, not making a sound.

"Now, my parents were quite... raucous in the night, and they always seemed very happy with each other. Even for all his military training, my father was a sweet man who dearly loved his wife. I have seven younger siblings, by the way: Nathaniel, Hope, Grace, Felicity, William, Rebecca, and Sarah. Hope, Grace, and Felicity are triplets. My parents loved all of us, but adored each other most of all."

The Black Rose rubbed her forehead, blinking. "Clearly. That is a dizzying number of children. Especially having three at once."

Ben shrugged. "It seems like a reasonable number to me, considering how long they were married and how often they made love..."

The Black Rose got a strange look on her face, and Ben realized she was probably mentally calculating how often *she* made love to *him*, and how many children *that* could potentially produce. Whatever number she arrived at made her go pale, a stark contrast to the fierce blush not twenty minutes previously. He waved his hand to try to disperse those thoughts as if they were smoke he had accidentally blown into her face.

"Anyway, even though losing my virginity was terrible— and my father warned me the first few times would probably be terrible—"

"Our first time wasn't terrible!" The Captain interrupted, indignant, hands on her hips.

Ben laughed, blushing slightly. "I'm also not seventeen anymore. Eight years make quite a difference. As does having an enthusiastic partner." He put a hand on her cheek. "That makes a *tremendous* difference."

"So, since I am apparently inclined to say and do stupid things after making love, I said something that made her slap me and call me 'a damn, daft fool,' and that it was a mistake, and she left. She wouldn't speak to me after that, and I threw myself into my work."

"Lo and behold, months later, as I was preparing for my first sailing as a junior officer, just shy of eighteen, her father, the Magistrate, appeared at my door demanding I marry her. She was with child." Here, the Pirate Queen gasped and held her hand over her mouth.

"He said I should do the correct thing and marry her to preserve her reputation and to give the bastard proper parentage. I tried to fight it, but in the end, his threats against my family and my career led me to go through with it." The Captain took his hand. Ben sighed deeply.

"It has been...suggested...that the Magistrate forced her to go through with it to teach her a lesson. Regardless, I found her unenthusiastic and unwilling to return my affections. She gave me a black eye on our wedding night because she didn't want me to touch her. I don't even remember when or how we consummated the marriage, but I spent more time sleeping in guest rooms than I did in the bed that was supposed to be ours. Every time I tried to be the doting or affectionate husband I wanted to be, she would slap me, or worse."

The Black Rose shook her head and clicked her tongue. She regretted slapping him for finishing inside her and telling her he loved her; that was probably the worst possible thing she could have done to this poor, sweet man.

"The child was..." Ben put his head in his hands and sniffled, "stillborn, a girl. I only found out because I bribed the midwife's apprentice for information. I'd been hoping for a daughter. I was going to raise her to be sweet and kind and gentle...but no, she was taken before I could even meet her." The Black Rose put her arm around his back, feeling him tremble.

"Oh, Ben, I had no idea. Doctora told me you were married very young and unhappily so, and not as...experienced...as one would expect, but never mentioned a baby. I'm so sorry." He took a deep, shuddering breath, eyes shimmering with tears.

"How could you have known? It's not something that is really spoken of, at least not among men. Most of the men I worked with, I haven't the slightest idea if they were married, let alone if they had children. I don't know how it is with women. Doctora and I discussed it once, and she told me about her Octavio. And even before she and I had *that* conversation, Felipe figured it out because of how I acted when he told me about Jackie, Alicia, and Abbie. I wanted to name my daughter Abigail, and..."

"And the way Alicia's husband acted after the birth upset you, didn't it?"

Ben nodded, his voice wobbling even as he snarled. "Prick got everything I've ever wanted, and threw it all away. Terrible!" Ben took a deep, calming breath through his nose, letting it out through his mouth

'And it was right before Christmas, too, so that time of year tends to be difficult for me. Just so you're aware, I tend to be broody and melancholic when December comes around. I don't tend to be fun at holiday parties."

"I love December," the Black Rose whispered before she could stop herself. She cleared her throat. "Sorry, please continue."

"Not much else to tell, honestly. Anne drifted further away, constantly criticizing and insulting me to my face and behind my back, physically fighting against any touch I attempted.

"To avoid being around me, she started dedicating endless hours to her flute lessons with Mr. Fulton. It was such a waste of money, honestly, because she doesn't have a musical bone in her body. Hours upon hours with Mr. Fulton, and she never practiced at home, so I could never follow her progress. Mr. Fulton this, Mr. Fulton that, Mr. Fulton some other damned thing... Why are you looking at me like that?"

The Captain's face had a look of pity, her brown eyes wide. She grimaced, clicking her tongue again. "Benny, I don't think she was learning to play the flute...or at least not the actual instrument."

"Then what do you think..."

The Black Rose made a motion as if she was trying to stimulate an invisible cock with her mouth, and the coin dropped. "Oh my gods!" he shrieked, slapping his forehead, hyperventilating slightly. It suddenly all made so much sense! "Even on Sundays?!" Ben's voice was strained. The Captain threw her arms around him again. He was shaking, so she held him tighter.

"Oh, Ben! I'm so sorry! That... bitch whore!" Ben turned to face the Pirate Queen, and a humorless laugh tore out of him. He was caught in a strange place at the intersection of despondency, rage, and relief, and his mind overloaded, leaving the Captain wondering if she had somehow broken her new navigator.

After a few moments, Ben flopped backward onto the bed, the laughter dying in his throat as he considered the pulley system above her bed. His eyes and his voice were incredibly far away when he spoke again. "All this time, I have been feeling like an adulterous arsehole for all my time spent in your bed, and she was fucking Mr. Fulton almost our entire marriage! She always...Oh my *gods*! She looked at him the way you look at me when you're about to rip my clothes off! *How* did I never notice?"

The Black Rose snuggled up next to him. He absently rubbed her back as he finished his tale.

"I decided to throw myself into sailing, working my way up the chain of command, studying and preparing for a promotion I never got. The day you captured the *Starling* was the day before we were supposed to make port and go on leave. The night before, I wished upon a shooting star that I would not have to return to Anne...and my salvation came in the form of the *Deception*, and the beautiful, mysterious Mistress of the ship." He looked up at her, and she smiled at him. "And I have served her faithfully ever since."

The Captain spoke quietly as she ran her fingers over his chest.

"So...I suppose you don't regret your decision?" Ben shook his head, capturing her fingers in his. He gently kissed her knuckles, his voice still soft.

"It was the best decision I've ever made, if I do say so myself. I'm to be the navigator on a beautiful ship, I have a freedom the Royal Navy would never allow me, and I get to regularly bed the most beautiful woman in the Caribbean, if not the world." Ben sat up, taking her with him. He pulled her close, kissing her forehead.

The Black Rose cleared her throat, choosing her words carefully. "I know I asked you before, but tell me again: you're not imagining her when you fuck me, are you?"

Ben winced. "I don't imagine you *as* her, if that's what you mean. I imagine making her *watch* me fuck you, so she can see what it's like to have a good time in bed. She would *never* let me try anything that I found in any of the dirty pamphlets that get passed around among boys on ships. For example, do you remember the first time I had you on your desk, and I told you I had only theoretical knowledge of pleasuring a woman with my mouth?"

"Yes. And might I add, your performance has only improved with practice."

Ben blushed at the compliment, pleased with himself. He was slowly coming back to his normal self. "Thank you, Mistress. Anyway, that was in one of them. I copied the diagram and tried to explain to her what I wanted to do when I was home for shore leave. She broke a plate and threatened me with a shard, called me a deviant, and wouldn't let me into our bed. Again. She made me sleep in a guest room on an entirely different floor of the house."

"Gods, she sounds like the worst, honestly." The Black Rose once more pushed Ben onto his back, and the two cuddled together in her silky red and purple sheets.

# Chapter 23

## Deeds of Desire

The air in the Captain's quarters was dense as she and Ben lay together. The helmsman was still as a statue, his mind on a dark shore leagues away, his eyes trained on the ceiling. The Pirate Queen began to fidget, rubbing a piece of his shirt between her fingers. She waited for him to come back to the conversation. He usually returned quickly when she touched him, but this was different. Had she actually broken him?

And not only that, learning so much about him at once suddenly felt directly contrary to her desire to keep this relationship, or whatever it was, on the lighter side. She had been granted seemingly forbidden knowledge about who Benjamin Harrington had been back in Jamaica, and the implications seemed larger than even her Black Rose of Cartagena persona.

And the longer he remained lost in his mind, the more complications might rear their heads. She was struck with a thought: if she could ease him back into a more lustful mindset, maybe it would bring him out of his stupor. Then she would be back in control of the situation once more.

The Captain pulled herself over Ben, tracing the tense muscles in his neck and shoulders with a single finger. He blinked, finally registering the weight of his lover on top of him.

"I'd love for you to diagram me and explain what you want to do to me," she whispered, giving him a tiny, suggestive smile.

The air suddenly shifted; the melancholy of the past few minutes was replaced by a flare of heat between them. Exactly as she'd hoped.

"Is that an order, Captain?" Ben asked quietly, his tone deep and seductive. It was unlike him, but it made the Black Rose tremble with delight.

"You know we can't right now, but we will certainly have to try that when I am better able to enjoy myself."

"I can't think of anything that I would like more at the moment. And now that I've been at least partially absolved of adultery...who knows what I'm capable of when you remove the guilt?"

"I shiver with anticipation to find out," the Black Rose said, raising her eyebrows.

"Would you like me to actually draw you sometime?" Ben asked, suddenly thoughtful. There he was. There was Benny. His grey-blue eyes studied her in the low light. "I think that could be quite beautiful and sensual. Felipe helped me buy these beautiful colored inks for our *Chronicles of the Deception...*"

The Pirate Queen rolled up onto her haunches, tugging at Ben's shirt. He sat up and pulled it off.

"Hmmm, that could be fun. I could be your own Scheherazade... but I feel like this conversation has taken a turn for the... lustful... don't you?"

She again traced the muscles of his shoulders and chest with her fingertips.

"I do, but I feel bad since you can't-"

The Black Rose waved a hand. "You have laid your painful story bare. The least I can do is make you feel better for having to reopen old wounds for me."

Ben cupped her cheek and gently pressed his lips to hers. When they parted, there was a twinkle in his eye. "Fancy a flute lesson?"

She giggled, playfully pushing his face away from hers. "Navigator Harrington, get your trousers off this instant and give me a flute lesson neither of us will ever forget!"

Ben obeyed, pulling off his trousers and tossing them aside. The Black Rose removed her shirt as well. Ben moved to the edge of the bed as she knelt on the floor.

"Look at this spectacular instrument," she purred, taking his cock into her hands. "Let me see, how should I use it? Hmmm..."

"Perhaps lick the tip to start?" Ben suggested, loosely twirling one of her curls around his finger.

She did as he suggested, and his cock jolted slightly. Ben remembered something she had said to him one of their first times together, when he had seduced her with a song, and repeated it back to her. "My body is your instrument. Play me a symphony."

The Captain nodded, but instead of attempting to swallow his cock as she normally did, she ran her lips up and down the length, dragging along his foreskin in the most delicious way. She then repeated the motion with her tongue, licking warm stripes along his skin.

"Oh, yesss," he sighed.

She smiled up at him, tugging at his hair so he leaned down. She closed the distance between them, and they kissed. Ben's cock rubbed against soft skin, and he groaned into her mouth. Their lips parted, and Ben opened his eyes.

His manhood was in the hollow where her sternum separated her breasts. While the Captain's bosom was not nearly as big as Talia's or Doctora's, it was still in good proportion to her figure. He adored her breasts, as they were part of his Princess of Stars, even if he did not usually lavish on them the attention they deserved. But seeing his cock nestled between them gave him an idea.

"Hold your breasts together," he whispered.

She did as he asked. They were just big enough to surround him, and he tentatively thrust. The purple-pink tip popped up between them before disappearing back into her cleavage. The Captain laughed, and he did it again.

"That feels so strange," she commented.

"It feels quite nice for me," Ben said. "It feels warm and close... like being inside you, but not... it would feel better if..."

He paused and thought for a moment. What did it feel like to be inside her? Warm, yes. Close and intimate, of course. Something was missing, but what?

As he was thinking, the Black Rose ran a finger around the head of his cock, licked her finger, and did it again. The second time, her saliva eased the pull where their skin met.

Wet. That was the missing sensation.

"Do you have some sort of oil or lotion we could use to reduce the drag?"

She nodded, stood, and went over to her dresser. After some consideration, she returned with a small jar of lotion that smelled like plumeria. That was why she always smelled like flowers. It reminded him of their time on Isla Rosa. She took a small amount, rubbing it onto his cock with two fingers. It warmed his skin, and she once again enveloped him between her breasts.

The difference was immediately apparent. Ben's cock slid against her with ease as he thrust slowly. The warming sensation was heavenly. The Pirate Queen chuckled, attempting to kiss the tip each time it popped out the top as though it were some sort of game.

"Are you enjoying yourself?" Ben asked, panting slightly. While he knew she was likely not having as good a time as she was used to, he wanted to know that he was not selfishly leaving her out.

"It's strange, but I like watching it. The way the skin moves up over the tip and then pulls back, it's fascinating."

She kissed the tip again, looking back up at him with a smile. Ben leaned down to kiss her lips as she held her breasts together and moved them faster.

"You're wonderful," he murmured against her lips.

"I think you'd like me even better covered in your seed," she whispered in response.

Ben pulled back. Could she read his mind? If so, he was in an awful lot of trouble.

"How did you know?"

She chuckled. "You aren't the only one with the powers of observation, Benny. You look at me differently when you release on my body. Like an artist admiring his work, proud and possessive."

She beamed up at him, that wicked little "goddess of lust" grin he adored. "I must say, it suits you. I like seeing you look powerful."

As she spoke, she moved her breasts against him a little faster, pressing them together a little tighter, and Ben moaned quietly. She continued, clearly trying to edge him closer to release.

"I like seeing the Benny who knows what he wants, who is willing to do whatever it takes to get it. I like it when you get out of your own head, when you show me how badly you want me, and how you're willing to move mountains so I want you as well. I like that version of Benny very much."

Ben felt like he was on fire. The heat was becoming almost too much, a fiery lust curled in his belly that would attempt to break free very soon. But something about it was hitting his brain strangely, even as his reason melted away.

"Then why don't you like it when I tell you that I love-" he asked, strained.

"Acta, non verba," she said simply, holding his cock still and licking the tip like it was a delicate sweet.

The combination of her speaking Latin, the warmth still radiating from her body, and the feel of her tongue and hands on him was far too much for Ben all at once.

"Mistress," he whispered, feeling his thighs vibrate.

She smiled up again, that beautiful, desirous smile, and she aimed his cock at her breasts.

"Fire at will," she said, an excited lilt in her voice as she stroked him.

Ben exhaled and allowed the pleasure to crash over him as he released his seed onto her. He painted her, marked her, claimed her. While he knew she was not fully his, at least not yet, in that moment she was. She had invited him to spend intimate time with her. He had finally told her about his wife. He had been partially absolved from the guilt of adultery, knowing that Anne had similarly been unfaithful. And the Black Rose chuckled between his legs, stroking him to make sure every last drop of his seed was accounted for.

"That's the Benny I like."

The Captain reached for a rag and cleaned them both off. She climbed into his lap, knocking him back onto the bed. They cuddled together.

"I didn't know you spoke Latin," Ben muttered against her forehead as he pressed light kisses to it.

"I only know that phrase because of Felipe. I know he has said similar things to you repeatedly. That is something he values greatly, and I suppose it has rubbed off on me a bit. But I don't even know enough Latin to get through Mass."

Ben cocked his head. "If your family was landed gentry in a Catholic country, how on Earth did you manage that?"

The Pirate Queen froze for a moment, eyes wide and again looking trapped. Ben tried to speak as though calming a skittish animal, low and slow.

"You don't have to tell me. It was just...you know...it seems...odd."

She let out a long, sighing breath, pasting a smile onto her lips. "I think we've had enough secrets tonight, Benny. Thank you for finally telling me about...her."

She spat the word.

"But really, I can't imagine what this Mr. Fulton has that you don't!"

"People skills? Social graces? Money?"

The Black Rose waved a dismissive hand, hovering her lips over his. "I would rather have a sexually generous man who brings me to release every time I invite him to fuck me, who can seduce me with a song, and who calls me Starlight."

"Even though I'm a walrus?"

She smiled, pinching his cheek. "Even though you are an awful walrus. But it's getting late. Did you enjoy your private company?"

Ben pressed a kiss to her forehead. "It was everything I hoped for and more! And I do not feel forsaken in the slightest. You are spectacular, Starlight, and I look forward to finally having business befitting my training."

The Black Rose smiled and rubbed her nose against his. "Excellent."

She kissed him again, gently pulling on the curls at the back of his neck.

"You shouldn't do that if you want me to leave," Ben murmured.

The Captain immediately let go. He shook his head before getting up to search for his clothes.

Ben left the Captain's quarters, after one last, lingering kiss, and made his way onto the deck, looking over the lights of Barranquilla, their conversations replaying in his mind as music, laughter, and snatches of things he didn't understand drifted on the wind. He kept returning to the Latin she had spoken.

*Acta, non verba.*

Deeds, not words.

That was likely a piece of the puzzle to win her fully. As a man who quite liked his words, that was going to be difficult, but Ben resolved to show her his love. He turned away from the city and scanned the early April sky over the harbor, but all the stars were where they should be tonight, so no wishes were to be had.

But it didn't matter in this moment, because he finally felt he was on his way down the correct path. He was going to be a navigator in two weeks' time at last, and he had a clearer heading to the Black Rose's heart.

Ben crossed the deck to the starboard side. After making a few quick calculations, which wrote themselves in glowing script in the air above him in the darkness, Ben raised his hands, extending his middle fingers in the direction of Jamaica, one for Mr. Fulton and one for Anne. While he knew he was still not free of their influence on his life and psyche, it made him feel a little better. And even though he knew how silly it sounded, the moment he said it, he allowed one spiteful curse to leave his mouth and fly into the night:

"I hope you choke on his flute."

# Chapter 24

## Sickness and Sleep

*Deception* left Barranquilla and made for Saint Lucia. Ben had been to Saint Lucia once before on a supply mission and was looking forward to seeing it again.

Unfortunately for Ben, once they reached the island, he made the mistake of immediately buying a seafood stew that tasted strange. Out of an excess of politeness to the old man who had sold it to him, he ate the whole bowl without complaint, even as Felipe whispered to him to stop eating if it didn't taste right.

They returned to the *Deception*, greeted Talia, and Ben immediately vomited over the rail. His illness was so violent that Doctora called for the sleepy tea, and Felipe, Andrew, and Jean-Luc carried Ben down to the sick room. Ben was out cold for their entire stay in Saint Lucia, although he did wake at some point to see the Black Rose and Doctora standing at the door with a man whose red hair was streaked with white.

"You must be old Doc Finney," Ben said before the world went black once again.

When Ben next awoke, he found Felipe and Doctora on the floor beside his bed, quietly playing cards and using buttons as currency. They didn't seem to notice Ben was awake, so he watched them flirt. Each of them was trying very hard to let the other win, to the point that it looked like neither of them had any idea how to actually play the game.

"We should play Ruff and Honors sometime. That way you can play as a team."

Doctora jumped slightly at Ben's voice breaking the silence, but Felipe chuckled.

"I was wondering if you had vomited your voice out. You do not usually stay quiet that long."

Ben was about to argue when he realized the older man was right.

While Ben was introverted, unless, of course, he had a guitar in his hands, he found it much easier to talk to these pirates than it had ever been to talk to anyone else he had known in his pre-*Deception* life, excepting his mother and closer siblings like Sarah.

He had told these people more about himself in a month and a half than he had told any of his shipmates on the *Starling* in years. As much as Ben liked words, it was still so strange to be around people who cared about his, and shared theirs with him in return.

Doctora was on her feet examining him, her long tawny fingers gentle on his face.

"Did you learn anything from your experience?" Felipe asked as Ben chewed some ginger root Doctora produced from a pouch on her utility belt. The sharp, biting flavor overwhelmed his senses and made the back of his nasal passage burn. It also, oddly, made him feel better.

"If it doesn't taste right, stop eating it."

The Frenchman nodded. "I imagine you probably would like to clean up before we let her know you're awake?"

Doctora asked. Ben nodded, and Felipe slipped out the door. The older woman smiled.

"She was very worried about you. Let's get you freshened up."

"How long was I out?"

"About four days. It was one of the worst cases I've ever seen. We'll get you some porridge to eat now, and maybe a banana, and then I'll have Xiang make you some plain noodles for supper. If you can keep all that down, you should be back to normal tomorrow."

She looked over her shoulder.

"Felipe, can you get-"

Before she finished the thought, Felipe had already returned with a basin of water, a sponge, a cloth, and some soap.

"Thank you," she purred, smiling widely up at him.

Ben imprinted the image on his brain to draw later: Doctora in profile, hands clasped under her chin, a brilliant smile on her face, eyes sparkling, a few tendrils of hair coming loose from her bun and framing her face. Felipe smiled back, the tips of his ears red.

"We'll let you get cleaned up first, then we'll have the Captain come down to see you. Come next door to my quarters when you're ready."

"Leave the basin when you finish. I shall take care of that," Felipe said, earning another big smile from Doctora.

Ben thanked them, and they left him alone.

As Ben scrubbed himself, he tried to remember if he'd had any dreams. Four days was an awfully long time to sleep, but it appeared that the sleepy blend tea was formulated to ensure total calm. That was probably why Doctora had suggested it for Tobin after Los Roques, if he was prone to nightmares.

As disgusting as he felt washing away four days' worth of sweat, grime, and who knew what else, somewhere in the back of his mind he wished the Captain were there to help him. It wasn't so much about wanting to be naked with her, although that was likely part of it, but about having a moment while she took care of him a little. Ben shook the thought out of his head.

The woman had a ship to run; she couldn't be expected to be at his bedside nursing him back to health. That was, in all senses, Doctora's job. She was the doctor, and the Black Rose was the Captain. Besides, he had to admit that he didn't want to be coddled and babied as much as he wanted the roles reversed. What he really wanted was the opportunity to take care of her.

He sighed, splashing cool water on his face. But as much as he wanted that, he also didn't want her incapacitated badly enough that she would be bedridden and need nursing. He allowed himself a few moments to imagine feeding her spoonfuls of soup as she snuggled in her bed, gazing adoringly up at him, then pushed the thought away.

His mother always said he was a nurturer by design, and he supposed she was correct. She never cared for Anne, and he wondered what she would think of her firstborn son becoming romantically entangled with a Pirate Queen.

Ben was brought out of his musings by a scratch at the door and a whine. He opened it, and Mar bolted in, wagging her tail and depositing something large and feathery at his feet, looking awfully proud of herself. Ben gagged a little, but fortunately, nothing came up.

"Oh, a seagull! Thank you, Mar, it looks delicious!"

He stroked her silky ears while avoiding her attempts to give him kisses.

"Damnit, dog," an exasperated voice rumbled from the door.

Tobin sighed, picked the bird up by its webbed feet, and tossed it out a small porthole. Mar paid no mind to the quartermaster's grousing, her tongue lolling out the side of her mouth. Tobin cracked, a small smile lighting up his face, and patted the mutt before turning his attention to Ben.

"Welcome back to the land of the living. I trust you learned something important during your spree? Mainly, don't kill yourself by being polite?"

"I think I may have had that lesson forced through my thick skull, yes."

Ben paused.

"Are we away, or are we still in port?"

"We set out last night. We unfortunately had to vote without you. We will be heading to Tortuga to sell the gems on the black market. We think we'll get the best price there without drawing too much attention. Then we'll go to Panamá for Xiang. Your promotion ceremony will be the night after tomorrow. It's Good Friday today, if you are inclined toward Christianity."

"Not particularly," Ben said with a shrug. "Never really made sense to me, at least not compared to everything else out there."

Ben once again found himself wishing he could still his tongue. But no, words just kept coming. And unlike the Captain, who had a vested interest in keeping his company, Tobin was under no such obligation to humor him.

"Every religion I've ever read about seems just as bizarre as the last. And many of them are just so damned unfair, and all the gods seem so mean-spirited. At least the Greek and Roman deities have some personality to make them interesting, in addition to being awful..."

Tobin snorted quietly. "That's something you and she have in common, then."

"She told me her... tarter bwaylo? ...was instrumental in converting the indios in Colombia. She did not seem too proud of that. And she doesn't know enough Latin to get through a Catholic Mass somehow?"

Tobin nodded. "She..."

The quartermaster paused, sucking his teeth, trying to decide how much to tell the helmsman. Ben kept his mouth shut, hoping against hope that Tobin's tongue would loosen.

"How much has she told you about her home life?"

"I know about her... tarter bwaylo..."

"Tatarabuelo, her great-great-grandfather."

"I know that because of him, her family is landed gentry in Colombia, just below the ruling governors. I know she has a younger brother named Bernardo. She ran away and became a pirate at fifteen. She told me her birthday is in October, but not the specific date, and she will be twenty-five, so she has been at this for about ten years."

Tobin thought for a very long moment.

"The information I am about to give you does not go in that thing you and Felipe are writing unless she tells you herself. Actually, anything I tell you is not to be mentioned to her unless she tells you herself first. Am I perfectly clear?"

Ben nodded. Tobin stepped into the room, closed the door, and leaned back against it, crossing his arms. The eye contact was intense as he began to speak, but Ben didn't want to give him the satisfaction of breaking it.

"Her mother died giving birth to her younger brother. I believe she was three or four. Her father put all his energy into his heir, and she was basically raised by the servants, as a servant."

Ben imagined the Captain as a child, a dirty, disheveled ragamuffin being worked to the bone, wondering why her father no longer loved her as he doted on her little brother.

"That explains how she knows how much work goes into caring for horses," Ben commented quietly.

Tobin nodded. While Ben didn't say it out loud, he supposed that also explained all the scars on her back.

"And why she can speak the Romani tongue of the gitanos. Their servants did not practice religion except by celebrating the December and January holidays, such as la Inmaculada Concepción, Nochebuena, la Navidad... that is, Christmas, and Three Kings' Day."

"That's why she loves December."

Tobin nodded again, finally looking down at Mar and allowing Ben to relax.

"But she was functionally atheist for eleven months of the year for ten years. And being worked to the bone, while her little brother was treated as a prince, rather damaged any inclination she had toward believing any of it.

"And then, when her father realized he could use her to get his son a more advantageous standing by marrying her off, he forced a whole lot of very unfair roles and rhetoric on her in a very short amount of time in hopes of securing her an advantageous match... Please close your mouth. You look like you're going to vomit again. It's quite unsettling."

Ben realized his mouth had fallen open, not just because he was stunned Tobin was so freely giving him information for once, but because the information was so damned horrible. He snapped his jaw shut with a click of his teeth. He also remembered what Doctora had told him:

The Captain has also had a difficult life, and has experienced immense cruelty from people who were supposed to love and protect her.

"Why are you telling me this?" Ben asked.

Tobin shrugged. "We could say that it was to test your belief system in a roundabout way. I can't come up with tests off the top of my head as easily as the old bastard can."

Ben chuckled, and so did Tobin.

"I know you get concerned about reacting to things correctly, so rest assured, that was the reaction I was hoping for.

"And since you still seem intent on pursuing her even with the rules she has set for you, and yes, she did tell me-"

"I rather thought she would, since they were your idea to begin with."

Ben couldn't keep the comment from escaping his lips. It sounded a little more accusatory than he would have liked. Tobin must have heard it too, because he scoffed.

"It is in her best interest to..." he began, taking a step toward Ben.

Ben held up his hands, shrinking away from the other man.

"I understand where you're coming from, truly. I know you and Xiang have rules for your relationship, and I know that helps you both feel content with each other. And while I may not like some of her rules, her reasoning makes sense. I can follow rules that make sense, even if I don't particularly like them.

"However, I truly believe that I can become the man she deserves, and I would very much like the opportunity to try."

Ben was not sure what Tobin would say or do after such a declaration, but the quartermaster retreated, giving him space once more.

"Good man," he said quietly. "She... she was worried sick about you. She took some of the shifts to watch over you, hoping you would wake up."

Ben's heart fluttered in his chest. She had been at his bedside, but he had missed her shift.

"She didn't have to do that. She has a ship to run!"

"I know that. And believe me, she knows that. Everyone knows that. Even the dog knows that."

Mar cocked her head and wagged her tail, oblivious to the information she was supposed to know, but happy to have the men's attention again. Ben patted her head.

"The Captain must like you more than she hates vomit, and that is saying quite a lot."

He poked Ben in the chest.

"Do. Not. Fuck. This. Up."

Ben nodded.

"Now, hurry up and get dressed. She's dying to see you."

Eliza had seen to it that his clothes were laundered for when he woke up, he made his way next door to Doctora's quarters. He was greeted warmly by Talia in the hallway.

"Och! Benny boy! Good to see ya standing up straight!"

Ben nodded in acknowledgement. She lowered her voice slightly, even though it was still louder than a normal whisper.

"Everyone's been most fashed over ye!"

"Thank you, Tals. I am very sorry we have not had time to talk about any music..."

Talia waved her hand. "I've got it all sorted. Jean-Luc disnae ken yet, but he is also getting promoted. Ya dinnae have to speak on that if ye dinnae want to. I ken Felipe wants to say some since Jean-Luc is on his gun crew."

"Jean-Luc has a strong arm and a steady hand. He will do well!"

Talia nodded. "And dinnae forget thaa we also are celebrating Juanito's adoption by the crew. We dinnae need ta do much, but I would like to perform a wee song for him. D'ya ken 'A Health to the Company'? Wee bugger likes that one best."

Ben chuckled. "That's an odd choice for a lad his age, but if he likes it best, then that is the one we shall play!"

Ben and Talia entered the quarters the boatswain shared with Doctora and found the physician and the gunner sitting on her bed, grinding some mint leaves. Well, Felipe was grinding the mint, and Doctora was "guiding" him, her hands on his rippling arm muscles, her chin on his shoulder as they whispered and laughed quietly amongst themselves.

The Frenchman must have said something particularly funny, and Doctora pressed her nose into his cheek, giggling. They were so adorable together that it warmed Ben's heart.

Talia sighed loudly and cleared her throat. Doctora jumped, losing her balance and nearly falling off the bed. Felipe caught her effortlessly before she could fall too far, but if looks could kill, Talia would have been dead, cut into a hundred pieces, the pieces burned to ash, and her ashes drowned in the ocean.

"¡Ay! ¡Por Dios!" Doctora said, flustered.

Felipe pulled her up onto his knee and held her close to his chest. He once again looked as though he would kiss her when the door was quite literally kicked open.

The Black Rose bustled in carrying a serving tray with a bowl of porridge, a banana, a cup of tea, and a mug of grog. Xiang followed in her wake, and while Ben still didn't understand his words, he understood the intent.

*Captain, please let me carry that for you. Be careful! Don't spill the tea!*

The Captain's brown eyes shone with starlight as she presented the tray to Ben.

"Good morning, Benny!"

"Good morning, Captain," he responded quietly.

She looked tired, bags darkening the skin under her eyes. But she smiled happily at seeing her lover up and about.

"You must be fah-me-shed!"

Ben blinked and shook his head slightly. "What?"

Surprisingly, it was Doctora who corrected, still perched on the gunner's knee.

"Famished, Captain."

The Black Rose seemed momentarily taken aback by the physician being quite literally on top of Felipe, but she said nothing, even as her eyebrows shot up into her curls.

"Ah. Yes, indeed. I am quite hungry!" Ben stuttered.

"Very good! Then sit, sit, sit!"

Doctora vacated Felipe's lap and forced Ben to sit on her bed. The Frenchman pouted slightly as he also stood, taking the mortar and pestle with him. Talia rolled her eyes at him, shaking her head in exasperation, and he made a face right back at her, with a middle finger subtly scratching at his eyebrow.

Doctora scooped the crushed mint into the tea and stirred it as the Captain deposited the tray onto the table. Felipe offered Ben a folding knife to cut up his banana. The younger man accepted it and began to slice the fruit. After he finished, he picked up the spoon, scooped a hearty spoonful, and realized everyone was staring at him.

"What?"

That seemed to break the spell. The Captain cleared her throat.

"We...we were really, very worried about you, Benny. I believe I speak for all of us when I say that we are thrilled to have you back."

There were nods and sounds of agreement, and then Ben's stomach rumbled loudly. The Captain snorted, kissed Ben's forehead, and said quietly, "Come find me when you're done. We'll go over last-minute details for the ceremony."

"Yes, Star... Mistress. Yes, Mistress."

She patted his cheek and was gone.

"Tals, Xiang, and I should be going about our business as well," Felipe muttered, looking longingly at Doctora, who was watching Ben eat.

Ben handed the Frenchman back his folding knife. Xiang said something to Doctora, who nodded.

"Yes, plain noodles for him tonight. I know he has a taste for spicy food, but we can't risk his stomach getting irritated again."

The cook bowed slightly, clapping Ben on the shoulder.

"Xièxie, Xiang!" Ben said after he swallowed.

When they were alone, Doctora busied herself tidying her massive dresser, putting all the medical instruments into order. The physician turned, trying to casually wipe down a massive blade as she spoke.

"She was very worried about you, even if it didn't appear..."

"No, I could tell. She looked tired. For someone who likes sleep as much as she does, I'm honored she thought me worth sacrificing all that time she could have been resting."

Doctora smiled kindly. "I think you would be surprised by who all volunteered to watch over you."

"Hmmm?" Ben asked.

The physician pulled out her journal, opened to a page, and handed it to him.

Ben took the book and looked over the list of names in her lovely script. The Captain did early watches every evening. Felipe did most mornings. Each of the children. Arturo. Jean-Luc. Maeve. Daichi. Matilde. Femke. Andrew. Eliza. Li Mei.

Doctora pointed at the page. "Frank did a shift, so I think we may have finally gotten Felipe off wanting to fight him. And Anya did a rotation. Do you have any idea how hard it is to get her to sit still for that long?"

"That's almost two-fifths of the crew," Ben said quietly.

Doctora's eyes sparkled. "And many more were lined up if you didn't wake this morning. All volunteers, Benny. Nobody was forced to sit by your bedside. Everyone who was there wanted to be."

Ben could feel his eyes watering. "Really?"

"Really. I thought you would like to know that."

Ben took a shuddering breath. "That is really nice to know, thank you."

They smiled at each other for a long moment. Ben sniffed and wiped his eyes before handing her back the journal.

"I realize she is probably going to want to... demonstrate how much she missed you... but I don't think it's a good idea. We need to see how this food sits, and how your bowels take it. I definitely do not think you want to be hit with... shall we say, indigestion... while you are being intimate."

Ben cringed and shuddered. "Eww, no."

"If she seems inclined to do that this evening, tell her I suggested saving it for after the ceremony."

"I will be sure to let her know. Thank you for taking care of me."

She patted his cheek. "It's my job, but we are really happy to have you with us, Benny. We are all incredibly proud of you. Even if you might put the rules of politeness over your own common sense sometimes."

After he was done eating, Doctora sent him up to see the Captain with a handful of mint leaves to chew if his stomach felt sour. Ben ascended the stairs and quietly knocked on the door of the Captain's quarters. It opened, and the Black Rose was on the other side in her dressing gown.

"Am I intruding, Mistress?"

She shook her head, inviting him in.

"I'm actually very glad you came. Can I...ask you...a very strange favor?"

The door closed, and she immediately latched onto him. Ben wrapped his arms around her waist and sighed, content. The lovely plumeria lotion again wove a seductive spell.

"Doctora recommends we don't make love until after the ceremony, just to make sure my body is ready and nothing-"

She shook her head. "No... not that... although I have been missing you. I..." she sighed, bouncing on the balls of her feet. "I need a nap. I... I was wondering if..."

Ben blinked at her owlishly, but he waited for her to finish. Was she going to say what he thought she would say?

"I... was wondering... if... you would let me... take a nap with you?"

Ben grinned widely. "Really? I thought you were worried you would never sleep if you let me stay the night?"

The Black Rose threw up her hands, flustered, a blush creeping across her cheeks.

"When I fell asleep on your chest that night? I felt like I had an entire night's sleep in the span of a few hours. I don't know if it was you, the wine, or both. But I want to conduct an experiment to find out. I want to see how I feel after a two-hour nap with you. Nothing else. And since it's your fault I'm at a deficit..."

Ben stopped her with a kiss. She melted into him, and he held her close to his chest.

"I can assure you I would love nothing more. But you realize that I have spent the last four days asleep, and..."

The Captain pointed at a pile of books. "I anticipated that. My animal book is there, along with some others I think you'd appreciate. Don't worry, no more Don Juan stories... stop smirking at me like that, you awful walrus!"

Ben laughed, kissing her forehead. "I would be honored to take part in your experiment, my Starlight Princess. Shall I remove my clothes?"

She shook her head. "No, your clothes smell nice. Eliza used some rose oil. Felipe must have bribed her again."

She pulled up the covers and let Ben get into bed. He grabbed a couple of books and made a smaller pile next to the pillow.

"I swear more of his pay goes to her than to anything else."

"So you know he pays her to take care of Doctora's things?"

She slipped out of her dressing gown and joined him under the sheets. He ran his hand along her leg.

"I do now. But the arrangement had quite an explosive start. It was fairly soon after we got her and Talia off the *Leonard*, and she was still recovering. Felipe decided her work didn't meet his standards, and he shouted at her. Andrew had to intervene before it got too nasty, and he took Felipe to task for upsetting her. First time he ever stood up to the old goat."

She cuddled close, settling her head on Ben's chest.

"How did you end up involved?"

"Andrew brought it to me. I think he wanted to ensure that it didn't happen again and undo all of Eliza's healing. He didn't want to bring a formal complaint, just... an incentive to help Felipe remember."

Suddenly, Eliza pulling a weapon on James on Andrew's behalf made infinitely more sense.

"So what did you do?"

"I sat them down together, the three of them. I made Felipe work with Eliza so he could see what she had to do to get the desired results. Once he understood, they negotiated a routine and price. Andrew observed the whole proceeding on my behalf.

"Then, as a penalty for his outburst, I made Felipe add another fifteen percent to the amount they agreed upon. He is not generally the type to speak abusively to women, but he gets so blinded when Doctora is involved that he forgets other people also have feelings. Eliza doesn't know about the 'bad behavior' tax; she thinks it's a bonus for her excellent work. She can't disappoint her best customer, even if he is the cause of most of her headaches. And Felipe now knows not to shout at her again if he wishes to keep his tongue."

Ben chuckled, running his hand up and down the Black Rose's arm, observing the contrast between his golden wheat-tanned skin and her naturally occurring honey-bronze.

"And you came to that compromise at barely twenty years of age? My goodness, you really are a natural at this!"

She burrowed her face into his shoulder, but he still felt the heat on her cheeks as she blushed.

"That's enough talking. I would like my nap now. Please wake me in two hours."

Ben checked his watch before kissing her forehead gently. Then he opened her animal book to a section about birds and began to read.

Two hours later, Ben prodded the Captain.

"My Starlight Princess, it's time to awaken!"

She groaned, snuggling into his chest. He began kissing her cheeks while making exaggerated noises, preparing his fingers to tickle if necessary.

"Come now, Darling, you have a ship to run."

The Pirate Queen snorted, but kept her eyes closed.

"Very well. You leave me no choice!"

He unleashed a tickle assault on her that made her eyes snap open, and she tried to wiggle out of his grasp.

"I'm awake! I'm awake! Nasty old walrus!"

Ben chuckled, pulling her close and kissing her lips. She relaxed into him, her fingers curling into his shirt.

"So what last-minute details do we need to discuss about the ceremony? I thought we pretty well covered everything we needed to in that meeting with the other officers?"

She tapped his nose. "We don't. I needed an excuse for you to come up here for a few hours. Everything is handled. Xiang is going to make you some Saint Lucian seafood stew!"

She chuckled as Ben grimaced.

"He would probably make it better, and he wouldn't serve it to us if it didn't taste right."

The Captain nodded. "And you know we have our fair share of... shall we say, assertive crew members who would have told him immediately if it was not up to standard."

"Maeve."

"Among others. Tobin would say something to protect Xiang's reputation. Natsuki probably would not let him serve it at all. Giselle actually has a fairly refined palate; she is usually the first to tell if something is starting to go bad. It's a shame she has no talent for cooking herself. I don't know if it is a real job, but she would be a wonderful taster for royalty, ensuring their food was not poisoned."

"That's interesting! Has she been trained in any way? Or is it an inborn talent?"

"Mostly talent, but Doctora is training her to recognize medicinal herbs by taste and smell. I think Felipe suggested training her on poisons, but Doctora won't hear a word of it. She thinks it's too dangerous, and that, somehow, Juanito will end up dead."

Ben snorted, and the Black Rose also began to laugh.

"He would, wouldn't he? Either by accident or because he made her angry on the wrong day."

It seemed rather a dark thing to laugh about, especially given that Ben himself could have died, but it felt good to laugh. He realized she was speaking to him.

"I'm sorry, Starlight, could you please repeat that?"

She smiled shyly. "I rather like being your Starlight Princess, but you need to be sure you don't say it in front of anyone else. You almost slipped earlier."

She pulled herself out of bed and began searching for her clothes.

Ben examined her back once more, but instead of focusing on the crescent moon burn scar on her shoulder, as he normally did, he focused on the crisscross of Xs. Her own father...

"What are you thinking about, Benny?"

Ben shook himself. The Black Rose stood before him, fully dressed, looking concerned. Ben sputtered, remembering Tobin's words. Fortunately, his brain supplied him with an excuse, something he did, in fact, want to know the answer to.

"I was just curious about the results of your experiment. Was your nap satisfactory?"

The Pirate Queen scrunched up her nose and grimaced. "It was unfortunately quite lovely, and I feel very refreshed."

"Why unfortunate?" Ben asked with a catlike smile.

She laughed and pushed his face away. "Because I don't want to become dependent on you, obviously. You just cannot help but be a walrus, can you?"

Ben caught her hand and pulled it to his lips, gracing the back of it with a kiss. "Clearly, I cannot."

He winked up at her, pleased to find he could still make her skin flare with heat and her breath hitch.

"Trim your beard and mustache before your ceremony. It's getting long again, and I will not have my new navigator charting a course for pleasure looking like a ruffian."

"Yes, Mistress," Ben said quietly, taking her into another kiss. "Let me know if you require any further cuddles this evening," he added with a smirk.

The Captain snickered and shoved him out the door.

# Chapter 25

## Holy Histories

Ben's stomach recovered fully, and he was right as rain the next day. There was a palpable buzz of anticipation on the ship. From what Ben could gather, April, July, and December were the great celebratory months aboard the *Deception*. If his birthday had been any indication, this was likely to be an incredible party.

While the Mohammedan, Jewish, and Christian holidays being celebrated all seemed wildly different at first blush, the Black Rose and her crew made sure that everyone felt seen and heard. The crew had held an all-hands meeting on the way to Saint Lucia, presided over by Andrew, to develop a menu based on criteria from each faith.

Andrew had revealed a talent for planning large celebrations, his clear brown eyes sparkling with excitement. It had been quite a lengthy process, involving meticulous note-taking by Tobin. Eventually, the winning suggestion had come from Halima: a mutton curry. However, since rice was forbidden for their sect during Passover, Anya had requested the compromise of noodles and an unleavened flatbread.

Ben had been floored by how calmly everyone conducted themselves. Even Anya, who could be as rough and snarky as one would expect a pirate woman to be, had made her substitution request meekly, with the understanding that she could be outvoted. Andrew had been able to diffuse a few particularly heated interactions with gentle jokes, and all factions had worked together and compromised for the good of the crew as a whole.

The order of ceremonies was settled with great attention to detail.

First, they would drop anchor for the celebration so everyone could take part. Ben's watch from Campeche kept excellent time, so they would use it to restart the bells after everything was over, allowing Gerda to celebrate with her parents instead of minding the hourglass and ringing the bell.

Supper would be served after sunset to break the Ramadan fast. From what Ben gathered, the Mohammedan crew observed a modified version of their holy month of fasting, since travelers were exempt from fasting, but traveling was their livelihood.

After supper, the crew would adjourn to the deck. Representatives from each faith would tell the stories of their beliefs. Hamza and Aisha would represent the Mohammedan crew, Anya and Gerda the Jews, and Andrew and Matilde the Christians. Despite the solemnity of the occasion, Andrew's retelling of the Easter story had been interesting enough that all the non-Christian crew had banded together and demanded that he be allowed to tell it again that year.

Some members of the Christian contingent argued that he wasn't serious enough, and that the year before he had gotten sidetracked into different Bible stories that had absolutely nothing to do with the celebration at hand. Ben noticed Andrew kept glancing at Eliza, and every time their eyes met, she favored him with a smile, which seemed to bolster his confidence even as he was berated for being too silly.

After the stories, Ben would be officially promoted, finally receiving his pin. Someone else would be promoted to the new helmsman, and while it was officially a secret, Ben knew from Talia that it was to be Jean-Luc. The younger Haitian man had no idea.

Then there would be toasts, music, and dancing. Talia and Ben would begin by leading the crew in "A Health to the Company" to celebrate Juanito, with Felipe on his fiddle and Tobin on his drum. Then it would be a matter of playing crew requests until everyone decided it was time to pack it in. Talia had told Ben that the crew very much enjoyed the opportunity to stump their musicians, but she was confident that between the four of them, they would be able to triumph.

Later, Ben moved his few possessions into the room he would be sharing with Felipe. Or rather, into Felipe's massive pile of bric-a-brac. Ben was still not entirely sure if the man slept, and if he did, where. However, the gunner did make good on his promise, and from somewhere in the depths of his hammock, he pulled three long, sturdy hooks. In a trice, he had them hammered into the wall, giving Ben a place to hang his guitar. He also produced a medium-sized looking glass, which he hung on the third hook.

"Merci, mon frère," Ben said, looking at his reflection in the mirror. "Would you be able to teach me some French?"

"Oui! What would you like to learn?"

"I'd like to learn the song you were singing that night we helped Frida in Barranquilla." He hummed a few bars.

The gunner laughed. "Ah, yes, it is called 'Chantons Pour Passer le Temps'. It is about a woman who disguises herself as a sailor to follow her betrothed. They end up on the same ship, but do not recognize each other. They sail together for..."

He stopped, a strange look on his face.

"What?" Ben asked, concerned the older man was having an apoplexy.

"They sail together for seven years."

Ben snorted. "Seven years on the same ship, not realizing they were in love with each other? Isn't that quite the coincidence! And how does that song end?"

The gunner rolled his eyes and flipped Ben a middle finger before answering.

"They recognize each other for who they are when they get off the ship. Between the two of them, they made enough to marry and have a fortune together."

"Hmm. Interesting! It sounded nice when you sang it. I know you don't think much of your singing voice, but I quite enjoyed it."

Felipe chortled. "You were so drunk!"

He clapped Ben on the back, nearly knocking the younger man over.

Ben joined in laughing. "So were you!"

"Well, I will leave you to get ready. I must go see Maeve and suggest to her and Giselle that Jean-Luc might want to put some extra care into his appearance this evening."

Ben nodded.

"I will be back to fetch you for supper."

After the gunner left, Ben asked Tobin to borrow some items to trim his facial hair again. Normally, cutting one's hair and fingernails at sea was considered bad luck, but he wasn't about to dismiss a request from the Black Rose. Especially since she had specifically mentioned getting his face between her legs. Bad luck or not, Tobin gave him what he asked for, although the quartermaster suggested Ben get his own set when they were in Tortuga.

"That reminds me," Ben said quietly as the quartermaster gathered up the items. "I was wondering, and you can absolutely tell me no, but I was wondering if I could perhaps have a small emerald as part of my share."

Tobin opened his mouth, and Ben raised his hands.

"I know, I know, but... it looked like the Captain was thinking of an emerald ring, and... I... might like to have one made for her."

Tobin sighed. "You noticed."

Ben nodded.

"Her mother left her an emerald ring when she died. It... was taken from the Captain under very unfortunate circumstances that are certainly not my place to tell you."

Ben nodded again.

"I am not sure I can sneak one of these out, but I can try. With one condition."

"Which is?"

"That you hold onto it until such a time as she is absolutely certain she wants you the way you want her. She may see that as a marriage proposal, and I'm hoping by now I don't have to explain myself further."

Ben nodded.

"Understood. I... used my mother's sapphire to propose to Anne when it was clear I couldn't get out of it. And she never even wore it! She thought it was hideous. It was perfectly lovely, if a little plain. I should have taken it back and given it to one of my sisters. She never would have even noticed. But I never did."

The Englishman shook his head.

"But I understand. I will see if I can get it set, but I promise I shan't give it to her unless she expressly tells me she wants to be mine."

Tobin nodded.

"I know you're a man of your word. I'll see what I can do. It may not be very big or of fine quality, because it will be even more suspicious if you don't get any pay at all."

He extended his large hand. Ben took it, and they shook.

"Very good, thank you."

"Now go make yourself presentable. Can't have our ship's very first navigator looking like an upside-down broom!"

Once back in his new quarters, Ben made quick work of trimming his beard and mustache to the Captain's liking. He considered cutting his hair, but knew he likely wouldn't be able to do a good job. Besides, the Black Rose seemed to like his curls a little longer. He wondered if he would have enough for a short ponytail by July.

Once he had cleaned up, Ben opened his parcel from Barranquilla with the two neatly folded shirts. He pulled the red one out and held it up to himself, looking at his reflection. He frowned.

This wasn't right.

This wasn't right at all.

While in the shop, the color had looked brilliant on him, complementing his dark hair and making him look strong and full of swagger. However, it didn't feel right for this. It was too bombastic, too overpowering. The color threatened to swallow him whole, like a flame of anger, or of Hell itself. It made him want to hide in his hammock and never come out. This absolutely would not do.

He put it down and held up the green, and the Ben in the mirror smiled back at him. This made him look calm, cool under pressure, serene. His grey-blue eyes transformed into a forest of new growth, a garden for meditating, like Felipe had told him was common among the Buddhists.

Perfect.

Ben dressed, then sat in his hammock playing nonsense on his guitar for a while to soothe his nerves. There was a knock at the door.

"Come in!" Ben called, pulling himself to standing.

The door popped open, and Felipe entered, a big smile on his face, which immediately fell as he regarded Ben's fashion choices.

"Why do you not wear the red? Make a statement, remember?" He clenched his fist and flexed his massive bicep. "You are strong! You are powerful! You are a red rose that stands with Black Rose!"

Ben shook his head.

"That's the wrong message for this ceremony. I am…" He paused. He needed to phrase this carefully so as not to insult the gunner's intelligence. "I am not here for my fighting prowess, but I will help her grow her fleet with calculations and measurements. I am not a red rose standing with the black; that is you and Tobin. I am the green stem, a… a vine, a branch, supporting all of you, holding you up. I'm not some… some peacock who dares to put myself on her level when I have certainly not secured that place…"

He paused, finding the chink in the armor of the Frenchman's stubbornness.

"James would wear the red."

Felipe snarled quietly at the mention of the other Englishman, bringing to mind a shaggy, protective dog.

"You are correct. James would wear red to try to make himself her equal. Connard."

His demeanor shifted, his hazel eyes twinkling.

"Also, peacock? I thought you did not know the animals?"

Ben laughed quietly. "I've been reading the Captain's animal book. Very informative. The peacock illustration was quite beautiful, so it stayed in my mind."

Felipe nodded, brushing a loose thread from Ben's shoulder.

"They are très beaux in real life. Until you make one angry. Then they scream very loudly, and can be very frightening. They are the Devil's own pet parrot, and they can be as good a watchdog as any mastiff."

Ben stared at him for a moment before shaking his head with a smile. "I'm going to have to give you some more pages in the book, you crazy old goat."

Felipe shrugged.

"Anyway, demonic hell-birds aside..." He trailed off and stopped, shaking his head. "And another danger is how damn pretty you look with green eyes. You do not mind being called pretty, oui?"

Ben snorted. Part of him was positively giddy at being called pretty by such an attractive older man. While the Black Rose was his goal, knowing that Felipe felt the same way comforted him.

"You have my permission to call me pretty. Especially if it gives you an incentive not to rearrange my face too thoroughly during training."

Felipe laughed too, clapping Ben's shoulder.

"It is a good thing you are spoken for on this ship, because everyone would be throwing themselves at you. I think even Anya could be convinced to forsake Zsófia for eyes like that! Very dangerous indeed!"

Ben blushed at the compliment. He sighed, looking at his reflection in the glass once more.

"I will wear the red when I have fully secured her heart, and have the right to count myself as one of her red roses."

Felipe nodded.

"And when you fight James! You must wear it to fight James. Even if your relationship with her is not to your standard, James will not know that. Let him reach his own conclusion."

Ben nodded and finally looked over the gunner.

Felipe was wearing a deep black shirt of fine quality. He looked very good as well, the pink tint of his skin making him look healthy and virile even with the white streaks in his dark beard and hair. He was not wearing a headscarf for perhaps the first time since Ben had met him.

He had long, thick, dark, glossy curls that hung halfway down his back, tied into a ponytail with the small, light blue ribbon Ben recognized as coming from the bundle of pencils from Campeche. Every drop of his aristocratic blood came together to create an incredibly regal appearance, like a stately black lion. This version of Felipe was definitely making a statement, and that statement was aimed squarely at one person, and one person only.

"Doctora is right, you look very pretty in black!"

The Frenchman smiled, taking Ben into an embrace and kissing him on each cheek.

"Thank you, Benny! Now let us go make a navigator of you!"

Felipe and Ben entered the galley, finding it bustling. Everyone was trying to get last-minute things together while Xiang, Natsuki, and Li Mei were trying to wrangle everyone into some semblance of an orderly line for supper. Frank was in charge of the distribution of beverages, with two large bowls filled with very different drinks. One was a blood-red wine punch with fruit chunks floating in it. The second was the spiced milk for the Mohammedan crew. As Ben approached, Frank smiled up at him, looking incredibly overwhelmed.

"Hello, Frank. What do we have here?"

"This," he indicated the red liquid, "is a wine and orange punch. It's apparently quite common in the Spanish-speaking countries for Holy Week. I think she called it sangría.

"And this... I don't remember what they said it was called, but it's special milk for Eid. It is very sweet. It has coconut, rosewater, sultanas, and some spices I don't even know the names for. It brings to mind a posset punch, except without alcohol."

"May I have a taste of the milk? Please?"

Frank looked like he was going to argue, but then thought better of it. He poured a small portion into a cup. Ben drank it.

It was as delicious as it sounded. Ben could taste the warming spices: cinnamon, clove, cardamom, and ginger. There was also a distinct nutty flavor and the delicate floral note of the rosewater. Ben stared into his empty cup for a long moment, a million different thoughts fighting for a place at the forefront of his mind. He finally looked up at Frank, who stared back at him, concern in his watery blue eyes.

"Do you ever think about how incredibly lucky we are to be on this ship with these people?" Ben asked.

Frank's confused expression melted away, and he suddenly got a far-away look in his eyes.

"Yes. It's difficult and strange sometimes, but I like it here."

Ben didn't have to turn around to know who Frank was staring at. Li Mei must have entered his field of vision. Ben chuckled. He was certainly familiar with that feeling.

Speaking of which, he felt a light hand on his arm, and he turned to find the Black Rose smiling up at him. She gasped when she looked into his eyes, her hand traveling to cover her mouth.

"Oh my goodness..."

"Yes, Mistress?" Ben said with a smirk, raising his eyebrows, consciously trying to open his eyes a little wider than normal.

The Pirate Queen was dumbstruck as she looked into her soon-to-be navigator's face. The new light green shirt was very becoming on him, with his tanned skin and black hair, even though she preferred the blue that brought out...

His eyes.

His eyes were not the color she was used to when he turned to face her. As if by some enchantment, his eyes matched the shirt he wore, a sparkling sea green that she often saw when algae bloomed off the coasts of certain islands. The effect was striking, and damn if that awful walrus of a man didn't know it. The Captain cleared her throat and stood up straighter.

"That is a lovely shirt, Benny."

"Oh, very glad you like it, Mistress. Have you tried some of this... Eid milk?"

The Black Rose chuckled.

"I have. It's delectable, isn't it?"

Ben nodded.

"But you really must try the sangría!"

She took a cup from Frank's pile and filled it. She offered it to Ben. He put the used milk cup down and took the wine, taking a sip.

"There's rum in this!"

"Isn't it wonderful?"

The Pirate Queen tapped her cup to Ben's and smiled at him.

"I think you will love the curry, too! Xiang let me have a taste earlier."

She took his arm.

"Come, Benny, you now officially have a seat at the officers' table!"

They both nodded to Frank and got in the food line. Ben accepted his bowl of curry from Xiang with a "Xièxie" and gave Natsuki an "Arigato" when she added some noodles. There was a massive tray of flatbread for the crew to help themselves.

The Black Rose and Ben sat down with Talia, Tobin, Felipe, and Doctora. Everyone was dressed in their best. Talia was wearing a deep purple blouse that must have cost a small fortune, her blonde hair in tight ringlets. Tobin was wearing a shirt of deep, ruby red, and Ben was glad he had decided against wearing red himself.

While Ben's red shirt had threatened to swallow him whole in his reflection, Tobin's suited him, complementing the Black Rose's red blouse. They looked like a unit, two sides of the same coin, leader and enforcer. There was no way Ben could have stood next to Tobin without looking like a little boy wearing one of his father's uniforms.

Ben was surprised to find that Doctora was not wearing her usual widow's black with baggy pants, but instead a long dress of the deepest midnight blue Ben had ever seen. In fact, he would have thought it was black, except the physician was sitting next to Felipe, who was wearing true black.

Her hair was not in its normal tight bun, but tied in a loose ponytail with another length of the light blue ribbon like the gunner's. They were both in good spirits, neither wanting to take their eyes off the other if they could help it. Doctora's hand kept running through the Frenchman's ponytail, and he once again gamely pretended not to notice.

Ben took a bite of the curry and found it very good, even if he did not normally care for mutton. It was nice to have such good food again.

After supper, the crew filed out onto the deck for the religious side of the celebration. Hamza and Aisha agreed to go first, telling of the Prophet Mohammad while Aisha voiced the Angel Jibril. It was clear they had rehearsed the story together repeatedly, and they were quite engaging. Hamza had a husky voice almost as deep as Tobin's, and Aisha's light, airy voice complemented it well.

Next, Anya told the story of Passover. Ben had heard it before, as his younger brother William had wanted to be a preacher when he grew up, and the story of Moses and the Plagues of Egypt was his favorite to practice. Gerda's role was asking questions, although Ben got the distinct impression that they were missing a meal of some sort, as the girl was asking about bitter herbs and dipping their food.

However, it mattered little, as Anya was also a charismatic storyteller, which Ben hadn't expected given their interactions. The holidays brought something special out in everyone, truly.

Then it was Andrew's turn to tell the Easter story, and Ben immediately saw why the rest of the crew had demanded he represent the Christian contingent.

Andrew was hilarious. While Ben knew this from tattooing him, the man had quite a talent for imitation. Jesus spoke with Felipe's accent, while the voice of God was a pitch-perfect Tobin. Other characters, when introduced, were subject to a vote. Ben found himself nominated as the voice of Pontius Pilate.

Upon winning the vote, Andrew turned Pilate's speech into a song on the spot, much to everyone's delight, even Matilde's. Ben wasn't sure how accurate the impression was, but the effect was impressive nonetheless. Was it blasphemous? Likely, but Ben certainly didn't care. It was lovely to see all these people from disparate places with different beliefs coming together and sharing.

Matilde kept Andrew in line, and when he arrived at the Via Crucis segment, Andrew's entire tone changed. He told the story of the Way of the Cross with the gravitas of a ghost story, allowing the weight of Jesus's death to hang heavily in the air. However, to celebrate the joyous resurrection, Jesus rose from the dead complete with a French accent.

When Andrew finished, there were raucous cheers from the crew, regardless of their faith, or lack thereof. Andrew bowed, then indicated Matilde, who sheepishly bowed as well. Andrew took Eliza into a one-armed embrace, and she scratched under his chin as if he were an over-large golden retriever.

"Ye done good!" she said with a laugh, her blue eyes sparkling. "Even better than last year!"

He said nothing, but smiled widely before resting his chin on the top of her head, his goatee disappearing into her golden-blonde hair.

And then it was time for the ceremony.

# Chapter 26

## The New Navigator

A hush fell over the assembled pirates as they cleared a space for the officers. The Black Rose stood in the center next to a small table that held the box with Ben's new pin and two cups of sangria. Tobin stood to her right, Xiang and Talia beside him.

Talia had her flute, and Ben snorted as he recognized a soaring rendition of her inferior version of "Jolly Roving Tar." Ben caught her eye and stuck out his tongue. The boatswain's emerald eyes twinkled, and she scrunched up her nose, but did not miss a note.

Felipe stood to the Captain's left, Doctora by his side. Ben waited until the Captain indicated that he should approach, then stood in the space between her and Felipe, who clapped him on the shoulder as he passed. The Black Rose smiled radiantly, her eyes full of starlight, and Ben couldn't help thinking again how lucky he was to be on this ship with these people, about to accept a promotion from this beautiful woman.

He was finally going to have the title he had always wanted, and having it bestowed upon him by the woman he loved made it surreal. Her hand brushed his, filling him with warmth, and she spoke, her words carrying into the night.

"Amigos, tonight we celebrate! The sea we all love so dearly is a fickle mistress. Up until now, we have survived and thrived on sheer dumb luck, and the poor, taxed brains of three people who, in all honesty, should not be trusted to do this much math."

The pirates laughed.

"And while Talia, Felipe, and I have done the best we could, I am immensely pleased that those days are behind us!"

A great cheer arose from the assembled.

"For we have finally found a man who has not only joined our crew with great enthusiasm but who has the knowledge and skills we have been yearning for!

"To survive these waters, we need a man who can not only read maps and charts, but can follow the stars and the sun. We need a man who can not only tell which way the wind is blowing, but can tell how fast just by how it feels on his skin. A man who can read a shadow and a sextant with equal accuracy. A man who can correct a map from memory with the most astounding veracity!

"And not only is he good with charts and calculations. In his time aboard, Ben has proven himself brilliant with scheduling, despite how some of you felt about being trapped in the doldrums with a ship full of cows in tow..."

There was another laugh.

"He is a wonderful teacher, a steady hand at the helm, adaptable and willing to do what needs to be done for the good of the crew, whether that be helping serve a meal if the galley line is struggling, or allowing himself to be tied to a mast and punched in the face so we could sell a story of mutiny."

She opened the box, removed the pin, and turned to face him. She shimmered under the lanterns, ethereal. Ben did his best to imprint this moment on his memory forever, his heart soaring.

"Ben, in the short time you have been with us, you have made your mark on the *Deception*. You were likely days away from being awarded this position on a Royal Navy vessel, and you decided to join us instead. You are a true scholar of the sea, and I have no doubt that your skills will help us grow our fleet, as well as create new routes for our enterprising ships. We, your fellow officers and your crew, place ourselves in your capable hands, and we trust you with our very lives. With this pin, you are now an officer of the good ship *Deception*!"

The Black Rose delicately pinned the small wooden rose to Ben's breast, twirling the small black swallowtail ribbon around her finger. She smiled up at Ben before embracing him and pressing a kiss to each cheek. He wished she would give him just one on the lips, but knew she wouldn't. Not in front of everyone. Hopefully, there would be abundant kisses later. She dropped her hand, giving his a stealthy squeeze before handing him a cup and raising her own.

"A toast to our new navigator, Ben. May your charts be accurate, may your stars be bright, may your wits be sharp, and may your..." She stumbled briefly, seeming to change her mind about something in her speech mid-blessing. She cleared her throat. "And may our journey together under your guidance lead us to untold adventure and wealth! Hip hip!"

"Huzzah!" the crew yelled back.

After the cheering died down and everyone took a drink, it was Ben's turn.

"And here is to you, Captain! May your spine always be steel, may your heart always be gold, and may we always find the safe harbors we seek! Hip hip!"

"Huzzah!"

The Captain raised her hand, and the crew fell silent once again.

"Not only are we promoting Ben tonight, but we are also naming a new helmsman. For that, I am turning it over to Felipe."

There were whistles, catcalls, and good-natured boos, including a boo from Doctora, which made the gunner laugh. The Frenchman immediately slipped into his role as showman. He slowly walked through the crowd as he spoke.

"Seven years ago, we captured a ship. On that ship, there was a boy—scrawny, frightened, and alone. But he had a fire in his belly and a spirit that refused to remain chained. And now that boy is a man, as fine as they come!"

Felipe finally arrived at Jean-Luc's side. Despite Maeve and Giselle helping him look his best, the younger man still seemed surprised by what was happening.

"Jean-Luc! Jean-Luc, mon frère, you have developed the eyes of an eagle and the steadiness of a tortoise."

"And the mouth of a parrot!" Giselle yelled across the deck, causing the crew to chortle.

"And the mouth of a parrot!" the older man agreed with a hearty chuckle. "I am very sorry, Jean-Luc, she is not wrong! Although it seems to run in the family, ma petite fille!" he shouted over his shoulder.

Another roar of laughter.

"But it has been an honor to see you grow, and I know that this is but another stepping stone to your greatness. I am so, so proud of you, mon fils. So may your hand be steady, may your heart be true, may fair winds fill your sails... and may you continue to prove those who doubt you wrong. Especially your sister!"

There was a big whoop from the crew and a "Hey!" from Giselle. Felipe took Jean-Luc into an embrace and kissed the younger man on both cheeks before pressing their foreheads together for a long moment, as if attempting to transfer some talent and wisdom by osmosis. When they parted, Jean-Luc wiped his eyes and sniffled.

"To Jean-Luc, our newest helmsman!" Felipe roared. "Hip hip!"

"Huzzah!"

Jean-Luc hiccupped and laughed nervously, still trying to get a handle on his emotions.

"You all know I can't do fancy words on the spot as well as this old bastard can, so here's to the old bastard!"

"To the old bastard!" the crew yelled back, everyone howling hysterically.

Doctora took off her spectacles, tears of mirth streaming down her face. Ben also couldn't stop laughing, watching Felipe embrace Jean-Luc again, whispering in the younger man's ear. While the gunner wasn't nearly as vocal about his affections for Jean-Luc as he was about Alizée, it was apparent that the two had been through a great deal together and cared deeply for each other.

Ben remembered the story of how Felipe had posed as Jean-Luc's owner to buy Giselle, and how they had also freed Maeve in the process. Pulling off a stunt like that was going to forge a bond not easily severed.

The pirates tapped their glasses with those of people nearby, and everyone drank. The Captain nodded to Talia, who produced Ben's guitar, Euphonia. Tobin pulled out his drum. Felipe gave Jean-Luc one more bear hug before returning to the front. Doctora handed him his fiddle and bow. The Frenchman whispered something to Doctora, who went over to where Juanito was standing and put her hands on the boy's shoulders.

"Alright you lot!" Talia's voice rose above the din. "We still nae done our celebrating! Nae only have we our new navigator and new helmsman, but we also cannae have our April celebration without celebrating our fair company adopting our Juanito! Lad, every day ye survive is a miracle!"

There was a jovial tittering and a "hear hear" from somewhere in the back of the crowd.

"But we love ya, ye wee daftie, and we are most chuffed ye've managed another year with our fine crew. So this here is fer you, lad!"

She nodded to Ben, and he began to strum his guitar.

"Kind friends and companions, come join me in rhyme
Come lift up your voices in chorus with mine..."

The crew joined him on the chorus. Ben still didn't quite understand why Juanito was drawn to this song, but damnit if he wasn't going to perform it to the best of his ability. The next verse was about a dear lass whom the singer loves so well. Did he dare sing it to the Black Rose? He looked in her direction, and they locked eyes. She smiled and winked, as if reading his thoughts. He smiled back and returned her wink. That wink was as good as a command, and the Captain would always get what she wanted from him.

The crew sang another chorus, and then Juanito was invited to sing the last verse. The lad's voice was a light falsetto, untrained but still very sweet. Ben wondered if he would be able to convince the boy to try some vocal training to strengthen his voice.

As if taking a cue from Ben, the boy took Doctora's hand and sang the last stanza to her. The physician looked as if she would cry, clasping her other hand over her heart. As frustrating as she found Juanito, their bond was palpable and incredibly sweet.

"If ever we should meet again, by land or by sea,
I will always remember your kindness to me."

There was a great cheer before the crew sang the last chorus together. After they finished, there was thunderous applause. Doctora embraced Juanito and kissed his forehead. He snuggled into her, looking quite pleased with himself. Felipe raised his hands to quiet the crew.

"In honor of our Juanito turning the lucky age of thirteen, and his path to becoming a man, I have a gift!"

There was an "oooh!" among the crew.

"Felipe gives the best presents!" Talia whispered into Ben's ear. "Ye didnae get one on account of being new to the crew, but he still gave ye a right lovely promotion speech. He worked on that for days! He bought me my flute for my last birthday, but he also owed me because I lent him some money to buy Doctora that there dress. He was short after paying Eliza extra for an experiment gone bad. Half the crew ended up covered in red ink!"

Felipe had been speaking the whole time, and as Ben focused back on him, he seemed to be doing a card trick. Juanito chose a card, handing it back to Felipe. Felipe rolled up his sleeves, flexing with a wink at Doctora, before rolling them back down. He took Juanito's card, put it into his own black shirt at the collar, and pushed it down the sleeve until a chain dangled out at the wrist.

"Oh, mon Dieu! What is this? Be a good boy and pull that for me."

Juanito did as he was told, and from Felipe's sleeve he pulled a small watch. The boy was awestruck, and another great cheer echoed into the night. The gunner smiled widely.

"Joyeux anniversaire, Mijo. To time well-spent, and joyous adventures to come!"

The watch was very similar to Ben's, simple, small, silver, with an hour hand and a minute hand. Ben could also see that it had an ornate engraving of the letter J on it. Juanito embraced Felipe around the waist, and the Frenchman ruffled his hair.

When the boy let go, Doctora put her arm around Felipe's waist, and they hugged as well. The gunner lightly brushed the physician's forehead with his lips before moving back to stand with the other musicians. Ben was quite literally shaken from his thoughts by Talia.

"Benny! As our new navigator, ye get to choose our next song!"

Ben glanced up at the Black Rose, and immediately knew which song he wanted. He had always wanted to play it for the woman he loved. When he had tried to play it for Anne, she had stood up and left the room, leaving him to perform it for a pair of maids and one of the butlers. While they had politely applauded at the end of the song, Ben had cried himself to sleep alone that night, having been once again locked out of the room he was supposed to share with his wife.

And while the fear that the Captain would react the same way was still there, he had to push against it. She might not love him yet, but she saw value in him. They all did.

He had to try.

"Do any of you know a song called 'Waly Waly'? Sometimes it's called 'The Water Is Wide'?"

Tobin shook his head, as did Talia, which surprised Ben, since he was fairly certain it was a Scottish song. Felipe raised his hand, his eyes still glued to Doctora, who was examining Juanito's watch.

"Is it this one?"

He hummed a few bars, and Ben felt like he could kiss the Frenchman.

"Yes! That's exactly the one! Do you know how to play it?"

"But of course, mon frère," he said with a wink. "I shall come in on the second verse, oui?"

Ben nodded enthusiastically.

"Perfect!"

He turned back out to the crew, taking a deep breath. He could do this. It would not go terribly. She will appreciate it. She will appreciate it. She will...

"Oh the water is wide, I cannot cross o'er,

And neither have I wings to fly.

Build me a boat that can carry two,

And both shall row: my love and I."

He tried not to stare at the Captain as he sang, he truly tried. Especially when Felipe's fiddle came in on the second verse, a hauntingly effective counterpoint to the bright notes of Euphonia. The Pirate Queen had her hands clasped under her chin. He moved on to the next verse.

Was it his imagination, or was she getting closer? No, she certainly was moving toward him, transfixed, her cheeks flushed as if they had just escaped to the cleaning closet for a quick fuck again. Maybe she was thinking about it. He had to keep going, but she was responding to his song exactly as he had hoped she would.

The Captain was so close now. He ached to put his guitar down and take her into his arms, but he knew he couldn't, lest she knee him in the groin again like that fencing lesson back in March. The Black Rose reached for him as if in a trance. Her hand touched his cheek and guided his face down toward hers. Was she going to kiss him in front of everyone? Would she get angry and blame him if she did?

Ben panicked and very gently blew a puff of air in the Black Rose's face. As childish a response as that was, it seemed to be exactly what was needed to break her out of her rapturous state before she embarrassed herself. She snorted and shook herself, coming to her senses and realizing where she was. She recovered quickly, kissing Ben on the cheek before turning to her crew.

"A most beautiful and excellent song from our new navigator, yes?"

A great cheer went up among the pirates, and Ben caught her hand. He brought it again to his lips, gracing the back of it with a delicate kiss while allowing her a long moment to look into the light green his eyes had become. He was immensely pleased that she shuddered with desire. If she hadn't planned to ask him to her quarters after the celebration, she was very likely to now. She smiled and turned away.

"Those are not the words I know," Felipe whispered when the Black Rose retreated.

"There are a few versions, but I was certainly not going to try to seduce her with a sad one," he said as quietly as he could to avoid Tobin overhearing. Even if Tobin begrudgingly accepted Ben as the Captain's lover, he still didn't want the quartermaster to hear him use the word "seduce".

Felipe laughed and clapped the younger man on the back.

"Oui, very good choice. You certainly left her wanting. Look at her!"

Ben hazarded a look at the Pirate Queen and found her taking large gulps of the sangria as she fanned herself with one hand, still watching him intently. He caught a tiny, naughty smile before she raised her cup again.

Oh, yes, she wanted him. Badly.

Excellent.

Next they played a song for Jean-Luc that Ben didn't know, but Talia and Felipe did, and Ben did his best to stomp along to Tobin's beat.

The party lasted long after midnight, and as things were starting to wrap up, the Black Rose approached Ben, her cup tight in her hands. She was swaying slightly.

"Benny," she whispered, "after everyone's done cleaning up, put your guitar away and then come up to my quarters."

"Yes, Mistress," he responded with a smile.

She gave him a wink and disappeared toward her room. Hopefully, she wouldn't fall asleep without him.

After everything was cleaned up, Ben went down to his room to deposit his guitar and run a comb through his hair. Fortunately, there was nobody else about, and he scurried back up the steps to the Captain's quarters. This was already so much easier.

He knocked lightly, and the door opened, a hand pulling him into the room. The Captain immediately attached herself to him, standing on her toes, her mouth searching for a kiss, which Ben gladly gave her. He had rather hoped she would change into her sheer white robe, but no such luck.

However, she had removed her cincher, so the fabric of her red blouse hung loosely from her frame. She had also lit her candles in the small lanterns again and was burning a long stick of incense. It gave her quarters an earthy, heady scent that made his blood run hot. They parted, and he pressed another kiss to her forehead as she laughed.

"Thank you for your prudence earlier," she said, burrowing into his embrace.

"It was certainly one of the most difficult things I've done recently, and that's saying quite a lot!" He nuzzled her forehead with his cheek. "You looked like you were under a spell!"

"That was a beautiful song. And you sang it directly to me. How did you think I would react?"

Ben shrugged.

"I wasn't sure. Your reaction was better than the last time I attempted to play it for the woman I was... entangled with. Much better."

The Black Rose rolled her eyes and sighed.

"That awful woman." She gently touched his cheek. "She didn't deserve you in the slightest."

She pressed a kiss to his lips, as hot as the red picante sauce from the elote in Mexico, burning, searing. Ben tangled his fingers in her curls as she opened her mouth and her tongue went exploring. Their bodies pressed close together, and she reached down and grabbed his cock, fondling him through the fabric of his trousers.

When they parted, she kept a firm but gentle hand on his manhood. They sat on the bed, sinking into her soft sheets, shimmying out of their clothing. Once the barriers were removed, they crashed into each other again, kissing hungrily.

"Navigator, please chart us a course for pleasure!" the Black Rose purred.

Ben twirled one of her curls around his finger, his mind racing as he considered what he wanted.

"When you say you don't want anyone on top of you, what do you mean by that?"

The Pirate Queen blinked, entwining her fingers in his.

"Isn't it obvious? I don't want a man on top of me. My chest... pressing down... I don't like feeling like I can't breathe."

She put a hand on her sternum, looking very uncomfortable. Ben thought for a moment. That was most unfortunate, as he had been thinking recently about how badly he wanted to make love to her as a proper gentleman ought. If he couldn't put weight on her chest, that would not work at all. He mentally replayed all the ways they had fucked, trying to think of what to do instead.

The Captain rolled over onto her stomach next to Ben. She crossed her arms under her chin, cocking her head, and watched him like an inquisitive cat, one foot popped up into the air. Her breasts pressed against the fabric of her sheets, and his loins stirred with need. That gave Ben another idea.

"Well, what if... what if you were lying on your stomach... just like this... and I took you from behind?"

The Black Rose looked pensive.

"I'm not sure. It might be good because I could lean up on my elbows so I can breathe better... We can at least try it."

Ben nodded.

"If you don't like it, we will stop immediately and I will think of something else."

"Very well."

Ben rolled over, allowing the Captain to occupy the space he vacated. She scooted over, pulling a pillow down to support her upper body. She glanced over her shoulder with a welcoming smile. Ben chuckled and got on his hands and knees, crawling over her, growling quietly. Again, her scarred and healed back was laid out before him, and he placed whisper-soft kisses on the injuries he imagined had hurt the most.

He arrived at her bottom and again fought the urge to slap it, to make her delightful, delicious flesh jiggle. He instead took the cheeks into his hands and gently squeezed them, causing the Pirate Queen to chuckle. Ben straddled her backside. She was slick with desire, and she purred low in her throat, a counterpoint to his growl.

"Whenever you're ready, Benny."

Ben nodded and slid into her, meeting no resistance. He held her waist as he began to thrust, the primal desire to smack her backside only getting louder in his brain.

Then the Black Rose did something unexpected.

She crossed her legs.

The change made her channel all the tighter around his cock, slightly limiting his range of motion. It was divine. Ben paused, getting his bearings, willing himself not to release, as that likely would have been the end of his lessons.

But she moaned, her head falling back. Ben leaned forward on his fists, finding his rhythm, kissing a line up her back, trying his best to stay off her. The Black Rose was very vocal this evening, making the most beautifully obscene noises. She turned up to him.

"Benny... ¡bésame! Kiss me."

Ben leaned down, still keeping his weight on his knuckles, and made contact, the whole of his chest covering her back. She turned and caught his mouth in a sloppy kiss with lots of tongue.

"May... may I pull your hair?" Ben asked quietly into her ear.

The Captain nodded, biting her lower lip. Ben slowed, adjusting his stance slightly before taking a large handful of her curls and pulling them gently but firmly. Her head fell back with a smile and a groan that was nearly silent. Ben chuckled to himself, pleased that this was working in his favor. He licked her neck the way she liked, and she began to pant as her legs tightened around him again.

"Benny, this is so... so good... please, harder! And faster! Please!"

Ben did his best to do as she asked, but it was becoming very difficult to keep himself from release. He paused again, willing himself to calm down. The tight slide inside her, how close he was able to get, the taste of her skin, and the thrill of victory, of finally achieving something he had set out to do over ten years ago.

He had finally made navigator, and part of his reward was getting to fuck this spectacular woman. His pleasure receded slightly, and the Black Rose wiggled her hips. She gasped as something hit the correct spot within. Ben knew what he had to do.

He began to thrust into her again, pulling her hair with one hand while steadying himself with the other. He felt the Captain tremble under him. She cried his name again, arching her back as her whole body shook. Thank the gods, he wasn't sure how much longer he would have been able to last.

He pulled out, and as soon as the air hit his cock he exploded onto her backside. He gasped for breath, stroking himself, letting his seed drip onto her honey-bronze skin. He exhaled before cleaning the Captain up again. She waited for him to finish, and he pressed a kiss into the center of her crescent moon scar.

"Excellent, Benny. Well done as usual. Cuddle with me a few minutes before you go."

Ben lay down next to her, pulling her close again. The Black Rose yawned.

"Oooh goodness!" she muttered, covering her mouth.

Ben stifled a responding yawn. The Captain's head fell forward, tapping onto his chest, and she pulled it back up with a snort.

"You have to go, please. I'm falling asleep. Surely you must be tired, too."

"Drained in all manner, Mistress. Are you sure I can't stay and help you sleep?"

She frowned, pouting slightly.

"And what was one of our rules to keep naughty walruses in line?"

Ben sighed. "I leave when you tell me," he responded flatly.

She put her hands on his cheeks and gently squished them together as though he were a puppy.

"But tonight you get to sleep in your own room! And it's right at the bottom of these stairs! Isn't that wonderful?"

Ben grumbled quietly. Maybe he should have let her kiss him in front of everyone. Ben imagined the whole crew cheering as they kissed. However, that musing quickly turned to horror as a voice from nowhere that sounded suspiciously like Anne's shouted, "Wait a minute! He isn't a true navigator! She's only promoting him because he's her bed pet!"

A chorus of voices, including Mr. Fulton, Ben's brother Nathanial, Lieutenant Thomas Blackwell, and Captain Reynolds, joined in the shouting curses and insults. The crew raised their swords and guns, crying, "Mutiny! Mutiny! Mutiny!"

"Benny!"

Ben felt light slaps on his cheeks and shook himself, finding the Captain holding onto his face, her eyes searching his in panic.

"Your eyes went so grey they were nearly white, and you were muttering something about mutiny. What is happening? Is this like Los Roques again?"

He had his hands locked onto her shoulders, digging into her soft skin. He flexed his fingers to release her before taking her into his arms. His breathing was ragged, and he took a deep, calming breath. Her hair smelled like coconuts and flowers. He could see the incense had burned down to the stub. He could feel the Captain's heart pounding against him, and she was also shaking. Shit, he'd given her an attack of nerves as well. That broke him the rest of the way out of his spiral, even without having to name things he tasted and heard.

"No, Mistress, I'm sorry. No, no mutiny afoot. You know Tobin and Felipe would suss it out before anything happened. I..." He took a deep breath and let it out slowly. "I suppose I am much more tired than I thought. It was a very long day."

The Black Rose nodded, rubbing her cheek into his chest.

"And you're still recovering from being sick, even if you performed very well in all aspects. Doctora said it might take a bit to build your stamina back after a hit like that."

Ben nodded, kissing her forehead. As much as he hated to admit it, keeping their relationship in the shadows was likely for the best. It still hurt tremendously, though.

"Thank you for the lovely evening, Starlight. I will do my very best for you in my new position."

She handed him his shirt, and he slid it on, the fabric cool against his skin. She smiled again at his sea-green eyes.

"I know you will, Ben. I have every confidence in you. I would have even more if you went downstairs and went to bed. Tomorrow is your first day as our navigator, and we need to chart our next courses after we're done in Tortuga. So give me another kiss, and please get some sleep."

Ben complied, and she rubbed the tip of her nose to his before putting a light hand on his backside and pushing him out the door.

# CHAPTER 27

## A COVENANT OF CONFIDENTIALITY

When Ben arrived downstairs to his new room, he found somebody waiting outside his door. They were seated on the floor, but rose to their full height, which was nearly as tall as Ben, Tobin, and Felipe.

Zsófia.

"Oh, hullo, Zsófia. Can I...?"

She indicated the door.

"Privately? Very well, after you."

Once they were inside, Zsófia turned, and Ben realized in that moment that he had never heard her speak before. Her voice was rich and deep, as if a dense, misty evergreen forest could speak. She spoke with the same Polish-Lithuanian accent as Anya.

"Benny, I know this is... awkward... but I wanted to make sure you have... no designs on taking Anya from me."

Ben felt as though he had been kicked in the head and was momentarily perplexed. Where on earth would she have gotten that idea?

"No? Why would I...? I mean, she obviously loves you with all her being. And I have the Cap..."

Ben slapped a hand over his mouth, the odd daydream of mutiny sending a few bubbles to the surface. He coughed and stood up straighter.

"No, I am not interested in Anya."

Zsófia breathed a sigh of relief.

"Felipe... the old bastard is too loud when he is excited. He said something earlier about you convincing Anya to forsake me, and I... I overheard. The door was open. You must understand, I... she..."

Ben raised his hand as if swearing an oath.

"I can assure you, the very last thing I want to do is destroy your family."

Zsófia swallowed hard, her hands fiddling with the ends of her long, dark hair.

"May... may I tell you a secret, Benny?"

Ben blinked. He was fairly certain this was the first time he had ever spoken a full sentence to Zsófia, and she wanted to tell him a secret. Why did most of these pirates just seem to trust him implicitly? It was so odd.

He realized Zsófia was staring at him, awaiting an answer.

"I'm sorry. Yes, if you would like, I will keep a secret for you."

She nodded and spoke so quietly that Ben could barely hear her over the creaks and splashing of the ship.

"I... I was born a man. But I have always felt that I was meant to be a woman. I will spare you most of the details, but Anya loved me as a boy, and as a man. Even after I told her who I really was, she still wanted me. She faked her death for me. She was thrilled when we had Gerda, after I began to live as a woman. But twelve years is a long time, and I... I worry sometimes... that she would love me more if I had remained a man. And she took a shift at your bedside when you were ill..."

"So when Felipe made the jest about me being able to take her from you, you were worried Anya would leave you if a more manly option presented itself?"

Zsófia bit her lip and nodded.

"Well, I hardly think most people would find me an acceptably masculine option, but please believe, nothing you said has changed the fact that I would not want to break up your family. You both clearly love each other, and you are raising Gerda well."

Zsófia let out a slow sigh.

"Yes, she is a good girl. She is the best of us. But it doesn't bother you? That I was born a man?"

Ben shrugged and tried to speak as reassuringly as he could. Even if society believed there might be something wrong with this person, Ben couldn't see how Zsófia's happiness in being her true self was any detriment to him and his life.

Zsófia was an excellent romantic partner for Anya, a wonderful parent to Gerda, and, unless she actively pulled a pistol or knife on Ben, she was no threat to him. And her love for her wife meant she would not be competing with him for the heart of the Black Rose. All of those factors meant Ben could focus his attention on the real menace: James.

"I don't see why it should. Being free to live the way you want seems to be the thesis of this fleet, don't you think? I would presume Doctora knows, and probably Felipe and the Captain. If they don't find a reason to be worried, then neither do I."

Zsófia looked like she might cry. Ben realized with a pang that this conversation probably didn't normally go very well for her. He patted her on the shoulder and smiled.

"But I have my own romance to pursue, and Anya is very much not my type."

Zsófia smiled back, a genuine grin, thinking of her wife.

"I can see what you mean. Anya... she is very intense. While I know you have a taste for powerful women, I can see where a line might be drawn. Thank you."

"Of course. You have a beautiful family. It's very sweet to see."

"Thank you, Benny. And congratulations again. You are already a great officer."

Zsófia clapped Ben on the back before slipping out into the hallway, leaving Ben alone in his new room.

# SUPPLEMENTAL

## ANYA, ZSÓFIA, AND GERDA'S TALE

*(Excerpt from The Chronicles of the Deception)*

*Preface, on the nature of names: Let it be known that Zsófia entrusted us with the name bestowed upon her at birth. After much deliberation, it has been stricken from these pages. That man died long before the woman we know ever set foot upon the Deception. He remains buried in the old country, and we honor the wife, mother, and gun crew member who entrusted us with her story.□*
*– BRH, FdC, & R*

Preface, on the nature of the interview: Unlike the accounts given thus far, this was an impromptu session, so no questions were gathered beforehand. Anya and Zsófia were assisting Felipe in sharpening blades in the armory, and I happened to wander in with the folio. They graciously agreed to tell their story as they worked, answering questions as they arose.

While they may appear standoffish, that is merely the stoicism of their home-land, a fact confirmed by multiple members of the crew. Do not mistake their silence for shallowness; their devotion to each other, their daughter, and the family they have found aboard the *Deception* burns brightly even under the ice.
– BRH

Anya and Zsófia were born in Poland-Lithuania, in a tiny village that rarely appeared on official maps. Their families were incredibly close. Anya was born first, and the two were betrothed the moment Zsófia was born a boy three weeks later.

Zsófia felt from a young age that she had been born into an incorrect body, a feeling that grew more suffocating with each passing year. While she fought an internal war, Anya fought an external one with the neighborhood children. While other girls focused on learning how to be good, traditional wives, Anya preferred exploring the wilderness and collecting dead creatures. She amassed an extensively macabre collection of pinned beetles and butterflies, as well as her own faltering attempts to preserve the remains of mice and birds.

While the other children were cruel, Zsófia served as Anya's stalwart shield. Even as she defended her friend, by the age of fourteen the weight of the masquerade had become unbearable. She began looking for a way to leave the struggle behind.

The turning point came one day after an altercation with the biggest, meanest boy in the village, who had taken Anya's jar of freshly caught butterflies and smashed it, cutting the poor creatures to ribbons. Zsófia came fiercely to her defense, standing victorious with a bloodied lip and bruised knuckles. In the aftermath, Anya kissed Zsófia. Anya claims it was merely the heat of the moment, that seeing Zsófia defend her so passionately awakened a desire within her.

But for Zsófia, it was a lifeline, a tiny spark in her chest that filled the void and inspired her to stay alive. From that day on, they became inseparable: the "boy" who felt dead inside, and the girl who thought dead things interesting and beautiful. Their families delighted in watching the two fall in love, unaware that the wedding, slated for the day after Zsófia's eighteenth birthday, would change everything.

As Zsófia's eighteenth birthday approached, the mask she wore felt more like a noose. As much as she loved Anya, the weight of it was unbearable. She refused to let the woman she loved enter into a union built upon deceit. On the night of Zsófia's birthday, the night before their wedding, she slipped over to Anya's house. She coaxed her bride-to-be out for a walk, and they made their way to the river. On its banks, with the rushing water concealing their conversation, Zsófia confessed her truth to Anya: that the "man" the village had celebrated that day did not exist. She was a woman who loved Anya too much to lie any longer.

Anya did not so much as flinch. For a woman who liked to look beneath the surface to see what was real, this was no different than removing the feathers from a bird and replacing them with different ones. She apparently passed through an incredibly odd phase while teaching herself animal preservation. She did not care about the shape of the vessel, so long as the heart within it belonged to her. Zsófia was the only person in that godforsaken town who did not find her off-putting or strange, and Anya would be damned if she let something so silly keep them from being happy together.

The next day, the pair wed with the blessing of their families and community. Despite some initial trepidation at occupying the role of "husband," Zsófia went through with consummating the marriage.

One might expect that Zsófia's struggles with her physical body would cause issues in the bedchamber, but that does not appear to have been the case. Zsófia admitted that being so physically close to someone who loves her so completely is a most magical experience. Even after twelve years, their flames burn brightly for one another, and on each shore leave they seek out accommodations in which to indulge each other's charms.

Anya wishes they could do so more often, stating that it is the only thing that makes her consider heeding the Call of the Land. Yet both understand the peril they face. To live as they wish, to be freely themselves with their daughter, they require a community willing to protect them as they are. Their deepest wish is to find a sanctuary on land with some of their chosen family from aboard the *Deception*, people they can trust to guard their peace. As the women spoke of their desire to create such a community, Felipe stopped sharpening the blade he was working on. He fell oddly silent, his hazel eyes somewhere else entirely. It appeared the old bastard had found another puzzle to solve.

Returning to their tale: the next day, at their wedding feast, they presented a united front. Zsófia declared that she wished to live as a woman, with Anya steadfast by her side.

The reaction was as disheartening and brutal as one might expect.

Zsófia's own brothers, fueled by a misguided sense of honor, dragged her from the room to the banks of the very river where she had revealed her true self and found comfort and acceptance with her wife. They beat her until her blood stained the water, then left her as a feast for the crows.

When the brothers returned, righteous and silent, something snapped inside Anya. The quiet, strange young woman was filled with a fierce rage. She reached up and tore the collar of her dress over her heart, performing the Kri'ah—a Jewish rite of mourning rooted in the story of Job. It is an act of holy anger, in which one symbolically rends the vessel so grief may leave and the strength of the True Judge may enter. She explained that normally one tears the right side for children and partners, the left side being reserved for mourning parents; she tore the left side to demonstrate the depth of her sorrow.

"If Zsófia cannot live as she wishes," Anya screamed defiantly, "then I have no wish to live at all!"

She fled to the river, intent upon following Zsófia to the depths. But it seemed a different plan had been laid for them, for a passing band of Romani had found Zsófia and were tending to her. They took one look at the young woman in the torn dress with the eyes of a warrior and immediately agreed to bring Anya with them. Zsófia believes it was for fear of what Anya would do if they refused. Regardless, they were both accepted into the caravan, leaving the only home they had ever known in the wagon's dust.

Zsófia's strength returned. At the coast of the Baltic, they bid their new community goodbye and set up a life for themselves. They posed as sisters, a convenient lie that allowed them to share a rented room and a bed without raising suspicions. For two years they built a life cleaning the homes of others, then retreated each evening to their sanctuary together.

This happiness was not to last, as it so rarely does. Their landlady barged in while they were in the throes of passion. The woman saw Zsófia's body, so there was no way to spin it. And even had she not, the evidence against the "sisters" would have been damning enough. With little more than the clothes on their backs and their meager jar of savings, they booked the first passage they could aboard a ship for the New World.

The crossing was arduous. In the belly of the ship, Anya became ill, wasting away, unable to keep even the smallest morsel of food down. Zsófia feared for her wife's life. The ship's doctor, a curt man more accustomed to amputating fingers than dealing with "woman troubles," dismissed it with a wave of his hand. However, the truth manifested soon enough: Anya was not dying, but with child. The doctor declared it a medical impossibility, a harsh lesson for the two women. He was blinded by his arrogance, so certain he was correct, that Anya and Zsófia both regard men in the field of medicine with a healthy distrust.

They finally arrived in Haiti, welcoming Gerda with the assistance of a fantastic midwife who, unfortunately, passed away not long afterward. Gerda was named for Anya's grandmother and is a source of great comfort to her parents. She blessedly carries little physically of Zsófia's family, favoring Anya's white-blonde hair and bright blue eyes. Like her mama, Anya, she prefers to keep her hair cropped close, while her mother, Zsófia, keeps her black hair long to her waist.

They came to the *Deception* about four years ago in another moment of desperation. Gerda, then only six, was beset by a vicious pox. Possessing little trust in the local male healers and even less familiarity with the local language, the family made their way to Port-au-Prince. Zsófia believes it was divine intervention that their paths crossed with Doctora, who took one look at Gerda and offered assistance.

Communication was a struggle, even for Felipe's extensive linguistic abilities. They resorted to pantomime and drawing in the dirt, but eventually Doctora convinced Anya and Zsófia to bring Gerda aboard the ship. They were further welcomed by the Black Rose, who addressed them in the language of the Romani who had kept them safe and healed Zsófia all those years before. The language barrier dispelled, they told the Captain their story as Doctora set about healing their daughter with salves and doses of an experimental "sleepy tea." Zsófia's true nature was accepted without so much as a sideways glance, and Gerda made it through her ordeal. The little family pledged themselves to the service of the crew that had saved them.

Today, Zsófia serves as a loader on the gun crew, lifting cannonballs with practiced ease. Anya has grown into a fighter whose ferocity is matched only by her devotion. They are both immensely proud of the education Gerda is receiving, knowing she would never have reached this caliber in Haiti, nor back home in Poland-Lithuania. The child's English is impeccable, and she writes in a finer hand than most adults. Felipe swears she has the makings of a boatswain, but for now she is content to observe and learn what she can as a child of the sea. She is only ten, after all.

Anya and Zsófia are another shining example of the world the Black Rose seeks to build. The world thought them broken and strange, and yet together they have built a home and a life of wood, oakum, and salt. May we all follow their lead, as crew members, as lovers, and as parents.

**Archivist's Technical Observation, RE: Physical Condition of the Folio (Alma, 2023)**: These specific pages of *The Chronicles of the Deception* show precise, intentional removal. The pages were cut from their original location toward the front of the folio, and the parchment was relocated further back among technical diagrams and schematics. Given the dangers of the era, it appears the authors created a secondary "vault" to ensure the safety of this particular family should the documents be seized. We are currently cross-referencing Roberto's private journals to see if we can find more information about this specific threat.

**Historian's Note (Phil, 2025)**: Anya and Zsófia chose the surname Wojciechowski, which means something akin to "joyful warrior" in Polish. It appears that Zsófia chose it as a gentle joke about Anya's legendary love of a good fight. On a personal note, I find their choice of name adorable, choosing to highlight joy above all else they endured.

**Marginalia Note (Mina, 2023)**: Reading this as a descendant of this crew is wild. My ancestors were documenting and protecting a trans woman's right to be herself in the 1700s. They really lived "trans rights" and "love is love" centuries before they were hashtags. So proud of my family!

# Chapter 28

## Charting a Course

The Captain approached Ben in the galley the morning after his promotion, all business. Despite their activities the previous evening, their almost-kiss in front of the whole crew had left her on edge, and she was stiff and overly formal in public.

"Benny, congratulations again on your promotion to navigator. I would like you to come up and get acquainted with our maps today. We need to plot our next course because Xiang is running low on his special ingredients."

Ben nodded, slicing thin ribbons of mango into his breakfast porridge. He matched her tone.

"Aye, Captain. I have to stop by my room for a moment, and then I'll be up."

"Good man."

The Black Rose slapped his back, but her hand remained on his shoulder a beat too long. Ben glanced up at her, eyebrows raised. She cleared her throat and withdrew her hand, her eyes darting to the next table over.

Juanito, Giselle, Toñiete, and Gerda were all watching the two adults interact with varying degrees of fascination. Juanito, who Ben knew was a romantic at heart, was deeply invested in what was happening. He had looked positively crestfallen when the Pirate Queen had not followed through and kissed Ben the night before. Since he had helped Ben learn the phrase "Veo todas las estrellas del cielo en tu mirada," Juanito knew exactly how their new navigator felt about the Black Rose.

Giselle seemed more interested in Juanito's reaction than in the flirting itself. Toñiete watched the Captain and Ben as though they were the subjects of an experiment, and Ben could almost see the calculations in the boy's eyes. Gerda was likely paying attention because they were the nearest people available to observe, though that only made them marginally more interesting than her orange.

"As you were," the Captain said, gently but firmly.

The children all became suddenly very interested in their porridge as the Captain walked away. Ben did his best to conceal his smile.

Ben arrived at the Captain's quarters some twenty minutes later, all business, as she had been. The Captain invited him in, opened the curtains to let in the sunlight, and spread the maps out on her desk.

The smell of old vellum and iron-gall ink felt like coming home.

Ben drew his spectacles case from his pocket, put them on, and bent over the first chart. Tiny writing bloomed into clarity beneath the smoky-tinted glass, and within moments he was lost in the work. He heard the Captain's breathing hitch, but paid it little mind. He had already corrected one of her maps. He would have to be vigilant with the rest.

The Black Rose, however, was floored.

The spectacles somehow made Benny, whom she already considered the most handsome man she had ever known, let alone bedded, exponentially more attractive. They were an unusual style, wrapping around his temples to his ears instead of perching on his nose like Doctora's. She had seen Felipe wearing a similar pair recently and now suspected the gunner had modeled his after Ben's.

Ben must have noticed her staring, because he looked up.

"Mistress?" he asked.

"Do you require spectacles normally?"

He shook his head. "No, but I find they help for reading, especially when I'm expecting delicate handwriting. Which, as it turns out, I was."

"Where did you get them?"

"I had them specially made back home in Jamaica when I was expecting a promotion. They were fortunately in my pocket when you took the *Starling*, because otherwise they would have been exceedingly difficult and expensive to replace. They stay in their case most of the time."

Then, just like that, he went back to the maps, tracing with his fingers, muttering under his breath, existing in a world that did not seem to include her at all.

The Pirate Queen felt heat curl low in her belly.

Those fingers had traced her skin. Those lips had said the most interesting things to her. Those intense eyes had seen the most secret and sacred parts of her body. And yet here he was, so engrossed in a chart that he was all but ignoring her.

She cleared her throat.

"Benny, I was fully prepared for this to be an entirely business meeting, but..."

He glanced at her over the top of his spectacles, and something in his expression undid her. She crossed the room, grabbed his cheeks, and kissed him with all the restrained passion she could manage. He kissed her back at once, hands finding her waist, mouth warm and hungry.

Then he pulled back, breathing hard.

"Mistress, do you want me to do my job, the job you just promoted me to do? Or do you only want to keep me as your bed pet?"

The directness of it made her pulse jump.

She pressed herself against him, stroking him through the fabric of his trousers. "Please?"

Ben shut his eyes for a moment, visibly mastering himself. "If I fuck you now, will you let me work afterward?"

The Black Rose nodded immediately, biting her lower lip.

"I promise," she said. "Those spectacles are something else entirely."

Ben gave a helpless little sigh, then caught her wrist and kissed the inside of it.

"Mistress," he said quietly, "this feeling you are having right now? This is how I feel every single time I see you."

"Then do something about it."

That did it.

He swept the maps aside in one impatient motion, the rolled vellum tumbling harmlessly across the desk, and seized her with a roughness that made her gasp. He turned her, bent her over the desk, and tangled one hand in her hair at the nape of her neck.

"Is this what you want?" he murmured in her ear. "Do you want me to take you right now, like this?"

"Yes," she breathed at once, dragging her trousers down. A moment later her shirt was on the floor. She arched against him shamelessly, rubbing her bare bottom back against his hips.

Ben lost the last of his restraint. He slapped her once.

The sound cracked through the room. She gasped and turned her head, eyes wide, and he immediately froze.

"Mistress, I am so sorry, I didn't mean—"

She reached back, grabbed his chin, and looked at him with pupils blown wide.

"Oh, Benny," she said, her voice smoky with lust, "if you're going to spank me, you need to mean it."

Emboldened, Ben gave another good slap, watching her backside jiggle. He reached down and grabbed the Captain's calf, bringing her knee up to rest on the desk, opening her up to him. His spectacles magnified her beauty. He reached between her legs. She was ready for him, but Ben wanted to toy with her a bit more. He slapped her bottom before sliding two fingers into her. She gasped and arched her back, pushing herself closer to him.

"Benny," she groaned, "more, please!" The Pirate Queen had one hand grasping the edge of the desk, and the other disappeared under her. Ben pressed a kiss into the crescent moon scar on her shoulder before using his free hand to tilt her chin up to look at him. Clearly, his spectacles were having quite the effect on her, because she made a quiet "ohhh" sound and shivered. The hand underneath her began moving at a much faster pace, and their fingers bumped.

"Benny, please fuck me!"

"Yes, Mistress," he breathed, letting his fingers slide out of her. He dropped his trousers to the floor and stepped out of them. He slapped her backside one more time before guiding his cock to her entrance; then he roughly grabbed her hips and thrust into her.

"Yes! Benny, please!" Ben found his rhythm first, before smacking her bottom as he thrust. The honey-colored skin was starting to turn red from the repeated slaps, but she moaned each time his hand made contact. The Black Rose looked back at him over her shoulder.

"Pull my hair again? Please?" Ben reached out and grabbed a handful from the back of her neck, gently pulling her back toward him as he smacked her again. "Benny!" The Captain shrieked, her body shaking, her hand rubbing her pleasure bud with lightning speed. Her inner muscles did their now-familiar flutter, and she released with a guttural sound.

Once he was sure she was finished, Ben pulled out, pulled the Black Rose off the desk, and spun her around to face him. He wordlessly pointed down at his throbbing cock. The Captain immediately complied, using both hands to stroke him. She sat down on the edge of the desk, working magic with her hands. Ben leaned forward and kissed the Pirate Queen fiercely, and she continued to roughly handle his manhood. He felt his body shaking, and he gently bit her lower lip as he shot his seed onto her legs and stomach.

Then, breathless and flushed, he kissed her once, found his trousers, and went immediately back to the maps.

Immediately.

The Black Rose stood there for a moment, still warm and bare and not entirely steady, watching him settle his spectacles back into place as though what had just happened had merely been an interruption to the true purpose of the morning.

She came up behind him and wrapped her arms around his waist.

"Why are you being so uptight today, Benny? Why do you want to get back to work so badly?"

The air in the room changed.

She knew at once she had struck something tender, something far deeper than irritation. His shoulders stiffened. His jaw clenched. He pulled off his spectacles and turned to face her, his face flushed with something much more dangerous than embarrassment.

"Because you gave me a job to do."

His voice rose sharply, and he flung a hand toward the maps.

"We have fifty people we are responsible for, and it reflects poorly on us if I don't do what I'm supposed to because I cannot seem to keep myself from between your legs. This is the first time I've been able to do what I was trained for, with the proper title. I need to be the best navigator the *Deception* has ever fucking seen, and even then, will that be enough for you? Or will I still be nothing more than your elaborate fuck-toy?"

The words hit her harder than she expected.

He dropped into the chair behind him as though his own anger had exhausted him, then struck the desk once with his fist.

"Benny," she said, moving closer.

He looked away.

Then her hand touched his face, and found it wet.

The sight of his tears knocked all the heat out of her in an instant.

She slid into his lap and stroked his cheek gently, wiping away the wetness with her thumb. His larger hand came up to cover hers.

"I apologize, Mistress," he said, his voice shaking, "but this"—he gestured toward the rolled maps—"is what I have wanted since I was a child. This always made sense, no matter what. This is what I love."

He was speaking faster now, words spilling out too quickly to contain.

"I love maps, and charts and calculations and sailing, and the sea and the stars, and—"

He broke off, swallowed, then forced the rest out.

"And I want to love you, too. And have you love me back. But you aren't letting me do either of those things. If you would let me do my job, or let me love you as more than just a cock to ride when you feel like it, I could be content. But you are giving me neither, and I don't think I can live like this. I... for fuck's sake, I don't even know your name."

By the end of it, he was openly sobbing.

The Pirate Queen pulled him against her and held him there, stunned by the force of what he had clearly been carrying for far too long.

"Ben," she whispered. "Oh, Ben. I'm so sorry."

He buried his face in her neck, and she could feel the hot dampness of his tears against her skin.

"You gave up everything you knew for me," she said softly, stroking the back of his head, "and I have not respected that nearly enough."

When his sobs had eased enough for him to breathe, she pulled back and cupped his face between her hands.

"Benjamin Harrington," she said, gentler than he had ever heard her, "allow me to reintroduce myself. My name is María Rosa Eliana Marcos-Gobernado. Henceforth, in private, you may call me Rosa, if you would like."

She held out her hand. He took it and kissed it reverently.

"And I really am from Cartagena."

That, somehow, made him cry all over again.

"I feel very stupid right now," he whispered between tears. "I should have been able to suss that out on my own, and yet it is so nice to finally meet you... Miss Rosa."

Rosa cradled his head against her shoulder and let him cry. She did not tease him. She did not rush him. She only held him, thinking more seriously than before about what, exactly, she had asked of him since bringing him aboard.

At last his sobs softened into sniffles.

"Let me ask you something, then," she said. "Do you want to end our arrangement completely?"

He shook his head against her hair.

"No. Mistress… Rosa. I wish to remain your…" He hesitated, then corrected himself. "Your student, as long as you'll have me. I was being truthful before. I am willing to take whatever you are willing to give me. I do not wish to forfeit my place in your bed. Merely…" He gave a watery laugh. "Enhance it."

That pulled the ghost of a smile from her.

"Does it make you feel any better to know you're the only one I've fucked since we met?"

He closed his eyes and took a long breath.

"It's a small comfort," he admitted. "But I'm not sure how I'll handle it if we find a prisoner willing and able to play by your rules. I'd rather not think about it."

"No use worrying about that now," she murmured. "We'll cross that bridge when we come to it."

He nodded.

"Do you want a stronger separation between work and play?"

Another nod.

"Would it help if these navigation meetings happened somewhere less private?"

"Yes," he said, then huffed a small laugh. "Either that, or invite the other officers. You are much better at keeping your legs closed when other people are around."

Rosa leaned back to stare at him in mock offense.

"Benjamin, are you calling me a harlot?"

"If the corset fits, Rosita."

That made her freeze.

"Please don't call me Rosita," she said quietly. "Someday I'll explain."

His fingers immediately entwined with hers.

"Yes, Mistress. My apologies. Rosa."

She wiped the last of his tears away.

"Do you feel better?"

"A little."

"Would you like another roll in the sheets, or would you like to get some work done?"

That finally earned a real smile from him.

Ben retrieved his spectacles, settled them back over his nose, and tangled a hand in her hair.

"I would like to work," he said. "But if you're a good girl, perhaps I'll reward you afterward."

Rosa shivered despite herself.

She kissed him quickly, retrieved a book from her shelf, and stretched out on the bed while he returned to the desk. This time, however, there was no bitterness in the distance between them. Only a clearer understanding of what they were doing and what they were not.

He worked in absorbed silence for some time, pencil in hand, compass moving, his whole face brightened by concentration. Rosa watched him over the top of her book often enough that she had to pretend she was reading more than she was.

Eventually she could not help herself.

"Can I ask one more question before I lose you completely to those charts?"

"Hmm?"

He looked up, and the grey-blue of his eyes seemed almost silver behind the glass.

She swallowed.

"Why did you take your spectacles off before you yelled at me? Were you afraid I'd break them?"

Ben shook his head. "Not in the least. It's because... well, I still want you to want to fuck me, Starlight. Besides, they get really foggy if I cry."

That nearly made her laugh and ache all at once.

"You are a very unusual man, Mister Harrington. They look very good on you."

Some time later, Ben finished plotting their course for the stops in Panamá and Mexico so Xiang could restock. The satisfaction that rose in him at a job well done was immediate, deep, and almost holy.

Then he looked toward the bed.

Rosa was still naked, sprawled on her stomach with her book open before her, absently twirling a strand of hair around one finger. He stood there for a moment, just looking at her, and felt that familiar, impossible rush go through him.

This time, though, the feeling was different. Less frantic. No less intense, but no longer tangled up in resentment.

He crossed the room quietly and climbed onto the bed beside her. Rosa looked up just in time to laugh as he tackled her gently into the mattress. They rolled together in a tangle of limbs and laughter until she ended up on top of him, hair falling around her face.

"So I take it I've earned another tumble?" she asked against his lips.

"Regrettably, Captain, you were a *very* good girl. So good, in fact, that I'm not sure you deserve all the terrible, naughty things I want to do to you."

"You *want* to do, or you're *going* to do?"

"Both."

"Well, you'd best make up your mind. You know I'm partial to men of action!"

"And my action, Starlight, is offering you your choice. You were such an *exceedingly* good girl, you may choose your reward."

Rosa's smile was so wide that Ben swore she outshone the sun coming through her window. "I wish to see your face, and the spectacles stay on."

This second joining was slower than the first, less like a sudden loss of control and more like a choice. Rosa settled into his lap facing him, wrapped her arms around his neck, and simply looked at him for a long moment as though memorizing him in this new form: tear-stained, spectacled, clever, earnest, ridiculous, and dear.

There was a twinkle in her eyes, and Ben again thought about how she clearly had to feel *something* for him, even if it wasn't love just yet.

"Rosa," he murmured once she had him hard beneath her hands again.

"Hmm?"

"Nothing. It's a lovely name. So is Eliana."

She smiled, then kissed him. "I was named after my abuelas, Rosa and Eliana."

As she spoke, she guided him into her and sank slowly into his lap, maintaining steady eye contact the whole way down. Ben nearly lost his mind on the spot.

Part of him wanted to look away from the intensity of her gaze. The rest of him wanted to drown in it.

The Black Rose stroked his hair over his ear and sighed. "You're so beautiful. While the green eyes were a pleasant surprise, I think I like this best."

"Bésame," Ben said, low and firm.

She obeyed at once.

They moved together slowly, almost languidly at first, kissing between murmured words and half-breathed laughter. When she shifted to grind against him instead of rising and falling, Ben made a rough sound in his throat and grabbed her backside. She kissed him harder. He answered by slapping her gently once, and the little moan she gave him went straight to his blood.

"Dirty, bad, naughty boy," she whispered.

"You're one to talk," he muttered against her shoulder.

Rosa laughed breathlessly, then broke into a shudder a few moments later when pleasure began to overtake her in earnest.

"Benny," she whispered. "Say my name."

"Rosa," he said, helplessly at first.

Then again, stronger.

"Rosa."

That was enough to send her over. She came apart in his arms with a guttural sound, collapsing against his chest. Ben followed moments later when she slipped from his lap just long enough to work him in both hands until he spilled onto her thigh and stomach.

Afterward, she leaned forward and rubbed the tip of her nose against his.

"I really like how you say my name," she murmured.

He smiled, still breathing hard. "Thank you for finally sharing it with me."

Her expression softened, and some of the warmth faded from it.

"I hope you understand that it's sensitive information, especially if we end up in Cartagena. There are people who believe me dead, and I prefer to keep it that way."

Ben nodded at once. He did understand, or at least understood enough not to pry. He only pulled her into his arms and held her.

"What's the matter, Benny?"

He shook his head, then kissed her temple.

"I'm sorry I yelled at you, Starlight."

"No," Rosa said, stroking his cheek. "I deserved it. It was your first opportunity to do your work as our navigator, and I let lust commandeer my better judgment and my authority as your Captain. But I think it brought us to a better understanding, yes?"

"Yes," Ben said quietly.

She smiled a little. "However, Benny, those spectacles may prove your secret weapon in your quest to become the most ridiculous walrus in the world."

That coaxed a laugh from both of them.

Ben gave her a crooked grin. "I shall keep that in mind. Perhaps I'll wear them in front of everyone, and you can suffer nobly."

She shoved his face away, laughing.

"You're awful. Get dressed, give me another kiss, and get out. Maybe if you're lucky, I'll invite you and your spectacles back this evening."

"Yes, Mistress Rosa, my Starlight Princess."

# Chapter 29

## Bartering and Bitterness

The excursion to Tortuga disappointed Ben in many respects.

Rosa ordered the other officers to keep a close eye on the new navigator at all times, and he was under express orders not to announce his title at any point for any reason. She was so adamant about it that it startled him into an anxious silence. Later, while he and Talia were stowing cables, he finally blurted out what had been needling at him.

"Are you all ashamed of me? You only just promoted me, and—"

The Scotswoman laughed at first, emerald eyes sparkling, but the mirth vanished when she realized he was serious.

"Nae, ya daftie. It's to protect ya because we like ya. Do ya want to end up on another ship with a gun to your head and their charts in your hands?"

The sudden solemnity of it was jarring enough to make Ben drop the rope he was carrying. He jumped back as it landed with a heavy thwump on the deck.

"Oh. Goodness. Of course not."

Talia clicked her tongue and helped him gather it up again, lowering her voice.

"This whole fookin' island is crawling with pirates. They aren't as nice as we are. Watch yer back and cover yer drink. dinnae trust any of the girls, either."

Ben sighed. "That makes sense, unfortunately. Since I volunteered for service, I forgot about the press gangs."

Talia chuckled and patted his unruly curls.

"There's a good lad. I ken you've been working hard with Tobin and Felipe, but you're still a high-value prisoner. If they dinnae steal ya outright, you're worth a pretty penny."

In the end, Ben elected not to disembark at all. Not only was he uneasy about his own safety, but his experience in Saint Lucia was still fresh enough to sour him on the very idea of vendors in port. At least one officer needed to remain aboard at all times, so Ben found himself left in charge of the *Deception*.

Everyone else had errands to run. Rosa and Tobin needed to sell the jewels so the crew would have pay when they reached Panamá. Xiang and Felipe went to market. Doctora went shopping with Anya, Zsófia, and Gerda. Talia had a rendezvous with one of her "tickle partners," a man named Gregorio, and she treated Ben to a long, explicit explanation of why she liked him before wandering off to her next chore.

When she was gone, Ben found himself wondering uneasily whether Rosa imagined he spoke of their private activities in the same way. It would certainly explain one of her rules. Unfortunately, nothing Talia offered was information he could use to win the heart of the Black Rose.

"Your main duty is to look out for any members of our crew who are staying aboard," Rosa told him as she and Tobin prepared to descend the gangplank with their pouches of gems, "and to prevent anyone unknown from wandering aboard."

Ben chuckled. "But isn't that how you ended up with Felipe?"

The Black Rose tossed her head, curls whipping in the breeze. She wore a high-quality red linen dress and a different perfume that day, something rich with cinnamon and spice. It took Ben only a moment to realize the purpose of both: she meant to look wealthier than usual. Even the way she held herself had shifted. She was fully inhabiting the Black Rose persona.

"That was La Habana, not Tortuga," she said. "Absolutely do not trust anyone in this port, even if they ask for help. If they ask for help, only give it if they are bleeding."

"And only if you can tell the blood is theirs," Tobin grumbled. "Tortuga is one of the places where our normal rules do not apply. Unless they are bleeding and you can see the wound, keep them off our ship until the Captain, Felipe, or I return. Do you understand? Don't even let Doctora examine them without one of us, because you know the old prick will have our hides if something happens to her."

Ben nodded at once. "Yes, sir."

Though Ben was now an officer himself, Tobin still outranked him, and calling the man sir was proving a difficult habit to break. Rosa gave his hand a quick squeeze, flashed him a radiant smile, and went ashore.

Ben spent most of his time in Tortuga sitting on a barrel at the top of the gangplank, working in his journals in the spring air while the breeze carried up the scent of hot sand from the beach. The inks Felipe had helped him purchase in Barranquilla were beautiful, and he began blocking out a portrait of Doctora in a bright blue dress: hands clasped beneath her chin, eyes sparkling, smile wide, a few strands escaping her bun. He took a little artistic license with the flare of the skirt, but hardly thought Felipe would mind.

Rosa and Tobin returned far sooner than Ben expected. The Pirate Queen looked dejected, and Tobin's eyes betrayed disappointment even as the rest of his face remained stony.

"They wouldn't give us a good price, but we also can't keep those jewels on our ship. It's not fair to the crew. We still got enough that we can pay everyone, but it wasn't nearly what they were appraised for in Colombia. We should have sold them there and let them go back into the community in Barranquilla," Rosa groused.

Ben squeezed her hand. He wanted to take her into his arms, but he knew better. Not here.

She pinched the bridge of her nose.

"I'm going to lie down. I have a headache after dealing with that nasty woman."

Ben looked at her questioningly.

"Yes, Benny. You are welcome to stop by and take a nap with me."

With that, she rubbed her temples and disappeared.

After she was safely ensconced in her quarters, Tobin turned to Ben.

"I wasn't able to get you an emerald. The woman hit us with such a low price I couldn't remove anything without them noticing."

Ben sighed. "I did say it was fine if you couldn't. I'm a little disappointed, but I'm more upset that she's upset."

The quartermaster shook his head.

"She's used to commanding a lot more respect. Unfortunately, pirate towns like this are different from our usual ports. To the communities we work with, she is a sort of Robin Hood, bringing work and money and freedom. But here? To most of these people, she's just some upstart wench who can't keep her legs closed. They don't see how much work she puts in, and has put in, for ten years."

He paused, then eyed Ben sidelong.

"She's been having you nap with her?"

Ben nodded honestly. "Indeed. Well, I don't sleep, but she does. She snuggles up on my chest, and I take the opportunity to read some of her books. It's only happened a few times, when she really needs it. She says I help her sleep better, so perhaps she thinks it will help her headache."

"Huh." Tobin looked briefly at war with himself. "I hesitate to say this and invite you to enjoy her more than you already do, but for me, one of the best ways to get rid of a headache is... uh... Xiang calls it gāo cháo..."

Ben stared blankly.

Tobin covered his face with both hands.

"It means to achieve release. In bed. Sexually." His voice climbed in pitch as it dropped in volume. "But I am absolutely not telling you to go in there and fuck her unless that is what she wants. If she wants a nap, she gets a nap. If she wants... that... you can give her that. I'll take over your post here. But please don't tell her I suggested it, or she'll use headaches as an excuse every time she wants to get you underneath her."

Ben chuckled despite himself. "I won't."

He bowed slightly and headed toward the Captain's cabin.

She didn't answer when he knocked. When he eased the door open, he found her already asleep with a wet cloth draped over her eyes. He stood there for a long moment, tempted to slip into bed beside her anyway, but decided against it lest he wake her.

So he went back up to the deck.

"She's already asleep."

Tobin quirked an eyebrow. "Hmm. Very well. Would you mind getting your guitar and playing for a bit? I think it would make us both feel better."

Ben smiled.

"I think that is an excellent idea, sir."

# Chapter 30

## Risqué Revelations

The rest of their time in port was uneventful, as were the sailing days that took them to Panamá. Ben wondered whether it was his promotion or if Tobin had put in a good word for him, but Rosa was quite sexually generous with him on the journey. Ben knew it would not last forever, because as May approached, so would her monthly course. But damn if he would not make the best of his situation.

One night, after Rosa slipped a note into his pocket at supper, Ben arrived at her door with his spectacles, his watch, and an idea.

"I would like to time myself and see how quickly I can bring you to release with my hands and mouth."

Wearing the spectacles was a strategic choice, and it paid off exactly as he hoped it would.

"Anything you want," the Captain breathed before kissing him. "Just don't take those off, you beautiful, awful walrus."

The night before they arrived in Panamá, Ben managed a personal best time of six and a half minutes. Rosa threw her arm across her forehead as she used her other hand to shield her womanhood from Ben's seeking tongue.

"You naughty walrus," she purred.

"You enjoy naughty walruses," he countered, kissing along her stomach and chest, up to her neck.

"Maybe I do."

"Tell me a secret, Starlight."

Ben wasn't quite sure why he asked. Perhaps he was hoping she would tell him the same story Tobin had about her family. The Captain thought for a moment, fanning herself with her hand. What she said thoroughly surprised him.

"Felipe and Tobin mutinied against me once."

Ben felt his jaw drop, the heavy ache between his legs momentarily forgotten. "What?" the navigator asked, flabbergasted.

The Black Rose chuckled. "It wasn't a true mutiny, but maybe... six years ago or so, we had a raid go badly. Not the one where I got burned, a different one. We had a string of bad luck.

"Afterward, we creamed the ship on an island that would become Isla Rosa."

Ben snorted quietly. One of his favorite quirks of hers was how Rosa could never quite get a handle on the word "careen". He cleared his throat.

"Sorry, Starlight. Please continue."

"Anyway, I sent everyone else on the crew off to explore in groups. I had the officers in my quarters, and I completely lost my composure. I screamed at each of them in turn, just viciously tore into them. Geraldo, Tobin, and Felipe stood there and took it. It was massively unfair to all of them, and I said many awful things that, to this day, I wish I hadn't.

"Once I was finished with Felipe, I turned to Doctora. You know she isn't even involved in raids. She hadn't done anything wrong other than come into the room with us. I'll never forget it. She was standing next to Felipe, hands over her mouth in shock, like she couldn't believe I was saying such terrible things. I turned to her, opened my mouth, said something unnecessarily cruel about Gustavo, and she just... crumbled. She started to cry..."

"Oof. I imagine Felipe didn't take that well."

Rosa shook her head. "Absolutely not. He didn't yell, which was somehow even scarier. He put an arm around her and said, so quietly I could barely hear, 'Zat ees enough, Rosa.'"

"He never calls you by name," Ben said in awe.

"No, he doesn't. That may be the only time he's used my name since I've known him. It startled me into turning back to him. But before I could start in on him again for insubordination, he picked me up, slung me over his shoulder, and carried me down to the brig. Tobin held the door for him, shaking his head and muttering to himself.

"They locked me up until I calmed down, which took much longer than it should have. I am incredibly lucky nobody else was aboard. I was only eighteen and didn't really know what to do with my anger. I screamed, cried, smacked the bars until my hands were red, had an entire tantrum, and they just sat and played cards until I got it all out.

"And when I stopped yelling, Felipe had me rehearse my apology to Doctora and the rest of the officers while Tobin fetched them. Only after I apologized and offered to make it up to them did they unlock the door and let me out. I know they did that for my own good, but it was a difficult lesson to learn. If you want to keep good people around you, you have to treat them well. I know I'm not perfect, but I try very hard. I'd like to think that's why we don't have the turnover some pirate crews do.

"And that's also why my continued leadership has only been put to a vote two or three times, and I've won each time. Usually, it's some upstart we get from a captured ship who doesn't understand what we're trying to accomplish here. I can all but guarantee that if we had taken on more members of the *Angelina Marie* besides just Frank, one of those cabrones probably would have tried it. But I think Frank is too scared of you, Felipe, and Tobin to try anything himself. Unless he thought it would impress Li Mei, perhaps."

Ben was dumbfounded, and Rosa pulled his face toward hers.

"If that secret is good enough, I would like one in return. And then I would like my naughty walrus to show me why I keep letting him into my bed."

The pair smiled at each other before Rosa leaned in and kissed him deeply.

"Hmmm..." Ben muttered as they parted. "Let's see... a secret for Rosa..."

What could he tell her? They had already shared quite a few secrets, including some big ones. Perhaps if he talked about his family and his father, she would open up about hers.

"My father... while he loved me, all of us, he never really appreciated that I didn't follow in his footsteps and join the Army. He felt that the Navy was unnecessarily treacherous, and he harbored a deep phobia of the sea. We argued about it quite often, almost every time I was on shore leave, from the time I went on my first ship, around age ten.

"The last time was after I married Anne. He... he saw bruises on my face. We had an awful row, and he... called me a coward. He said I was running to sea to run away from her. It was such a strange thing for him to say, because he and Mother were both normally very supportive of us, even if they knew we were making a mistake. I told him that if I wanted to be spoken to like that, I could report early and ship out. He said maybe I should. So I did. Anne was thrilled I was reporting early so she could be rid of me. I was away for a month. When I returned, my father... my father was gone. He'd had an apoplexy in the middle of supper one night. I didn't get to say goodbye, and neither Anne nor her father attended the funeral in my stead. So my father died thinking I was a coward."

Rosa's hand was gentle on his cheek, and she touched the tip of her nose to his.

"He called you a coward?" she asked, moving her fingertips to the back of his neck.

"Well, he didn't actually say it, but he strongly implied it."

The Captain looked confused.

"What do you mean? I thought you said your parents did well explaining things so you understood them. So why would he not have been plain with you about that?"

"He..." Ben began, then stopped. "It was rather out of character for him. Wait a tick..."

The navigator went quiet as he tried to sort his memories.

"What did he say, Benny?" Rosa asked, snuggling closer.

"He said, 'I raised a man, not some sailor boy who flees to the ships whenever things get difficult. If you want to be a father, a good father, you're going to have to confront your problems. For your sake, and that poor babe's.'"

For a long moment, neither of them moved before Rosa gingerly removed Ben's spectacles and placed them on her nightstand, as though she could see the torrent about to hit.

"I... I don't think he was calling you a coward," she said quietly.

"Oh no." Ben slapped himself hard across the face, even as it felt as though an anvil had dropped into his stomach. "Oh my gods, he wasn't. He was telling me I needed to stand up to her. That I had to protect my child and myself. Oh no."

The pain in his gut migrated up into his chest as Ben realized he had misinterpreted his father's words, twisting them into a weapon to flagellate himself with for the past eight years.

"That's why he looked like he was going to cry when I stormed out. I... he... Anne... my brothers and sisters... Mother..."

A tidal wave of emotion crashed into Ben, and he began to sob. As he cried, Rosa pulled herself onto his chest, running her nails through his hair and making small, soothing noises. Somewhere in the depths of everything he was feeling, Ben did appreciate how safe he felt in his emotions with Rosa. She never called him a whiny little bitch or made him feel like less of a man for expressing his feelings. And she had the foresight to take off his spectacles.

After a few minutes, Ben sniffled, running a hand up Rosa's thigh. She made a low purring noise in her throat. She really was like a cat of some sort.

"I'm so sorry, Benny," she whispered into his ear.

"I think that might be why, after Mother passed, none of my siblings would talk to me anymore except Sarah. They all saw me yelling at him when all he was trying to do was inspire me to lead a better life and create a safe home for my child. I suppose once she... once I no longer had to worry about the child, I stayed with Anne to punish myself. I... I never did stand up to her. And ultimately, I kept running away..."

Rosa clicked her tongue as she nuzzled Ben's cheek.

"You did make a choice to do something. You all but begged a Pirate Queen to take you with her. Maybe you didn't force Anne to confront how she treated you, but you removed yourself from her. I certainly know it can be quite frightening to cut all ties and burn all bridges and just disappear. But I'm making it worth your while, yes?"

Ben inhaled deeply, taking in the sweet scent of plumeria, and nodded into her shoulder.

"You know it's infinitely better. You would be..."

He stopped himself before he told her what a wonderful mother she would be. She probably would not take that very well.

Rosa looked at him expectantly, waiting for him to finish. Ben decided to occupy his mouth otherwise before he said something stupid, so he pulled her into another kiss. After they parted, the Black Rose wiped Ben's tears away with her thumbs.

"He wanted you to be happy. I'm sure they all did."

Ben nodded. "You're probably right."

"However," the Pirate Queen muttered, trying to turn the conversation back to lighter topics, or better yet, no talking at all, "if you're going to keep having revelations with lots of crying, I may have to ban secrets from my bed as well. I invite you here to indulge in pleasures, not to take confession."

Ben snorted, pulling Rosa closer. "It's only because you're so easy to talk to, Starlight. I would like to think both my parents would be happy that I've found you."

He kissed the place beneath her ear that made her squirm, and she sighed happily. Ben's eyes slid to her large mirror, and he caught sight of his reflection.

The Ben in the mirror looked... actually, he wasn't sure. Bored? Frustrated?

His face was uncharacteristically blank, his grey-blue eyes burning through the gloom at him. They stared hard at him, even as Rosa smiled with her eyes closed. He was about to make love to her. Why wasn't he smiling? Would his parents be happy if they knew his situation? Was he even happy in this situation?

"What can I expect in Portobelo, Mistress?" he asked quietly, trying to distract himself from the man in the mirror.

"You are going to love Buenaventura. They treat us like royalty. The first mixed couple to marry, Keiko and Raúl, are expecting a baby fairly soon, if she hasn't already had it. They're all so wonderful. I can't wait for you to meet them.

"We don't actually put in at the official port. We use the natural harbor around the peninsula, to the southwest." She drew a map of the coastline through his chest hair with her finger, continuing to trace a battle plan as she spoke. "We'll drop anchor and use the dinghies to go ashore on the beach. The village is right up the hill. If you need anything from the city proper, I'm sure someone will be able to escort you. Buenaventura is about an hour's walk from the port…"

She looked up and found Ben staring at her, his arm moving slowly.

"What?"

She followed the motion of his arm to find his hand stroking his cock.

"I really like you drawing maps on me."

She chuckled, settling lightly on his chest.

"You want to take part, or are you just going to watch?" Ben asked, his voice strained.

"I do enjoy watching. You should let me watch you more often."

"What about you? Maybe you should pleasure yourself and let me watch."

Rosa grabbed Ben's hand and pinned it to the bed. She leaned forward, her breast brushing along his chest, his manhood sandwiched between their bodies.

"Maybe next time I tie you up, I'll let you watch. I bet you'd like that."

"Maybe I would," Ben growled back as he slapped her bottom with his free hand.

She chuckled again, entwining her fingers with his, their lips brushing.

"You're so beautiful, Starlight. I would watch you do just about anything."

The Black Rose settled herself so she was on top of his cock without him being inside her. She slid along his length, forward and backward, and Ben made a frustrated little sound.

"Like what?" she asked, that dare in her voice again.

"I'd love to see you dance dressed as Scheherazade. Dance of veils, wiggling your hips while wearing jingling bangles… You're quite beautiful in red, and all that luscious skin showing? I would watch that for the rest of my life… although I would also settle for watching you ride my cock right now instead of teasing me like this."

Rosa bit her lower lip before leaning over to retrieve Ben's spectacles from the nightstand. While she was bent over, Ben squeezed her breast, drawing a laugh from her.

"If you want to watch me ride your cock right now, it might help if you could see better."

Ben chuckled as Rosa gently placed his spectacles on his nose, wrapping the wires around his ears. They kissed, sweet and slow, as the Black Rose adjusted herself, sliding onto his cock. Ben sighed happily. They regarded each other for a moment, enjoying the sensation, before Rosa took Ben's hands, pinning them on either side of his head as she began moving her hips furiously. Ben's eyes rolled back.

"No. You want to watch me, you're going to watch me," Rosa snarled, grinding harder against him.

Ben's eyes snapped open, the tempestuous grey-blue meeting the deep mahogany brown. Rosa shuddered, leaning forward, her fingernails biting deliciously into Ben's wrists.

"You're so beautiful, Rosa... Princesa... Starlight... You're always beautiful, but you're most beautiful when you're just like this. When your body is an extension of mine, when we are joined in the dance of..."

Rosa leaned down and kissed him fiercely before he could say the word love, which she was fairly certain was coming.

"If you have the capacity to speak that poetically, clearly I'm not fucking you hard enough," she rumbled as if she had been taking voice lessons from Tobin.

"You know me, Mistress. I will accept whatever fucking you give me... but I agree, you could be fucking me much harder. Why don't you see if you can fuck me so hard you leave me speechless?"

Ben smirked as he felt Rosa's inner muscles clench around him.

Challenge clearly accepted.

"I'm going to fuck that naughty walrus smile right off your face," she growled, releasing his wrists long enough to rake her nails across his chest before pinning his arms over his head again, her grip tight.

Ben gasped as she began to move with speed and force. He tried to move his arms, tried to touch her, but she held fast. This woman was much stronger than he had realized. She bit her lip, staring intensely into his eyes. It was amazing, the effect something as simple as his spectacles had on her. Amazing, too, how they evened the playing field a bit, a way he could send her a message.

I want you to want me.

And so far, it had a one hundred percent success rate.

"Bésame, Princesa," he whispered.

She did as he asked, sliding forward on him, her mouth hot and sweet on his, turning her head to avoid smudging the glass. She let go of his wrists, guiding his hands to her breasts instead. Ben gently squeezed, and she moaned against his lips, running her hands through his hair and scratching his scalp around his ear just as he liked.

It was all just so wonderful.

This was the life he deserved, exploring pleasure with this exquisite woman.

Ben's skin was hot, and he was getting close to release. He needed Rosa to release first, even though he had already taken care of her once that night, so he could pull out and achieve his bliss as well.

"Mistress... Mistress, please..." he whimpered. "I don't... want... to upset you..."

"I know, Benny. I... just need... a little more..."

Rosa wiggled her hips slightly and found what she needed. She threw her head back as Ben squeezed her breasts harder. She shook in his lap before falling forward onto him, panting hard.

"Mistress..." Ben's voice was strained, his face bright red.

She rolled off him, taking his cock into her hands.

"Sorry, Benny. Now you may."

Ben's eyes rolled back as her hands stroked frantically. It felt amazing, as always. Rosa bent down and kissed him deeply as he allowed himself to give over to the pleasure coursing through his body. His cock contracted, his seed shooting onto his own stomach. The Captain slowed her movements as she pressed her nose into Ben's cheek with a smile. Ben sighed.

"Thank you, Starlight," he murmured as she kissed his cheek before cleaning him up.

Once that was taken care of, Rosa flopped across Ben's stomach. He stroked her back down to her bottom, which he lightly slapped. She snickered.

"No more tonight, Benny. We've got a big day tomorrow."

"I know. But that was spectacular as usual, Princesa."

She rolled off him, but curled up next to him, her chin finding the hollow of his shoulder.

"It was, Benny, thank you. Even if I didn't fuck you speechless."

They kissed again, rubbing their noses together, before Rosa pulled Ben up to a sitting position and they sought their clothes. Ben's reflection still stared judgmentally at him as he pulled on his shirt.

After they dressed, Ben gave Rosa a passionate kiss goodnight, perhaps as a message to his reflection, entangling his fingers in her curls. After they parted, she wrapped her arms around his waist and held him for a long moment.

"I don't like seeing you cry, Benny. I really don't."

"Well, I wasn't exaggerating earlier. You are quite easy to talk to, and when it comes to people skills, it's easier for me to talk it out. Since I never had anyone I could tell about my last argument with my father, it just stewed in my brain for eight years. Besides, the unexamined life is not worth living."

Rosa's face lit up. "So-crates!"

Ben laughed, kissing her cheek. "SOCK-ra-tees, Starlight."

"Socrates!"

"My goodness, you really must invite me for more naps so I may read more of your lovely books. Our fair Captain is as intelligent as she is stunningly beautiful."

She laughed. He kissed her again on the forehead.

"Goodnight, Princesa."

"Buenas noches, Benny."

Ben exited her quarters and made his way out onto the deck. Now that the warm, fuzzy feeling of satisfaction was fading, he needed a moment. He looked up at the sky, scanning the heavens briefly before the constellations began connecting themselves with glowing lines before his eyes.

Eight years.

For eight long years, he had carried the scar of his father's last words to him. It had not been an indictment, but a plea. He had not been telling Ben to stay for Anne; he had been begging his son to grow a spine for himself and his grandchild.

Ben leaned over the rail, listening to the rhythmic slap of the waves as he forced himself to examine his wife through a realistic lens. Her physical beauty masked a selfish spirit. She struck and berated her husband and servants, poisoning the air with cruel words. In no version of the story would she have been the doting mother he wanted for his daughter. She had been nothing more than a pretty green-eyed prize for an idiot boy. The contrast with Rosa was staggering.

A movement of light caught the corner of his eye, but Ben did not treat this falling star as a wish to be made so much as a message to his father.

*I am so sorry it took me so long to understand. I hope you see the man I have become, and I hope you and Mother are both proud of me. Please watch over the rest of the family, especially Sarah, and...*

He squeezed his eyes shut.

*Please guide me in my relationship with Rosa so that I can find a way to be as happy with her as you were with each other.*

Ben took a deep breath, and from somewhere in the night wind came, inexplicably, the scent of lemons. Ben's eyes snapped open.

His mother had kept a lemon tree since before Ben was born, treating it as if it were her ninth child. She loved how the fruits smelled and tasted. She cooked and baked with them, and would often rub some of the oil onto her skin. The scent of lemon may as well have been a hug from her carried on the wind.

But the look of his reflection in the mirror nagged at him. Was he happy here? He sighed, running his hand through his hair. Perhaps he was just tired.

Besides, tomorrow was going to be a big day.

# CHAPTER 31

## THE PRINCES OF PORTOBELO

Ben tried to remain calm up in the rigging as he fed instructions to Jean-Luc at the helm to bring the *Deception* into the small natural harbor outside Buenaventura. They had sailed past the main port in Portobelo with Spanish colors flying in the wind, but had replaced them with the Black Rose's banner once they were out of sight. As stated in Xiang's story, there was a forest of massive trees on the peninsula, shielding the village from the larger town.

Talia elected to stay aboard the *Deception* while the other officers went ashore, muttering something about how the Buddhists were not that interesting. Ben held his tongue, since it did not feel right to start an argument over non-confrontational, nonviolent people. Despite Talia's opinion, Ben was so excited to meet these people that he felt as though he had fuzzy lightning in his veins instead of blood. A whole group of people like Xiang, living in harmony with the native Panamanians. Fascinating.

Those going ashore gathered at the rowboats and split into teams. Tobin and Xiang, Doctora and Felipe, Natsuki and Jean-Luc, and Rosa and Ben each took charge of a dinghy, heading a group of six. Everyone else would remain aboard the ship with Talia.

Ben had been the one to decide the groups, and everyone seemed quite pleased with their assignments. For his good work, Ben had received a stealthy squeeze on the rump from the Black Rose in addition to a sparkling smile. The Captain gave instructions before they dispersed.

"Each team has at least one Spanish speaker and one Japanese speaker. Please stay together as much as you can. If you do not speak either language, please stay with one of the translators. We do not want anyone to get lost or for anything to happen to any of you. You are accountable to your team leaders, and you are to follow their instructions as if they were my own."

There were nods and choruses of "Yes, Captain."

Once they reached the shallows, Ben, Frank, Arturo, and Andrew jumped out and pulled their boat ashore. The men on the other dinghies did the same. Ben watched Felipe reach up and effortlessly spin Doctora in an elegant twirl as he helped her off their rowboat. Ben looked up at Rosa.

"Don't you dare," she said, her voice quiet and far away. Though her words were firm, her eyes were soft and full of longing.

"Maybe just a little?" Ben whispered back.

Rosa nodded, biting her lower lip, and allowed Ben to grasp her by the waist to help her down onto the sand. She was wearing the fancy, spicy perfume again.

"Thank you, Benny."

Something caught her eye, and she waved as a smile crossed her face. Ben turned and saw a gathering of people at the top of the beach. There was a great ruckus as the mass of humanity came down to meet them, speaking a jumble of Japanese and Spanish that, to Ben's untrained ears, sounded like aural soup.

"¡La Rosa Negra-gozen!" some young children shouted as they reached the pirates first.

The villagers gathered around Rosa like an illustration in Ben's family Bible of Jesus meeting the masses. The people were dragging her away from him, and Ben felt a freeze creeping through his body, as if he were possessed by a ghost stealing all the warmth from him. Rosa's brilliant smile faded slightly as her eyes locked with her lover's. She stopped, and the sea of humanity stopped with her. All eyes turned to him.

"Tío Benny-senpai, nuestro navegador."

Ben weakly raised his hand.

"Hola," he said, feeling more than a little faint.

Rosa made her way back to him, and the masses parted. She took Ben's hand and squeezed it, offering some sort of explanation in Spanish Ben could not even begin to follow. But the squeeze warmed him, beating back the chill of panic that had threatened to overtake him. She was in front of him. Felipe and Doctora were on either side of him. He was surrounded by friends. He was meeting new, interesting people. It would be fine.

He let out a breath, nodded, and loosened his grip on Rosa's hand. As much as he wanted Rosa to ease his nerves, the Black Rose was holding court. He had to let her do her job. She smiled, curled her fingers around his, and pulled him along with her as she talked to the villagers.

Panamá was beautiful, and when they reached the top of the hill overlooking the beach and the harbor, Ben turned and was treated to a sparkling expanse of ocean. His heart sang to see how far away the horizon was from this vantage point. The sea was vast and endless, as if it stretched all the way to the edge of the world itself. This was why he had always wanted to be a sailor. He felt fully like himself again, and Rosa let go of his hand as the village elders approached.

There was an old Panamanian man, an even older Panamanian woman, and a Japanese man in red robes. Felipe and Xiang stepped up to Rosa's side, and they all bowed to the elders, who bowed back. When everyone straightened again, there were smiles, a flurry of embraces, kisses, and another cacophony of language. Felipe did an admirable job of keeping pace with three different languages at once.

The group made their way into the village proper, and it appeared that almost everyone had come out to meet them. Everyone except a couple, about Ben and Rosa's age, who were sitting on chairs outside their home. The man was Panamanian, the woman Japanese. She was massively pregnant and looked a little ill. This must be Raúl and Keiko.

Doctora rushed over to the pair and embraced Keiko before asking rapid-fire questions in Spanish as her long tawny fingers ran over the smaller woman's body. Felipe abandoned his translator duties to stand with her. With every answer, the physician looked more and more agitated. Felipe put a large hand on her back and rubbed it gently. Doctora said something very definitive, stamping her bare foot, and Raúl and Keiko stood, the husband leading the wife into the house. The Boricua turned to the elders, and even though Ben did not understand the words, he recognized the emotion.

Doctora was furious.

Her tone was low and icy, her arms crossed tight against her bosom. Ben had only seen Doctora this angry once before, when Felipe, Tobin, and Talia were hazing him with smoke bombs on his first day and he had nearly fallen overboard. She must have truly believed Keiko's well-being was at stake to speak to a woman nearly twice her age like that.

"She's saying they've let the baby go too long, and it's dangerous," Giselle whispered to Ben.

He had not realized the girl was next to him, and he jumped.

"She's demanding they induce Keiko now. Abuela Gabriela says they don't have the proper herbs, and Doctora says she knows they do. There's a grove not far from here where they grow. She hopes it's still in season."

"Thank you," he muttered, again amazed at how well-rounded the children's education was aboard the *Deception*.

Doctora said something to the assembled group, which Felipe translated into Japanese.

"She is going to need some volunteers to come with her to gather the herbs to bring the baby out."

"Ooh, herbs. Me. Me, Doctora!" Giselle excitedly raised her hand, as did Juanito. Three children from the village also raised theirs. Felipe volunteered, grinning at Doctora, who smiled back adoringly. So did the Black Rose. Ben felt his own hand rise as soon as he saw Rosa's go up. The village elders said something else to Doctora, and she sighed, but nodded.

"Looks like it's just us, then," Giselle said, looking up at Ben. "Since they didn't know we were coming, they want to welcome us properly."

Ben nodded, and he and the girl went to stand with Doctora. Rosa addressed her crew.

"Right. Everyone not coming with us, please assist them in any way possible. Anyone who needs a translator, pick someone and stick with them."

Felipe was speaking to the village children who had volunteered. They were a Japanese boy, a Panamanian boy, and a Panamanian girl. Felipe made introductions to the *Deception*'s crew. The girl, Sandra, was the youngest of the trio, about six years old, and the boys, Kaito and Eduardo, looked to be about seven or eight. Sandra and Eduardo were siblings. Ben realized, after doing some quick math, that Kaito's mother must have been pregnant when they were on the *Gouden Zee*. Looking at the villagers, Ben saw there was quite a noticeable gap: there were no Japanese children between the ages of eight and fourteen.

All of those children had either been taken and converted, or slaughtered in the name of a supposedly loving God.

The Black Rose took Ben's hand and squeezed it again.

"Benny, you look upset," she whispered, and Ben schooled his features back into a more neutral expression.

"Just thinking, Mistress."

She cocked her head, confused, but then her eyes softened.

"Your concern does not help those who are already lost. We need to focus on Keiko."

Ben nodded. Rosa was right; he had to be here, now. Xiang would be proud.

Ben also noticed Andrew haltingly asking Abuela Gabriela for an audience, with Arturo acting as his translator. The bilge rat was fidgeting with a blue piece of cloth that looked like a handkerchief. Ben was not entirely sure, but it looked as though it had a small E embroidered on it. Odd. The older woman rubbed her hands together with a huge smile. She said something and paused for Arturo.

"She says she was wondering when you were going to come speak to her. Come, she will give us some chicha and talk."

As the old woman led them away, Ben saw Doctora smile and clasp a hand over her heart. Whatever was happening must have been incredibly positive to break through the physician's frustration, even for a moment.

Doctora shook herself and turned back to look over her volunteers, determination returning to her dark eyes as she set her jaw. Ben, Rosa, Juanito, Giselle, Kaito, Eduardo, and Sandra. Felipe took her hand and squeezed it as she exhaled. She seemed calmer with the gunner's steady hand in hers.

"There's a grove about twenty minutes' walk outside town that I'm fairly sure has the plants we need," Doctora said. "Juanito, Giselle, stick with us for now. Once I show you what we're looking for, you can explore a little with Kaito, Eduardo, and Sandra, ¿vale?"

"Vale," they responded dutifully. She had them very well trained.

"One herb will be brewed into a tea for her to drink. The other she will have to chew, so we will need a lot of that one. There may be a third that will help bring in her milk, but we need the other two first before we worry about that."

"Sí, Doctora."

She smiled brightly, ruffling Juanito's hair and gently tugging one of Giselle's braids. Out of the corner of his eye, Ben saw Felipe with his hand over his heart, watching the woman he loved interact with the children they had all but adopted.

"Bueno, vámonos!"

# CHAPTER 32

## PLANTS AND PIGS

The group of four adults and five children set out to find the plants. Once they were out of sight of the village, Rosa took Ben's hand, entwining her fingers with his, and led them in singing a simple song in Spanish that even Ben could follow about an old dance called "La Bamba."

The second verse was almost entirely made up of cognates, and Rosa took great joy in singing that she was not a sailor, but in fact the Captain. She laughed and skipped with the children, her eyes sparkling. The song repeated, and this time Ben clumsily sang along.

Sandra weaved in and out between Rosa and Ben, and he allowed himself to imagine for a fleeting moment that Sandra was their daughter. Almost as if she subconsciously knew what he was thinking, Rosa picked a flower from the side of the road and tucked it over the child's ear.

She really would be a wonderful mother.

Someday.

Presently, the group found the grove they were seeking. Doctora and Felipe began searching, explaining what they were looking for in Spanish, and Ben was once more lost. Dancing La Bamba only needed a little grace, but finding these herbs was slightly more complicated. And he was just a sailor, after all.

"Doctora!" Giselle called, pointing to a clump of short shrubs with tiny yellow flowers.

"Excellent work, mija. Benny, this is rue. Please collect as much as you can, because we're going to need a very strong tea. Meanwhile, Giselle and I need to find—"

"Jules! I found it! Come!" Felipe shouted from across the clearing, and Doctora patted Ben on the arm, leaving him to his task.

The herb stank, a sharp scent that stabbed at his sinuses, one he recognized from Doctora's quarters. Ben began to gather great handfuls before realizing he had nowhere to put them. As if sensing what he needed, a large red square of cloth appeared on the ground. Rosa had taken off her crimson headscarf, and her curls danced in the breeze.

Ben smiled at her and laid the rue in the fabric. Rosa smiled back before kneeling next to him. It was slow work, and it took nearly an hour to pick as much as Doctora seemed to think they needed. After the initial shock of how medicinal the plant smelled, Ben eventually picked up citrusy notes that smelled a little like bitter orange.

"How do you like Panamá?" Rosa asked, breaking the silence.

"It's beautiful here, and it's so interesting to see the villagers living together." Ben paused, wiping his brow. "What does *gozen* mean?"

The Black Rose shrugged.

"Felipe tells me it's like the title of lady. It's incredibly respectful, like addressing a noblewoman. All those words they tack on at the end are varying degrees of familiarity or respect. I can't keep most of them straight."

"So what is my title?"

"Uncle Benny, and I think senpai is like... a mentor? Not quite a teacher..." She shrugged, flustered. "I'm not entirely sure."

Ben decided to steer back toward a language she was comfortable with. "¿Bésame?"

The distraction worked, and Rosa laughed, allowing Ben to take her into his arms.

"Is your response to everything asking for kisses?"

He shrugged, giving her a crooked smile. "Is there something wrong with wanting kisses? Nobody can see us."

"Besides us?" a French-accented voice came from immediately next to them, and Ben nearly jumped out of his skin while Rosa fell over in a fit of laughter.

Doctora shook her head, but also laughed from Felipe's other side. "We already know what you two tortolitos get up to," the physician said. "You know we won't tell if you indulge in a little romance."

Despite the reassurance that all was well, Rosa still noticeably stiffened when Doctora said tortolitos.

"Is this enough?" Rosa asked, looking around. "Where did the children go?"

The Captain persona replaced Rosa as she stood up, quick and straight, holding their massive bundle of herbs. Ben scrambled to follow suit.

"That should be plenty, and we've been gone long enough. They can dry anything left over. We collected the other one we needed, so I sent them a little farther into the forest to try to find one last herb for me. Giselle knows what to look for. I told them not to wander—"

As if on cue, there was a chorus of screams in the brush, and the four adults paused, looking toward the source of the sound. Out of the undergrowth burst Juanito, Giselle, Kaito, Eduardo, and Sandra. They were screaming, but not in a children-enjoying-themselves way. This was genuine fear.

Behind the children, snorting and squealing, came three wild pigs with massive tusks: two large males, foaming at the mouth and running at full tilt, and a smaller female trotting behind as if she were curious to see what would happen.

The children ran past the adults, the little Panamanian girl falling behind. She stepped on a large rock, her ankle turning at an unnatural angle, and went down hard. She began to cry, clutching her leg. The pigs showed no sign of slowing.

Without fully thinking it through, Ben moved quickly to put himself between the pigs and Sandra. He could not outrun the creatures, but he could at least try to stop them. He raised his arms and spread his legs to make himself look bigger.

There was a rush of feet, and someone slid in the dirt next to him, kicking up a small cloud. A sword pressed into his hand, the cool metal contrasting with the heat of the moment. Ben took his eyes off the beasts long enough to glance at his companion, expecting to see an older Frenchman with a smile on his face, ready for a fight.

What he saw instead was a wild tempest of curls, a head shorter than he was, and a fierce determination in dark brown eyes that sparkled like stars.

Rosa stood next to him, also holding a sword.

She must have taken them from Felipe. She bared her teeth and snarled. Ben hazarded a look behind him and saw that the gunner was carrying Sandra back to Doctora.

"Benny!" Rosa barked. "Aim for the shoulder joint."

She pulled Ben out of the path of the first pig as it reached them, pushing him protectively behind her.

"They bite!" she added as she took a swing, nicking the animal's back. It grunted, running in a wide arc to make another pass as the second male approached. This one was much slower than the first.

Rosa frantically tapped a spot on Ben's back where his neck met his shoulders, her head on a wild swivel.

"There's a spot right there. If you stab it there, you'll kill it."

Her words were breathless and clipped. She shoved Ben away, and as the pig passed between them, the Captain stabbed down into its shoulder. The borrowed cutlass went deep, and the pig fell with a loud squeal, attempting to compensate for the loss of a limb, blood pouring from the wound in gouts. It opened its mouth, and Ben could see the massive tusks. Overtaken by fear, Ben kicked the creature in the snout as hard as he could, thankful he had chosen to wear his boots ashore.

"Kill it," the Black Rose screeched, her eyes pivoting back to the other male. "Before it takes our ankles!"

The female decided she was no longer interested in the outcome of this fight, turning tail and fleeing back into the forest. Ben tried to remain calm and examined the writhing animal, attempting to find the point the Captain was referring to. His pulse pounded in his ears, drowning out all other sound.

Time slowed. Standing out of range of those awful, javelin-like teeth, he found what looked like the correct spot and stabbed down. It was tough to punch through the hide, so he pushed harder against the sword. The animal convulsed with a gurgle, a pool of deep crimson spreading across the dirt beneath it.

"Benny!" Rosa cried, balletically dodging out of the first pig's way. It was coming straight for him.

He tried to yank the sword out of the pig, but instead slipped in the blood and fell hard on his knee. A sharp pain shot through his body, seemingly to the tips of his hair. He tried again to pull the cutlass free, but to no avail.

Shit.

"Benny!" Felipe yelled, throwing something toward him in a wide arc.

A large stick flew at him, and Ben's field of vision filled with calculations. Either he could try to catch it midair, or let it hit the ground and risk it skidding away. He decided to risk it and reached. His fingers wrapped around the lumpy bark, and there was a large, roundish knot at the top. It resembled a shillelagh. His father had taught all his siblings how to use one for self-defense, though he called it a walking stick when teaching the girls. Ben had an idea what to do with this.

Both knees wet and sticky with blood, lungs refusing to hold air, Ben swung the stick as hard as he could. His internal voice, rather dry and detached given the circumstances, told him this was incredibly stupid, and that he should brace for impact.

But if it's stupid and it works, it's not stupid.

The knot connected with the top of the pig's head. Its front legs splayed slightly. Disoriented, it tripped over the body of its companion, landing face-to-face with Ben, who got another look at the massive teeth. Rosa swiftly moved into place behind it. She took the cutlass in both hands, stabbing down with a precision that told Ben she had done this before.

The beautiful patroness of violence had returned, her teeth bared as she made sure the animal was dead. There was a streak of red on her cheek, a flame in her eyes. He knew Rosa was fierce and powerful, but this was something else.

Holy shit.

She sighed, wiping her cheek with her sleeve and smearing the blood. The spell was broken, and she reached out a hand to Ben.

"Very good, Benny. You can be very stupid when you're being brave, do you know that?"

Ben chuckled nervously, allowing her to help him to his feet. His knees refused, buckling again. She reached out a gentle hand to steady him.

"I've been told that before, yes. Give me a moment."

Rosa rubbed his back as Felipe brought Juanito and the other boys over to prepare the pigs to take back to Buenaventura. Once Ben caught his breath, he took Rosa's hand in his own.

"That was... incredible... Captain."

She smiled, her hair falling in a curtain between them, then went to check on Sandra. Giselle was picking leaves off another plant and tasting them. She seemed pleased with whatever it was and offered some to the little girl. Sandra was pale and shaking, but she was safe. She ate the plant Giselle offered her without complaint.

After a quarter hour, the group was ready to depart. Ben was holding one end of a stick with a dead pig hanging upside down by its trotters. Felipe held the other. Juanito and Kaito carried the other one.

"What are these things, anyway?" Ben asked the Captain.

She walked between Ben and Juanito, carrying her headscarf full of rue. Behind them, with Felipe and Kaito, Doctora carried Sandra piggyback while Giselle and Eduardo walked beside her. The cabin girl was carrying two other parcels of herbs, chattering as she tried to make conversation. The Panamanian boy was quite shaken, hovering protectively around his little sister and giving one-word answers.

"Coyámel," Rosa explained. "They can be aggressive if provoked. If I had to guess, these two were likely fighting over the female when the children disturbed them. While Juanito tends to be our little bad-luck charm, we are fortunate. They tend to live in much larger groups of twenty, thirty, or more. A stampede would have ended poorly. These ones are on the larger side... *What?*"

Ben shook his head, but he smiled.

"You're remarkable, Starlight," he said quietly.

She blushed slightly, waving the compliment away. "I just like my animal book."

"And I just like well-read, intelligent women."

Ben knew there had to be more to it than just reading, and he glanced at her expectantly, hoping she would favor him with an explanation. Rosa looked away, her honey-bronze skin sparkling in the sunlight, but her small smile did not reach her eyes.

# Chapter 33

## Petals and Preparations

Once Buenaventura was in sight, Rosa sent Eduardo on ahead to fetch their parents to tend to Sandra. Whatever plant Giselle had given the child must have soothed her, because she was asleep on Doctora's back. Her ankle was swollen and bruised, purple and blue.

Sandra and Eduardo's parents came to meet them, as did some of the other villagers. Abuela Gabriela seemed pleased that Doctora had been able to find what she was searching for. They were also incredibly pleased to see the two dead coyámel, as the larger males in their herd had been causing a great deal of trouble lately. The pigs were taken away, and Doctora handed Sandra to her father.

Giselle was to go with them and keep watch over the child until Doctora came to examine her, after she had given Keiko a dose of the tea. Giselle nodded dutifully and followed Sandra's family back to their home, chattering animatedly in Spanish. Kaito likewise was led back home by his mother. Juanito was given instructions to find Tobin and stay with him to avoid any further trouble. Felipe left to fetch Xiang.

Doctora set Ben to work breaking down the rue and the other herbs they had collected. Ben still did not know what they were all called, and he was not sure now was the time to ask. Rosa sat beside him, helping, mumbling an excuse to no one in particular about wanting her headscarf back. She looked tired, the energy from their fight with the pig fading. Ben, by contrast, was still energized, his fingers making quick work of the herbs.

Felipe reappeared with Xiang and a woman introduced as Song Mei. Ben remembered that Song Mei was the woman Xiang secured some of his ingredients from, and her eyes lit up at the sight of such a bountiful harvest. She explained that the pigs terrorizing the area around the grove with the herbs were the main reason they had not been able to induce Keiko yet. No one had been brave enough, or foolish enough, to go to that part of the forest to harvest the plants, so they had been waiting for Keiko to go into labor on her own.

"Why didn't anyone warn us about them, then?" Ben asked after Felipe translated everything for him. Even though the woman was Japanese, she was speaking Spanish beautifully. Or perhaps not; Ben had no idea. But Song was a very appropriate surname for her, as her voice was musical and sweet. "If everyone was so scared to go there because of the pigs, why didn't they just tell us?"

Felipe asked Song Mei Ben's question, and the woman laughed. What she said in reply made both the gunner and Doctora blush, and they avoided looking at each other.

Rosa pulled Ben close and whispered in his ear. Her warm breath against the sensitive spot made his body tingle.

"She says it's because they figured if Doctora was angry enough, it would make Felipe angry enough that he would take out the whole herd if he had to," Rosa whispered. Her low tones made him shiver, raising goosebumps along his arms despite the heat of the day. "It sounds like Abuela Gabriela put her up to this. She finds it funny."

Xiang and Song Mei disappeared, returning a few minutes later with other, different flowers and asking Doctora for approval, which was granted. Xiang took a couple of great handfuls of the stripped herbs Ben and Rosa had prepared and disappeared again.

Felipe and Doctora were playing a strange game in which they avoided each other's gaze while still watching each other intently. Xiang and Song Mei reappeared a quarter hour or so later with a massive flask wrapped in a towel. Doctora clapped excitedly.

"Thank you, Xiang! Gracias y Arigato, Song Mei!" She stood, beaming. "Come! We need to get Keiko to drink this!"

"What happens after she drinks it?" Ben asked.

He barely remembered Anne going into labor. He had become so wound up that he had been physically removed from the house, spending the day with his sister Sarah. It was only after nightfall that word came through a servant that the child had not survived.

Ben had rushed home to be with his wife, only to find she had locked him out of their room. The midwife's apprentice, a girl hardly older than Giselle, was still cleaning up. He had given her a coin to tell him something, anything, about what had happened. The girl had looked up at him, eyes wide, and said three words before taking her bag and bolting:

"Was a girl."

"Benny!" Doctora called, lightly tapping the navigator on the cheek to bring him back to the moment. She sighed.

"Sorry," Ben began, and she shook her head.

"No, I should have expected that. Once Keiko drinks the tea, we will wait for her water to break. We will give her tea every two hours until it does. Then we give her the other herb to chew, which will help with the pain. It should also help with bleeding. May I see your watch?"

Ben produced the timepiece, and she squinted at it, adjusting the spectacles on her nose. She pulled out her own from a pouch on her utility belt, winding it to match Ben's before handing his back.

"If we are lucky, she will start laboring by sundown. If we are less lucky, it looks as though I will be spending the night." She looked at Felipe, who made a gesture as though he were crushing something between his massive hands, a question in his eyes. "I'm sorry, we will be spending the night."

The Frenchman's expression softened into a small smile.

"That is not a problem, Jules. Anything you need, you know I will happily assist."

"Would it help if I stayed?" Ben asked quietly.

He was not entirely sure what possessed him to volunteer. Felipe and Doctora had a silent conversation of raised eyebrows, head tilts, and pursed lips before Doctora nodded. Ben also caught Rosa's horrified expression out of the corner of his eye. He knew she hated being away from her own bed, but he ignored it. He wanted to help.

"I'm sure it would not be terrible to have you. I'm certain we can find something for you to do when the time comes."

The physician spoke nonchalantly, but Ben had an inkling Doctora already had a task in mind. She turned to her Captain.

Rosa's arms were crossed tightly over her chest, her face pinched as she bit her lip. She stared hard at her officers for a long moment before throwing her hands up.

"Fine," she snarled, as Doctora and Felipe tried to hide their smirks.

Ben reached out and squeezed Rosa's hand. She deflated a little, but still looked annoyed.

"Captain, you don't have to..." Doctora began, but Rosa waved a hand.

"I am somewhat responsible for this, after all. Maybe not as much as Tobin and Felipe, but this happened on my watch and under my command, so..."

Ben clapped his hands with a wide grin.

"This is so exciting," the navigator said, buzzing with enthusiasm.

The Black Rose sighed, looking entirely unconvinced.

"If you say so."

# Chapter 34

## Rendezvous and Requirement

The Black Rose dismissed everyone back to the ship if they did not want to wait for Keiko and Raúl's baby. Tobin decided to return to the *Deception*, as no one was thrilled by the prospect of Talia being left as ranking officer for an entire night. The last time she had been left in charge overnight, the boatswain had gotten into some paint, which was why her and Doctora's room was entirely blood red.

Everyone was still annoyed at the waste of paint, and Doctora thought it made her quarters look like a brothel instead of a place of healing. Ben saw Felipe bite his lip, but the navigator was not sure whether it was because the gunner wanted to laugh or because that detail was now coloring some of his private thoughts about his lady love. The tips of his ears turned red, so Ben guessed it was the latter.

Natsuki was distressed at having to leave so that the crew would have breakfast in the morning, since Xiang staying ashore overnight was a given, but Frank and Li Mei promised they would run the galley. Xiang and Natsuki gave them some last-minute instructions and seemed confident in their crewmates' abilities. Arturo, Toñiete, and Andrew promised to help as well.

Before he left, Abuela Gabriela took Andrew's cheeks into her hands, pulling him down to her level and planting a kiss on his forehead before tousling his shaggy blond hair. He nodded, his clear brown eyes glossy with tears as he straightened again.

In the end, Xiang, Natsuki, Daichi, Rosa, Ben, Giselle, Doctora, and Felipe stayed. Tobin said they would leave a dinghy on the beach just in case, and the rest of the crew would return in the morning. The quartermaster gave Rosa and Xiang hugs before leading the rest of the crew back to the ship.

The larger man held his lover for a long moment, and Ben realized they probably did not spend many nights apart. Xiang said something to Tobin about Mar, and Tobin nodded before disappearing, leading the crew back to the beach.

In the meantime, those who were staying needed accommodations. That was hastily worked out with the village elders while Doctora went to check on Sandra and fetch Giselle. Xiang, Natsuki, and Daichi would stay with Song Mei. Doctora, Felipe, and Giselle would have to be with Keiko when she went into labor. That left Rosa and Ben needing a place to stay.

The Captain was adamant that Ben not be left alone without someone who could translate for him. Abuela Gabriela appraised the pair with a smirk before saying something. The Black Rose turned to her navigator.

"She says she has beds for us, Benny," Rosa said with a tight smile. Ben knew she was thinking of her large, soft, sumptuous bed back aboard the ship. There was no way this old woman had anything like that. Ben nodded to the old woman with a quiet "Gracias."

It turned out Abuela Gabriela lived just a few houses down from Keiko and Raúl, and she walked with them. Rosa went in to look at their room while Ben saw Doctora and Giselle approaching. He made his way over to them.

"How is Sandra?" he asked haltingly in Spanish.

Doctora smiled, speaking slowly and pantomiming. "She is sleeping, but her ankle hurts very much." She switched to English. "She'll have to stay off her feet for a few days, but it's not as bad as it looks. Pobrecito Eduardo is beside himself. Turns out they stumbled on the two males fighting over the female, and he decided to throw rocks at them. That made them angry and caused them to charge. And here I thought it was somehow something Juanito did."

"Well, that would be a fair guess, given his usual record," Ben muttered. "But the Captain was right. That's exactly what she thought happened."

"The Captain is very intelligent," Doctora began, switching back to Spanish before saying something Ben did not follow. Whatever it was, it drew a laugh from Giselle.

Speaking of the Captain, the Black Rose approached, looking grumpy. She nodded to Doctora and Giselle before turning to Ben.

"Abuela Gabriela was not lying," Rosa said flatly. "She has a bed for us. Singular. One."

Ben's eyebrows shot up. Odd. He would have thought an older Catholic woman would want to keep an unmarried couple as far away from each other as possible.

"This is what I get for not going back to the ship with everyone else."

She grabbed Ben by the wrist, dragging him into the house.

Abuela Gabriela's house was bigger than Ben expected, but cozy, and smelled like freshly baked bread. She had a room for herself, a second bedroom, and a large kitchen and living area. The Black Rose dragged her lover into their room, let go of his arm, and indicated the bed.

The bed looked as though it had been intended for a child. It was only by the grace of Ben's lanky frame that they would both be able to fit. Rosa trembled with frustration.

Ben stood behind her, rubbing her shoulders. He pulled her body against his and kissed a slow line up her neck.

"Is it really so bad to share a bed with me, Starlight?" he murmured against her skin. "I thought you liked how relaxed and refreshed you were after a nap with me."

"But... but that's in my own bed. Look at this thing," she griped, turning into his embrace.

Out of the corner of Ben's eye, he saw Abuela Gabriela smiling in the hallway. She nodded at him, waggled her eyebrows, then held a finger to her lips. With a wink, she closed the door.

Oh.

Oh.

Rosa thumped him lightly on the chest with her fist before looking up at him.

"Stop smiling, you awful walrus. I swear, it's like you willed this into existence."

Ben chuckled, cupping her face in his hands. She playfully attempted to bite his thumb.

"I could sleep on the floor if you'd like," Ben said with a slight pout, trying to give her the puppy-dog eyes he knew she had a hard time resisting.

She sighed deeply, as if the weight of the entire world were leaning on her. He cracked, knowing he had won.

"You don't have to sleep on the floor, but at least stop smiling like that. No naughty business."

She gently pushed him away and turned to examine a decoration hanging on the wall. Ben grasped her around the waist from behind, pulling her back against his chest again, whispering against her neck as one hand roamed over her shirt.

"Of course. No naughty business at all. Only perfectly normal sleeping, with me holding you very close to prevent you from falling off the bed."

Rosa turned to face him, pulling him down into a kiss.

"I hate you sometimes. I hope you know that," she breathed before kissing him again, fiercely and passionately.

"Oh, yes, Mistress. I can just feel the hatred flowing through you," Ben joked as they parted.

She chuckled, pinching his nose before blowing out the candle Abuela Gabriela had left.

"Then I suppose we should get some sleep. I have no idea when we're going to have to do what."

As they settled in, they realized it was easier said than done. Ben's long legs hung off the edge of the bed, and he had to hold Rosa even tighter than was comfortable for her to feel secure that she would not fall off. The Captain groused under her breath, and Ben was beginning to understand why she did not like sleeping off the ship. He buried his face in her neck. He was getting excited, but felt as though he had Abuela Gabriela's blessing to engage in at least a little naughty business.

Rosa was agitated, feeling his cock pressing into her backside. Why did it have to be so big and obvious… and absolutely wonderful? It was always difficult to say no to him when he was hard and willing, and his lips on her neck made it even worse. He held her so close, hands sliding under her shirt and cupping her breasts, rubbing small circles around her nipples. She wanted nothing more than to claw his clothes off.

She flipped over to face him, losing her balance slightly and throwing her leg over him to keep from falling backward onto the floor. He grabbed her hips, pulling her toward him as the bed made a creaking noise. She purred as he nibbled the skin of her neck, his mustache and beard setting a thousand tiny fires between her legs.

His breath was hot and shallow, and he was doing his best to be quiet. The Captain squirmed against him as Ben slid his hand into her trousers, his fingers searching for the pleasure bud hidden where her legs met. Said legs fell open slightly before she snapped them closed again.

"We can't," she breathed, even as she held him closer. "Not in someone else's house."

"I know. That's what makes this all the more delicious. It's all part of my dastardly plan to make you desperate for me."

They kissed again, and Rosa growled quietly into his mouth.

"I have no idea if you're joking or not, but it's certainly working. How dare you," she whispered as Ben laid a possessive hand on her breast. "I hate you so much, Benny."

Despite her words, she palmed his manhood through his trousers.

"And you know I love you, Starlight. Let's get some sleep, but promise me we'll do something about this when we're back aboard the ship."

"I don't know if I can wait that long," Rosa grumbled, her skin hot with desire under Ben's fingers.

"We could go for a walk, find somewhere quiet outside of town, and make love under the stars again."

He wiggled his hips, and her hand curled around his cock. Despite the layer of fabric separating them, it throbbed under her touch.

"You know I like that, Mistress."

"I hate you," she snarled, "but I don't think either of us will be able to sleep unless we take care of this. Come on."

The two scrambled out of bed, nearly silent. Rosa quickly folded a spare blanket and put it in her rucksack. She put a finger over Ben's lips.

"Quiet as mice. We are going to sneak out, quickly and quietly find a suitable place, quickly and quietly fuck, and quickly and quietly come back as if nothing happened. You do not say a word to anyone. Understood?"

Ben nodded, kissing her finger. She shuddered, her composure hanging by a thread.

"Come on."

The door to Abuela Gabriela's room was closed. Ben and the Black Rose stole out of the house and made their way by moonlight. The night was clear and warm, and Ben felt a rush of excitement and lust. As much as it would have been spectacular to fuck in that tiny bed, Rosa was right.

It would be most unseemly to make love in someone else's house, even if the older woman seemed to give her blessing, especially when they were waiting for Keiko to go into labor.

Rosa's hand was warm in his as she led him toward a secluded hilltop overlooking the natural harbor where the *Deception* was anchored. The grass was as high as Ben's waist, so they would likely be well hidden from the footpath as long as they were quiet.

The Captain took the blanket out of her bag and spread it out. They both looked out over the expanse of sea and stars for a moment before Rosa pulled him down to the ground with her.

"Benny, please."

Ben nodded, taking her into an embrace, his lips hot on hers as he laid her back and removed her trousers.

"Six minutes, Mistress. But remember to be quiet."

She nodded, and Ben set about his wonderful, wanton work.

Rosa sighed, looking up at the stars. Her monthly course would be upon her soon, and the looming red tide must be the reason she wanted Benny so badly. She should not have agreed to this, but it was going to be difficult to sleep in such a small bed with him otherwise.

They may as well both get it out of their systems. She gazed up at the spring sky as Ben kissed up her thighs, his mustache igniting the fire in her loins once more. She ran her hands through his hair as he began to lick her slit, manipulating her with his fingers.

Rosa hated to admit it, but it was absolutely magical. Stars filled her vision, a warm breeze drifted across her skin, and Ben was using her favorite warm, sloppy tongue.

As he predicted, it took just about six minutes for her to reach release, and she threw her arm over her mouth to stifle the sound of her moan. He was infuriatingly good at that. Once he was done pleasuring her, Ben crawled back up beside Rosa, kissing her deeply. The taste of herself on his lips was as intoxicating as ever.

"How may I make love to you, Mistress?" he whispered in her ear. The vibration of his voice seemed to travel through her body, igniting her lust all over again.

"Whatever you intended to do to me in that little bed."

She felt his smile against her neck as he wiggled out of his trousers. His manhood pressed once more against her bottom, but now that there was nothing between them, all bets were off.

Ben held Rosa's legs open slightly so he could enter her, reaching around to rub her pleasure bud as he took her earlobe into his mouth. Rosa covered her mouth to keep a moan from escaping as her lover found his rhythm. His other hand went beneath her, cupping her breast and pulling her close.

"Benny," she moaned quietly, allowing the delicious warmth to run through her body. The tight, possessive hold he had on her limited his range of motion, almost as if he were trapped inside her. The head of his cock rubbed against the internal pleasure center like Aladdin rubbing the lamp. A powerful wave of euphoria was waiting to be released. She ached for it.

"Rosa," he whispered in her ear, making her shiver. Ben kept moving, the sensitive area begging for just a little more of him even as his fingers stimulated her nub. Her skin felt hot, and all her muscles coiled in anticipation. Rosa turned as best she could and caught Ben's lips with hers, but in order to turn far enough, she had to close her legs.

The result was explosive.

Her inner muscles clamped down on his manhood, locking him into place in exactly the spot he needed to be. He squeezed her breast roughly with his other hand, their lips crashing together. Rosa's whole body seized, enraptured. She curled into Ben, his mouth on hers, a guttural groan flowing from the very depths of her soul until her body stopped shaking and the warm, good feeling receded slightly.

They parted, Ben moving more slowly now, panting, squeezing her breast to try to calm himself. He would have loved nothing more than to release with her, but he did not want to make her angry, especially when they did not have access to her tea. It was taking every ounce of control he had to keep from releasing inside her.

"Rosa... Rosa, please..." he whispered in her ear.

Rosa pulled off him, flipped over to face him, and slid down to his crotch. She took him into her hands, sucking and stroking, allowing him to fuck her mouth.

"Rosa... please... please, please, please..."

The Black Rose nodded against his leg, and Ben finally allowed himself to give in to the ecstasy. Rosa felt his cock contract in her hand, and she shoved his manhood into her mouth just in time. Ben's world was full of light and warmth as he released into his lover's mouth.

"You're wonderful," Ben murmured as Rosa pulled his trousers back up and then her own.

"You are too, Benny. That was absolutely spectacular."

They cuddled, sharing more kisses and watching the stars, before Ben got a strong feeling they needed to go back. Rosa grumbled, giving him another kiss before they got up. As Rosa packed the blanket away, Ben saw a flash of light. But instead of making a wish about himself and Rosa, Ben's thoughts turned to Keiko and Raúl.

*May their child be healthy, beautiful, and may she join their community together in bonds that cannot be broken.*

Rosa stood, hefted her rucksack over her shoulder, took his hand, and led him back to the village. As they approached, they saw people moving around in the street outside Abuela Gabriela's house. It was Doctora, Felipe, and Raúl. Abuela Gabriela was at the door, and she smiled when she saw the couple approach. Doctora rushed over, breathless, Felipe hot on her heels. Raúl remained standing in front of Abuela Gabriela, looking a little shell-shocked.

"There you are. Thank goodness. Captain, get cleaned up, you'll be assisting us."

"What? Wait. Why me?" Rosa asked, panic in her voice.

Felipe put his giant hands on her shoulders. "Madame, Keiko asked for you. She wants you to be there. Would you really have me tell her no?"

Rosa suddenly looked very small, her skin paling in the moonlight.

"No," she whimpered, the Black Rose persona nowhere to be found.

Felipe picked a piece of grass out of her curls and flicked it away. "Excellent, Madame. Then let us have a baby."

"Who is with Keiko?" Ben asked, feeling stupid as soon as the question left his mouth.

"Giselle," Doctora answered as Rosa handed Ben her rucksack. "But we can't leave her alone too long. This is her first human birth."

Suddenly, Giselle's presence made much more sense. As Doctora's protégée, of course the girl would be involved in as many procedures as Doctora could manage. And since the physician was no longer in the habit of attending women in labor, the teacher in her would naturally pounce on the opportunity to have Giselle assist with a birth. She had likely witnessed a litter of puppies or kittens, but a human birth would be a different story entirely.

Rosa embraced Ben, and she was shaking slightly.

"You'll be fine, Captain," he whispered in her ear as she squeezed him tighter.

"I don't want to, but I can't refuse to help her. Take care of Raúl for us."

Ben nodded, kissing her cheek before she and Doctora disappeared into Raúl and Keiko's home. Felipe steered the father-to-be toward Ben, speaking in low tones in Spanish and indicating Abuela Gabriela, who stepped aside, beckoning the men into the house.

"What do you expect me to do?" Ben asked the older man. "I don't speak Spanish."

Felipe paused, reaching into his pocket and pulling something out: a deck of playing cards.

"That will not be a problem. Teach him a card game. Jules says these herbs work fast, so hopefully you will not have to wait long. I will come fetch him when it is done."

"Wait, why do you—?" Ben began, but the gunner was already gone. Raúl looked at Ben, his eyes wide, finally registering the other man's presence.

"Hello. I am Raúl. My English is not the best, but I speak some. We play cards until my baby comes, yes?"

"Yes, of course. My name is Ben. A pleasure to meet you. Come."

Ben checked the time when they went into Abuela Gabriela's house. It was a little before midnight. Abuela Gabriela lit some candles and provided the men with a sweet, warm corn drink called chicha, the same thing she had offered Andrew and Arturo earlier in the day. Raúl's English was actually quite good, so the two men were able to teach each other a few card games before their conversation turned to the topic that was clearly weighing on both of them.

"You are more nervous than I am, Benny-senpai. Do you have children?"

Ben shook his head, shuffling the cards. "No. And that is why I am nervous for you."

They looked at each other for a long moment in silence before Raúl shook his head.

"I will not think like that. Keiko said the child was still kicking and strong. I trust Tía Doctora and Tío Felipe to help her bring the baby into this world. We have both God and the Buddha on our side, and we both received the best fortunes at Ōmisoka. I fear nothing."

"What is Ōmisoka?" Ben asked.

"The New Year for the Buddhists, January first. They brought with them a tradition of drawing lots for fortunes for the year. Keiko and I both drew dai-kichi, the greatest blessing for the year. I have to believe it is correct, or I will be lost in despair."

Ben nodded. "Keiko is strong, and she is in the best possible hands."

The men spent the next few hours talking about how the Japanese Buddhists had changed the Panamanian town, how Ben found living on a pirate ship after years in the Royal Navy, and anything else they cared to discuss. Ben felt an odd kinship with the man, as if Raúl understood him on a deep level.

A little after three in the morning, a loud knock startled them, and Abuela Gabriela shuffled out of her room, a blanket over her shoulders. Felipe entered the house, bags under his eyes, but his body betraying his excitement. Raúl scrambled to his feet, and the Frenchman swept the younger man into a big hug. He said something, and Ben caught the word hija. Feminine. Raúl grabbed Felipe's arm.

"¿Y Keiko?"

"She is tired, but happy. Come!" the Frenchman said in Spanish before switching to English. "You too, Benny. Madame needs you."

The men collected up Felipe's cards and handed them back to the gunner, who tucked them into his pocket.

"How did Rosa and Giselle do?" Ben asked as Raúl embraced Abuela Gabriela.

"Giselle did admirably, considering this was not a litter of puppies. She still has much to learn, but this was an excellent first experience. Madame... well... eh... you will see."

Felipe opened the door, and Raúl bolted toward his house, leaving Felipe and Ben scrambling to catch up.

"It's a girl?" Ben asked, his heart swelling on behalf of his new friend.

The gunner nodded. "She is strong and beautiful. And big. Jules is right, they let Keiko go too long. It is good Keiko has large hips, otherwise..."

He stopped when they reached the door of the other house. Raúl had rushed inside, and Rosa met her officers at the door. She looked haggard and haunted.

"How was it, Captain?" Ben asked.

"It was disgusting," Rosa said, her body language wrapping her in prickly spikes like a cactus. Despite this, she took Ben's hand and squeezed it. The navigator could feel her trembling.

"It was beautiful," Felipe countered. "Bodies are wonderful, amazing things."

"You don't need to kiss Doctora's arse. She isn't even here."

Felipe laughed. "Non, I say it not because of her. I say it because it is true. But my Jules did an excellent job, as did Giselle."

Rosa shook her head.

"I want to go to bed. Can I have some tea to help me sleep?"

Felipe nodded, handing the Captain a flask. The Black Rose took a big swig. She swallowed, licked her lips, and took another big mouthful.

"Benny, I am going back to Abuela Gabriela's. Don't be long, because I will require some cuddles after all that, and this batch is strong."

Ben nodded as the Captain beat a hasty retreat. He watched her leave as Felipe shook his head. The younger man turned to the gunner.

"So why are you allowed to help with giving birth? That's very unusual."

Felipe opened his mouth and then shut it a few times, looking like a fish as he tried to decide what to say. He finally found an answer.

"I will not answer your question fully, as I fear it may upset you. But suffice it to say, Jules needs someone stronger than she is in case things go badly."

He clapped the younger man on the back.

"She has not yet needed me to do anything... disgusting... at least not acting as a midwife. Besides, Madame kept her eyes shut for most of it, so Jules needed someone who is not... how you say... delicate?"

Ben stared at him for a long moment before he started to laugh. Felipe gave him a strange look.

"I'm so sorry. I know what you mean, but it's funny to imagine the Captain as delicate."

Felipe thought for a moment and also snorted.

"Non, I understand. She is understandably uncomfortable with childbirth, considering..."

The Frenchman slapped a hand over his mouth. "Merde," he mumbled.

"Tobin told me, but I don't officially know."

Felipe nodded, lowering his hand. "Oui, Madame gets very upset over birthing and babies. She does nicely with children, but les enfants? Non. She gets very out of sorts. We only had her help because Keiko asked. Had Keiko not specifically requested Madame, you both would likely be asleep."

As if on cue, Ben yawned.

"What are they naming her?" he asked, shaking himself.

Felipe shrugged. "In Japan, they name the child on the seventh night. It is called Oshichiya. I am not sure whether they will observe that tradition or not. Keiko has not said anything. But that can all wait for the morning."

The younger man nodded and bade his brother-in-arms goodnight.

Ben made his way back to Abuela Gabriela's house, finding Rosa waiting for him in the tiny bed.

"Benny," she murmured, her voice thick.

Ben lay down next to her, taking her face in his hands. Her cheeks were wet, and her nose was running.

"Oh, Starlight," he murmured, holding her close.

She sobbed against him.

"Why did they make me do that?"

Ben held her as she cried herself to sleep, hoping it was stress and exhaustion, and that she would feel better in the morning.

# Chapter 35

## A Feast and the Future

Ben was startled awake by Rosa crying and screaming. He looked down at her in an unfamiliar bed, and she was massively pregnant.

"The baby!" she screamed, a torrent of blood and water running from under her skirts. "The baby is stuck because my hips are small!"

There was a crash as Felipe kicked in the door. "I am here to do something disgusting," the Frenchman cried, picking Ben up and throwing him bodily out of the room.

Ben woke from his nightmare when he hit the floor. Rosa grumbled in her sleep, stretching out in the small bed. Ben sat up, rubbing his shoulder, his heart pounding as he caught his breath. Sunlight streamed in through the window, and, tired as he was, there was no way he would be able to go back to sleep after that.

He may as well get up. His watch read half past six. He kissed Rosa on the cheek before going about his morning business.

Once he was ready, Ben made his way back to Raúl and Keiko's house. He found Felipe and Xiang sitting outside in the chairs, drinking tea together before

Buenaventura awoke. Xiang's tea smelled citrusy and was an earthy orange, meaning it was the pep-up tea; Felipe's was green and flowery, the jasmine calming tea. Neither man looked as though he had slept. Both showed every moment of their ages, the eldest and third-eldest members of the crew.

"Buenos días," Ben greeted them.

The men greeted him in return. "Did she sleep?" Felipe asked.

Ben nodded. "She did, eventually. She—" He was going to tell them she had cried herself to sleep, but caught himself. That was probably unnecessary. "She was quite upset. She is still sleeping, so I left her be."

Felipe clicked his tongue, and Ben continued. "Obviously, you did not sleep. Did Doctora? Did Giselle?"

The older man nodded. "They are both sleeping now, as is everyone else. However, I expect the baby will be waking soon. She is very precise, like clockwork. That is an excellent sign."

As if on cue, the door opened, and Raúl stepped out, carrying a blanket-wrapped bundle. Felipe and Xiang stood as he approached.

"I wish for you to meet her," the new father said quietly to Ben. Raúl offered him the blanket, and Ben looked between the other three men.

"Go on," Felipe whispered. "She will not bite."

Xiang made some soothing noises, smiling broadly.

Raúl gently placed the little girl in Ben's arms, and Xiang made sure the navigator supported her head. She weighed more than Ben expected, even after Felipe had mentioned she was big. She was also incredibly cute. The little girl blinked up at him, and Ben was smitten almost faster than he had fallen in love with the Black Rose.

"Hullo, darling," Ben said quietly.

She had a mass of downy black hair, large dark eyes, and the tiniest little nose. She smelled like milk, a scent that took him back to the first time he had held his youngest sister, Sarah, when he was nine. The baby reached up and uncoordinatedly tapped Ben's own large nose with a burble. Ben caught her hand, and her fingers wrapped around one of his.

Her skin was so smooth and soft, and each tiny fingernail reminded him of a fancy doll Anne had from England that held a place of honor on her bureau. The baby yawned, showing a little pink tongue. Ben's heart did not know whether it wanted to swell, shatter, or both. His eyes blurred with tears.

"Preciosa," he whispered, giving the child a gentle hug before handing her back to her father, who beamed proudly.

"Yes," Raúl agreed.

The baby began to fuss. After a quick consultation with the other men, it was determined that the child was hungry, so Raúl took his leave to bring the girl to her mother for feeding. Felipe also went inside to check on Doctora and Giselle, leaving Ben and Xiang outside.

The navigator watched them go, trembling, rooted in place. Once the door closed, Xiang pulled Ben into a tight bear hug, and the dam of emotions broke. Ben sank to the ground, and the cook pivoted, rubbing his back and whispering to him.

Another body appeared at his side, a hand on his back. Doctora, looking exhausted, her hair in a loose ponytail instead of her usual tight bun on the crown of her head.

"Oh, Benny," she muttered.

Ben turned and latched onto her, crying into her hair.

"It's okay, Benny. Someday."

"But... Rosa..." Ben blubbered.

Doctora squeezed tighter, as if she intended to crush Ben's soul out of his body. Or perhaps back into it. The pressure was comforting and calming.

"She is young still and has a lot to work through. You have time."

Ben hiccuped, sniffling. "She's so beautiful... and so tiny," he said wetly. He pulled away slightly, wiping his eyes.

"She's very beautiful," Doctora agreed. "Another little heartbreaker to add to our protection."

"I'm glad Raúl took it better than Alicia's husband. I'm not sure what I would have done if he had been angry."

The physician gave him a handkerchief to wipe his eyes and nose.

"He was more concerned for Keiko. It did not matter to him whether the child was a boy or a girl, so long as Keiko survived."

Xiang made a small noise of agreement before Doctora continued.

"Raúl is... well, he's a lot like you in many respects. He's very smart, but he also doesn't work well with people. He's good with language, like you are good with calculations and maps, but he does not do well with the... I suppose, the emotion behind the language. He spent all his time by himself, reading and teaching himself different languages. Let me see..."

She counted on her fingers. "Spanish, English, Latin... He speaks and reads four languages. Geraldo says he would never have found a wife if Keiko had not literally shown up on his doorstep. They needed all available beds, and since Raúl's sister, Marilena, married a man in the city, her bed was not being used. Keiko took a liking to Raúl immediately. Her interest confused him for a bit, but he learned her language as fast as lightning, and now he speaks Japanese almost as well as Felipe does."

Xiang said something, and he and Doctora chuckled.

"I'm sorry, better. She is also teaching him to write the kanji, which is a wonderful way to preserve her history. He was tasked with teaching the Buddhists Spanish, and he and Keiko give language lessons together. They're two drops of water." She chuckled. "He's an entirely different person now that he knows where he belongs. Surely you relate, no?"

Ben nodded.

"But Keiko is doing well, and so all is right in his world. And today, there's more in it."

A mass of curious bystanders, both Panamanian and Japanese, began to gather outside the house. They stood, eyes wide and expectant, but nobody said a word. Doctora and Xiang helped Ben to his feet.

"We have to wait for the elders to come," Doctora explained, waving to the townsfolk. The lines around her eyes looked deeper than usual after her late night. "If we announce it before they come, we'll never hear the end of it." She turned to Ben, eyes twinkling behind her spectacles. "I was very surprised Abuela Gabriela offered beds to you and the Captain."

"It was one bed, sized for a child. But I can't help feeling she was attempting to drive us closer together."

Doctora and Xiang both raised their eyebrows before laughing.

"No, that sounds like Abuela Gabriela. They say she has an eye for matchmaking. Nobody in this town is allowed to marry without her blessing. If she did that immediately after meeting you, she must see potential for you as a couple. You should see the nonsense she orchestrates to get me to confess my feelings to... ah, speak of the devil, and she appears."

Abuela Gabriela was approaching with the other elders. They walked up to the front, standing before Ben, Doctora, and Xiang.

Doctora raised her hands, speaking Spanish slowly so Ben could pick out some of the vocabulary he had been learning over the past few months. He gathered she was announcing the birth of a daughter around three in the morning; the parents were happy; and they would name the child at the Oshichiya Felipe had mentioned.

When she was finished, Xiang repeated the message in Japanese. Everyone held their cheers and applause until Xiang finished, bowing to the abbot monk and to the gathered townsfolk.

Abuela Gabriela raised her hands, and any confidence Ben had gained in his Spanish listening comprehension went out the window as the older woman spoke. There were cheers, nods, and applause before the crowd dispersed.

"They will celebrate our visit and the birth with a feast tonight. Tobin and the others should be coming back soon," Doctora told Ben. "They will make sure to bring food for Keiko and Raúl throughout the day and the week."

Ben nodded. "What should I do? Is there anything I can do to help?"

Doctora patted the younger man's cheek. "You can make sure the Captain is not too distressed by what she saw last night. I may try to get a little more sleep, and hopefully Felipe will, too. Giselle was exhausted, so she will likely be out for a few more hours."

Xiang said something, pointing to himself with a big smile.

"Yes, it was fitting for you to be the first to see her." She turned back to Ben. "He has a little prayer he says over the child for health and luck, and it was a beautiful moment." She sighed. "That child is destined for something great."

She gave Ben one more squeeze and then pushed him toward Abuela Gabriela's house. "Go. You still look tired, too. Maybe you should also have a nap in the tiny bed before the feast."

Rosa was still asleep when Ben returned. He tried to arrange himself without waking her and knocked over the decorative wall hanging while trying to climb around her. He froze as the large weaving fell to the ground with a clatter, but Rosa did not stir.

Felipe had previously mentioned she was a heavy sleeper. Ben decided he could be a little less careful and managed to comfortably situate the two of them in the bed without Rosa waking. The woman truly did like her sleep. Ben rested his head on Rosa's breast, listening to her heart beating slowly. His eyelids grew heavy, and soon he was asleep as well.

A tickle under his ear woke him, and his hand caught Rosa's. Her chest rose and fell as she chuckled, and he turned to face her.

"Buenos días, Benny."

"Good morning, Starlight," he mumbled. "How are you?" His eyes did not want to open.

"Much better now that I've had some sleep, but I saw some things last night I don't know if I will ever be able to get out of my head."

"What about the things you felt?" Ben asked, his hand possessive on her breast again. He was still mentally foggy, and his shoulder still hurt from falling out of bed.

"The part with you was wonderful. You quite outdid yourself. But everything after that was..." She shuddered. "Quite unnecessary. I hate not being able to say no when people ask for help."

Ben finally managed to pry open his eyes. "I'm sure it was good for you."

She scrunched up her nose before pushing him off her chest and wiggling out from under him.

"She's beautiful, though," Ben said, rolling onto his side as he watched Rosa walk around the room gathering her things.

"Have Tobin and the others come back yet?" she asked, changing the subject.

"Not sure. They weren't when I came back to bed, around seven." He pulled out his watch. "But it's about ten now. The village is holding a feast for us tonight."

Rosa sat down on the bed, kissing Ben on the forehead. "Excellent. You're going to love it."

Ben and Rosa exited Abuela Gabriela's house to find Buenaventura abuzz. There was an energy to the town that had not been present the day before, even with the arrival of their favorite pirate crew. Rosa took Ben's hand and led him to the festival grounds, where they found Tobin and the other members of the crew.

Tobin was following Abuela Gabriela around with a piece of paper, taking notes as the old woman talked. Xiang, Natsuki, and Song Mei were tending a massive fire pit. The two pigs Ben and Rosa had killed the day before were roasting, along with a massive quantity of vegetables.

Doctora was sitting beside it, watching the cook and his assistants work. Giselle was asleep with her head in the physician's lap, and Felipe dozed with his head on Doctora's shoulder. The older woman still looked tired, but happy to be exactly where she was. She smiled to see Ben and Rosa approaching.

"Good morning, Captain," she chirped. "Benny."

Her voice and movement woke Felipe, who snorted and blinked. The gunner scrambled to his feet.

"Madame," he said. "None the worse for wear, I see."

Rosa glared daggers at him.

"Do not make me do that again," she hissed.

Doctora bit her lip, trying not to smile, and gently tugged on one of Giselle's braids to wake the child. Giselle shook herself and sat up. She rubbed her eyes.

"Jean-Luc. Maeve. I delivered a baby," she shouted before scampering over to her brother and her auntie, chattering excitedly in a mix of French, Spanish, and English.

"Again, Madame, she asked for you. And you agreed to help her because she asked." Felipe helped Doctora to her feet. "And, despite your misgivings, I think you being there gave Giselle confidence as well."

"She did an excellent job," Rosa said. "She is well on her way to becoming a talented physician."

Doctora beamed.

"They are just about ready to serve," Tobin's voice rumbled from behind Rosa and Ben. "Song Mei and Xiang will deliver some plates to Raúl and Keiko later."

There was such a wide array of food that Ben did not know where to start. Some of the Buddhists appeared to be strict vegetarians, so there was a wide variety of plant-based dishes. The only meat available was from the pigs.

As he was considering his options, Ben found himself cornered by an old woman. She was older than Doctora, but younger than Abuela Gabriela. She spoke excitedly, reaching up to pull Ben down to her level and offering him a fork with something on it.

Pork.

Shit.

"No... no gracias," he said weakly.

The woman's smile left her eyes, and she spoke faster, poking him on the chest. He got the very distinct impression she was telling him that, since he had killed the pigs, he should taste them. Ben did not want to argue. He forced a smile and accepted the pork from the old woman.

"Gracias," he said, his throat tight.

He took a bite, and despite the spices, the flavor and texture of the pig brought back a series of traumatic memories.

Memories of wrecking a ship on Los Roques during a mutiny when he was twelve.

Of killing a man with a rock to save his own skin.

Of having to eat the bodies of his shipmates to survive.

*Of swearing silence to Captain Llewellyn as the captain burned the logbooks detailing why he and Ben were the only survivors.*

In the present, Doctora, Felipe, Rosa, and Tobin were all watching Ben with concern. Ben continued to chew, eyes watering, as he felt hot bile rise in the back of his throat. He calmly placed his plate on a table, walked a little way behind some flowering bushes, and vomited violently.

As Ben expelled the entire contents of his stomach for the second time in a month, he felt a gentle hand on his back. When he stood, he found the hand was attached to Rosa. She, Felipe, and Tobin all wore varying degrees of exasperation, while Doctora dug around in one of the pouches on her utility belt.

She found a thumb of ginger, flicked open her folding knife, and cut him off a small coin. Ben nibbled on it, allowing the strong flavor to coat his tongue and throat and drive away the taste of bile. As expected, Felipe spoke first.

"What did we tell you about eating things that will make you sick just to be polite?"

"I couldn't..." Ben began.

The Frenchman shook his head. "Non. Jamaal, Halima, Zahra, and Aisha, they did not eat the pork just to be polite. Anya, Zsófia, and Gerda also do not eat the pork. They all very sweetly said, 'No, gracias,' and ate something else that did not touch the pork. Very simple, oui?"

"But they did it for us," the navigator mumbled weakly, feeling his face flush more from Felipe's disapproval than from being ill.

Doctora tsked at the gunner and put a gentle hand on Ben's arm.

"You and the Captain killed the pigs. They cooked the pigs. It was not necessarily for you both so much as to use what they had. And to celebrate the birth of Mariko."

Everyone's head snapped up. Felipe grabbed Doctora by the shoulders, his annoyance with Ben forgotten.

"Is that the name? You found out the name?" he laughed giddily. For such a large, frightening man, he could be incredibly childlike sometimes. "That is a most excellent name."

The physician smiled, putting her hands on top of his. "Raúl's family wanted to name her María, but Keiko wanted to name her Kokoro. So they compromised. Mari. Ko. Mariko. They will announce it on her seventh night, per Japanese tradition, but since we won't be here, they told me."

"It is an excellent name. I knew a Mariko once, and she told me her name meant 'child of a genuine village.' If that is how they choose to write it in Japanese, it is perfect."

Tobin cleared his throat. "Back to the matter at hand. Benny, you really must stop putting politeness ahead of your own well-being. If you don't want to eat the damn pig, then for fuck's sake, don't eat the damn pig. We can't afford for you to keep making yourself sick. Please."

Rosa squeezed Ben's hand. "Please stop torturing yourself for other people's approval. Especially people you've only just met."

"Everyone, please," Doctora sighed, taking off her spectacles and rubbing her eyes. Her long day and a half was clearly catching up to her. "You all know Tía Faustina can be pushy." She turned to Ben. "Do you feel a little better?"

Ben nodded.

"Good. There are plenty of other things to eat, but if you start to feel ill again, stop eating and chew some more ginger."

"Thank you, Doctora."

Ben tried valiantly to push memories of Los Roques away and enjoy the present moment. He concentrated on eavesdropping on Spanish conversations and trying to pick out words he recognized. That proved to be an excellent distraction. Ben also found a pepper salad that he really liked, and it paired well with noodles. There was a great air of celebration. At one point, Raúl appeared and was showered with hugs and kisses.

The poor man looked immensely uncomfortable, much as Ben imagined he probably did when he was about to freeze. Thankfully, Xiang and Song Mei swooped in, gave him plates piled high with food, and shepherded him back to his wife and child.

As the shadows grew long, the Black Rose and her crew started saying their goodbyes. Rosa especially wanted to be back on the ship before bedtime. Ben found himself face-to-face with Abuela Gabriela, who took his hand and led him away from the rest of his crew.

"Umm, muchas gracias... su... uhh... hospitality?" he said quietly.

She beckoned him down to her level, and Ben bent slightly. She took his face into her soft, wrinkled hands. She stroked her thumbs over Ben's cheeks and, with great effort, spoke quietly in English.

"You remember me of my married man, Ignacio. I ache without. I was proud as a young, and fault many years, many years I could have been his woman. We wed many years, but could was longer. Rosa is good girl, but stubborn. Girl is blind if no see good man you are. Almost stupid like Julieta and the French goat. They clearly love too, fault many years playing baby games. I am content that Andrew not follow the bad example they give."

She shook her head. "Nobody is made young again. I hope I help you and Rosa pass good night together. You are good man, brave and smart. I see you with baby, you will be good father. Care for Rosa. Care for all of them. They are good family. Maybe a little stupid, but a good family."

Ben nodded, taking the woman's hands in his and standing back up.

"*Thank you very much. Rosa and I... many kisses... with the stars... very romantic*," he pieced together in Spanish. It was jerky and did not flow musically, but she seemed to understand.

The woman smiled, showing a number of missing teeth. "Qué bueno. You welcome to come share little bed when you return. And no eat pig if pain the stomach."

The old woman and the young man chuckled together before she patted his cheek and walked away. Ben felt a hand on his shoulder.

Rosa.

He looked over his shoulder and smiled at her. A good girl, but stubborn indeed.

"Come, Benny, back to the ship!"

# Chapter 36

## Presents and Panic

Once the *Deception* was away from Panamá, with the promise to return in early autumn, Ben threw himself into his training with Tobin and Felipe. He was running out of time to ensure he beat James so decisively that the other Englishman would not be able to twist the situation in his favor. The older men tried to incorporate more dirty tactics into their fights, which Ben hated.

Why did James have to be such an arsehole that they couldn't trust him to fight fair? It was not the first time he'd had this thought and it came to him again as he shielded the sensitive area between his legs from Tobin's knee. It did not help that Rosa kept looking over at them, one steady hand on the helm.

She was likely watching to keep Tobin and Felipe from "damaging the goods," but it made Ben incredibly self-conscious. The last thing he wanted was for her to see how weak he still was.

Rosa was also not as sexually generous as usual after her experience helping Keiko through labor. Even though, according to both Felipe and Doctora, it had been completely normal and unremarkable, the Captain was skittish about letting Ben into her bed. It did take Ben a day or two to figure out that she was also likely dealing with her monthly course, and that realization made him feel a little better.

Rosa invited him into her quarters one evening to read what Ben and Felipe had recorded so far for the *Chronicles of the Deception*, making annotations of her own as she went. After she was done reading, Ben pulled her into his lap for some kisses and cuddles. She began to roll her hips out of habit before stiffening and rolling off him. She sat beside him, her hair falling in a protective curtain as she put her face in her hands.

"Starlight?"

"Benny, no, you don't understand..." She shook her head, her voice muffled. "A whole head... a whole... *child*... came out of her. It was..." She shuddered. He put a hand on her shoulder, and she leaned over onto his chest. "I'm sure I'll get over it, but it was so..."

Ben kissed her forehead. "I'm sure you will, Starlight. But you're allowed to think it was upsetting, regardless of what Doctora and Felipe say. And besides, we're careful. You drink your tea. We won't worry about that until you decide we're ready for it. Now, what can I do to make you feel more relaxed and comfortable?"

Rosa sat up, blinking in confusion. She reached over to her chest of drawers and pulled out the plumeria-scented warming lotion. She hiked up her shirt and lay on her stomach on the bed.

"Rub my back?" she asked, indicating the swath of skin she had left exposed.

"Of course, Starlight." Ben rubbed the lotion into her lower back, singing softly to her. He was oddly pleased that she fell asleep under his touch. He moved her into a more reasonable sleeping position, and as he pulled the covers over her, he gently kissed her forehead.

"I love you, Starlight, and I will win you yet," he whispered. She mumbled something back in Spanish, but he definitely heard her say "Benny." His heart fluttered as he showed himself out.

The following week, during the next officers' meeting, Ben wore his spectacles. As they hashed out the next few ports of call, he made sure to look at her repeatedly over the frames. Rosa's cheeks flushed, and her hand traveled up his leg under the desk as she knelt next to him, once again playing her lusty game of chicken.

He pretended not to notice, keeping his voice and hand steady as he sat scratching small Xs into the map. He let her get within a hair's breadth of her quarry before he caught her hand and winked, enjoying the spike in her skin temperature.

Once everyone was satisfied with the next few weeks' sailing, the other officers filed out to go about their business. The Captain caught Ben by the back of his collar, and he smirked as she pulled him back into her quarters. Once the door was closed, Rosa took Ben into a deep kiss, turning their joined bodies around and backing herself into the door. Ben pressed up against her, relishing the warmth of her body against his.

"You're a very naughty girl, Starlight," he said against her lips.

She nodded, tugging at his curls as they kissed again. "You're one to talk, you walrus. Wearing your spectacles to seduce me."

"I was wearing them to work. And what about you, trying to touch my cock in front of everyone? It seems the walrus may in fact have been you all along."

The couple stared at each other for a long moment before collapsing into a fit of laughter. Rosa's head fell forward onto Ben's shoulder.

"Please make love to me, Mistress," he whispered into her ear as he maneuvered her hips against his.

She gently pushed his pelvis away from hers. "Benny, we can't..."

"But perhaps delicious release will help you forget about it," he murmured against her forehead.

"It's not that, Benny..."

There was a knock at the door. Rosa smiled, eyes twinkling, and pulled it open. Felipe, Talia, Doctora, and Tobin all scrambled back into the Captain's quarters, conspiratorial grins on their faces. Felipe carried something large and vaguely phallic, covered with a sheet. Doctora and Talia had large baskets that looked very heavy. The Frenchman deposited his item onto the Black Rose's desk, adjusting the cloth to make sure it remained covered. The women dropped their parcels on the floor, shoving them under the desk.

"He doesn't suspect a thing," Tobin said quietly.

Then Ben remembered.

Xiang's birthday.

There was another knock at the door, and Natsuki, Daichi, and Andrew also slipped into the room.

"Li Mei and Frank are keeping him busy," Natsuki said with a breathless smile. "Frank accidentally on purpose let Mar into the chicken run, and Li Mei may have riled her up considerably, so now it will take all three of them to give her a bath."

Doctora snorted, and Felipe raised a finger. Andrew anticipated his question.

"Don't worry, we gave Eliza some coin... and other favors... to play along," he said, his clear brown eyes twinkling with amusement.

The Frenchman nodded, and Ben laughed. It was delightfully absurd how much respect Eliza commanded, even if, in Ben's opinion, she absolutely deserved it. Ben had always had issues with the feel of his uniform fabric on his skin, but the laundress somehow magically kept all his clothes and his blanket soft without his worrying that they would fray or tatter.

They always smelled nice, too. As far as he was concerned, the woman was a fae creature with a talent for cleaning clothing, but she would raze the ship if angered. He wondered when her birthday was.

"Did you get the saké from Osamu-sama?" Rosa asked Natsuki, who nodded before taking a basket off her back and putting it on the desk next to Felipe's sheeted tower. Felipe and Tobin pulled out the bottles and examined them, and Tobin nodded, pleased.

The plan for Xiang's birthday would require quite a bit of distraction for the cook, who was always surprised that his crew made a big deal of his birthday. Especially with his Buddhist background, he was often overwhelmed by the gifts given to him, so everyone made sure, whenever possible, that the gifts would also benefit the rest of the crew.

As everyone planned and chattered excitedly, Ben began to think about what he could offer Xiang for his birthday. Xiang was the first member of the crew to truly welcome him, and he had learned a great deal from the little Buddhist man.

Ben was drawn from his thoughts by a knock at the door. Apparently, he was the only one who heard it, so he went to answer. He opened the door to find Giselle and Maeve on the other side. Maeve looked unperturbed, but the girl looked absolutely horrified, clutching her sides.

"We need Doctora," Maeve said.

Ben nodded and turned, waving Doctora over. The physician pouted slightly at having to leave Felipe's side.

"Hello, Maeve... Giselle, what's wrong, cariño?"

The girl burst into tears and threw herself into Doctora's arms. Maeve sighed.

"Chile is a woman now," she said matter-of-factly.

Doctora's face softened, and she nodded. "It's alright, Giselle. I'll give you something for the pain, and we'll talk about what's happening with your body. Meet me downstairs."

The girl sniffled, nodded, and detached herself. Then she and Maeve made their way down the steps. Doctora whispered something to Rosa and Felipe, and they both nodded.

The look of disappointment on Felipe's face reminded Ben of the bet they had made back in March, the one that had resulted in the gunner becoming his co-author for the *Chronicles of the Deception* project. The Frenchman had wanted Ben to man the infirmary and give Doctora the night off.

While Ben was not entirely sure he would be the best person to have a "Congratulations, you're a woman now" talk, he had overheard some of it when his mother had delivered it to the triplets. She had included a piece of advice that rang in Ben's ears now, something he wished he had followed more closely to save himself eight years of pain:

"Now that you are capable of bearing a child, think long and hard about the men you allow to know you in that way. Make absolutely certain he is the sort of man you want raising your child. And if he is not, do not let him near that part of you to even invite that possibility."

If only his father had said something similar, maybe it would have stuck. Thankfully, all of Ben's sisters had taken that advice to heart, with assistance from Nathaniel, who took his protective older brother role far more seriously than Ben did. The triplets in particular had been incredibly choosy with suitors, especially after the experience with Ben's classmate, Joshua.

"Benny-kun?" Natsuki asked quietly, putting her hand on Ben's arm.

He jumped slightly, his memory of Hope, Grace, and Felicity twirling back into the darkness of his mind.

"Sorry, Natsuki… Say, I have an idea. Would you be willing to help me?"

The next evening, the night before Xiang's birthday so he would not suspect, the plan was put into motion. Ben's role was to "accidentally" spill grog on Rosa, drawing Xiang from behind the counter. They waited until the supper line was finished, ensuring nobody went hungry. Ben walked over to Daichi, holding a full mug of grog. As the navigator and the Japanese man exchanged pleasantries, the Black Rose slunk up behind them.

Before Ben could make his move, the plan spiraled out of control. Juanito, attempting to get Rosa's attention, tripped, knocking the Captain into her lover. Ben's grog sloshed over as he stumbled backward onto Rosa and the boy.

Juanito reached up to grab the edge of the table and knocked Daichi's mug onto the dogpile, spilling it right in Ben's face. Ben sputtered, rolling off Rosa, thankful he did not weigh enough to hurt her.

Rosa was stiff as a plank, pale, her breathing fast and shallow. Ben remembered her similarly panicked during his first flying lesson. Being pinned to the ground evoked the same primal terror as her fear of heights. Ben squeezed her hand, and she looked up at him, eyes wild. She was having an attack of nerves, not unlike his own. Juanito scrambled away like a pup avoiding a swat to the rump, and Xiang approached with rags and a mop.

"Captain, breathe," Ben said quietly, rubbing small circles on her hand. "Concentrate on my voice, and come back to me. Tell me one thing you can hear."

"Your voice," she muttered with a shaky breath.

"One thing you can feel."

"Wet. I feel... I feel wet."

Not exactly what he expected, but not incorrect.

"One thing you can taste."

"Blood. Blood." She stuck out her tongue, which was, in fact, bleeding.

"That's definitely blood, yes. One thing you can smell."

"Grog. It's in my nose."

"Yes, everything smells like grog. And one thing you can see."

"Xiang is coming."

Ben took some deep breaths, and Rosa mimicked him. The cook knelt, offering the rags to his fellow officers.

"Captain?" Xiang asked.

Rosa nodded. "I bit my tongue, but I think I'm okay now. I'm sorry, Benny..."

"No, Captain, I'm sorry. I didn't mean to land on you like that. I lost my balance, and I know you don't like that."

As Ben nervously helped Xiang wipe the grog off Rosa's skin, he watched over Xiang's shoulder. Felipe quickly placed the large tower thing on the counter, removing the sheet with a grand flourish. The sudden movement deflected the crew's attention, eliciting quiet gasps and whispers.

It was a tall, three-tiered serving platter, each layer carved with intricate flowering vines. Each tier was divided into sections, which Natsuki and Doctora rapidly filled with nuts, dried jerky strips, and small fruits like grapes and berries.

Talia, noticing Rosa's distress, put a finger to her lips before picking up some oranges. She proceeded to juggle them rapidly, her past as a traveling acrobat shining through. Her grin dazzled, but her emerald eyes held very serious concern for her Captain. Once everything was set up, the Frenchman nodded to Ben with a thumbs-up. Ben helped Rosa to her feet. She put a hand on Ben's arm and exhaled shakily, smiling weakly at Xiang.

"Surprise," she said quietly, pointing to the counter.

Xiang turned and gasped to see his gift and his fellow officers standing behind it. He dropped the mop in shock. Andrew picked it up and made quick work of the mess on the floor before retreating to stand with his co-conspirators.

Talia, still juggling her fruits, caught them with a flourish and a loud "Ta-da!" Xiang's eyes went wide as he moved back toward the counter and examined it. He said something, and the gunner, physician, and boatswain all beamed. Felipe glanced at the Captain and Ben before launching into his showman voice.

"Oui. Jules had an idea around Christmas. She thought it would be most lovely if we had a rotating serving platter to complement the fruit bowl. It was a most excellent problem to solve. She carved the leaf design."

Doctora pushed it gently, and the whole tower turned around, gliding smoothly on some sort of mechanism. Ben thought it sounded like balls rolling through metal tubes. While the rest of the crew was enraptured, Ben took the opportunity to give Rosa a hug. She was still shaking, but she accepted his embrace. Ben squeezed her as hard as he dared and felt her relax in his arms.

"Then I gave them the idea to make the wee bowls. And I helped carve them. Look!"

Talia popped the snack-filled bowls out and set them on the counter as Felipe and Doctora put other items onto the now-empty platters. Once they were finished, there was an array of glass jars and vials on each tier, and on top sat a potted plant with the tiniest little pepper Ben had ever seen.

"Happy birthday!"

"Joyeux anniversaire!"

"¡Feliz cumpleaños! And we got a baby pepper plant from Song Mei, so we will never be without her special chiles!"

Xiang said something with the word yīqǐ, which Ben knew meant "together," and they all nodded. He bowed deeply to them and, for the first time, said something in Mandarin that Ben understood entirely.

"Thank you. It is beautiful. I like it very much!"

They bowed back and gave him a massive group hug. The smaller Chinese man kissed both women on the cheek, and Felipe kissed Xiang on the forehead.

Once they let go, Felipe shifted, fumbling in his pocket.

"I realize it may be in poor taste to give someone else a gift on your birthday, but I know you will understand. I have a gift for Tobin."

The quartermaster looked up from examining the serving tray, confused.

"I know your birthday is not for a while, but they are finished, and I want you to have them now. Summer comes swiftly." He handed Tobin an elegantly carved box, bowing slightly. "Jules carved the case to match the serving tray."

Tobin took the box and popped it open.

Inside were a pair of spectacles made of bronze wire and brown-tinted glass. Tobin gingerly put them on and stepped over to the porthole, looking out at the setting sun.

"You son of a bitch," he rumbled, his voice full of emotion.

Doctora put her arm around Felipe's waist, grinning proudly.

"We think they will help your headaches," she said, her hand on the Frenchman's chest.

Tobin turned back to the group, took them off, and put them back in the case before catching the gunner around the waist and rubbing the top of the older man's head with a closed fist.

"They're wonderful, you old bastard. I can already tell they'll help!"

Felipe laughed as he broke out of the younger man's hold.

"And thank you, Doctora!"

She beamed as he hugged her. Ben looked down at Rosa, who was still clamped around his waist. Her color and breathing had returned to normal. After a moment, she gave him a squeeze, lightly kissed his chest, and let go. The Black Rose stepped away from him, standing up straight, cracking her neck, and clearing her throat, her Captain persona in full effect.

"I also have a gift for you, Xiang, but it comes with a caveat. I'm sure you will know exactly what it is." She reached under the counter and pulled out a massive basket with a cloth over it. She removed the cloth, revealing that it was full of coconuts and a large bag of sugar. Xiang's eyes went wide, and he covered his mouth with his hands. Ben could immediately tell why: that bag of sugar must have cost her entire last share. The cook spoke, and Rosa shook her head.

"Yes, I did. And I wanted to. But I think you see what I want you to do with it?"

Xiang nodded and bowed deeply, nearly folding himself in half. Ben racked his brain, but then he remembered: Xiang wanted to experiment with making sweets, and one of his favorites to make was a three-ingredient coconut thing. Coconut. Sugar. Water. The Captain smiled broadly and clapped her hands. When he stood, the Black Rose swept her cook into a big hug, and they traded kisses on the cheek.

Ben had his gift for Xiang as well, but the thought of presenting it so publicly after everything else that had just happened made him want to vomit. Instead, he sidled up to Tobin, tapping him on the leg with the small scroll. The quartermaster tore his eyes away from his lover and his little sister, and the navigator held it out.

"It's for Xiang, but I don't want... I can't... there are too many people... especially after all that... and I don't even know if he can read English..."

Tobin snorted slightly, taking the scroll. He unrolled it, scanning Ben's neatest handwriting.

On the evening of his choosing, I, Benjamin R. Harrington, will cover the supper line in Xiang's stead. If he so desires, I will also teach Frank and Li Mei to make his noodles for the next day's supper. Natsuki has agreed to assist.


Underneath Ben's script, Natsuki had written something in Japanese, but had neglected to tell Ben what it meant. It was clear from Tobin's questioning look that he did not know, either.

"No, she didn't tell me. But I'm assuming it will mean something to him."

Tobin nodded, rolling the scroll back up and tying it. "Thank you. He will be pleased. I'll give it to him later."

"Xièxiè, Tobin."

The quartermaster nodded even as he tried to hide his smile. "And good work with the Captain's attack of nerves. She..."

"I know, she doesn't like weight on top of her."

Tobin nodded again.

Rosa turned to her crew, looking no worse for wear. "Let us move this revelry up to the deck. What say you all?"

The Black Rose was greeted with a great cheer from the crew.

# Chapter 37

## Birthdays and Barometric Pressure

As there usually was with celebrations on the *Deception*, there was much singing, dancing, and laughter to celebrate their beloved cook. Xiang's favorite song, according to Tobin, was "Fathom the Bowl," which Ben did not really believe until he noticed Xiang mouthing along to Talia's singing. The man spoke much more English than he let on. A lot more.

After a while, Talia took Euphonia from Ben and nodded slightly in the direction of the Captain with a wink. She began to strum a jaunty tune on Johnny Jump-Up, which made Rosa squeal with delight.

"And it's all for me grog, me jolly, jolly grog!"

Ben arrived next to Rosa, who took his hands and began to twirl.

"I love this song," she shouted above the noise. "It's my favorite!"

Ben nodded and sang along with Talia as he allowed the Black Rose to lead him in a dance. After the song was over, they ended up in a small group with Felipe, Doctora, and Tobin. Talia was playing a tune Bjorn had requested, and the Swede was singing in a deep, mighty voice. Xiang was talking to Natsuki, Li Mei, and Frank, so Ben guessed they would be retrieving whatever they would use for the birthday toast soon. Ben looked down at the Captain.

Rosa sneezed with a quiet "ow," then rubbed her cheeks just under her eyes. Suddenly, a look of terror slowly crossed her face.

"Oh no."

Felipe, Doctora, and Tobin all looked up, and immediately the same look of panic colored their features as well.

"Merde."

"Ay, joder."

"Shit."

The officers had a wordless conversation of raised eyebrows, grimaces, nods, and head shakes. They seemed to be debating what to do. The Black Rose looked between her officers and mouthed, "Vote?" Her quartermaster, gunner, and physician all nodded. Rosa looked at Ben.

"I didn't quite follow. Whatever you decide is fine with me," he said quietly, so as not to draw attention to them.

"Do we interrupt Xiang's birthday to prepare for the coming storm?" the Captain whispered.

Ben nodded. His first real vote on an emergency matter as an officer, and it was to ruin a birthday celebration. And not just any birthday, but the birthday of the sweetest man Ben had possibly ever known.

Felipe put a hand on the navigator's arm. "I know it is difficult, but this is being an officer."

Ben nodded. The Black Rose wordlessly counted on her fingers at waist level, and Ben grimaced as he lifted an open hand on three. It was only logical that if Rosa knew a storm was coming, they would have to ready themselves. They were in the middle of the open ocean, with no safe harbor within a day's sail, and the *Deception* was quite a large vessel.

They had to be responsible and prevent anyone from getting drunk ahead of preparations. He fully expected everyone else to show closed fists, especially Tobin, and was surprised to see a unanimous showing of open hands. They were all in agreement; they had to stop the party.

"We have to let them know before the saké comes out. Xiang will understand," Tobin rumbled, and Ben could hear the disappointment in his words.

Rosa nodded and cracked her neck. She climbed up onto a barrel, holding on to a piece of the rigging. Felipe put two fingers in his mouth and whistled, loud and long. All the chatter, music, and laughter stopped. All eyes were on Rosa, who once more melted away to reveal their Captain, the fearsome Black Rose.

"I am sorry to interrupt your celebration, Xiang, but we've got a storm coming, and it's going to be bad. Worst one we've seen in a good while. We decided it was better to tell you before the saké came out. We can still do a toast, but we need everyone sober and ready when it comes. And I know some of you will be trying saké for the first time."

Xiang stepped forward, bowing to the Captain. Ben heard the words *wǒ míngbái, I understand,* and *nǐ de zhìhuì, your wisdom.* Even so, Ben could tell the man was saddened to cut the celebration short, even as he endeavored not to show it.

"Very well," the Black Rose said. "We shall still have our saké toast, but if you are not familiar with it, maybe take a smaller portion."

Xiang said something else to the Captain, whose eyebrows shot up and whose eyes went wide.

"Oh. Xiang says if anyone wants to join the Mohammedan crew in a non-alcoholic toast, he understands."

There were murmurs among the crew. While Xiang was generally the most generous man aboard the ship, the juice the Mohammedan crew drank for toasts was not usually offered so freely. Ben was torn. On one hand, he had never had either drink; on the other, saké would likely come out again. It was very unlikely he would be offered something specifically made for the Mohammedan crew again.

"Everyone who wants saké, please line up in front of Natsuki. Everyone who wants juice, line up in front of Frank."

There was a great shift as almost the entire crew formed a line in front of Frank, who looked surprised. Ben could hardly believe it, and apparently neither could Xiang, who laughed nervously. He grabbed Natsuki and Frank, and they disappeared below with Tobin and Felipe following. Rosa dismounted from the barrel and sauntered over to Ben.

"I thought for sure you would jump at the chance to try the saké," she said quietly.

"There will be saké again. This particular opportunity, on the other hand..."
She nodded. "You'll like it. It's delicious."

As they waited, Talia handed Ben Euphonia, which he presumed meant he was in charge of amusing everyone until the toast was ready. He wove through the line of his crewmates, taking requests, feeling like a bard of old. He spied Giselle, who still looked a little ill, toward the back of the line with the other children. Juanito still reeked of grog, and he averted his eyes from the Captain, who came to stand in front of them.

"¡Hola, Giselle! How are you feeling, cariño?" the Captain asked in Spanish with a smile.

The girl cast her dark eyes down to the deck. "I feel better. Thank you, Captain," she replied, smiling weakly. "Doctora gave me something, but we'll have to experiment with the dosage to find what works best for me."

The Captain nodded kindly. "Ah, yes. I know exactly what you're referring to."

"Eh, Juanito!" Maeve said, tugging the boy's ear. "Ya got something to say to the Captain and Benny?"

The boy began to mumble something, still looking at the deck. Maeve tapped his chin, clucking her tongue. He looked up at the adults and began again.

"I'm sorry I ran into you and caused such a mess. I was going to ask the Captain if we were doing anything for Xiang's birthday, and, well..." He indicated the celebration around them.

Rosa laughed stiffly, and Ben could see her smile did not quite reach her eyes. She was still sore about having an attack of nerves in front of the entire crew, despite the efforts to remove attention from her.

"It's fine, Juanito. I know you get excited sometimes."

"And did you see Talia juggling? That was so wonderful! Do you think she would teach me?"

Ben tried not to laugh at the look of horror that crossed Maeve's face at the mere suggestion that Juanito learn to juggle. The Haitian woman was biting her lips, eyes wide and sharp, telling Ben he had better change the subject. He cleared his throat.

"Who knows? Say, Giselle, do you have a request for me?"

Giselle thought for a moment. "I liked that song we sang in Panamá, the 'Bamba Bamba' song. Do you think you could play that?"

"I believe I can, darling, but I will need some help remembering the tune. Could you help me?"

Ben was easily able to play along to the song, and when he had finished, Giselle seemed in much higher spirits. As did Rosa, but as soon as she turned away from the children, her smile fell again, and she squeezed the bridge of her nose.

"How are you doing, Mistress?" he asked quietly as they left the youngsters to their own devices.

Rosa sighed. "I'm not sure. It doesn't do to show weakness like that..."

Ben stealthily took her hand and squeezed it. "I know. But with this crew..."

He never finished his thought, his reassurance that their crew adored her, because from below came forth a small parade of casks. Felipe and Tobin each hefted one by themselves while Li Mei and Frank carried a third, and Xiang and Natsuki the fourth. Ben put Euphonia down to help distribute cups for the toast.

After what seemed like ages, everyone on the crew had their cup. Ben was not sure what he expected, but he was somewhat surprised to see Tobin stand to toast his lover.

"Xiang, it has been seven years since we found you, a golden nightingale singing in a prison. Since then, we have learned more from you than we ever expected. We have learned compassion without condition, generosity without expectation, and wisdom without condescension."

"Maybe a little condescension," Felipe muttered, which earned a hearty laugh.

Tobin snorted and continued. "With your guidance, we have learned to find calm, even as the storm may rage outside. We have learned not just to hope for a better future, but to take steps to build it ourselves."

Tobin turned away from the cook, addressing the crew.

"Every soul aboard this ship is here because they were looking for a place to belong. Some were freed from literal chains. Others cast off metaphorical shackles."

The quartermaster looked pointedly in their direction, but Ben was not sure if he was looking at the navigator, the Captain, or both.

"And all of us directly benefit from the vision that crystallized when we found you. It's the same spirit that we invoke whenever we open our arms to a lost soul. And now, because of you, we are seeing a whole new generation of love and connection. We did that. The world has more love and light in it because of us, and we do what we do because of you."

He raised his cup, and so did everyone else.

"To you, Older Brother. May you continue to fill our hearts as you fill our bellies, and may we strive to be the people you believe we are. To Xiang!"

"To Xiang!"

Everyone took a sip of their juice. An explosion of citrus danced across Ben's tongue, and it momentarily stunned him into silence. He completely missed whatever Xiang said in return, but he likely would not have understood most of it anyway. This drink was a delightful little puzzle he wanted to piece together.

He could taste orange, which must be the base. He knew that Xiang often extracted the juice from oranges to use in flavorful sauces. The cook even had a little machine, designed and built by Felipe for his birthday the year before, that crushed the juice out of halved fruits with the pull of a lever.

There were other fruits as well, but Ben was not quite sure he could parse them. He took another sip, swishing it around in his mouth. A bright, tart flavor came to the forefront.

Passion fruit.

He did not normally care for passion fruit, even though he rather liked the flavor. He could not stand the texture and how it felt in his mouth, but in juice form, it was perfect.

He was not entirely sure, but he thought maybe there was guava in it as well. He had only just had guava for the first time recently. Doctora had offered him some *guayaba* with a salty cheese, and Ben, remembering Rosa had said she liked it, had tried some. Tobin had also taken some, thanking the physician profusely for the guava. Apparently, the combination was very common in her native Puerto Rico, and the quartermaster really enjoyed it.

"So do you like it?" Rosa asked Ben over the rim of her own cup as she took another sip.

"I do. It's quite nice. What's in it? Orange...?"

She nodded. "Orange, guayaba, and maracuyá."

"Is maracuyá a little purple fruit with squishy yellow seeds?"

The Captain nodded.

"In English, we call it a passion fruit."

Rosa raised her eyebrows as she considered that. "That is an interesting name." She dropped her voice. "Why? Is it making you feel something?"

They both chuckled.

"You know I don't need fruit for that, Mistress. I feel plenty for you on my own."

Ben was suddenly struck by how Tobin's speech for Xiang had not made any mention of their relationship. But then, he only saw it because he knew to look for it. As open and accepting as most of the people on this ship appeared to be, there were still taboos yet. Zsófia and Anya referred to each other as *małżon-ka*—which Ben was pretty sure meant "wife"—and were usually physically close to each other, but they did not touch very often in front of the rest of the crew. At least, they did not display their affection like Natsuki and Daichi did, or even like Felipe and Doctora.

Xiang and Tobin also rarely touched in front of others, even though they shared a room with only one bed. Ben realized that must be part of the under-standing the quartermaster and the cook had. They were exclusive bedfellows, but their relationship only took place behind closed doors or when they knew nobody would be paying attention to them, like dancing together on Isla Rosa, off to the side where nobody would pay them any mind.

And that appeared to be how Rosa wanted her relationship with Ben, too. And while Ben was not entirely sure he could blame her, he ached to be able to announce his love for her, shouting it from atop the mast. He wanted everyone to know he loved the Pirate Queen and wanted her to showcase her love for him in return. But Zsófia, Anya, Tobin, and Xiang probably wanted to do that, too, to bring their feelings out of the shadows and into the light.

Ben was lost in thought when a giant hand landed on his shoulder, snapping him back to the moment. Felipe.

"You like this juice?" he asked, shaking Ben slightly.

"Yes, it's very nice."

"He normally does not make this much, as it is quite difficult with all the passion fruit. It requires quite a lot. That's why it took so long. All the passion fruits, they are now gone."

Speaking of gone, so too was Rosa, having been pulled away by some of the Mohammedan crew, who were chattering happily with her.

"Thank you for distracting everyone so I could calm her down. She was truly frightened when I fell on her."

The gunner nodded. "She does not get like that very often. She looked like you do when you freeze. But I knew she was in good hands if we put on *un petit spectacle*. It is a shame she has been hit in the face with a coming storm. She is likely having a terrible headache."

"Did you check the barometer?"

The Frenchman nodded again. "The barometer shows low pressure. This will likely be a quick but dangerous storm. However, I still choose to believe that Madame is magic."

Ben sighed as he watched the Captain tap her cup with Halima, Aisha, Zahra, Jamaal, and Hamza. They were laughing about something, and despite her current pain, Rosa once more sparkled like starlight under the glow of the lanterns. Ben raised his cup to the Frenchman, who tapped his own against it.

"Aye, she is, Felipe. She certainly is."

# Chapter 38

## A Hurricane and Harassment

Xiang's birthday dawned dark grey and windy, lending credence to Rosa's prediction that a storm was coming. There was an air of anticipation as the crew prepared what they could.

Rosa wanted as few people on deck as possible, and everyone out there would either have a harness or a rope tying them to a mast. Ben was to man the helm with Jean-Luc as support. Talia and Arturo, Daichi and Jim, and Aisha and Tenoch would each take a mast in teams of two. Zsófia and Henri would join the officers on deck.

Everyone else would stay below with various jobs: Frank and Li Mei were to keep the chickens safe, Eliza was to keep Mar safe, Maeve and Anya were to keep the children safe, and everyone else was charged with securing their possessions and the goods in the hold. Ben looked over the lists and realized there were twelve harnesses and fourteen people who would be out in the weather.

"We'll tie Doctora to the mast. I don't usually wear a harness unless I have to," Rosa said nonchalantly when he pointed out the discrepancy.

Ben cocked his head. "That's ridiculous. What if—?"

"She said she doesn't wear a harness, Benny," Tobin growled. "Don't be insubordinate."

Ben wanted to argue, but the withering look Tobin gave him frightened him into silence. The quartermaster seemed tense over the whole situation.

Ben wondered if it was because it was Xiang's birthday that he was acting so bull-headed.

Finally, everyone was in place as rain began to fall, thick, fat drops soaking them almost immediately. Then the wind picked up, and the seas began to churn. Fortunately, they were far enough out in deep water that Ben was not worried about hitting anything, but he did not want to be blown too terribly off course.

He was also deeply concerned about keeping the ship upright, especially if Rosa insisted on running around the deck without a harness. The recklessness seemed unlike her, and Ben wondered if she was somehow trying to make up for her attack of nerves the night before by proving she was still a brave leader.

It made his heart ache.

Once the storm hit in earnest, it took all of Ben's strength and control to keep his hands on the helm and the *Deception* steady. Suddenly, he had an odd feeling, much like he had before Los Roques.

Something was terribly wrong.

He looked around, and his eyes stopped on Juanito.

Juanito? Wait, what the hell? What was Juanito doing on deck?

"You're supposed to be below with Maeve and Anya!" Ben shouted above the gale.

The boy scampered over to him, sliding through a large puddle. "I should be out here with my crew!" the lad yelled back. "Doctora is out here!"

"She's tied to the mast, and you are not. And we don't have any more harnesses. Go back downstairs, and that is an order."

The boy made a face as though he wanted to argue, but he was not about to disobey a direct order from the ship's third in command. He saluted with a massive pout and made his way back toward the stairs. He slipped again in the same puddle. Before he could scramble to his feet, a large wave walloped the *Deception*, and the ship pitched hard onto her side. To Ben's horror, Juanito began to slide across the deck.

Ben remembered his first day aboard, the deck disappearing from under him as he nearly fell out through the drainage hole. But Ben was a good thirty centimeters taller than Juanito and had much longer arms. His wingspan was what had kept him from taking a bath that day.

Juanito was not that lucky.

"Juanito!" Ben screamed.

"Man overboard!" Talia yelled from her position on the mast before blowing a few short, shrill notes on her whistle. Felipe, Doctora, Tobin, Henri, and Rosa ran for the rail.

"Talia, harness, now!" the Captain called as she sprinted to the side of the ship. Before Ben could register what she was doing, Rosa had a harness around her waist and was up on the rail.

She dove cleanly into the drink.

"Rosa!" Ben screamed after her. He grabbed Jean-Luc and shoved the Haitian man toward the helm before lunging for the rope. Ben kept his eyes on the red scarf tied over the Captain's hair as she surfaced and wiped the water from her face. That tiny crimson spot in the endless grey was his lifeline. The Black Rose looked around and finally saw Juanito. She struck out toward him, but the rope was too short.

"Let the line out!" Tobin bellowed, appearing at Ben's side along with Talia, Felipe, and Doctora. "She needs slack!"

Tobin and Talia both reached for the rope. Felipe had a spyglass trained on the Captain, and Doctora clutched the gunner's waist, fear written on every line of her face. She had already lost Octavio and Gustavo; she could not lose Juanito too. Ben focused back on Tobin, who was still shouting at him.

"Let go!"

"No. She—"

"Let the fucking line out!" Tobin repeated, shoving Ben's shoulder hard.

"No!"

Ben's hands clenched tighter around the rope, praying he would feel her weight on the other end. He could not, not with Tobin and Talia holding it too. Panic rose hot and sharp. He could not feel her. She was somewhere in that churning grey, and he could not feel her. Juanito was out there too. His mind seized on the worst possibilities all at once.

Everything was wet and cold and too loud. Tobin was shouting at him. His clothes were plastered to his skin. Salt spray hit him in the face. He could not breathe.

And Ben did perhaps the worst possible thing he could have done at that moment.

He shut down completely.

Everything went quiet, and time slowed to a crawl. Ben's mind was a whirlwind of panic, but he could not make his body do anything. It was calm here, detached, almost peaceful. Eventually even his thoughts began to slow.

He felt Tobin's large fingers lace into his own, trying to pry Ben's grip loose from the rope. The quartermaster was much stronger than he was, and it hurt—a lot. The pain brought him back to his body, back to the deck of the *Deception*. A searing bolt of agony shot through his hand and up his arm as Tobin pinched a pressure point in his wrist.

Nope. Not time to die just yet.

But he still could not feel Rosa on the other end of the line.

Ben's panic, his pain, his terror for Rosa's life all burst free at once, and it came out as rage. The brute in him—the one willing to kill Felipe, kill James, kill anyone who dared hurt his beloved Starlight Princess—surged to the front. He dropped the useless rope and punched Tobin in the face.

"Don't touch me!" Ben screamed, taking a step toward Tobin, who met him so they were nose to nose. The rope fell from the quartermaster's hands, and somewhere far away, Talia screamed in pain and surprise. Right now, all that mattered was Tobin, and Ben was ready to kick his arse. Tobin seemed to feel the same, growling and baring his teeth.

Both men were snapped back to the moment when Felipe grabbed each of them by an ear and hauled them close, yelling above the wind like an enraged father on the verge of reaching for a belt. "Will you both put your bites back in your trousers and help us? Merde!"

Ben and Tobin broke apart. Ben shook himself and looked again for the red scarf in the heaving grey sea. He found it and saw the Captain floundering, trying to secure the boy with the rope and waving up at them while spitting saltwater from her mouth. Tobin, Ben, Felipe, and Talia hauled on the line, even as Talia's voice, usually so strong and clear, wavered.

"Heave!"

"Ho!"

"Heave!"

"Ho!"

They managed to pull the Captain and Juanito to the hull. Rosa hoisted the boy over her shoulder and scrambled up the side with everyone hauling. She all but threw the lad over the rail to Felipe and Doctora, and then Tobin and Ben helped her over the side, bringing gallons of the Caribe with her.

Doctora immediately bent over the boy, using her breath to bring him back. She paused, and Henri and Zsófia rolled the lad from side to side before she tried again. Ben moved to embrace Rosa, but she was focused entirely on Juanito and on getting the harness off her waist. He tried to follow her, but Tobin blocked his way, arms crossed tight, a snarl on his lips.

Then the boy vomited seawater and began coughing. Rosa helped him sit up with a tired smile. She looked up at her officers, and her face shifted to horror.

"Talia!"

Ben and Tobin turned to see Felipe comforting Talia, whose hands were bloody and raw, the skin seemingly flayed from her palms. She was crying and shaking. Ben had never seen the outgoing, energetic boatswain look so small and fragile.

"Take her and Juanito to our quarters!" Doctora yelled.

Rosa caught Talia by the arm as Felipe scooped the boy up and carried him.

"The rest of you to your business. Storm is almost over!" Rosa called over her shoulder.

As the Captain had predicted, the storm was over a quarter hour later, with no further injuries and no one else overboard. The moment he was sure he could slip away, Ben left Jean-Luc at the helm and went down to Doctora and Talia's room. He met Tobin on the stairs, and while the quartermaster did not say a word, he did shoulder past Ben hard enough to be deliberate. Ben ignored it. All he cared about was Rosa. He had to see her, hold her, reassure himself that the worst had not come to pass.

Doctora's door was open. Rosa was wrapped in a blanket, her sopping clothes discarded into a large bowl. Doctora bandaged Talia's hands. Talia looked away from Ben with a huff.

Ben opened his arms to Rosa, and she let him pull her into an embrace. She was shivering.

A few moments later, Felipe came in, also very obviously avoiding Ben's eyes.

"Xiang has Juanito in front of the stove and is brewing some tea. He will bring you some." He cracked his neck and set his jaw. "Madame, Talia and I would like to speak to you." He looked pointedly at Ben. "Privately."

Rosa looked from Felipe to Ben, clearly confused even as her teeth chattered.

"Uh, very well. Ben, please go warm up my bed."

"Yes, Mistress," Ben muttered, brushing the barest ghost of a kiss across her forehead. He did not care that it was in front of the other officers. She was alive, hale, and whole.

He made his way up to the Captain's quarters and stripped off his wet clothing, wringing it out the window before hanging it on the small rope clothesline Rosa kept by the windows. He tried to dry his hair with a towel before climbing into her bed.

Brave or not, what she had done had terrified him. Still, he could not deny how fiercely she had gone after Juanito. Of all the unlucky things that had happened to the boy, this had to be among the worst. Though the snakebite had been terrible too.

After what felt like ages, Rosa finally entered her quarters holding a mug of flowery jasmine tea and the bowl with her clothes. She wrung them out, hung them beside Ben's, and climbed into bed. She leaned against the headboard, blowing across the tea before taking a sip.

"Benny, be a dear and help me warm up?"

"Yes, Mistress," he said quietly, laying a hand on her leg. He stifled a gasp when he found her skin as cold as the grave. He put his head on her chest and wrapped his legs around hers.

"Sing to me? Please?"

"Of course, Starlight."

Ben sang the first thing that came to mind, which happened to be "Lavender's Blue, Dilly Dilly," a rhyme his mother used to sing to him and his siblings. It seemed fitting, given the line about keeping warm. He rubbed whatever skin he could reach, using friction to coax heat and circulation back into her body.

She finished her tea and wriggled down under the blankets with him, holding him tight. Her teeth had stopped chattering, but she was still well below normal temperature, her curls frizzing from damp and cold.

"Benny, I think I know how you can warm me up."

As Rosa said this, the coldest thing that had ever touched Ben found its way to the inside of his thigh. He yelped, caught her hand, breathed warmth over the chilled skin, and rubbed it briskly.

"Are you asking me to make love to you, Mistress?" he asked, pressing warm kisses along her fingers.

"I am, Benny. So if you could please let me get on top of you, we'll make a nice little tent of heat."

Ben slid down toward the middle of the bed, taking a pillow with him. Rosa lifted the blankets and pulled them over them both like a cocoon. She leaned down, and Ben dutifully took her breasts into his hands, rubbing and licking them warm. Concentrating so closely on his favorite part of her body made him hard at once, and he pulled her down roughly onto his cock.

The Black Rose gasped as he impaled her; the contrast in their body heat was oddly exciting. She bent low over him, their breath mingling in the enclosed warmth. Ben ran his hands over her back, barely holding the intrusive thoughts at bay.

What if she had not reached Juanito?

What if she had not come back at all?

She moved rapidly on top of him, still bent low over his chest, and soon their little world under the blankets was as sweltering as any rainforest either of them had ever visited. Rosa's breasts warmed quickly from the friction, followed by her torso, then her legs and arms. She released the blankets and braced her hands on either side of his head. Ben could still feel the chill in her fingers.

"Rosa," he whispered as she bent to kiss him again. He held her as he felt her inner muscles flutter and her body tremble on top of him. With another kiss, she slipped off him and slid down his body. Her icy fingers wrapped around his cock, and Ben swallowed a screech.

It was not pleasant, but only for a moment before her mouth replaced her hands. Her tongue worked magic, and her breath was blessedly warm. The friction did seem to be helping, and by the time Ben crested, Rosa felt almost back to normal.

"Mistress, please..." Ben choked out as he neared release. The Captain threw the blankets back, and cool air hit his skin as he spilled over his stomach. She kissed the tip of his cock before reaching for a rag to clean him up. As she wiped him down, Ben rubbed her back, grateful simply to feel her breathing. Once she finished, she flopped down beside him, and he pulled the blankets back over them.

"Please don't do that again," he muttered.

"Don't fuck you again? I thought you enjoyed that?" Rosa snarked, a twinkle already back in her eye.

Ben scrunched up his nose and let his head fall back. "You know that's not what I mean. I mean don't jump off the ship in the middle of a storm. Don't jump off the ship, period, really. I don't know if I have ever been more scared in my adult life than I was watching you do that."

"Somebody had to," she replied, her voice small. "I'm probably the strongest swimmer on the crew. Talia does fairly well, but she was up on the mast. Tobin certainly wasn't going to. Felipe might have, perhaps. So who else was going to get him?" She tilted her head. "Come to think of it, I think we should make sure the rest of the crew knows how to swim. I know some of them think it's bad luck, but I think that's silly. But regardless, I'm quite pleased we aren't planning a funeral this evening."

"Me too, Starlight," Ben muttered, kissing her temple.

They cuddled a while longer before Rosa decided she was ready for a nap. Ben kissed her, wrapped himself in a towel, took his clothes from the line, still soaked through, and hurried downstairs to his own hammock to rest.

There was a dry pair of trousers on his dresser, though they were a little short for him. It hardly mattered. Once he was decent and his own clothes had been wrung out again and hung to dry, Ben climbed into his hammock and immediately felt something oddly crunchy and gritty under him.

He rolled back out and turned the canvas inside out. A shower of crushed hardtack biscuits rained down, skidding across the planks and settling into the seams.

What the hell?

He never ate in his hammock, and Xiang hated hardtack and rarely served it. How would that have ended up there? Unfortunately, he was too exhausted to puzzle over it for long. He climbed back in and fell asleep almost at once.

A notable miasma of bad feeling hung over the *Deception* in the days following the storm. At first Ben thought it was concern for Juanito, but the boy was soon back to his usual duties, none the worse for wear.

Instead, Ben found that Talia, Felipe, and Tobin refused to speak to him, communicating only through notes or through other people. He also realized that Talia's boatswain mates and many of Felipe's gunnery crew were going out of their way to make his life inconvenient.

Ben tried to ignore it, assuming it was perhaps belated hazing for his promotion. When he tried to ask Rosa about it, she only sighed heavily and rolled her eyes, mumbling something about her officers needing to act like adults. That confused him further. Rosa also developed a slight cold after her misadventure, and he did not want to burden her more than necessary. She spent most of her free time napping, so Ben kept to himself as best he could.

It all came to a head about four days after the storm, though the isolation made it feel much longer, as everyone gathered for breakfast in the galley. The Captain was eating with the children, chatting animatedly with Juanito, Giselle, Gerda, and Toñiete. Ben tried to keep his head down as he picked up his bowl of porridge and an apple. Talia appeared in what he could have sworn had been an empty space, and Ben bumped into her, slopping porridge down the front of her blouse.

In the next instant, she was surrounded not only by her own mates but by six of the eight members of Felipe's gun crew. Zsófia was sitting with her wife, ignoring the whole thing, and Eliza was nowhere to be seen. Ben backed away, only to find himself blocked by a support beam. He became acutely aware of how loud the galley suddenly seemed; poor Xiang looked overwhelmed by it as well. Ben searched for help.

Tobin stood nearby, arms crossed and smirking. Talia certainly was not about to discourage her defenders. Felipe sat with Doctora, also pointedly ignoring what was happening while the Boricua shook his shoulder and pointed at Ben. The Frenchman scratched his forehead with an extended middle finger, and Ben noticed the bandage on Felipe's wrist. It covered the tattoo that matched Ben's own. Then Ben realized Talia's matching tattoo was similarly covered, though it was harder to tell because of the bandages on her hands.

They had purposely covered the tattoos that symbolized their brotherhood. They hated him.

How could he have been so blind?

The boatswain mates and gun crew pressed in, and the noise in the room rose to a fever pitch. Ben looked to Rosa, pleading for her help.

Thankfully, the request was not only received, but honored.

The Black Rose slammed her bowl onto the table, startling the children, and stood on the bench. She put two fingers in her mouth and whistled, sharp and piercing, cutting through the uproar. Once she had everyone's attention, Ben saw that she was shaking with rage. When she spoke, her voice carried through the room, though she did not yell.

"I will not have my crew behaving in such a manner. Benny, Tobin, Felipe, Talia. My quarters, immediately. The rest of you have business to be about."

She took a pistol from her belt and stepped down, yanking another from Felipe's belt as she passed. He opened his mouth to protest, but Rosa shoved the barrel under his nose with a snarl. The older man swallowed and raised his hands in submission.

She thrust both pistols at Eliza and Andrew, who had just wandered in together, utterly oblivious to the scene they were entering. Eliza's cheeks were flushed pink, and some of Andrew's shaggy blond hair stuck straight up in the back. Their giddy smiles vanished as their furious Captain handed them guns.

"If anyone acts up, you have my permission to shoot first and ask about it after. I am ready to start keelhauling people. Do. Not. Test. Me."

Eliza and Andrew looked at each other, hopelessly confused, but nodded.

"Uhh, of course. Aye, Captain," Andrew said with an awkward salute.

Rosa turned back to her officers, who were all still staring at her. "What are you waiting for? Now."

Once the Captain had her four officers together, she slammed the door so hard her mirror wobbled on the wall. The dried bouquet Ben had bought her in Campeche bounced on its ribbon before settling against the glass. Rosa took several deep breaths, but exhaled them as growls. Finally she spoke, her anger barely leashed.

"I am immensely disappointed in all of you, and if I could slap all of you at once, I would. We are supposed to be parts of a whole, and you are falling apart—and dragging the rest of the crew with you. I did not interfere because I thought you were all adults capable of communicating like adults. However, since you've forced my involvement, we are getting to the bottom of this now. We are going to have it out, get over it, and move on before I force all of you onto different ships."

At the threat of being removed from the *Deception*, Ben felt as though he had been slapped. Judging by the faces of Tobin, Talia, and Felipe, they felt the same. The Captain stood tall and surveyed her officers.

"Each of you will have your say. You will not interrupt each other. After everyone has spoken, then you may discuss. I do not want this to end on the beach with guns and ten paces, because I am fairly certain we all know who would win."

Everyone looked at Felipe, who shrugged.

"Tobin, you may begin."

Tobin stepped forward. "During the storm, when you went after Juanito, Ben left the helm and grabbed the rope tied to your waist. He would not let it out so you could swim to the boy. He not only abandoned his post, but froze at the exact moment he needed to act in the best interest of the ship and her crew. Then he became insubordinate when I tried to get the rope from him. He punched me."

The Black Rose nodded and looked at Ben. He dropped his gaze to the floor, cheeks burning, throat tight. This was all his fault. They were angry with him. Furious, even.

"Mistress, I was selfishly more concerned with keeping track of you and keeping you safe than I was with Juanito. In the moment, Tobin wanted me to let the rope out, and I was so afraid of what might happen to you that I could not make myself put you in further danger. I couldn't feel you on the line anymore, and there was too much happening at once, so I panicked and shut down. Then, when Tobin started forcing the issue physically, the pain brought me back, and I lashed out."

"Very good. So you both stopped speaking because your loyalties clashed. Tobin's loyalty to the crew as a whole crashed up against Ben's loyalty to me as..." Rosa faltered, visibly searching for the word.

"Madame," Felipe sighed, rubbing his eyes, "respectfully, please just call him your lover. We all know, and it explains his actions well enough."

"My... lover," Rosa repeated quietly. She nodded. "Very well, then. Talia, your turn."

"I was holding the rope with them. I wasnae paying much attention to what they were doing until they both let go. Cap'n, I love ya, but you and Juanito both soaking wet are a mite more than I can pull on my own. Also, when the rope flew out, it took my palms with it. I was angry because neither of them even seemed to notice or care, since they were too busy raging at each other."

"As you have every right to be. That was the nastiest rope burn I've ever seen. And Felipe?"

The gunner cracked his neck and rolled his shoulders. "I am angry that these two were in a bite-measuring contest when they needed to take charge, and then, after all was said and done, neither of them apologized to Talia. Or to you, for that matter." He turned to Ben and Tobin, drawing himself up as tall as he could, his temper flaring.

"I may be the oldest *salopard* on this ship, but I know my place. You two *connards* are second and third in command, and you outrank the two of us. When we needed you most, you both abandoned your leadership and decided to fight each other like a pair of angry *coqs* instead of getting Madame and Juanito back on board without maiming our boatswain."

He turned back to the Captain, his voice softening at once under the force of his respect for her. "A thousand apologies, Madame. I realize that between my crew and Talia's mates, we have a fair number who answer to us. Even without saying anything aloud, they read our anger well enough and chose not to cooperate with Tobin and Ben as they should have. That caused the fracture in the crew. I am very sorry if it looked to you like a mutiny was afoot. I promise you no such thing will happen against you on my watch."

Rosa nodded. "Thank you, Felipe. So, to summarize: Tobin wanted to help me reach Juanito. Ben wanted to keep me safe. Talia is rightly upset that those clashing priorities physically harmed her, and Felipe is upset that neither Ben nor Tobin apologized to Talia. Ben abandoned his post, and Tobin abandoned his command. Am I missing anything?"

There was a chorus of "No, Captain."

Ben took a deep breath and stepped forward, his skin burning with shame. This was the best crew he had ever been part of, people he had begun to think of as family, and now they all hated him. His vision blurred as hurt, frustration, and sadness surged up all at once. They were surely going to throw him overboard for real now.

"Mistress, this was all my fault. I thought I was acting in your best interest, and I did not think about what was best for the crew as a whole."

He turned to the quartermaster. "Tobin, I'm sorry for my lapse in leadership and for taking it out on you. You outrank me, and I should have let you take control of the situation without argument. I am also sorry I struck you outside of training."

Next he turned to the boatswain. "Talia, I am incredibly, deeply sorry that my negligence hurt you so badly. I was not thinking, and failing to apologize to someone I have harmed is not how I was raised. Please tell me how I can make it up to you."

Ben then looked at Felipe and hesitated. "Do... do I actually need to apologize to you? Or are you angry on behalf of the ladies?"

The gunner held up a hand. "Non, Benny." He removed the bandage from his wrist, uncovering the compass rose tattoo that matched Ben's. Talia did the same. "Thank goodness," Felipe muttered, scratching at his skin. "That was getting *très irritant*."

"Are... am I going to be flogged? Or worse?" Ben asked quietly.

The other officers exchanged looks. Ben kept going, since he had already begun digging his grave anyway. The Captain's handwriting in the Articles floated before him.

*Any person found guilty of cowardice or drunkenness in times of engagement shall suffer what Punishment the Captain and the Majority of the Company shall think fit.*

"I don't know whether this exactly counts as a violation of Article Nine, but on a Royal Navy ship it would be close enough. I abandoned my duties because I was too much of a coward to lose... the Captain."

"I don't... I don't think you need to be flogged..." Rosa began.

Tobin shook his head sharply. "Flogging is too much. I was thinking a couple of raps on the knuckles for insubordination."

"But now we might have to do something bigger, so the crew can ken they're allowed to get along with him again," Talia added.

Ben shook his head. This was probably not the moment to be pedantic, but Baffling Benjamin could never keep entirely silent. "The Articles state that my punishment shall be whatever the Captain and the majority of the company think fit. I am willing to accept almost any punishment..." He took Rosa's hand. "Anything except the loss of your favor and our... lessons... even if that is what got me into this predicament in the first place. So if you can assure me that will not be my punishment, I can take anything else. Even a flogging."

Rosa looked to the other officers. Another wordless exchange passed between them and then they all held up open hands. Ben, unsurprisingly, had followed none of it. The Black Rose rose onto her toes and kissed him on the cheek.

"That is fair. I promise the loss of my tutelage is off the table."

Felipe clapped his hands and rubbed them together with a maniacal grin. "Whelp. We shall rally all hands. It looks like we shall have a proper pirate trial."

Talia was already at the door, blowing her all-hands-on-deck call.

"Wait, what?" Ben asked, the blood draining from his face.

Rosa squeezed his hand. "You'll be fine. Think of it as a big improvised play. Play up the chivalry and the unrequited romance, and you will likely be fine."

"What do you mean, 'likely'?"

Rosa did not answer. Instead, she loosely tied Ben's hands in front of him with a length of rope. Then she kissed him on the lips, lingering just long enough to leave him dazed, before heading for the door.

"And what do you mean, 'unrequited'?" he yelped after her, cold panic sweeping over his skin.

She put a finger to her lips and winked before disappearing, leaving him alone in her quarters.

# CHAPTER 39

## A TRIAL AND TOMFOOLERY

Ben stood in Rosa's quarters, his mind spinning in a hundred directions.

What the hell just happened? Where had this trial nonsense come from? Why had Rosa said his feelings were unrequited? Did she really feel nothing for him? Was she like that Hinata woman Felipe knew, who only felt what she was paid to feel? Did Rosa really only care about what Horsecock Harrington could offer her? Was she starting to tire of him outside her bed?

After a few minutes of spiraling downward in his own mind, Felipe came back to retrieve Ben. The gunner's excited smile fell when he saw the navigator's pallor and heard him breathing fast and shallow.

"Oh, Benny," the older man said, putting his giant hand on Ben's shoulder. "What is it you say? Something you can hear?"

"Your voice."

"And smell?"

"Your pipe tobacco."

"Taste?"

"I think I'm going to vomit."

The Frenchman cocked his head. "Does that count?"

Ben took a deep breath, shaking his head. "No idea. I feel your hand on my shoulder, and I see that you wear a ring on a cord around your neck. I never noticed it before."

Felipe pulled on the length of braided leather around his neck and held the ring up so Ben could examine it. It was a signet ring, impressed with a knight on a horse charging with a leveled lance. Ben's panic began to ebb, replaced by curiosity. He could not quite read what it said. Fortunately, the gunner filled in the blanks for him.

"My *nom de famille*, de Chevalier. It signifies that I am from a long line of knights. This ring is all I have left of my past and my family, and while it means very little here in the New World, it got me out of a few scrapes the last time I was back in France. It also leaves a nice imprint on sealing wax."

"Very interesting," Ben said, before letting out a deep breath and squaring his shoulders.

Felipe nodded. "I want you to know, I did not enjoy avoiding you, but I feared I would lash out in anger. I did not want to do anything I would come to regret. I am glad you apologized to those you wronged. That shows a true man." He clapped Ben on the shoulder, but then his smile faded, and he sighed, again looking his age. "Unfortunately, since Talia got more of the crew involved, we must adhere to our Articles. Even the officers are not above them."

"What is going to happen?"

"It is very simple. Have you ever watched a trial before?"

"I have been involved in some court-martials. Not because I did anything wrong, but the Royal Navy convenes them whenever ships are lost. I had to give testimony when I was twelve."

Felipe nodded, stroking his beard. "You will be charged with negligence that resulted in harm to your fellow officer. We shall not call it cowardice."

"Thank you. I appreciate that," Ben muttered.

"Tobin will represent Talia. We agreed not to mention you striking him, either. I am going to be your defense. I asked Jean-Luc if he would participate, and he said no. You know he does not improvise well. Jules and Zsófia agreed to sit on the jury, so you have at least those votes in your favor. Zsófia respects you very much. She is a good person to have on your side, like Eliza. Eliza and Andrew may also be on the jury."

"What will Ro... the Captain be doing?"

"Madame will preside and will likely give some testimony. Juanito may as well. But we will do our best to present it as an accident, and that you did what you did because of your feelings for Madame."

Ben looked at the older man, tears of stress beginning to prick at the corners of his eyes. "Do you think that's wise? She said my feelings are unrequited. Do you think she was lying?"

Felipe's face went blank for a moment. "I do not…" He paused. "I do not remember what that means in English."

Before Ben could explain, there was a knock at the door. Tobin poked his head in, wearing his new dark sun spectacles.

"We're ready."

Felipe nodded, squeezing Ben's shoulders. "You have made great strides since you have been with us. You have many people who adore you on this ship. Look." He held out his left wrist. "I am your brother once more. You will be fine. All I ask is that you trust me once more."

Ben gulped and nodded, allowing Felipe to lead him out onto the deck by the loose rope around his wrist.

There was an amazing cacophony, not unlike the birthday celebrations aboard the *Deception*. Felipe kept a firm hand on Ben's shoulder, anchoring the younger man.

"You will be fine. Stay calm. You have more people on your side than against you," the gunner said quietly.

He raised a fist in the air. At first, Ben was not sure why, but then he realized it was Felipe's left arm.

The one with the tattoo.

Felipe indicated a small crate to one side, and Ben sat. He was grateful for the seat, as his legs were shaking. He busied himself by fidgeting with the rope around his wrist. The rough texture gave him something to concentrate on, and his fingers something to do.

Rosa stood at a makeshift table wearing a powdered wig that Ben recognized as belonging to the captain of the *Angelina Marie*. It still shed a little flour when she moved, snowing onto a black cloak around her shoulders that must have been Talia's. The Black Rose banged a mallet on her table, and the crew went silent.

"Amigos, we gather because one member of our crew has done harm unto another. You all know that here on the *Deception*, we are a large, floating family. There will always be squabbles, but sometimes bigger issues are found. Before us, our navigator, Benjamin Harrington, stands accused of a crime against his crewmate and fellow officer, boatswain Libertalia Scott."

It was jarring to hear Talia's full name, and the murmurs that passed through the crew proved Ben was not the only one who thought so. The Captain turned to her quartermaster.

"Tobin, please explain the charges."

Tobin stepped forward, standing straight and tall, adjusting his dark sun spectacles. He looked quite stately, the sun blazing off his bald head. "We accuse Benny of neglecting his duty, which resulted in Talia sustaining quite a severe injury. Therefore, we are invoking the latter portion of Article Eight: 'Anyone who neglects his business shall suffer what Punishment the Captain and the Majority of the Company shall think fit.' So we shall present the evidence, vote on his guilt, and if he is found guilty, we shall vote on his punishment."

There were gasps from the crew. Some, like Anya, seemed to be playing along with the spectacle, while others, like Eliza, seemed genuinely concerned for Ben's safety and well-being.

"Very well. Now we shall hear from the defense."

Felipe stepped forward, also standing tall, his showmanship once again on display. "*Mes amis*, I stand before you not just as your Gun Master, but as someone who could be considered the pappy of this crew. While it breaks my heart that Talia suffered injury because of Benny, I believe it was not because Ben was neglectful. Therefore, I shall prove unto you, beyond the shadow of a doubt, that if nothing else, Benny was doing too much, thereby causing an accident."

More tittering from the crew, and Rosa banged the mallet.

"Very well. Tobin, you have the floor."

Tobin stepped forward once more. Felipe lit his pipe, holding it in one hand while keeping the other steady on Ben's shoulder. The tobacco had a faint vanilla scent that Ben found very comforting, especially in conjunction with the gunner's large, heavy hand. The combined warmth of smell and touch kept Ben from slipping into the icy abyss of a freeze. He would have to find some way to thank Felipe for this. Maybe he would give Doctora a night off so the old goat could finally confess his love to her.

"I call Talia to give testimony."

Talia smiled, waving her bandaged hands to the crew as she stepped forward. She blew a kiss to Felipe, who stuck out his tongue in response.

"Talia, please give your version of events."

Talia was absolutely relishing the opportunity, her emerald eyes shining with mirth.

"Oh, aye. It was during that big wee storm. I was up on the mainmast with Arturo. Somehow, in the middle of it all, poor wee Juanito fell in the fookin' scupper, and the lad went full well overboard. The Cap'n, she called for a harness, and then she dove into the drink after him!"

There were more murmurs, and the Black Rose blushed.

"Oh, aye. Ye ken she is a most wondrous swimmer. She dove in, and I came down to the rail. Since part of my duties is to care for these ropes and cables, I took up the rope attached to her harness." She paused, her voice becoming deeper and more somber. "However, suddenly, my rope, which I thought was being anchored by Tobin and Benny, was nae anchored any longer, and it ripped through my palms, giving me some right terrible rope burn that I'm still healing from."

"Thank you, Talia," Tobin rumbled before nodding to Felipe. "Your witness."

The Frenchman stood up straight, removing his hand from Ben's shoulder.

"Talia, do you know what Ben was doing before the rope ripped through your hands?"

Talia shook her head.

"Nae. We were keeping our eyes on our fair Cap'n and Juanito."

Felipe made a small *hmmm!* noise and turned to the crew.

"Interesting. She does not know what Benny was doing before the rope slipped through her hands. Very interesting, to try to prove negligence when you do not know what he was doing."

Talia scoffed. "I dinnae ken what he was doing, but I'm nae the only witness. So if you are done asking me, we have another person to talk to. Are ye done with me?"

Felipe raised a single finger, opening and closing his mouth before narrowing his eyes in frustration.

"No further questions, Talia."

The gunner walked back over to Ben, once more placing his hand on Ben's shoulder. Ben laid his own hand over Felipe's and squeezed it, letting the older man know he appreciated it. Even if this was meant to be a silly show, it was nice to feel that someone was fighting for him sincerely, and knew him well enough to keep him tethered to reality.

"Very well, Talia, if there are no further questions..." Rosa began.

Talia walked to where Tobin was standing, wearing a smile like a cat that had cornered a bird. "And now it is my turn. I call Tobin to testify!"

"Wait a minute. That is not fair. They cannot do this!" Felipe sputtered, caught off guard.

Rosa shrugged, sending another dusting of white powder down onto her shoulders. "It's unusual, but they both should offer testimony. You and I both know that if Talia herself had not been the one injured, she would be your opponent. But she cannot question herself, so that is why I allowed them to work together. Should I hold you in content of court?"

Felipe tipped his head back and sighed. "It is 'contempt,' Madame. And no, I suppose that is fair enough."

He exhaled slowly and bent to whisper in Ben's ear. "If you have not yet realized why she is called 'the Lawyer,' you are about to find out."

Ben nodded. Talia had earned that nickname ostensibly for her ability to talk herself out of nearly any scrape with law enforcement. Since the final straw that had seen her bound for indenture in the New World on the *Leonard* had been her attempt to protect some children in her troupe of travelling mechanicals, it was reasonable to assume her silver tongue had a great deal to do with that as well.

And then, of course, there was her myriad of tickle partners. Ben could barely manage trying to keep one lover happy, so it stood to reason that Talia's charisma and skill with words at least got her foot in the door with someone in every port they visited.

"Now, Tobin, please share with the crew yer version of events."

Tobin stood up straight and cleared his throat. His deep bass voice carried a slight growl as he spoke. Felipe must have heard it too, because he gently squeezed Ben's shoulder.

"We were on deck during the storm, and somehow Juanito ended up out there with us. He was talking to Ben, but he slipped in a puddle just as the ship pitched. He slid out the scupper and fell overboard. The Captain was not harnessed, but she called for one so she could go in after the boy. Ben grabbed onto the rope and wouldn't let it out, so she could swim to Juanito. He left his duty, and he attempted to interfere with the Captain's rescue attempt."

"I see, I see. And what was Ben's business at the time of the storm? What was he supposed to be doing?"

"He was supposed to be manning the helm. Instead, he shoved that duty off on Jean-Luc. Again, so he could interfere with the Captain's rescue attempt."

"And since my back was turned, could ye please explain the circumstances of my injury?"

There were notes of sadness and curiosity in her question, and for a moment Ben was entirely convinced Talia truly did not know what had happened. He knew she was an excellent actress and performer, but for some reason, this still threw him.

Her question hung in the air, waiting for Tobin to answer. This would be the moment of truth. What would the quartermaster say had happened? He had said the charge was negligence, Article Eight, not insubordination, and certainly not violating Article Six, the rule against striking a fellow crewmember.

Tobin turned to face Ben and Felipe. "Benny froze," he spat, frustration dripping from each of those two syllables.

There were a number of nods and little "ohhh" sounds. Clearly, the crew was now quite aware of their navigator's tendency to shut down.

"He was thinking too much and wouldn't do anything. I was trying to get him to let the rope out for the Captain so she could reach Juanito. We both dropped it in the rain, and that's when it hurt you."

He cleared his throat and stood straighter.

"Also, I would like to publicly apologize for my part in your injury. Your air team and the gun crew have both made their thoughts on my behavior very clear, so I am sorry I did not do more to keep you safe."

Ben let out a small, shuddering breath. There was a certain comfort in knowing the quartermaster had likewise had a hard time with a large part of the crew over the past few days. More than that, Tobin had lied on Ben's behalf. A huge, glaring lie by omission.

"Och, well, thank you, Tobin, I'm right touched. But aye, our teams did have a wee bit of fun with you and Benny these past few days," she said with a chuckle. "Though I will admit, it was right fun watching ye be so frustrated."

Tobin shrugged. Talia turned to Felipe and Ben.

"Nae further questions. Yer witness."

The gunner gave Ben's shoulder another squeeze. "I have no questions for Tobin at this time, but I would like to thank him for apologizing to Talia."

Ben got the distinct impression that Felipe would have loved nothing more than to ask Tobin any number of asinine questions, to throw the quartermaster off balance, make him look like a fool, and otherwise make his turn as witness even more ridiculous for the sake of the spectacle. However, the Frenchman's words were clipped and serious, and he clearly wanted to get this over with, probably for Ben's benefit. Ben appreciated Felipe's attentiveness.

But then Ben remembered they were plotting to win this.

That meant there would be some big, humiliating revelation sooner or later.

The thought made his muscles tense, his whole body folding inward as if he could make himself smaller. The hammer would have to fall eventually, and his feelings for Rosa would be unfurled like their banner during a raid. He realized the quartermaster was speaking again.

"I call to give testimony..." Tobin turned and looked at Felipe with an evil little smile. "Doctora Julieta Pérez de Colón!"

The crew gasped as one. This was the drama they had been waiting for.

"You absolute *connard*," Felipe whispered under his breath, obviously regretting not taking Tobin for a ride when he had the chance.

Doctora looked caught off guard by being called to testify. She stood from her place among the jury and picked her way forward. Felipe rushed to take her hand just as she lost her balance trying to step over Toñiete. The gunner caught her and pulled her upright. They gazed adoringly at each other for a moment before Tobin growled:

"My witness, if you please."

Felipe dropped her hand, and Doctora pouted slightly before walking over to stand beside Tobin. She crossed her arms tight over her chest, tapping one bare foot impatiently.

"Doctora, you treated both Juanito and Talia, did you not?"

Her annoyance at the quartermaster manifested in a tight smile and a tone like poisoned honey, deadly sweet and snide. "Who else was going to treat them, Tobin? That is my job."

"Could you describe Talia's injuries?"

"How disgusting would you like me to get?" she asked in return, tilting her head innocently.

"Not very, honestly," Tobin conceded, holding up his hands.

"As stated previously, Talia suffered some fairly bad rope burn. Her palms were bloody, and some skin was scraped off. However, her wounds have been mending nicely, thanks to my healing paste and her changing the bandages frequently. In about another week, it will be as though nothing ever happened."

Tobin nodded. "You were also on deck during the situation. Do you have anything to add to Talia's telling of events?"

Doctora shook her head. "No. In truth, I was so worried for Juanito, and so frightened by the thought of losing him, that it was the only thing I could focus on at the time."

Tobin nodded. "No further questions. Your witness."

Felipe stepped forward, seemingly forgetting about Ben for a moment. "Jules. Hello. How are you doing this fine afternoon?"

Doctora raised her eyebrows, adjusting her spectacles as they threatened to slide off her nose. "I would be doing much better if you stopped worrying about me and focused on getting Benny out of trouble."

Felipe waved a hand. "Yes, yes, I know. Jules, you are privy to a great deal of information and many secrets on this ship, *oui*?"

"Yes, I would certainly say so. Keeping fifty-four people, a dog, and our chickens healthy means I have to know a lot of intimate details."

"Without going into too many details, would you say Benny had a difficult life before joining us?"

The physician narrowed her eyes slightly, trying to discern the Frenchman's angle. "Everyone on this ship has their reasons for being here, but none of us would be here if we had been content with our lives ashore. So yes, Benny has some things in his past that understandably turned him to piracy."

"You were one of the first people aboard to have an intimate conversation with him, *oui*?"

Doctora nodded.

"Could you please describe the man you met that day, and compare him to the man who is now before you?"

"The Ben I met that day was deeply sad, and clearly very lonely. He had endured many things that society says men should ignore, stiffen their upper lip, and pretend they are not bothered by at all. But Benny is so sweet and sensitive, and those things weighed heavily on his heart."

"And is that same Benny the one in front of us, Jules?"

Doctora looked over at Ben, her expression softening, and Ben could hear all the affection she harbored for him in her voice as she spoke.

"No. The Benny in front of us is, for the most part, more confident, more certain of himself. While he is still sensitive and sweet, he has truly blossomed into a dependable officer, and he is one of the most intelligent and quick-minded people on this ship. It is wonderful to see that he has found his place here, and I have no doubt he will continue to do great things for us."

Felipe nodded sagely. "And what do you think brought about his change? What, or who, do you think inspires him to be a better man for us?"

The physician bit her lip and looked to Rosa. Rosa nodded ever so slightly, giving permission.

Doctora looked back at Ben, apology writ large in her eyes. "I think he has become a better man because..." She screwed her eyes shut, balling her hands into fists. "Because he is in love with the Captain!"

The statement hung in the air, and the silence that followed was deafening. There were no dramatic gasps, nobody swooned, nothing to suggest this was some enormous revelation. Ben was surprised. It seemed Rosa, Felipe, and Doctora were also confused by the utter lack of reaction from the crew.

The stillness was broken by Juanito's nervous laugh. "Well, obviously."

He was rewarded for his observation with a slap to the back of the head from Maeve, who shushed him.

Rosa took it upon herself to heighten the melodrama. "Benny? Is in love with me?!" she asked, clutching one hand over her chest.

Ben's heart dropped, a white-hot stab of nerves sending heat and cold through him at the same time. Up until that moment, he had trusted the other officers to get him out of this. And for a few agonizing seconds, he actually believed Rosa had no idea how he felt about her. She was a good actress, perhaps on par with Talia. His logical side reminded him that it was ridiculous.

She knew exactly how he felt. But the louder, more animal part of his mind, the part that wanted to run and hide and never come out into the light again, believed her. That part believed she was hearing this for the first time, and that she was not going to be pleased. That she was going to be furious it was coming out so publicly.

Even though it had been almost entirely her idea to begin with.

"And Jules, what makes you say that?"

Felipe's voice came from so close that Ben jumped. The gunner's hands once again settled on the younger man's shoulders, gentle despite their size and weight. Ben landed back in his body as though his mind had been shot from a catapult.

"Why do you say Benny is in love with Madame?"

Doctora chuckled quietly, her smile kind. "The way he looks at her. He always smiles a little when he sees her. And he always looks at her when he sings romantic songs. He looks at her as if she were some beautiful goddess who has deigned to grace our ship, and he feels fortunate simply to breathe the same air as her. It's sweet."

"Would you say that Benny's affections for Madame have any bearing on his work?"

Doctora nodded fervently.

"Oh yes. I think he works harder. He wants to succeed. He wants to deserve his place on her ship and at her side. Every time I see him, he seems so happy to be here, so willing to get his hands dirty and do what needs doing, not just for himself and the Captain, but for the crew as a whole. If his affection for her has inspired him to do well, it stands to reason that his actions are explained by how he feels for her. He wanted to protect the woman he loves."

Felipe stepped out from behind Ben toward the woman who owned his own old, scarred heart. The gunner took the physician's hand, entwining his fingers with hers. "And that is the magic phrase, Jules. That is to be my argument."

He turned back to the crew, still holding Doctora's hand.

"Benny neglected his duty because he wanted to protect the woman he loves. He was so concerned for her that nothing else mattered. He could not stand by and let Davy Jones claim her. Not when he would do anything for her.

"And truly, did he neglect his duty? Yes, he left the helm, but he had Jean-Luc take his place. He had the presence of mind to ensure that our beloved ship was placed in capable hands before he tried to help Madame. You cannot call that neglect.

"And while Talia did end up injured, Tobin's testimony agrees it was an accident. Accidents happen all the time on this ship. Right, Juanito?"

There were titters of laughter among the crew as Juanito blushed. Felipe turned back to Doctora, who was completely enraptured. He kissed her hand and winked.

"Gracias, Julieta. No further questions."

Doctora melted entirely when he called her by her full name. She sat back down with the jury, and Femke produced a small hand fan. Doctora accepted it, removed her spectacles, wiped her face, and fanned herself.

"Tobin, Talia, do you have any further witnesses?" Rosa asked, once again allowing the stern Black Rose to take over.

"Nae, Cap'n."

"No, Captain. We're done. The prosecution rests."

"Very well. Felipe, please present the defense."

Felipe indicated for Ben to stand. The younger man did so, even though his knees shook and he feared they might give out entirely. His throat was tight. The gunner walked over and stood beside him, slipping the ropes from Ben's wrists, which were falling off anyway. The Frenchman placed a firm hand on the younger man's back again, drew a few deep, slow breaths, and Ben copied him.

"Very good," he began. "Benny, I ask you before anything else: Are you in love with Madame?"

Ben looked around at his crewmates. They all knew. They had known the whole time. Perhaps he and Rosa were like Felipe and Doctora, and no one made snide remarks out of respect for their Captain.

"I am."

No reaction from anyone except Rosa, who once more looked as though she was being told the biggest secret in the universe. "What?!"

Ben took another deep breath. "I am in love with her. I have been from the moment I met her. She's spectacular."

Felipe chuckled, patting Ben's back. "Oui, she is. Benny, please tell us your side of the story."

Ben shrugged. "I was at the helm. Juanito was supposed to be below, but he snuck onto the deck. I ordered him to go back down, but he slipped and fell out the scupper. Ro... the Captain... she was not wearing a harness, even though I thought she should have been. Or at least tied to the mast like Doctora. But she called to Talia for a harness, and she dove into the water after Juanito."

"You expressed concern for her during preparations, did you not?"

Ben nodded. "I did. I believed she was being unnecessarily reckless, and I said so. While Xiang may be the heartbeat of this crew, the Captain is certainly the spine. Without her, none of the rest of us work together. We, as a crew, would likely fall apart if anything happened to her."

There were murmurs of agreement among the pirates. Ben could hardly believe how eloquent he sounded under all this pressure. Hopefully he could keep it up.

"A most excellent metaphor, Benny. So how did you feel when Madame dove off the ship?"

"Terrified. I know she swims well enough in calm waters, but I was not sure she was strong enough to swim in open ocean during a hurricane. So, when everyone ran to the rail, I had Jean-Luc take the helm so I could take up the rope and try to keep track of her."

"Did you think you were going to help her?"

Ben shrugged again, letting his hands fall so they slapped lightly against his thighs. "I suppose I did, that I would pull her and Juanito up. But mostly I just wanted to be able to feel her moving on the end of the line, so I knew she was still alive, still fighting."

"But then Tobin wanted you to let the rope out. It was too short."

Ben nodded. "Yes. He and Talia took up the rope as well, and I could feel them, but I could not feel her anymore. Between the rain, the noise, and all the awful things that might happen to her running through my mind, I... yes, I froze. Tobin had to bring me back, but in doing so, we dropped the rope."

Felipe nodded solemnly, turning to the crew. "And you may know, Tobin and I are training Benny for a duel against James in July."

There were enthusiastic boos and jeers at the mention of the other Englishman.

"We have been trying to break this habit of freezing. While Benny has been getting better, sometimes he still gets overwhelmed. This was unfortunately one of those times.

"He also apologized profusely to both Talia and Tobin. He acknowledges his wrongdoing and wants to make it right. He is willing to endure any punishment we may deem necessary. Even a flogging."

"No!"

A chorus of dissent rose from the crew, the loudest voices coming from Zsófia, Eliza, and Doctora.

"He doesn't deserve a flogging!" Zsófia exclaimed, uncharacteristically impassioned, tears streaming down her face.

Rosa banged her mallet. "Order!"

Even though she was not on the jury, Anya scooted closer to Zsófia and took her wife's hand. Gerda handed her a handkerchief before settling back down between her parents.

"But we could also vote that Benny is not guilty," Felipe reminded them, his voice rising as the charismatic showman fully took over once more. "And then he would endure no punishment. He did what he did because of love. Had he truly neglected his duty, he would not have had Jean-Luc take the helm. But he wanted to make sure our beloved ship was handled and that our beloved Madame was safe. Unfortunately, it all became too much for him. Yes, it caused an accident, but he was not negligent."

He punctuated the statement by once more holding his left fist in the air, sleeve rolled up to reveal his tattoo. For a moment there was silence. Then a great cheer and a round of applause went up from the crew. Ben found himself applauding too, a little dazed. Tobin, Talia, and Rosa all looked taken aback. The Frenchman bowed low, then gestured toward Tobin and Talia.

"Your fucking witness!" he declared exuberantly before once more laying a hand on Ben's back.

Tobin and Talia conferred for a moment before the quartermaster cracked his knuckles.

Uh oh.

The quartermaster approached with all the delicacy of the hurricane that had started this trial in the first place.

"What makes you think you deserve her?" he asked, getting right up in Ben's face.

Ben shrank back, only to be nudged forward again by the gunner beside him.

"Objection, Madame. Intimidation!" the older man called.

Rosa nodded and pounded the mallet again. "I agree. Tobin, back up."

Tobin took a step back, and Ben relaxed by a fraction. He willed himself not to look over at Rosa. If he did, he might start crying. As passionate as Felipe's defense had been, this was becoming too much. Even with the steady, comforting warmth the Frenchman offered him through the hand at his back, Ben wanted nothing more than to hide in his hammock for the rest of the night. Or perhaps the rest of his life.

He took a few deep breaths before answering.

"I'm... I'm not entirely sure I do, honestly. I just know that she is the most wonderful person I have ever met. She's... I mean, she's beautiful, well-read, charismatic, kind, generous, and an excellent leader. I like who I am when I'm with her. But it is not for me to decide whether I deserve her..."

Ben clenched his fists, set his jaw, and stood straighter.

"And it is not for you to decide either. Nor Felipe, nor Doctora, nor anyone else on this ship. The only person who gets to decide whether I deserve the Captain is... is... is the Captain herself."

There were whistles and whoops from the crew, and Ben remembered something Felipe had said to him in Barranquilla.

"I want her to be happy, like keeping a fire lit. If anything I do for her can bring warmth and light into her life, why wouldn't I do that?"

Felipe chuckled beside him, and Ben thumped the older man on the back. A chorus of *aw* and applause rose from the crew, and Tobin snarled quietly.

The quartermaster looked from the navigator to the gunner and sighed. "And what are your thoughts about your future with her? Where do you envision this going?"

There were a million ways Ben could have answered. He paused to gather his thoughts, looking out toward the sun, which was dropping toward the horizon. He took another steadying breath, feeling Felipe's hand at his back and the wood of the *Deception* beneath his bare feet.

There was Felipe's pipe tobacco, and Rosa's faint plumeria lotion. A gull cried in the distance. He felt oddly calm. Despite everything he wanted for his future with her, it was not really about him, was it? He had to defer to his superior officer, even if she was his lover.

"I guess... wherever she wants it to go... as long as I may go with her."

That was apparently the perfect answer for the drama of the moment, because a wild uproar rose from the crew. Ben looked to Tobin, who had the slightest smile on his lips.

"That was the correct answer," he muttered beneath all the noise.

Rosa pounded her mallet again, calling for order, but no order was to be had. After a few moments, she put two fingers in her mouth and whistled. Silence fell across the deck once more.

"Tobin, Talia, do you have any further questions for Benny?"

Rosa's voice seemed far away, even as it carried cleanly across the ship.

The quartermaster looked back to the boatswain, who shook her head. He sighed. "No further questions, Captain." He nodded to Ben and Felipe and turned away.

More applause broke out from the crew, and Felipe leaned in to whisper in Ben's ear.

"We are almost done. One more witness. It may not seem like it, but Tobin and Talia are playing nice. You are doing well. Keep it up."

He gave Ben's shoulder one more strong squeeze and stepped away.

"And now, to give testimony, I call: the Captain!"

There were gasps, much like when Doctora had been called, and even Rosa herself seemed taken aback.

"Oui, I call the Captain of our ship, the Black Rose, to testify!"

# CHAPTER 40

## GRIEVANCES AND GREENSLEEVES

The Captain daintily removed the powdered wig before stepping around her table, dramatically flaring out the cape as she came around the corner. Ben sat back down on the crate and once again felt his body go hot and cold with nerves. What on earth was this woman going to say after his public profession of affection?

Fortunately, Felipe stayed by his side.

"Bonsoir, Captain. How are you?"

"I am well, Felipe. Are you enjoying yourself?"

"Oh, but of course, Madame. You know I enjoy defending my crewmates from injustice."

"Of course. Well then, let's get started, shall we?"

Felipe nodded, again squeezing Ben's shoulder. "Madame, did you know of Benny's feelings for you previously?"

Rosa shook her head. "I had no idea he felt as strongly, or as deeply, as all that."

An obvious lie, and Felipe clearly knew it, but he let it pass.

"And do you return Benny's affections?"

There was a beat of silence. A long, heavy beat. The Captain shrugged.

"I... I feel very warmly toward Benny too, I suppose."

Ben felt as if he had been stabbed through the heart with a flaming blade. His whole chest burned, waves of ice washing over it.

Noises of protest rose from the crew. Anya had to clap a hand over Zsófia's mouth. Andrew and Femke both had to keep Eliza from standing, even as the laundress growled something about making the Captain see sense. Felipe shot Eliza a Look, and she settled back down, folding her hands in her lap and staring daggers at the Black Rose. Andrew kept one hand clamped around the laundress's ankle, lest she end up on trial next.

"Let us keep the insubordination in check, *s'il vous plaît*."

The gunner turned back to the Captain.

"Now, Madame, do you not think that is being a little, shall we say, dismissive?"

The Black Rose raised her hands defensively. "I love all the members of my crew as if they were family. Benny does not get any special treatment."

More quiet muttering rippled through the deck. Felipe's grip tightened on Ben, and for a moment Ben worried the gunner might actually throw him overboard. However, when the Frenchman spoke again, there was only exasperation in his tone.

"Madame, I am sure you know that your crew wants your happiness, and if that happiness is to be found with Benny... well, I hardly think anyone would consider that special treatment so long as he continues doing his job correctly."

There were nods and murmurs of agreement, but Rosa stood straighter, resolute. Ben could see the wall of stubbornness going up.

"I'm sorry, Felipe. I didn't realize I was the one on trial here. Nor did I realize embarrassing me was on the docket."

Felipe held up a finger. "One moment, please."

He bent down and whispered in Ben's ear.

"Is this what means 'unrequited'?"

Ben nodded wordlessly.

"Merde. That is such bullshit. I have never seen her commit to a lie this strongly."

"So do you have any more questions for me?" Rosa asked, irritation sharpening her voice as she glared at Ben and Felipe.

Ben gulped, trembling under the negative attention of the woman who had, mere hours ago, kissed him and assured him of his safety and his place in her bed.

The Frenchman coughed. "Well, uh, same question I asked Jules. Was the man who surrendered to you in February the same man who sits here before you now?"

Rosa's demeanor shifted at once, like a child putting on her father's work clothes and pretending to be him. She was modeling herself on Felipe.

"The Benny I met in February was quite pathetic. Let me tell you about Lieutenant Benjamin Harrington."

What the hell did she think she was doing? Ben felt his skin go hot again, sweat rising over him.

No, no, no.

"Please don't," Ben whispered, his throat refusing to give the words any more volume. But if Rosa heard him, she ignored it completely.

"Benjamin Harrington was not very popular with the people who knew him because his mind works a little differently. He worked hard and did the very best he could, but in his pursuit of book learning, his people skills faltered. All the same, he became enraptured by the charms of a girl called Anne."

"Please don't," Ben whispered again, but it was useless.

"Anne is a horrid, awful woman, a spoiled little rich girl. But we all know how Benny can be when his mind is set. He decided she was the one he wanted for some stupid reason, and he was relentless in his pursuit, even when it should have been glaringly obvious she wanted nothing to do with him. He was but a fool in love, as he apparently still is.

"Then one day, she agreed to accompany him to bed, not because he had finally won her heart, but to get back at her father. But she did not fully appreciate him, and that awful bitch even slapped him when they were finished."

Sounds of pity moved through the crew, and Ben wanted a sea monster to rise from the water and swallow him whole.

"That, of course, was not the end of it. She ended up with child, and her father, the Magistrate, forced Benny to marry her. He was but seventeen."

More noise, louder this time. Rosa raised her voice to ride over it.

"The child was stillborn, but Anne physically beat our Benny, mocked him relentlessly, and sought comfort in the arms of another man, all while our Benny strove to be a sweet, doting husband. She starved him of affection."

The crew was completely invested in the story, clearly on his side, but Ben felt his heart cracking into a million pieces.

*How could she do this to him?*

Despite Felipe's grip on his shoulder, Ben began to drift away from the moment. He tuned out anything else she said, praying for an apoplexy that would kill him on the spot. Or perhaps Felipe would do him the mercy of throwing him overboard. Anything, anything to make her stop talking.

A memory floated back to him.

*I tend to be... quite explosive. I can throw quite the tantrum, and I can be unbelievably cruel with information shared in confidence.*

She had warned him. She had told him plainly, back in March after kneeing him in the groin. And he, stupidly, had chosen to believe it would somehow be different with him. He had trusted her with his past because she had asked.

"Captain. Objection."

The voice that cut through the noise did not belong to Talia, Tobin, Felipe, or Rosa.

It was Doctora.

Rosa stopped mid-sentence, one finger raised to make a point. She cocked her head.

"Doctora, you... may approach?"

The physician bustled forward and seized the Black Rose by the arm. Her voice dropped to a low hiss as Felipe, Tobin, and Talia closed ranks to give them a moment. Felipe's hand remained on Ben's arm.

"Captain, stop it. Can't you see you're upsetting him?"

She gestured toward Ben, and Rosa finally looked at him, truly looked.

Ben was shaking as though he sat in ice water, his lower lip trembling, his stormy grey-blue eyes wide and bright with unshed tears. He twisted his fingers together, a tight knot of nervous energy with nowhere to go.

"Oh no, Ben."

Rosa stepped toward her lover and took his hand. He came back to himself and looked up at her like a child who had just endured a vicious beating and was still trying to understand what had happened through the pain and shock. He stared at their joined hands for a moment before taking his back and placing it in his lap, where she would be less likely to reach for it before everyone.

"Why did you tell them that?"

Ben's voice was the smallest Rosa had ever heard from him, smaller than when he had told her about Anne, smaller even than when he had admitted to cannibalism to survive after being shipwrecked on Los Roques at twelve. He was trying to put on a brave face for show, but his control over his emotions was fraying.

"Wait, so all of that is true? You did not just bullshit a good story?" Felipe asked, looking gobsmacked.

The Frenchman knew pieces of Ben's past, but apparently a broader conversation about how bad the marriage had truly been had never taken place. Ben nodded.

Felipe's expression changed, and he stood straighter, his voice turning very paternal and very disappointed.

"Rosa..."

Rosa looked startled to hear him use her given name instead of *Madame*. Ben remembered that the gunner had only done that once before, when Felipe and Tobin had locked her in the brig for making Doctora cry.

"Jules is right. That is not fair. We want them to feel *sympathique*, not make him the... merde. I don't remember the English. But the, uh, uh, *hazmerreír*... of the ship."

Whatever that word meant, it triggered something defensive in the Captain, and she began justifying herself to Doctora and Felipe in Spanish.

Soon a hushed but heated debate was underway, the Frenchman and the Boricua against the Colombiana who outranked them both. Tobin translated for Talia and Ben in a low voice.

"Doctora and Felipe think this will make everyone laugh at Ben. Rosa thinks he has won enough goodwill that they will see how much he has grown and changed. Now…" He clicked his tongue and tilted his head. "Doctora just said something I am not going to repeat, but it was to the effect that Rosa denying her feelings publicly and then dragging Ben's past out like that is immensely cruel. And Rosa, once again, says she is not the one on trial here."

The quartermaster sighed and rubbed his eyes, his sun spectacles riding up onto his forehead.

"What an absolute orgy of idiocy."

Talia took Ben's hand and squeezed it. Ben squeezed back weakly, careful of her still-healing palms. The boatswain gasped and lit up. Ben started, thinking he had hurt her.

"Benny, I have an idea."

Her bright emerald eyes met his, and he saw a sincerity in her expression she did not often show.

"D'ya trust me?"

Ben exhaled and nodded. It was not as though this could get much worse.

Talia whispered something to Tobin, who moved behind the Captain's table and took up Rosa's mallet.

"Order!" he roared above the din. "This proceeding needs to come to order!"

While everyone was distracted, Talia whispered something to Felipe. The older man's face was red, his frustration with the Captain palpable, his hand clenched around Doctora's, though neither of them seemed aware of it. His hazel eyes softened at Talia's suggestion.

The boatswain nodded and bit her lip.

The Frenchman stepped away from Ben, raising both his voice and his hands.

"Merci beaucoup, Jules. I am done with this witness!"

Instead of returning to her place among the jury, Doctora pushed past the Captain and wrapped Ben in a crushing hug.

"You're fine, Benny. Everything will be fine," she whispered, pressing a light kiss to his forehead.

Ben nodded, though he most certainly did not agree.

Rosa looked flustered, but there was a flicker of remorse in her eyes as she looked at Ben. Could she finally see how close she had pushed him to breaking?

"Nae further questions," Talia said, all but shoving Rosa back toward her place behind the table.

Tobin handed the Captain her mallet, and she plopped the wig back on top of her curls.

"Are we done?" she growled. "This has gotten completely out of hand."

The gunner held up both hands. "I certainly agree. May I be excused for a moment? I have one last witness, but I must fetch her."

Rosa looked as confused as Ben felt, but nodded nonetheless. Did Felipe mean to interrogate Mar? Ben had to admit that questioning the dog was unlikely to make this any stranger than it already was.

Felipe disappeared for a moment, and before he came back onto the deck, his voice carried up the stairs.

"For my last witness... I call... Euphonia Harrington!"

A great cheer rose as Felipe strode back onto the deck holding Ben's beloved guitar.

"My... my guitar? What? What the hell?"

Ben was spiraling again, and another shutdown loomed until Felipe pulled him gently to his feet and placed the instrument in his arms. The feel of frets and strings beneath his fingers, the smell of the wood, the sparkle of the inlay in the golden light of the setting sun, the familiar weight pressed to his chest, pushing his pounding heart back into his ribcage where it belonged.

Felipe slipped the strap over Ben's shoulder and whispered in his ear.

"Talia says to play 'Greensleeves.' Trust us, Benny. We end this now."

Then, much louder:

"Yes, I call as a witness Benny's guitar, Euphonia. We all know a musician's instrument is the very door to their heart. Let us ask Euphonia to show us what lies in Benny's."

He gestured to Ben, and the younger man began to play a song he knew intimately, one of the first songs he had ever learned. At first he sang quietly, but his voice grew stronger. He looked once, briefly, at the Black Rose.

This was no longer a joke.

He was actually cutting open his chest and laying his heart before her in front of everyone.

He could only hope she would recognize it for what it was.

He dropped his gaze to the deck before his feet.

"Alas, my love, you do me wrong,
To cast me off discourteously.
For I have loved you well and long,
Delighting in your company..."

Ben had not been this nervous to sing for these people since his second night aboard, when he had played "Red is the Rose" to try to win the goodwill of these pirates. That had only been back in mid-February. So much had happened since then.

He was beginning to understand why Talia had chosen this particular song from all the ones he knew. It rang painfully true. Ben really had staked his life on a Pirate Queen's affections. Affection she could not be bothered to admit to when pressed, even if the crew approved of their romance, even if in some cases they seemed to demand it.

Ben could not help it. He began to cry as he sang.

This was all so stressful and humiliating.

Here he was, begging Rosa to love him back in front of the entire crew.

What would his father think?

"And that yet once before I die,
Thou wilt vouchsafe to love me."

Ben saw that he was not alone in his emotion. Much as he had won over the crew back in February, there were very few dry eyes on deck. Stranger still, it was sincere. Even Talia was crying in earnest, though it had been entirely her idea.

Ben could not bring himself to look at Rosa. If she felt nothing in response to his plea, he did not want to know. He may as well throw himself overboard and save everyone the trouble.

As the last notes faded into the sunset, Ben sank to the deck. He could not make himself remain standing any longer. The crew burst into raucous applause, whistles, and whoops of approval. Ben simply sat there, clinging to his guitar for dear life.

A heavy hand once more landed on his shoulder, and Ben drew in a deep, shuddering breath.

"And so!" Felipe's theatrical voice rose above the din. "We can see that Benny, despite everything he has suffered, has his heart set. Our Captain is his true North, and he has his heading. He made certain our fair ship was cared for in a moment of crisis. He has acknowledged his wrongdoing to Talia and to Tobin, and he will endeavor to correct it. I urge you to vote that he is not guilty of negligence, and that no further punishment is required. What he is enduring right now is punishment enough!"

He turned to Tobin.

"Your witness, *mon frère*."

"No further questions," the quartermaster replied.

The Captain banged her mallet again.

"Does the jury need time to discuss?"

There was some murmuring on the floor before Zsófia, who sat in the first position, rose and wiped her eyes.

"We do not need any time, Captain."

"How do you find?"

Zsófia's voice, though soft, carried through the dusk air. It was earthy and steady, an anchor that kept Ben from drifting away again.

"In the matter of Libertalia Scott versus Benjamin Harrington, we find Benny not guilty of negligence. He had the peace of mind to ensure the *Deception* was in Jean-Luc's capable hands. What followed was an accident that could have happened even under the best of circumstances. We recommend that he find a way to make it up to her, but we demand no punishment from the crew."

Rosa nodded.

"Very well. On the count of three, we shall vote. An open hand is agreement, a closed fist disagrees, and no raised hand is an abstention. On the count of three. Uno... dos... tres!"

A flurry of movement followed, and a sea of open hands rose. Some people, like Felipe and Eliza, raised two.

"Very well, Benny is hereby declared not guilty!"

A great cheer rose from the crew, and Felipe squeezed Ben's shoulders, shaking him slightly. Rosa pounded her mallet with a smile.

"Now, how about we get some supper and celebrate!"

# Chapter 41

## Rage and Resolve

The post-trial revelry lasted well into the night, but Ben still felt stupefied and detached after everything that had happened. It was nice that everyone seemed to be on his side again, but some of the things that had been said still hurt immensely.

A deeply sad, lonely man.

Quite pathetic.

A fool in love.

Starved for affection.

*What made you think you deserved her?*

And then to have his whole past with his wife laid bare before the entire crew? Something he had told Rosa in confidence? And for the stillbirth of his daughter, the worst moment of his adult life, to be given barely a passing mention? It did not matter that it had won him some sympathy. He had told the Black Rose something that had broken him, and she had used those shards to fashion a weapon, a blade to reopen all his old wounds.

The Captain laughed as though nothing was wrong, even while keeping a hand on his arm for a good part of the night. Even after denying she felt anything more than warmly toward him.

Did he want this? Was this what loving the Black Rose meant? Was he, as he was so often reminded, just an elaborate fuck-toy to her? It was too much, too loud, too many people. He needed quiet. He needed time to think. He had not been given any real chance to decompress after all that, and if he was going to find time alone, he would have to make it happen himself.

He found an opportunity to disappear and took it. Rosa wandered away for some reason or another, and he slipped quietly down to his quarters. He closed the door, hung up his guitar, got into his hammock, blessedly crumb-free, and pinched the bridge of his nose. His ears were ringing, his chest was tight, and he felt like a complete idiot.

Ben was not sure how long he sat there staring at the ceiling, trying to figure out what to do. He should leave. Claim he felt the Call of the Land the next time they made port somewhere English-speaking. He could start over where no one knew him. Change his name. Claim he was a widower or something. He had enough tragedy to invent a convincing backstory. If having a navigator was that fucking important to Rosa, maybe she should not treat his heart like a toy.

But, he realized with a pang, he did not want to live in a world without her in it either.

Her adorable laugh and her habit of mispronouncing words she had learned from books.

Her sweet kisses.

Her warm embrace.

Her magnificent hands on his body.

The way she trusted him, believed in his abilities, and never seemed to think he was strange.

A knock at the door startled him. It was quiet, tentative. He guessed it was probably Doctora.

"It's open," he said.

The door opened, and the Captain entered, looking worried. "Benny!" She rushed to his side, the familiar flowery lotion filling the room. The scent was heavy and made the space feel even smaller. "Are you not feeling well?" Her fingers ghosted over his forehead and cheeks, checking his temperature. "I must say, that was a fantastic performance. Everyone loved it."

Performance.

A white-hot spark of anger ignited in his chest. No, she was not going to call that theater. He had to say something. He had to do right by his father's memory and not let himself be trapped in another miserable relationship.

"You know, I don't appreciate you telling everyone about Anne. Now they all know I couldn't make my wife happy."

Rosa cocked her head, the ghost of a smile still on her lips. "Why not? Now they all know she was a rancid bitch who didn't deserve you."

"And what makes you think you do, Rosa? What makes you think what just happened was any better? Do you think feeling warmly toward me makes that much of a fucking difference?"

Ben looked up at the Black Rose, incredulous, unshed tears of frustration burning at the corners of his eyes.

"Benny," she said with a quiet chuckle, trying to cup his cheek, but he turned his face away. "Benny, come discuss this upstairs in my quarters."

"Why? So you can fuck me back into compliance? Because if you touch my cock enough, I'll go along with whatever nonsense you decide? Because I'm that starved for affection and that much of a fool in love?"

"Benny, come now. It all worked out brilliantly." There was something distinctly maternal in her tone, as though he were the one being childish. "May I sit in your hammock with you?"

Ben sighed, a low growl under the breath, then swung his legs over the side and planted his feet on the floor so she could sit beside him.

"May we have a cuddle? Or are you too upset for that?"

"What's the point?" Ben murmured.

Rosa reached for his cheek again. He had not been this upset since she kept lustily interrupting his work right after he was promoted. But that had mostly been frustration. She could deal with anger. What sat before her now was different. He looked small, hurt, and nothing like the confident, capable pirate he had become over the last few months.

"Benny, please listen to me. Please?"

He swatted her hand away and crossed his arms tightly over his chest, speaking with quiet defiance.

"I've listened plenty, and I don't think I much like what you have to say. Actually, I have something to say to you, Rosa."

Even though his touch had been light, barely more than a brush, his words cut. She bit her lip, but kept silent.

"I saw a side of you today that, although I knew it lurked in the shadows of who you are, I chose to believe you cared enough for me that I would never have to see it. You took this tattered, scarred heart that I thought you were helping mend, and you... you ripped it out for the whole crew to see. You paraded my pain as a jest, a twisted Punch and Judy show I never actually agreed to be part of."

Ben sighed heavily.

"I know what I sang, but you know what? I will not beg for your love, Rosa. I absolutely refuse. I crawled on hands and knees over broken glass for Anne's affection, respect, tenderness, any scraps she would deign to throw me, and all I got in return was scars on my heart, laughter, and insults ringing in my ears." His voice wobbled. "I thought you were different. I thought you believed I was worthy and wonderful, that you cherished my mind and my company despite my imperfections. You claim I have grown, that I have improved, that I have become a better man since boarding this ship. If that is so, then this... this is where I draw my line."

"I still wish to earn your love, but I absolutely will not grovel at your feet. Not for you, nor for any woman. Never again. I owe my father that much. So if you are going to make me beg to be seen as anything other than your plaything, then I do not think I want to be involved in this arrangement any longer. Drop me at an English port, and I will figure something out on my own."

"But if love, or partnership, or whatever this is or could be, is a ship, then trust and respect must be the keel. And you damaged it badly in a tempest of your own making, Rosa. The boat carrying the two of us is now adrift, directionless, and taking on water." He drew in a long breath and let it out slowly. "So the question is this: do we abandon ship and let it sink, each going our own way? Or do we salvage what we can, navigate to safer harbor, and repair it together?

Because I cannot, no, I will not do this alone. We bail together, or we sink separately. It is your choice, Captain."

He spat the last word as though it tasted foul.

Rosa sat in silence for a long moment, confusion still plain in her large brown eyes. "But... but we got you out of trouble. My crew is whole again." She waved one hand dismissively. "I concede, we should have warned you, because you don't like surprises, but I think it made it all the more authentic. Talia's idea to have you sing a song was brilliant. And Tobin coming at you all big and scary. 'What makes you think you deserve her?' Ooh, it was so dramatic. And Eliza was ready to fight me. We could not have scripted a better reaction than that."

Ben's head fell back, and an exasperated sound rose from deep in his throat. Was she really this immature?

"This really is a joke to you, isn't it? You took advantage of my trust in you and in my fellow officers. And you think I'm going to reward you for that by coming up to bed with you?"

Rosa scoffed as she stood. "And again, you think you're in love with me? Ben, I do not know how else to explain to you that I haven't even known you for three whole months. I feel affection for you, yes, but love?" She straightened, cracked her neck, and squared her shoulders.

"You're being ridiculous. You're acting like a boy who still believes in faerie stories. I don't need that. I need a man in my bed, and if you are not willing to be that, then perhaps we should take some time apart from each other. Maybe I should declare James the winner of your stupid little duel and give him what he wants."

Ben sighed, suddenly exhausted. The argument was pointless, and a heavy fog had begun settling over him. He had reached the end of his strength for the day.

"You don't mean that, Rosa."

"I do," she said, stomping her foot. "So are you coming upstairs or not?"

Ben shook his head, swung his feet back up into the hammock, stretched out, and stared at the ceiling once more. His eyelids refused to stay open. Perhaps he would feel better after sleeping.

"Ugh, fine!" Rosa snarled, spinning on her heel and stalking out. She slammed the door so hard Ben's guitar rattled on the wall.

Ben woke some time later to silence aboard the *Deception*. He pulled out his pocket watch and tilted it toward what little light there was. It was roughly three in the morning. He stretched and caught another whiff of Rosa's flowery lotion. It was suffocating, and with it came the full force of what had just happened. Part of him felt panicked.

What on earth had he done? Another part thought his father would indeed be proud of him. But the largest part felt like an icy snake coiled around his chest, squeezing tight around his heart. He was an idiot. And so was she.

Regardless, the smell was too strong, and he needed air.

Ben hauled himself out of his hammock and climbed the stairs. He snarled quietly to himself as he passed the Captain's door, his hands clenching into fists. His most spiteful impulse wanted to pound on the door, wake her, shout at her, cause a scene, ruin her sleep. But he did not know who he could count on as an ally after the spectacle of that day. So much for brotherhood and unity among the crew.

A seductive gust of fresh spring air hit his skin, a siren song luring him into the night. He followed it, the serpent within him coiling tighter. It was a good thing he was used to tamping down his feelings and pretending they did not exist.

The sky was inky black and strewn with stars, and the waves were quiet. The breeze was warm and salty, smelling of adventure. It was his favorite kind of night. The evening watch paid him no mind except Jean-Luc, who was manning the helm. The younger Haitian waved him over with a broad smile.

"Good evening, Benny," he chirped as Ben approached. "How are you tonight, sir?"

"I'm... fine, Jean-Luc. How goes it?"

"Steady, sir. Steady as she goes."

"And how are you adjusting to your new position? I apologize that I haven't had a chance to speak with you since your promotion."

"It's wonderful, sir. I do rather like the overnight watch... I miss Giselle a little, though. It's too late for her."

"Indeed. I know you love her very much. Felipe..."

Ben stopped. Felipe had told him Jean-Luc, Giselle, and Maeve's story, but he wanted to hear it from them. Did they see it differently?

He coughed.

"Felipe and I are collecting the stories of the crew members. He mentioned that you, Giselle, and Maeve have quite the tale."

"Aye, sir. Anya mentioned that you had a little project. I think it's intriguing that a man such as yourself is interested in people like us."

"People like... who? Pirates?"

Jean-Luc snorted, then stretched out his arm beside Ben's. The navigator did the same, blinking. It took him an uncomfortably long moment to understand what the Haitian meant.

"Oh."

Jean-Luc laughed and clapped him on the back, a hammer striking an anvil. The weight of that simple observation settled into the navigator's bones, sank into his marrow, and hardened there. The icy snake around his heart loosened a little beneath the heat of that new resolve.

Rosa thought it was too soon to fall in love with him? Fine. There were still over forty souls aboard this ship whose stories he had yet to hear. His project, *The Chronicles of the Deception*, would be unlike anything else ever written. And it would never be finished if he spent all his time moping and pining after her.

This was a test, a forge.

The far cry of a seabird in the night sounded like a summons, clear and full of promise. Despite his anger and heartache, this was where he was meant to be, in these fires, burning away what no longer served him.

And he would use every drop of those expensive inks while he was at it. He would collect every tale and sketch every face aboard this ship, even if it meant he never wrote another word afterward. The world would know these people had existed.

"Do you mind if I go fetch my folio and pencils, or would you rather wait until Giselle can join us?"

Jean-Luc's smile shimmered in the dark.

"I have fourteen years to tell you about before she was even born. Go get your book. I'll be here."

# Chapter 42

## Epilogue

### Phil's Plan

Phil Baxter stared at the email on the screen in front of him. Doctor Pettice, his advisor, had sent it twenty minutes ago, and he had received it immediately. He read her message twice, then three times, then four. For some reason, it simply would not settle into his brain.

*Phil,*

*This would be the perfect research year for you! Warm, sunny Puerto Rico, the chance to be at the forefront of new information in your field, and that Benjamina girl is a cutie! I think you and she would make an adorable couple, haha! If you want to take part, I've already written you a reference and gotten Dr. Tutti and Dr. Iglesias to write you something as well. We can meet and discuss paperwork and funding later this week.*

*Let me know what you think, but I know you're smart enough not to let this opportunity pass you by.*

*Dr. P*

Phil opened the article, which he had already read a hundred times thanks to a news alert he had set for anything with the keyword *pirates*. It was by a reporter in Florida named Becker Rolland, and Phil had found he rather liked the person's reporting style, which was why he kept rereading it. For the first time, however, he actually focused on the woman in the photo.

She had bronze skin, curly brown hair streaked with teal, big chocolate-brown eyes, and a brilliant smile. She wore purple rubber gloves and held an incredibly well-preserved pirate flag in front of a stacked bookshelf. The flag was crimson, bearing a black skull and a lacy, lily-like flower. The flag was amazing. And all the books behind her.

*Benjamina Johnson de la Rosa, 26, with the flag of the pirate ship Deception. Miss Johnson de la Rosa found a sea chest hidden in the archive room at the Rose Academy, founded by Eliana and Roberto Huerta de la Rosa and their business partners. It now appears that the founders were all pirates, opening and operating the Academy under assumed names.*

Phil had most of the article memorized at this point, but he read it again anyway. He was already intrigued by the Academy's mission, to make formal sailing education more accessible in the Caribbean. While sailing courses were offered, they also prided themselves on being at the forefront of scientific research in the region. Their newest program, a Doctorate in biomedical engineering, had received accreditation the previous spring.

There were further descriptions of Benjamina's ancestors and their business partners, but what interested Phil were the books.

*The Chronicles of the Deception.*

This man had collected his crewmates' stories and drawn portraits of each one, color portraits. And his private journals detailed everyone's relationships and how they had ended up on a pirate ship from all around the world.

This. This was exactly what Phil wanted to research.

Phil was not merely interested in the legendary names, but in the average working pirate aboard a ship. As a social historian, this was exactly his wheelhouse.

Phil had been fascinated by pirates for as long as he could remember, ever since seeing *Muppet Treasure Island* as a child. That fascination had grown into a habit of devouring every piece of pirate media he could get his hands on: *Treasure Planet, One Piece, Black Sails, Our Flag Means Death, Pirates of the Caribbean*, Errol Flynn films, and countless hours of History Channel documentaries.

He had also found solace in reading his father Liam's old, worn copy of *Treasure Island* after Liam died suddenly when Phil was ten. Liam had been the sort of man who annotated books, a habit that drove Phil's mum, Kathy, mad. But after he passed, both Kathy and Phil took comfort in seeing his handwriting in the margins. Two particular notes from *Treasure Island* had always stayed with Phil:

"Man cannot discover new oceans unless he has the courage to lose sight of the shore. — André Gide, French writer."

and

"The greatest treasures are often found in unexpected places. Keep an open mind, open eyes, and an open heart."

For a timid ten-year-old with a nervous disposition, adrift in grief, those words had felt like fatherly advice reaching across time, space, and the veil of death itself. Those simple sentences had carried Phil through a great many things, as had a series of quotes Liam had marked with yellow highlighter.

*Sir, with no intention to take offense, I deny your right to put words into my mouth.*

*Seaward ho! Hang the treasure! It's the glory of the sea that has turned my head!*

*You can kill the body, Mr. Hands, but not the spirit.*

And Phil's personal favorite:

*We must go on, because we can't turn back.*

And now here Phil was, standing on the edge of an adventure, if only he had the courage to lose sight of this familiar shore. He had to go on and not turn back. Doctor Pettice was handing him a wonderful opportunity on a silver platter because she thought he and this Benjamina girl would be cute together.

Open mind. Open eyes. Open heart.

Phil looked at Benjamina's picture again for a long moment before sighing, taking off his glasses, and rubbing his eyes. He took another swig of his iced coffee from Legal Grounds Café. The strong scent of vanilla soothed him, reminding him of his mum's perfume. He sat there absently tapping the space bar with one finger as he thought, but not hard enough to make it do anything.

This was ridiculous.

What on earth was he thinking?

She was pretty, certainly, but there was no way someone like her would be interested in someone like him... right?

Besides, in his admittedly limited experience, women with streaks in their hair were usually loud extroverts who were fiercely protective of their studies. There was a girl in his cohort with neon red streaks, Cristina.

Cristina's focus was on the Adelitas in the Mexican Revolution because she was supposedly descended from one, and she certainly behaved as though bold, brash revolutionary blood coursed through her veins. For someone as shy and soft-spoken as Phil, engaging with Cristina felt like trying to hold a conversation with a steamroller blasting German death metal.

She was exponentially more overwhelming when drunk, and over the course of their program she had made multiple uncomfortable advances toward him. He had finally found the courage to turn her down once and for all, and in no uncertain terms, at the department holiday party.

She had then gotten drunk and touched Phil in a way that triggered a massive panic attack, which had, of course, caused a huge scene. Phil still was not entirely over the embarrassment, even with multiple people, including Dr. Pettice and his therapist, Dr. Ford, reassuring him that it had not been nearly as bad as he believed. A year away from her would be rather nice. Perhaps it would give her time to find someone else to focus her attention on.

But unlike Cristina, with whom he had very little in common beyond being in the same cohort, he and this Benjamina girl shared a passion for pirates.

And Phil could talk about pirates for days.

*Miss Johnson de la Rosa is working toward completing her Master's thesis in history with the information she discovered. She is considering extending it to a Doctorate.*

"There's so much here. I think it will keep me busy for years to come. And I can't wait to meet other like-minded people who love history... and pirates!"

*The Rose Academy is opening its doors to researchers to help Miss Johnson de la Rosa with everything she's found...*

The article then listed ways to contact the Academy and get involved in the research. Phil leaned back in his chair and stared up at the Union Jack tacked to the ceiling. Something about all of this tickled a receptor deep in his brain.

What if Dr. Pettice was right?

What if he went, and he impressed Benjamina?

What if they became best friends, bonding over a love of pirates?

What if they co-authored papers or books together?

And what if they became more? What if they were a cute couple? Was he even capable of something like that? He had always been surrounded by aesthetically pleasing people, but he could not remember ever feeling any magnetic pull toward any of them radiating from his general groin area.

He had been dragged along on blind dates arranged by friends of friends who would supposedly be perfect for him, but his shyness smothered any flame before it could catch in his heart, or anywhere else. He often thought sexual attraction was like a treasure map that everyone else had received, and he had simply been home sick the day they were handed out.

But there was still something about this girl, the reverence with which she held that flag, the way she spoke about wanting to find people who loved history and pirates. People like him.

Something sparked inside him, and even if it did not lead where he thought it might, he was willing to at least try.

He shook his head, clearing his mind.

No. Best not to pile so many expectations onto it.

Three steps.

Get there.

Meet Benjamina.

Do research.

Anything else would be extra.

But still...

He had to lose sight of the familiar shore.

Open mind. Open eyes. Open heart.

"Doctor Benjamina Johnson de la Rosa and Doctor Phillip Baxter, pirate researchers," he said quietly, stumbling a little over the Spanish portion of her last name with his English accent. "Doctor Johnson de la Rosa and Doctor Baxter, experts on the Black Rose crew. Doctor Baxter and Doctor Johnson de la Rosa, co-authoring the best academic papers and books on pirates the world has ever seen. Doctor Johnson de la Rosa and Doctor Baxter, visiting beautiful beaches in warm, sunny Puerto Rico..." He tried to trill the R in *Rico* and failed miserably. "Doctor Phil Baxter, who hates the blasted cold and might not have to freeze his bollocks off this winter."

He punched the air triumphantly, then sat up straight again. He took one more long look at Benjamina's picture.

Open mind. Open eyes. Open heart.

Have the courage to lose sight of the shore.

Phil pulled out his phone and pressed the first name in his favorites. A sweet voice answered.

"Hullo?"

"Hi, Mum. I think I might have a lead on my research year... what do you think about Puerto Rico?"

**END OF BOOK II**

# ACKNOWLEDGEMENTS

To my husband, S, for the opportunity to pursue my dreams. I hope to pay you back for your support tenfold.

To my daughter, T, I hope I inspire you to never give up on yourself. Mommy loves you!

To Ocean, my beautiful heart dog, preserved in these pages as Mar. I know you still can't read, but you are the best girl, and I love you so very much.

To my parents, for all the sacrifices you made for my education. I'm sure this isn't quite how you envisioned me using it, but here we are. Thank you anyway.

To Isla, for my beautiful covers, and the crew at Spellwings for taking a chance on my "pirate smut," and allowing me to be part of your community. You all make the hard days a lot easier to deal with. Thanks for the laughs. All hail Coke Peach, the Patron Saint of Spellwings!

To my editor, Emma, for ripping this story to shreds so that I could rebuild it into something better. I still won't apologize for the exclamation marks, though. Let my pirates be excited!

To Kate, Tamara, Eric, and Sher. Without you all, *The Deception of the Black Rose* wouldn't have happened, and without *Deception*, I wouldn't have *Crew*. Thank you for believing in me and my story.

To my favorite rubber duck, Dr. KL, for your continued support and encouragement. None of this would have been possible without you, and I forever appreciate you.

To VW, for letting me take an awful moment in your life and turning it into a powerful fictional moment. You've always been so eloquent, and I hope I did your pain justice. I love jou, my seester from another meester!

To my favorite Marshmallow, JM, for beta reading and loving my book even as you were struggling yourself. Your kindness and smiles mean so much to me. Thank you for lighting the fire under my ass to get this story out into the world, if only to ensure that you get to read it all.

To my squad of cheerleaders, my first fans, who kept me excited and hyped up about my own work even through the slogs. This includes all my extra moms, dads, aunties, uncles, spouses, and siblings I've acquired. To list all of you would make this book another hundred pages, I'm sure.

To LM for the Black Rose's pirate flag. Thank you for this essential piece of my 'author brand'. Go Birds!

To the crew of the Tall Ship Providence, especially Andrew, Bryce, and Carly, for sharing information and excitement. Here's to many more voyages. Fair winds!

To the real Dr. Pettice, for sharing your knowledge, pushing me to learn more about the world when I was a student, for your encouragement, and for letting me steal your name. As with my parents, I'm sure this isn't quite how you envisioned me using my degree, but thank you all the same.

To the Longest Johns and their amazing Discord community, especially Mod Andi(pants) for maintaining the Wiki and saving me a ton of work with the music acknowledgements. Thank you for the music, the community, and for being such a Joyfully Dorky™ group and showing me what a positive fandom space can look like. Truly Adequate, the lot of ya.

To the writing community I have found on TikTok, for celebrating my wins and commiserating on the hard days. I appreciate every laugh, every pep talk, every tag, and every update. Here's to us all staying off government watchlists with all the weird crap we have to look up.

To the giants on whose shoulders I stand, especially Emotional Support Dead Guy™ Robert Louis Stevenson; his super-cool wife, Fanny Vander Grift Stevenson; Ray Bradbury; and Eiichiro Oda. And to Norton Juster for the spark that ignited my lifelong passion for reading.

To all the people who threw rocks at me on my journey, literally and figuratively. Thank you for helping me build my castle out of equal parts love and spite.

And to my readers. I hope these stories delight you, frustrate you, and inspire you. Fair winds, following seas, and happy reading!

To Mike, Mariko, and Chelsey, the three little birds I have carried in my soul since that fateful November day. With your inclusion in these pages and future ones, your memory will live on forever.

To Mr. Ray, for showing me from a young age that chosen family can be a powerful bond that even death cannot break. Thank you for those lessons, and I hope you're proud of me, wherever you are.

And to my Grandmom, who had the soul of a poet and the spirit of a pirate. I hope I live up to your name.

# About the Author

KG has been fascinated by pirates as long as she can remember. She began writing during a very difficult time in her life, and it has been a source of comfort and a means of escape for well over a decade. The tale of her pirate crew has grown and morphed into "The Chronicles of the Deception", becoming a full, rich, diverse world within her mind, and she is thrilled to share it with you.

KG lives on the East Coast of the United States with her family, including her husband, who is incredibly supportive of his future sugar mama.

You can help KG become her husband's sugar mama by following her on Facebook, Instagram, TikTok, Bluesky, YouTube, or Patreon for more side quests! Search KG Ryder – Author on all platforms!